Moroccan Roll

MOROCCAN ROLL

A Novel

Steven Stanley

iUniverse, Inc.

New York Lincoln Shanghai

Moroccan Roll

iUniverse books may be ordered through booksellers or by contacting:

iUniverse
2021 Pine Lake Road, Suite 100
Lincoln, NE 68512
www.iuniverse.com
1-800-Authors (1-800-288-4677)

Because of the dynamic nature of the Internet, any Web addresses or links contained in this book may have changed since publication and may no longer be valid.

This is a work of fiction. All of the characters, names, incidents, organizations, and dialogue in this novel are either the products of the author's imagination or are used fictitiously.

ISBN: 978-0-595-45324-5 (pbk)
ISBN: 978-0-595-69401-3 (cloth)
ISBN: 978-0-595-89638-7 (ebk)

Printed in the United States of America

To all friends, past and present, whose comments, suggestions, and encouraging words have led to the novel you now hold in your hands.

OCTOBER 1976

CHAPTER 1

▼

The pretty redhead seemed to be everywhere in the classroom at once. At one moment she was standing near the blackboard, at the next she was walking between the aisles of desks, the eyes of thirty-seven students following her, their faces bright and smiling, full of eagerness to learn the English language.

Pointing to the hand-drawn sketch she held, Janna Gallagher asked: "Where's the camel?"

Almost instantaneously she pointed to one of the dozen or so hands she could see raised.

"The camel is in the house."

The classroom was filled with laughter, which Janna quickly quieted with a stern look. She was small in stature but obviously in control, and it was clear that the students loved her and that this class was a time of recreation in a day otherwise filled with physics, mathematics, literature, and geography courses.

"Good!" exclaimed Janna. "Where's the monkey?

"The monkey is …," several students started to answer at once, but stopped. With only a glance in their direction, Janna had made them realize that they were out of turn. "One answer," she insisted softly but firmly. "Abdellah?" she asked, looking in the direction of the handsomely tanned, intelligent, but painfully shy Arab teenager who always sat in the back corner of the room.

"The monkey is under the table," answered Abdellah, slowly but confidently, his confidence gained after several weeks with this teacher who was so unlike any others he or his fellow students had ever had.

To begin with, she was an American. There were only four of them in the small Moroccan town of Aïn El Qamar, whereas there were over fifty French, the latest of the many invaders Morocco had known throughout its long history. Even today, in 1976, twenty years after independence, the French presence was still acutely felt in the North African kingdom. For example, over half the teachers in this secondary school, Lycée Mohamed Cinq—named after Morocco's first post-independence king—were French. Some of them had never intended to teach, but were taking advantage of an easy, well-paid two years abroad to fulfill their military service. The Americans were different, and students like Abdellah could sense it, even though they didn't know that, for example, they were paid less than their Moroccan counterparts and only half of what the French received because they had come to Morocco as Peace Corps volunteers. The students knew only that these teachers walked rather than drove expensive cars. Their housing was more modest than that of the French. They could speak Arabic, the language of the Moroccan family, and not just French, the language of the conquerors, which had greatly permeated the government, the media, and the schools. But most of all, the students recognized a difference in attitude. Teachers like Ms. Gallagher really liked and respected their students. And the students returned this feeling.

Abdellah adored Ms. Gallagher—she said "Ms." meant it was no one's business whether or not she was married. (She wasn't.) He thought he would do anything for her. It angered Abdellah that a small group of students had recently begun gossiping about her, spreading stories about a supposed romantic relationship between her and one of her pupils from last year who was now a foreign exchange student in the United States. Abdellah had heard the stories about private Arabic lessons which seemed to extend later and later into the evenings. Someone even claimed to have seen Lahcen Cherqaoui, Ms. Gallagher's student, leaving her house in the early hours of the morning. Abdellah refused to believe this of Ms. Gallagher. True, he had seen the couple at the post office together once, and teachers were not supposed to be seen fraternizing with students in public, but Abdellah wanted to believe that Ms. Gallagher had done nothing wrong, and so that was what he believed.

Abdellah watched eagerly as Ms. Gallagher continued her lesson. A few weeks ago, he had spoken not a word of English. Now, though his sentences were limited, he was able to express simple, basic ideas, and he realized with satisfaction that these ideas would become more and more complex as the year went on.

"Where is the mouse?" asked Janna, and pulled a Mickey Mouse toy out of her pocket. The class laughed as she put the toy on the floor next to a chair. "Driss?" said Janna, and an eager but somewhat slow-witted fat boy in the front row stammered out "The … the moose …"

The class laughed louder, and Driss chuckled with them at his mistake. "Mouse," corrected Janna, smiling warmly, and had the class as a whole repeat the word so that Driss would not feel that he was alone in his error.

"Mouse," repeated Driss. "The mouse is on the floor," he said self-assuredly, with none of his usual hesitation.

"That's good!" exclaimed Janna, who gave a shriek as she glanced at the toy mouse, and jumped onto the chair beside it. The class roared with laughter at her pretended fright, but once again quieted as Janna asked in almost a whisper, "Whe … where is your teacher?"

Shit! thought Janna Gallagher. Is the fucking bell ever going to ring! Then, realizing that the hour was not yet half over, she smiled at her irritation, a smile which her students saw and mistook to be part of the lesson. Ordinarily her heart was in what she was doing, but today she wished only that the noon bell would ring, that this interminable hour would end, and that she could rush to the *salle des profs*, or teachers' room, to see if a letter had arrived from Cleveland, Ohio. Lord, I never thought I'd be waiting for mail from Cleveland, Ohio, of all places, she said to herself. But Cleveland was where Lahcen had been sent just two months ago. And it was with Lahcen that her thoughts were now on this morning in late October, not on the lesson she was teaching.

Lahcen. Lahcen. She could hear the name echo again and again in her mind. Why had it been so easy to leave her friends in Washington D.C. when she came to Morocco last year, but so difficult to say farewell to this one human being? Departures were common to Janna. First from her Irish-American family at seventeen, away from the stifling atmosphere of Boston, of a family where one brother had become a priest and a sister a nun. Thank God she chose that vocation before it was my turn, Janna had often exclaimed. She had spent two years at the University of California at Berkeley during a period of student uprising—two years spent protesting the Viet Nam war, drinking beer and smoking grass, and making uninhibited love. But she had left Berkley without regrets for a year of back-packing across Europe. Oh, the fascinating people she had met there, and yet she had gone on with her life and never looked back. After finishing her university studies in Washington D.C., she had worked in the office of a U.S. Senator, but three years of being a virtual secretary was all she could take. Eighteen months ago, she had eagerly packed her bags and left the States in order to teach English in Morocco. She was sick and tired of being thought a sex object. She liked sex, but damn it, she was a person, and in Washington no one ever seemed to think of her as anything but a body with a pair of legs and a pair of tits attached to it in the proper places. So she had said good-bye to Washington, not only without regrets, but with pleasure.

Janna wished now that she had taken more seriously the warnings she received before leaving for Morocco. One friend had told her that the women's lib movement in America would seem centuries ahead of its time once she had lived for a while in North Africa. American women have it made, her friend had claimed. But Janna would have none of this. It can't possibly be that bad, she thought naively.

God, had she been innocent! Now she knew that it was true. In Aïn El Qamar, women were either saints or whores. Your mother and your sisters belonged to the first category, other women to the second. Foreign teachers were especially suspect. The married ones dared to go unveiled, wore make-up and suggestive clothing. The single ones sometimes smiled flirtatiously at men or accepted rides with bachelors. Worst of all, they often lived alone.

Still, Janna had scarcely realized this during her first three months in Morocco. She had been one of forty sheltered Americans training for their teaching assignments in the modern capital city of Rabat, and though they studied Arabic six hours a day, they found that the Rabatis usually spoke to them in French. The Moroccans who lived in the capital dressed so much like Europeans that they were often indistinguishable from the French.

It was not surprising, then, that Janna's arrival in the small town of Aïn El Qamar had come as a shock. She found herself so different from both traditional Moroccans and the sophisticated French that her first reaction had been to retreat from this strange and sometimes frightening new world. She had spent the first weeks in Aïn El Qamar living within a triangle made up of her house, the nearest grocer's, and her school. Then, one day, Janna had rebelled; she just couldn't keep hiding any longer. That day she had taken a walk to the downtown marketplace, ignoring the young males who followed her, some making comments in Arabic whose meaning she could guess even though she didn't know the insulting words, other telling her she was "byootifool" in their broken English, still others hissing to let her know she was hot stuff. She had walked halfway across town, done her daily shopping, insisting that the shopkeepers serve her in Arabic, and returned to her house. Upon entering, she had started to tremble uncontrollably, her body wracked with sobs. But soon she was laughing, laughing because she had won. Never again would she hide from the painful realities of life in Aïn El Qamar. And little by little she had found it easier to walk alone. People started recognizing her, students said hello to her politely, and the remarks she still heard in this her second year in Aïn El Qamar became easier and easier to ignore.

She had learned to love Morocco for its beauty, not only the magic and splendor of such historic and exotic cities as Marrakesh to the south and Fez and Meknes to the north, but Aïn El Qamar with its thirty thousand inhabitants as well. At the foot of the pine covered Atlas Mountains, surrounded by olive groves where young children played and students met to review their lessons, Aïn El Qamar was truly a fascinating place to live.

It was, Janna had come to realize, quite typical of other middle-sized communities in Morocco. Its dozen or so *quartiers*, or neighborhoods, lay spread out around the central town square, the Place de l'Indépendance. The houses in most *quartiers* were simply rows of two-story flat-roofed dwellings, each attached to the other. There was little emphasis put on outside decoration; the houses were mostly drab white or beige, rain streaked, and many had not been painted for years. This did not, however, indicate a lack of appreciation for beauty on the part of the inhabitants. The focus was on interior embellishments, with the three or four rooms of a traditional house's first floor surrounding a central patio, and relatively few windows facing the narrow streets, thus shutting out the noise of passing cars, animals, and children at play. Some wider streets had sidewalks, but these were usually earthen, with shade trees growing here and there to provide relief from the summer heat and winter rains. The streets themselves, though paved, were frequently strewn with "natural" litter, orange peels, apple cores, old crusts of bread, and the like.

Besides houses, each *quartier* had its own small grocery stores—countless one-man *hanoots*, which competed for neighborhood business and were frequented more for the personality or reputation of their owners than for the quality or variety of their merchandise, since they all dealt mostly in staple products, leaving meat, vegetable, and fruit sales to the specialized vendors who each operated in a section of town set aside for their particular goods. The butchers, for example, occupied a narrow street leading off the Place de l'Indépendance, their individual stalls displaying the hanging carcasses of sheep which were slaughtered daily, although the more prosperous shops had refrigerators in which meat could be preserved during the hot summer months.

Aïn El Qamar had become Janna's home over the past year, and slowly but surely her neighbors had become her friends. It was unusual, even unheard of, for a foreigner to speak Arabic. Hers was halting, and she often made embarrassing mistakes, but her neighbors loved her for her efforts and had invited her into their homes for delicious copious meals, *couscous, tajine, pastilla*, dishes unknown in America, but so tempting and exotic. However the invitations were offered somewhat less frequently these days, and Janna was concerned that it might be because of Lahcen. Her neighbors were willing to believe the best of her, but some of them must have noticed how frequent his visits had become and how long they had lasted near the end.

How ironic that it had been precisely to please them that she had first hired Lahcen Cherqaoui, one of her brightest students, to tutor her in Arabic. Lahcen was only seventeen, but already a senior in high school. Most of his classmates were several years older than he and considerably older than their American counterparts. As a third year English student, he was able to express himself with relative ease. Janna wondered what would have happened if he had not been able to communicate with her. If they had only been able to speak in her hesitant Arabic or rusty French, would their affair ever have started? Perhaps not, but that was beside the point now. History could not be changed. Nothing could alter the fact that Lahcen had become her lover, a lover she could not forget, despite the thousands of miles that now separated them.

"Ask a question starting with the word 'what.'"

Janna heard herself as if from afar. This morning's lesson was continuing satisfactorily, but her thoughts remained elsewhere.

"What is on the blackboard?" asked a student.

"Good question!" exclaimed Janna.

The smile was there, the warm look of approval in her eyes. But she was not thinking about what the student had said. She was recalling a day five months ago. That day she would never forget. It was the first time she and Lahcen had made love.

*   *   *   *

It was one of those beautiful late spring days that made her wonder how Morocco could ever have been stereotyped as a desert land. Here in Aïn El Qamar, with the rich foliage of the Atlas Mountains as a backdrop and waist-high wheat growing green for miles around, the desert on the other side of the mountains seemed an eternity away. The winter rains were forgotten, the heat of the summer soon to come but still easy to push aside from one's mind. School had recently ended. A year of hard, often exhausting classroom work was over. And for Janna Gallagher it was a time to relax, both physically and mentally, a time to enjoy the beauty of the fascinating worlds which surrounded her.

As she walked down Avenue Hassan Deux, the main street of Aïn El Qamar, carrying a basket of groceries, she smiled at the thought that what was foreign and exotic to the visiting tourists she saw alighting from the touring bus parked in front of the Hotel de la Paix—the donkeys carrying produce and merchandise on their backs, the men wrapped in their long flowing hooded woolen robes called *jellabas*, the women wearing either *jellabas* or the often colorful sheets called *haïks*, which made them look like flower-covered ghosts, horse drawn wagons, vendors pushing carts loaded with oranges and plums—all this was somehow natural and commonplace to her after nine months as a resident here. Of course, evidence of modern life was everywhere around her as well. The traffic was relatively heavy; Simcas, Renaults, Fiats, and Peugeots raced along the main street, honking at bicycle riders and swerving to avoid donkeys and children. Students wore inexpensive but often surprisingly stylish clothing. The girls went unveiled, with usually only a scarf and a smock to maintain modesty. Janna passed the recently constructed Volvo showroom, a fancy new apartment complex which was being built to house the well-paid French or affluent Moroccans, and the Epicérie Mondiale, which looked surprisingly like an old-fashioned small town American corner grocery store and was stocked with everything from peanut butter to French *pâtés* to kleenex and deodorants to Swiss chocolates. Looking at all that surrounded her on this warm afternoon in mid-May, Janna was once again struck by this blend of worlds, the old which resisted change with the strength and steadfastness of the mountains against which Aïn El Qamar lay cradled, and the new, which arrived from Europe and America with the speed and force of a supersonic jet, but which had only partially succeeded in breaking the barrier of ancient customs and attitudes.

In front of her Janna could see two examples of these incredibly different worlds. One of her students was walking towards her now, accompanied by his traditionally veiled mother.

They stopped to say hello, the student's mother astonished at Janna's greeting in Arabic.

"*Kataarf l'arabiya!*" exclaimed the woman to her son. "She speaks Arabic!" How often had Janna heard these words, surprised and shocked that so few of the French, whose presence had been felt for more than half a century, had ever bothered to learn the language of the local inhabitants.

"I am going with my mother to the dentist's. She has a toothache," said the student in English, using words which Janna had taught him that year. "She is a little afraid."

"Don't worry, *alala*," said Janna to the woman in Arabic, addressing her as "madam." "Everything will be all right. *Kull shi la bass!*"

"*Kull shi la bass*," repeated the woman, with less than total confidence, and Janna wondered if they were going to the French-trained dentist whose offices were in one of the new apartment buildings, or to one of the many traditional Moroccan practitioners who operated at the *souk*, or outdoor market. She hoped that it was the former, but feared from the woman's expression that she would soon be facing a pair of pliers and returning home with one less tooth.

Everywhere Janna looked as she continued on her walk she saw familiar faces. She was nearing the side street on which her house was located, and here too there were students, walking in groups, laughing and talking excitedly now that there were no more classes until next October. The boys were all smoking—it seemed that the entire male population could not exist without tobacco. The girls laughed coyly and Janna guessed that their topic of conversation was the boys they saw but could not associate with publicly. Once again, the conflict of worlds, thought Janna. They dress so much like Westerners, but their heads are halfway in the past.

Janna caught a quick glimpse of Claudette Verlaine, forty-something and the town's most celebrated and glamorous single Frenchwoman, as she sped past in her Renault 12. Claudette, who taught with Janna at Lycée Mohamed Cinq, lived in a world which rarely involved the Moroccans of Aïn El Qamar except while she was working. Her reputation as a teacher was excellent, although it was not as a teacher that she was best known, but rather for the life and vivacity she brought into the sometimes monotonous day-to-day existence of Aïn El Qamar's foreign community, with daily get-togethers at her house and parties which she occasionally threw. Aïn El Qamar would not be the same without the ebullient exuberance of Claudette Verlaine, or "Miss Claudette," as she was often called.

Janna realized with a start that she had reached the side street where she lived and she turned to walk along it. As she approached her house, the friendly faces of her neighbors smiled at her, greeting her warmly in Arabic, the little children running up to her to grasp her hand for a moment. What a contrast to the welcome she had received at first, the disrespectful comments from the men and boys, the cries of *nisrania*, or Christian woman, from the Moslem children, the whispered gossip from the women. It was true that she still heard such things outside of her neighborhood, but here, where she was known and liked, all that had ended. Janna supposed that her early experiences had been due to ignorance and fear, both on the part of those who had been rude and insulting, and on her own as well. Knowledge of each other had ended that, thank God, and Janna was grateful that unlike certain of her friends from training who had left Morocco at their first setbacks, she herself had decided to stay on.

Janna arrived at her house, which she had originally thought of as an apartment on the first floor of a concrete chunk of similar dwellings. Later she had changed her terminology. It could not be called an apartment in the American sense, as each unit was constructed by a different builder and owned by a different landlord, thus making these Moroccan homes a striking mishmash of styles and degrees of wealth. Janna's own was comfortable, but hardly as luxurious as that of Claudette Verlaine or the other French teachers who lived in the French *quartier*. It had a rather spacious high-ceilinged living room with a colorful tile floor and several large windows, though before Janna had furnished it, the room had been little more than a rectangular block. She had therefore needed to use all her ingenuity to transform it into something livable, placing plants around the room and hanging colorful posters on the walls. The mostly inexpensive furnishings consisted of two *banquettes*—narrow mattresses on wooden supports, a coffee table, a bookcase, a desk, and several leather *poufs*, or hassocks. The *banquettes*, at least, were beautiful, upholstered with the same dark blue brocaded fabric which covered the matching cushions propped up against the walls. Also, the wooden *banquette* stands had been carefully varnished to show the grain of the wood

It was refreshingly cool inside now, though Janna had heard that it would eventually be hot even indoors once summer finally arrived. She looked at her watch. It was nearly four o'clock and Lahcen would soon be here to give her today's Arabic lesson. Janna went into the kitchen to put a pot of water on the three burner counter-top stove. Lahcen had discovered that he liked Lipton tea, and they always had several cups during their lessons. His taste was in marked contrast to that of most Moroccans, whose national drink was sugary sweet mint-flavored green tea. Though Janna had learned to love this hot fragrant drink, a cup of *thé noir* always made her feel a little closer to home.

She dashed into the bathroom now to run a brush through her short wavy red hair. She wore little make-up, so her freckles were especially prominent after her walk in the sun. Janna was not traditionally beautiful, but she sparkled with life and energy and thus had always been considered attractive. She wondered how Lahcen found her, then told herself she was being foolish. He was eight years her junior, and it was ridiculous of her to have such thoughts.

Still, Janna knew that she found Lahcen dangerously good-looking, with his curly dark brown hair, his warm almond-shaped eyes, and the smile which lit up his entire face and made her stir with desire and, she was afraid to admit, something very close to love.

I'm a fool, Janna told herself. He's only a student. He can't possibly be interested in me. And even if he were, a relationship between us would be impossible!

It was annoying to have to worry about one's reputation, something Janna had never bothered to do before, but the fact remained that this was Aïn El Qamar and her neighbors were friendly only because they had put her into the category of saint. It would be so easy to become what they considered the only alternative.

Damn, she was living like a nun! Not since Christmas and a brief fling with another Peace Corps volunteer in Marrakesh had she had sex. The intervening five months had seemed endless to her, and yet Janna feared that her feelings for Lahcen exceeded, or could exceed, a mere desire for sexual pleasure.

Have you lost your mind by falling in love with your student? she asked herself as she heard the doorbell ring and went to answer it.

He was there, tall and strong for his age. He smiled and Janna was forced to face the truth.

"Hello, Lahcen," she said to him. You fool, she said to herself.

"I think we can stop now," suggested Janna in English. "It's already past five and my head is spinning from all the new vocabulary you taught me."

She took a cigarette and offered one to Lahcen. He lit them both, his own first. Janna smiled whimsically. The men always remained in control here.

"I think I must go now," said Lahcen, but he made no move to leave. Sensing his hesitation, Janna said to him:

"Is something bothering you?"

"It's nothing."

"Come on now, Lahcen. You haven't really been here in this room since you arrived. Is it the *bac* that you're worried about?"

Janna saw by his expression that she had guessed correctly. The *bac*, or *baccalauréat* examination, was less than three weeks away and its results would determine the futures of all high school seniors in Morocco. It was a nationwide standardized examination which covered a year's worth of material and was given over a five-day period in June. Passage meant going on to the university. Failure meant repeating the entire year or dropping out of school. Janna could sense the tension in all her senior class students whenever she met them. The exam was not written by their own teachers, nor would it be corrected by them. Anything was possible, everything had to be relearned, and their lives literally depended on the exam results. For Lahcen, passage meant that he would become a foreign exchange student in an American high school next year, and so he was under additional stress. He had often told Janna of his dream to visit the world outside Morocco, and she had been glad to recommend him to the American Field Service as one of her smartest students and the one she thought would best be able to adjust to American life. He seemed so much more open and broad-minded than his fellow classmates.

"I'm scared, Ms. Gallagher," said Lahcen. "We have so much to learn and there is not enough time. Sometimes I think I am going crazy."

Janna involuntarily reached out to take his hand in hers, then jerked it back, fearing that Lahcen might misinterpret such a gesture. However seeing the fear and worry in his eyes, she regretted her misgivings and reached out once again.

"You've got to have confidence in yourself," she said, feeling the warmth of his hand and sensing its strength. "You know you can achieve whatever goal you set for yourself. You're an incredible young man, Lahcen. You're gifted, and charming, and …"

Janna could scarcely believe her ears as she heard her own voice revealing her deepest feelings. Her hand, which Lahcen's enfolded, was becoming moist with sweat. This can't be happening, she thought. He's my student! And then it was Lahcen's voice she heard saying:

"You are so wonderful, Ms. Gallagher. You make me feel I can do anything."

Astounded at her own boldness, Janna reached up with her other hand and touched his cheek, and it was not the touch of a teacher.

Suddenly Lahcen's own hand was there, holding hers against his face, guiding its caress.

I shouldn't be doing this, thought Janna as she brought her lips towards Lahcen's. But her thoughts were silenced as Lahcen's mouth touched hers, at once tender and demanding. She felt her own open, felt their tongues meet and caress. She ran her fingers though his soft thick hair.

Then his hands were at her blouse, unbuttoning it, reaching inside her bra to fondle her breasts. She could feel her nipples rising, becoming hard to his touch.

She began removing Lahcen's shirt, savoring the hardness of his hairless chest, the warmth of his smooth skin. At the same time one of his hands was under her skirt, between her legs. After so long without sex, she found herself coming almost at once. And then, before she knew it, she was lying back on the *banquette*, and he was inside her, sending electric waves of excitement through her body. His mouth bruised hers, his hands were everywhere, his erect manhood plunging deep inside her, filling her with a satisfaction she had rarely known before because this time, she realized with a start, she was sharing it with a man with whom she had fallen totally and passionately in love.

Afterwards, he tried to apologize and Janna could see the shame in his eyes.

"Don't say you're sorry," she told him. "There's nothing to be sorry for."

"But, I should respect you. I should not touch you. You are my teacher, I …"

"Lahcen, you can love and respect a woman at the same time. It's perfectly natural. Can't you see that?"

But Janna could tell from his puzzled expression that such an idea was new to him. It was doubtless foreign to his contemporaries as well in this society where the sexes were separated from puberty on. Girls were merely objects, toys. How could love and respect coexist between people who never really spoke to each other? Here, friendships were primarily between men, and between women. How could it be otherwise, considering the make-up of society?

In the weeks that followed, Lahcen learned that things could indeed be otherwise. Janna taught him the joys of long, lingering kisses and caresses, that sex was not just five minutes spent in a sleazy room with a prostitute. Sex and love could be one, she said, and words of love and an exchange of ideas were as important to a relationship as the final moment of sexual release. Janna and Lahcen had many long conversations about their lives, their beliefs, and their dreams. She soothed him as he prepared with seemingly inexhaustible energy for the *baccalauréat*, and when they learned that he had passed, they celebrated together.

During all this time, they did their best to change as little as possible their public manner with each other. Lahcen still came to give her Arabic lessons, and if he stayed somewhat longer than before, Janna hoped that the neighbors would not notice. Their attitude seemed not to have changed, due she supposed to the months she had spent building up their confidence. Lahcen continued to sleep in the high school dormitory, and he insisted to her that he never revealed to his friends what was happening between them. He told Janna that his schoolmates had no suspicions, and she hoped for both their sakes that he was right. Lahcen's family did not live in Aïn El Qamar, and that, at least, was something to be thankful for.

When summer came, they traveled. Lahcen had relatives with whom he could stay in several of the big cities. Janna would check into a motel, one where unmarried couples could meet in private, and there they would make love, tenderly, passionately, until it was time for Lahcen to leave. Janna knew that there was a possibility of word reaching Aïn El Qamar, even though they did their best to be discreet. Still, being in love, nothing was going to stop her from living as her heart willed.

One day, Lahcen surprised Janna with the news that he had decided not to go to the United States after all, insisting that he could never leave her. Shocked at his decision, she argued with him for hours before finally persuading him that he must go. Janna knew that it meant sacrificing her own happiness at being with him, but she was willing to do so in order for Lahcen to have a once in a lifetime chance at experiencing another culture.

Their parting was painful. Luckily, Lahcen had already said good-bye to his parents and relatives in the town where they lived, so he and Janna were able to have a final farewell at the Casablanca airport. They kissed, a long deep kiss, oblivious to the shocked stares and rude comments which surrounded them, before Lahcen tore himself away to board the plane. It was only then that Janna became aware of the kind of insults which had first greeted her when she arrived in Aïn El Qamar. She shivered, wondering what life would be like once she was back in the town she now called home. There would be no more Lahcen, and she realized that she would now have to face the consequences of a liaison which could not have completely escaped the attention of her neighbors, her fellow teachers, and her students.

✳   ✳   ✳   ✳

"Mademoiselle Gallagher!" The commanding voice brought Janna back to the present, back to the classroom where she stood. She paused in her lesson and turned to face the *jellaba*-clad man who had just entered. It was Monsieur Rhazwani, the new *proviseur*, or principal, of Lycée Mohamed Cinq. This was only the second time Janna had encountered him personally. The first had been at a meeting of the school's five English teachers and her initial impression had not been favorable. Monsieur Rhazwani was in his forties, a large gorilla-like man with cold black eyes that did not smile even when his mouth attempted to. She had disliked him at once, sensing in him the type of Moroccan male who considered women to be second-class citizens and mistrusted any female who dared to assume the role of teacher. His attitudes towards education were equally rooted in the past. Students should learn by rote memorization and should be able to recite without hesitation what they had learned by heart. Those who misbehaved should have their knuckles rapped, or worse. Janna and her fellow teachers had been apprehensive about their meeting with the new *proviseur*, and with reason. He had rapidly dismissed their request for new textbooks to replace the old long-outdated ones. Janna had wanted to take a stand, but felt she did not speak Arabic or French well enough to do so. Thank goodness her colleagues Dave Casalini, another volunteer, one who spoke fluent French, and Michèle Perrault, a Frenchwoman who had recently arrived to teach English, had stood up to the *proviseur* and at least gotten him to agree to supply them with enough paper and mimeograph stencils to prepare their own handouts. Still, it had been evident from Monsieur Rhazwani's sour expression that he disapproved of Michèle's insistence, no doubt expecting her as a woman to assume a subservient role.

This new principal was certainly different from Monsieur Mahraoui, the considerate forward-thinking *proviseur* of the previous year who had been transferred to a better post in Meknes. No wonder everyone on the faculty, French, Moroccans, and Americans alike, was worried at what further encounters with Monsieur Rhazwani might bring. Now, it seemed, one such encounter was about to take place.

"Mademoiselle Gallagher," he repeated. "*Je suis venu observer votre classe.*"

Janna could feel the fear and dislike emanating from the students, which she shared; however she had no choice but to welcome him in to observe her class.

He stood at the back of the classroom and for the next twenty minutes or so Janna continued the lesson, feeling herself trembling slightly at first, then slowly gaining confidence but nonetheless remaining concerned about how he might interpret her teaching technique. She tried to make her questions less playful than usual. Keep the toy mouse hidden, and no more jumping up on chairs, she cautioned herself, sensing that the *proviseur* would not understand her belief that students could be entertained and learn at the same time. Janna wished she could continue teaching as if the *proviseur* was not there, but she had to face the facts. The man was her boss, and if she wanted their relationship to remain harmonious for the rest of the year, she'd better give him more or less what he wanted. As for what happened in her classroom when he wasn't around, well that was none of Monsieur Rhazwani's business.

It seemed now that the *proviseur* had at last decided to leave. Janna breathed a sigh of relief, but her relief was short-lived. "Come to my office when you finish," ordered Monsieur Rhazwani, and left.

"*Hellouf!*" said several of the students almost in unison. Janna knew that they had insulted him by calling him a pig, but she pretended not to have understood, and did her best to go on with the lesson until the bell finally, mercifully, rang.

After answering the questions of several of her students, Janna walked with some trepidation across the dirt courtyard around which the classrooms were situated and toward the office of the *proviseur*.

She told his secretary why she had come, and the veiled woman wearing a traditional *jellaba* asked her to wait. For a moment, Janna debated simply leaving the office and going home. It had been a long morning with three classes in a row, and she still had two more to go after the two-hour noon break. She was hungry and eagerly looking forward to a leisurely lunch. And if that weren't enough, there was still the matter of getting to the *salle des profs* to see if a letter had arrived from Lahcen. The nerve of Monsieur Rhazwani, to summon her to his office and then to make her wait!

Ten minutes passed, and Janna was about to either enter his office unannounced or walk away without bothering to give an explanation when the door opened and Monsieur Rhazwani beckoned her to enter.

The office looked markedly different from the way it had appeared when Monsieur Mahraoui had been *proviseur*. As soon as Monsieur Rhazwani had arrived, he had insisted upon more space, and so the rear wall of the office had been torn down to double its size. This had meant moving the *surveillant général*, or vice principal, into smaller quarters, and it gave a clear demonstration to faculty and staff alike exactly who was in charge of Lycée Mohamed Cinq this year.

Looking around the room, Janna saw that Monsieur Rhazwani had made good use of the other man's office space, choosing to completely refurnish the room at the school's expense. A pair of luxuriously upholstered *banquettes* now sat at one end of the office. Opposite them was a table whose top was an expensive round engraved silver tray. There were also several European-style armchairs and a mahogany sideboard against the wall. Monsieur Rhazwani's desk was also made of mahogany. It stood at the other end of the office and occupied nearly twice the space of Monsieur Mahraoui's much more modest one.

"Please … have … seat, uh … Miss Gallagher," said Monsieur Rhazwani as he settled into the high-backed armchair behind his desk.

Janna could scarcely restrain herself from laughing once she realized that the man was attempting to speak to her in broken English. Then she got an idea.

"Why, Mr. Rhazwani, you speak my language," she replied in her rapidest English. "I must admit I'm quite impressed. I had no idea you'd studied English or that you'd learned it so well. It's really quite a thrill for me to know that there's someone with whom I can converse here at Lycée Mohamed Cinq in the language of my birth! Tell me, how many years did you study? In what school? Have you ever traveled abroad to England or the States, for example?" Janna managed to get out this speech in record time and without pausing to take a breath. She was really quite proud of herself.

"*Humph, eh bien …*" stammered the *proviseur* in French, then continued in that language, "I did not ask you here to test your English ability. I am confident that you speak it adequately."

"*Lash brhiti tshufni?*" asked Janna in Arabic. "Why did you want to see me?" Screw you, she thought. I'll be damned if you make me speak French when my Arabic is much better. You think that speaking French makes you more cultivated than other Moroccans. Well, this is one game I'm not playing with you.

"*Je voulais discuter votre leçon avec vous*," continued the *proviseur* in French. "I wanted to discuss your lesson with you."

"*Wakha*," said Janna in Arabic. "I see." Although she was almost enjoying this sparring match, she couldn't help wishing that she knew French fluently, as did her three American colleagues, Dave Casalini, Kevin Kensington, and Marcie Nelson. It would make it so much easier to gain the *proviseur*'s respect. Janna had only had two years of high school French, and that was ages ago. At least, though, she knew enough to follow what Monsieur Rhazwani was saying.

"I'm proud to say I understood your lesson perfectly," the *proviseur* commented.

That's not too great a surprise, thought Janna, who had been teaching a class of beginners.

Rhazwani continued his "critique," but Janna paid little attention until she heard him mention her new friend Michèle's name.

"… unlike Mademoiselle Perrault."

"Excuse me?" interrupted Janna.

"I was saying that at least you dress respectably, unlike the incompetent Mademoiselle Perrault."

Oh my God, this man's an idiot! thought Janna. Michèle Perrault was a rarity, a French teacher of English who could speak the language perfectly. She had lived in the United States for several years, so her English was rapid and idiomatic. This was her first year in Morocco, but already Janna had heard students commenting on what an excellent teacher she was. It was true that Michèle's faded jeans and peasant shirts were a new phenomenon at Lycée Mohamed Cinq. Janna herself had wondered if such casual attire was advisable, but Michèle had told her, "I wear the clothes I feel comfortable in. What's that got to do with my ability to maintain discipline in class? I'm an experienced teacher. Wait and see. You won't find me having any problems with students." And Michèle had been proven right. She maintained the authority necessary to control the sometimes unruly Moroccan boys and girls, and the ownership of a car prevented her from ever having to go anywhere on foot as did Janna. It seemed that the only person really bothered by her clothes was Monsieur Rhazwani. He must be some kind of Neanderthal to assume that Michèle was a bad teacher simply because of what she wore.

"I see," said Janna, trying to hold back her indignation. "Was there anything else?"

"Only one thing," said Monsieur Rhazwani. "I myself personally take care of all discipline problems at Lycée Mohamed Cinq. You are to send any student who misbehaves to my office immediately, for suitable punishment."

"But there are no discipline problems in any of my classes," insisted Janna.

"That is for me to decide!"

Janna could scarcely believe her ears.

"You may leave now," said Monsieur Rhazwani. "My lunch is waiting. Good day."

He rose to reveal a protruding belly and held out his hand. Janna wanted to ignore the gesture, but she was afraid of being too obvious.

"*B'slama, Si* Rhazwani," she said in Arabic, nearly jerking her hand out of his sweaty grasp. "Good bye."

"*Au revoir, mademoiselle*," he answered in French.

Outside his office in the sunny courtyard, Janna lit a cigarette and inhaled deeply. She made it a rule not to smoke in public, but today was going to be an exception. She could see several students lingering around the classrooms looking in her direction, and she knew that they must be commenting on her cigarette.

"Ms. Gallagher is smoking at school?" asked an amused voice behind her, and Janna turned to face Kevin Kensington. Like Janna, this was his second year in Aïn El Qamar. He was younger than she, though, perhaps only twenty-two, pleasant looking, of medium height, with sandy colored hair. He shared a house with Dave Casalini, and no two people could have been more dissimilar. Dave was tall, built like a football player, outgoing and fun-loving, and quite willing to tell close friends that he was gay. Kevin, on the other hand, never discussed his personal life, if indeed he had one.

"You're damn right I'm smoking," she said to him. "You'd be too if you'd just been through what I have."

At that moment, Monsieur Rhazwani emerged from his office and Janna gestured to Kevin to move away. As the *proviseur* got into his Peugeot to drive off to the villa he occupied on the outskirts of town, Janna said, "With luck, he'll get run into by a truck!"

"What's he done now?" asked Kevin.

Janna told him about her interview with Monsieur Rhazwani.

"I can't believe that man's gall!" exclaimed Kevin. "What qualifies him to evaluate your teaching? According to Kacem Hajiri, Monsieur Rhazwani was given his first administrative post just to get him out of the classroom."

"That wouldn't surprise me," said Janna. "He probably only got this job because he's related to somebody."

"I wouldn't doubt it," agreed Kevin.

"Have you heard his English?" asked Janna

Kevin laughed. "He tried to show it off when Dave and I first met him a few weeks ago. Dave looked him right in the eye and told him in French, 'I'm sorry, *monsieur* but I don't understand Arabic!'"

"Oh God, I wish I'd been there," exclaimed Janna, "if only to have seen his expression. Unfortunately, neither my Arabic nor my French is up to making sarcastic remarks."

"I'd say you did pretty well for yourself today. But I must admit I agree with the *proviseur* about Michèle's clothes. They're not professional."

"Kevin, it's the seventies, for God's sake. You can't expect schoolteachers to dress the way they did twenty years ago!"

"This isn't the United States, you know," said Kevin.

"I realize that," admitted Janna. "But that doesn't mean I have to go along with every antiquated belief the natives may happen to have."

"I've never heard you talk this way, Janna. You sound like you're carrying some kind of grudge."

"I don't know, Kevin. Maybe I am," replied Janna, wondering if the grudge she was carrying was against Lahcen, for leaving her, or against herself, for letting Lahcen disappear from her life. "I've got a lot of things on my mind. Forget what I said. Listen. I'll see you later. I have to get to the *salle des profs* and check on my mail."

"I think I saw a letter there from the States with your name on it."

"Really?" Janna's face beamed. "I'll keep my fingers crossed."

"Be seeing you Janna. I've got to run. I'm invited to Kacem Hajiri's house for lunch. Bye."

"*B'slama*, Kevin," said Janna, thinking to herself: That's the second mention of Kacem Hajiri in just over a minute. Could little Kevin have set his sights on that handsome new Moroccan physics teacher? Maybe it wasn't just teaching that occupied Kevin's mind after all.

Janna turned to walk towards the *salle des profs*. It was certainly nothing like an American high school faculty lounge, just an unused classroom where teachers could meet between hours. There were a few old chairs inside and a large table on which the *shaoush*, or messenger, dropped the mail delivery twice a day.

Janna ran up to the table, then felt a stab of disappointment. As far as she could see, there was nothing there with her name on it. Kevin must have been mistaken. Damn, damn, damn, she thought. It's been over two weeks since Lahcen wrote, and I've already sent him three letters since I last heard from him.

Dejectedly, Janna left the school by the main gate and began the short walk to her house, not hearing the greetings of the students she passed along the way. She was too busy thinking of Lahcen in Cleveland, Ohio, wondering how he was adjusting to American life, wondering what could have prevented him from writing her for so long.

"Miss. Eh, Miss," said a voice almost at her ear. Startled, Janna turned to see who had spoken to her. It was a student-aged youth with unkempt hair and a day's growth of beard.

"Yes? May I … help you?" she asked cautiously.

"You want I walk home with you?" he asked in heavily accented English. His breath was putrid. "Maybe you are little lonely?" he added with a smirk on his face.

"No, thank you," she replied coolly, drawing away from him. "I'm perfectly fine. And the correct grammar is 'Do you want me to …'"

"Oh, you are very good teacher," continued the student in his oily way. "My teacher, she's Miss Nelson. She is new teacher. Maybe you are teaching the best. Some student say so. You know …" He winked at her.

"Miss Nelson is a very good teacher. I think that you probably just need to study harder."

"You want helping me?" asked the young man slyly.

This student was really getting on Janna's nerves. "Please leave me alone!" she said sharply, and turned quickly away, heading on towards her house, hoping that he was not following her.

Janna's first thought as she walked away was: What on earth provoked that?

And then it hit her.

Oh no! Could Claudette have been right? The glamorous Frenchwoman had told her she was getting into dangerous waters the day Janna had confided in her about her affair with Lahcen.

"Janna, you are being very stupeed," Claudette had said in her charming Gallic English. "I am in Aïn El Qamar seence six years, and I 'ave 'ad quite a few Moroccan boyfriends. But never, never here, in zees town. I always 'ave my Arab men in big cities like Casa and Rabat. You must think of what zee other people are saying. *Réputation*, you know."

Claudette gave many parties and wore daring clothes. In her ten years in Aïn El Qamar, she had become a legend. But Janna realized that what she said was true. In order to protect her standing in the community, she had never been seen dating a Moroccan bachelor inside Aïn El Qamar.

I should have listened to Claudette, Janna said to herself as she approached her house. People did notice my relationship with Lahcen, and they can't understand! They're making something trashy out of the most beautiful experience of my life.

Janna looked up the street and saw Michèle's Renault 4 parked in front of her door. With few telephones, unexpected visits were frequent, pleasant surprises in Aïn El Qamar. Janna hurried past the smiling neighbor children and went into her house.

"Michèle?" she called out.

"I'm in the kitchen," answered the Frenchwoman, and Janna went to find her. "I was just admiring your maid's cooking skills, but I haven't been able to tell her so."

"That's hardly surprising. Halima doesn't speak a word of French, which is lucky for me. She's been a great help in learning Arabic."

"*La bass*, Halima?" she asked the maid.

"*La bass*, Miss Janna," answered the heavily wrinkled sun-darkened Moroccan woman who was dressed traditionally in a brocaded silk caftan with a colorful scarf covering her hair. When outside she would cover this with her *haïk* and veil her face, in order to preserve modesty.

"*La bass* is about the extent of my Arabic," commented Michèle. "*La bass*—'How are you?' and *La bass*—'I'm fine.' It's like '*Ça va*' in French. The question and the answer are the same."

"It's really a shame you don't know Arabic, Michèle."

"Well, we French may make more money than you Americans, but you at least are trained in the language and the culture. They think a few days preparation before we arrive is enough for us."

"Let's go into the living room and have something to drink," suggested Janna. "I'm sorry I don't have anything cold to offer you, but on my salary there's no way I can afford a refrigerator. American necessities are luxuries for us here, you know. But I've got red wine, tea, or coffee, whichever you'd like."

"Coffee sounds fine," said Michèle.

"Could you bring us two coffees, Halima?" asked Janna in Arabic. "I'll eat later."

"*Wakha*, Miss Janna," answered the maid.

Michèle followed Janna into the living room and sat opposite her on one of the *banquettes*. "It's cute how Halima calls you 'Miss Janna' even in Arabic. And speaking of Halima, if you can't afford a refrigerator, how can you afford to have a maid? I thought that you American volunteers were supposed to live at the level of the people."

"Oh please, Michèle. You know how cheap hired help is in Morocco. It's not as if Halima works every day like your maid does. She only comes to do the washing and ironing, and she's the one who insists on cooking for me. She thinks I need some healthy Moroccan food. All told, she only works two mornings a week, and even though I pay her double the standard wage, it still hardly puts a dent in my pocketbook. Besides, she's been working for Peace Corps volunteers for years. It's almost a requirement to hire her. She also cooks and cleans for Dave and Kevin, and for Marcie too."

"Lucky lady," said Michèle. "No wonder she hasn't needed to learn French."

Halima arrived carrying a tray with two cups, a pot of coffee, sugar and cream. She set it on the table between the two women.

"Tell her I like her caftan. It's just beautiful," said Michèle.

"*Mademoiselle galet bin ajebha el qaftan dyalek. Galet bin zuween bazaff.*"

"Bravo, Janna!" exclaimed Michèle.

"*Barakallahoufik, mademoiselle,*" thanked Halima, and smiled to reveal a set of perfect teeth.

"They can't be hers!" exclaimed Michèle as Halima left.

"You mean the dentures? They're not. Those teeth are the result of years of saving. That's why she loves to show them off."

Janna poured two cups of coffee. Michèle added cream and sugar to hers; Janna took hers black.

"So, how was your morning?" asked Michèle.

"You shouldn't have asked. I was so pleased to see you that I nearly forgot." Janna told Michèle about her conversation with the *proviseur*.

"*Salaud!*" said Michèle when Janna was through. "That means son of a bitch in French. I'll be damned if I change my wardrobe just to satisfy a sexist pig! Besides, even if my jeans are tight, there's not enough meat on my bones to excite a Moroccan. Now if I had Miss Claudette's figure …"

"Well, I just thought I'd warn you," said Janna.

"Thanks," replied Michèle. "I appreciate it. And now, I really have to run. Domino is probably waiting for me to bring the wine for lunch, and I still haven't picked it up yet."

Michèle got up to leave. Then, snapping her fingers, she took something out of her purse. "I almost forgot my reason for dropping by. This," she said, handing Janna an envelope, "was in the *salle des profs*. I thought you'd left already so I decided to bring it over to you."

"Thank you!" cried Janna, trembling with excitement. "Oh thank you, Michèle!" she exclaimed, and threw her arms around the slender Frenchwoman.

"You're welcome," said Michèle, somewhat overwhelmed by Janna's enthusiasm. "And now I've got to fly. Be seeing you."

Janna wasn't aware of Michèle's departure, didn't hear the door shut or Michèle's car driving away. Her hands shaking, she tore open the letter which had finally arrived from Lahcen!

CHAPTER 2

$\blacktriangledown$

Michèle Perrault had only been in Aïn El Qamar slightly more than a month, but already she regretted not having come sooner. Still, she was not sorry for the three years she had spent in the United States, four if you counted the year she had lived there as a teenager when her father was sent to New York on business. After completing her university studies of English in Paris, she had returned to the States to teach French at a small college in Southern California. She had loved her life there, loved speaking English, loved the freedom she had felt. The climate had been ideal, of course. Michèle had spent long hours on the beach, even in January. She used to write back to her friends in France about this, knowing how envious they would be, and savoring their envy. She had even fallen in love in California. Unfortunately, though, the man had been married. Doubtless their relationship could have continued on indefinitely, but financial cutbacks had reduced her school's foreign language budget and no other teaching jobs had been readily available. So Michèle had said good-bye to her married lover, sorry at their parting but grateful that she could make the break, and when the offer to work in Morocco had come, she had jumped at the chance to discover another foreign world.

Unlike the American Peace Corps volunteers, Michèle and her French col- leagues, called *cöopérants*, were extremely well-paid, much better so than their Moroccan counterparts. Their ample salaries, provided in tandem by the French and the Moroccan governments, permitted them to buy new cars, to live in attractive apartments or houses, to travel extensively during school breaks, and still to transfer a considerable portion of their salaries into French bank accounts. Knowing Janna Gallagher had given Michèle a better perspective on Morocco than most of her French colleagues. That was one of the reasons she felt fortunate to have Janna as a friend. They had clicked right away, much better in fact than had Michèle and Dominique Moulin, the Frenchwoman with whom she shared a house. Michèle wished that she were living with Janna instead of the sour Dominique, but the American could never have afforded to split the rent of a place as pricey as the two Frenchwomen's. Janna had introduced Michèle to several Moroccan teachers whom she might not have met otherwise, and she found them friendly and less traditional than she might have imagined. One in particular, Kacem Hajiri, she thought she could grow to like. He was one of the handsomest men she had ever seen, but seemed shy and reserved around her, and so Michèle had only spoken to him once or twice. She was an outgoing person, but fearing that her attempts at friendship might be misinterpreted, she had decided to wait and see what time would bring.

Wait and see—that basically was her attitude as far as Morocco in general was concerned. Her car and her house in a *quartier* almost exclusively French had prevented her from having the unpleasant experiences that had greeted Janna upon her arrival. For the most part, Michèle had liked what she had seen, was fascinated by the new and exotic culture, worlds apart from either France or Southern California. She was nearing thirty, though with her short brown hair and boyish figure she looked closer to twenty. Still single, she enjoyed her liberty and the new life she had recently begun to live.

Now, as she drove away from Janna's house, she smiled at the children playing soccer with a dirty yellow plastic ball that had obviously seen better days. Other children carried miniature satchels as they returned home from primary school. Women, their heads and bodies covered with *haïks*, some white, some pastel colored, some bright with flowered patterns, trudged along lugging baskets filled with vegetables and fruit from the market or buckets of water from the neighborhood fountain. Many houses had running water, but obviously not all, thought Michèle.

She turned onto the main road and headed in the direction of the Epicérie Mondiale, the grocery store where most of the French shopped for staples. On the way, she glanced towards the now deserted market grounds where once a week the *souk* was held. Janna had taken her there soon after their first meeting, and Michèle had been fascinated by the myriad tents filled with everything from rainbow-colored fabrics, to shiny new kitchen utensils, to fragrant spices, to fresh produce. And of course there were the animals: sheep, goats, chickens, rabbits, all for sale, and not as pets. Michèle and Dominique's maid Aïsha, did much of their shopping at the *souk* each week, and Michèle had to admit that the fruit and vegetables she purchased there were far tastier than those sold at the indoor market where many of the French shopped.

Michèle was going to the Epicérie Mondiale to get one of the few things which Aïsha, as a Moslem, was forbidden to purchase—wine—although more than once Michèle had spotted Moroccan men leaving the store with suspiciously shaped bags and had surmised that a good deal of *vin rouge* was being sold under the counter.

There were almost always several cars parked outside the shop. It did excellent business with the French and with the Europeanized Moroccans of Aïn El Qamar, and carried most everything that could be found in a much larger grocery store in Casablanca or Rabat. Michèle parked, locked her car for safety even though she only expected to be inside for a minute, and entered the shop. As usual, the shelves were piled high with merchandise.

"Ah Michèle!" called out a voice, and as Michèle's eyes became adjusted to the relative darkness of the shop, she saw Claudette Verlaine, the famous Miss Claudette of Aïn El Qamar. Today the voluptuous Frenchwoman was wearing a clingy green silk blouse and tight white slacks which she had tucked into a pair of knee-high black leather boots.

Claudette was in her forties, though few would have guessed, for the obvious care she took with her appearance. She was tall, perhaps five-ten, with a thick mane of auburn hair and spectacular green eyes. Michèle thought that the expertly applied make-up she wore was a bit more appropriate for evening than for daytime, but then Miss Claudette had a reputation for doing everything to excess—driving fast, playing hard, and making love like a tigress.

"Just coming from class now?" asked Claudette.

"In a round-about way. I stopped off to see Janna Gallagher."

"A charming girl," exclaimed Claudette. "*Absolument charmante*. She lets me speak my atrocious English and never corrects a single one of my many mistakes. *Je l'adore!*"

Michèle found herself somewhat tongue-tied at Claudette's exuberance, but the glamorous Frenchwoman did not seem to be waiting for an answer.

"*Mon Dieu*," she continued. "School has only just started and already I am in need of a vacation. Not that I don't adore my little angels. But they can be little devils at times." Claudette's pre-teenaged students were in *première* and *deuxième*, the first two of the seven years of study offered at Lycée Mohamed Cinq. "I tell you, Michèle, I need a long vacation with a wonderful man who will make love to me from dusk to dawn, and then again from dawn to dusk."

Michèle remained at a loss for words in the presence of such enthusiasm. Fortunately, Claudette had turned to the pudgy, balding shopkeeper and begun to read off her shopping list.

"*Eh bien, monsieur*, I shall have one bottle of Pernaud Blanc, one of Martini Rouge, and three of Gris de Boulaouane ...," she was saying, and Michèle could only stand in open-mouthed admiration at this instantaneous change of persona. Speaking to the shopkeeper, Claudette was both aloof and commanding. Without being condescending, she nonetheless was able to keep her distance. It was quite an impressive performance, thought Michèle, who could see now how Claudette had managed to live for so many years in Aïn El Qamar despite her sexy ways and provocative attire.

As the shopkeeper's youthful assistant raced around the shop to fetch Claudette's requests, sometimes climbing up a ladder to reach the higher shelves, Claudette continued her conversation with Michèle, and once again she had become her usual ebullient self.

"So we were talking about vacation, *n'est-ce pas*? It is not yet November and already I am planning my December holidays. This year we shall have a longer period than we normally do because Christmas vacation coincides with the Moslem fête of *Aïd El Kébir*—you do know that means 'big holiday,' don't you? They will celebrate by slaughtering sheep, and I shall celebrate by making love day and night for two glorious weeks. And let me let you in on a little secret, *chérie* ..." Claudette leaned over to whisper in Michèle's ear. "I think I've found just the man to satisfy my urges. So tall, and handsome, and strong, and in his tennis shorts—a stallion! Now if I can just get him out of those shorts and between my bed sheets!"

A flustered Michèle noticed that the shopkeeper was again trying to attract their attention.

"*Oui, monsieur?*" said Claudette, resuming her nearly regal air. "Yes, that will be all. You have totaled it up in my book? Excellent!"

She signed her name in the notebook where her account was kept and noting that it was almost the end of the month, said, "I shall bring you a check within the week." The shopkeeper handed the bag containing Claudette's purchases to his young helper who proceeded to carry it towards her car.

As Claudette was leaving she called back to Michèle, "Oh, *chérie*, I almost forgot to tell you. I've decided to throw a magnificent party, the event of the year, on December 18th. That's the first night of the Christmas holiday, so don't leave town until after you've attended. Jot it down in your date book. It's sure to be an unforgettable night! *Au revoir.*"

"*Au revoir*," said Michèle, thinking to herself that Claudette could definitely be depended upon to bring life, energy, and excitement along with her wherever she went. It should be quite a party, Michèle told herself, happy to have something to look forward to, even though weeks away.

"And how is *mademoiselle* today?" asked the shopkeeper in French.

"*Très bien, monsieur*," answered Michèle. "I'd like a bottle of Valpierre Rouge."

The young shop assistant, who had returned, now scurried towards a door which led to the room where wine was stored.

"Valpierre rouge, an excellent choice," commented the shopkeeper.

"I thought that Moslems weren't allowed to drink."

"That is true, *mademoiselle*, nor may we eat pork, and all must fast during the month of Ramadan. I was only repeating what my customers have told me about this wine."

Michèle thought she noticed a slight twinkle in the man's eyes, and she wondered if he had indeed never sampled his merchandise. "What a shame for you to live in a country which produces such splendid wines, and yet not be able to enjoy them."

"*C'est bien dommage, mademoiselle*," agreed the shopkeeper, and again Michèle was unable to tell if he was speaking seriously.

The young assistant came out of the storeroom carrying the wine in a brown paper bag which he handed to the shopkeeper who in turn gave it to Michèle. "Will there be anything else?" he asked.

Michèle's eyes scanned the shelves quickly from top to bottom. There was so much to see: canned vegetables and pâtés, cooking oils, tissues and paper towels, aluminum foil, bags of pretzels and potato chips (much of this imported from Europe). Finally, on one of the shelves she noticed a huge jar of black olives.

"Are they fresh?" she asked.

"Naturally, *mademoiselle*. Fresh *zitoon* from right here in Aïn El Qamar."

"I'll take four hundred grams, please. That and the wine will be all."

Michèle watched as the shopkeeper placed the olives in a plastic bag and weighed them. These were not only cheaper than any olives she had ever bought before, but also more delicious, and they came from the groves which surrounded Aïn El Qamar. Just a week before, she had eaten at Janna's and Halima, the maid, had served a savory chicken and olive *tajine*, or stew. Michèle decided that she and Domino would have the olives with their evening aperitifs.

Like Claudette, Michèle signed her name in her account book, making a mental note that the month was nearly over. All the French bought on credit, a great convenience which Michèle had been pleasantly surprised to discover upon her arrival in Aïn El Qamar.

"Have a good day, *mademoiselle*," said the shopkeeper as Michèle left.

Michèle drove quickly towards the exclusive *quartier* where she shared a Moroccan-style home with Dominique Moulin. The houses there were similar to Janna's, but newer and more comfortable, with large kerosene heaters in each room, porcelain bathtubs, small gardens out front, and of course refrigerators, ovens, and high-priced stereo sets within. The *quartier* was called Cité Jamila, the beautiful city, and at least compared with the other *quartiers* in Aïn El Qamar, it was. Also, it was almost wholly occupied by French *cöopérants*.

Michèle pulled up her car in front of her house, reached into the back seat to grab her groceries, and got out, once again locking the door. Aïn El Qamar was not a dangerous place to live; indeed she felt safer here than ever before in her life. But an open car door was an invitation to petty thievery.

Michèle noticed that Claudette was not yet parked at her house just down the street, and she wondered where the woman had gone after their meeting at the Mondiale. Perhaps to the four-star Hotel El Qamar located a mile or so out of town? Miss Claudette often went to the hotel for a few sets of tennis before lunch.

Michèle realized that Jean-Richard's car was missing as well. Jean-Richard Moreau, Aïn El Qamar's handsomest and most eligible bachelor and its most notorious playboy, lived with Claudette. He had been in Aïn El Qamar for as long as Claudette and at first, it was said, they had lived together as lovers, though they now seemed more like brother and sister.

Apparently, like Claudette, Jean-Richard was out at the moment, and Michèle wondered what woman he was with today. Jean-Richard had made a pass at her soon after she had arrived in Aïn El Qamar, which she had skillfully resisted. She found the Frenchman quite handsome—tall, tan, and blond—but he seemed superficial and much too slick for her. She certainly was not interested in becoming another of his conquests.

Dominique, her roommate, poor plain Domino, had not protested however when Jean-Richard had taken her to bed. But that had been once, and once only, several weeks ago, and Jean-Richard seemed to have lost interest almost immediately. Poor Domino. Michèle feared that she was not going to have an easy two years in Aïn El Qamar. She hated the town already, bitched about it constantly, and had she been a volunteer, she would doubtless already have left. But unfortunately she had a contract, like all the French, and breaking it would mean having difficulties finding an equally well-paying teaching job back in France. Poor

Domino, Michèle repeated. You came here for work and for the money you could earn, but you'll never be happy with such a negative attitude.

Michèle unlocked the front door to their second floor house and skipped up the stairs. She was damned if she was going to let Dominique Moulin's negative feelings depress her. "Domino, Domino, I'm home," she called.

She left the olives in the kitchen where their maid Aïsha was putting the finishing touches on lunch. After a quick greeting in French, Michèle went into the living room, setting the bottle of wine on the large dining table which occupied one end of the room and which Aïsha had already set for the noonday meal.

"*Salut*, Domino," she said.

"*Salut*," replied Dominique half-heartedly from the *banquette* at the other end where she sat correcting papers. "Idiots! These Moroccan students … brainless dunces every one!"

And one wonders why Moroccans accuse us of being racist, thought Michèle. Out loud, she said, "That bad?"

"*Dégoutant*! They have understood nothing!" exclaimed Dominique.

And what do you expect? thought Michèle as she sat down on a *banquette* facing the other woman. These are country boys trying to learn algebra and geometry for the first time. But she said nothing. She had already advised Dominique to make a greater effort to explain in a way that would take into consideration their rural background. But Dominique had snapped back that she had no intention of lowering her "standards." Thank goodness I teach English, Michèle told herself. Students who had already studied French and Classical Arabic found English a breeze. I'm really very spoiled, she thought, as she poured herself a drink from the Martini and Rossi bottle on the coffee table.

"I think I'm going to lose my mind," said Dominique, "if I'm not killed or raped first."

"You can't be serious, Domino," exclaimed Michèle. "I feel in absolutely no danger whatsoever here in Aïn El Qamar. Nor should you," she added, thinking: Especially the way you look, with your mousy brown hair and dowdy skirt and blouse. What on earth prompted Jean-Richard to sleep with you? Simply the desire for another conquest, I suppose.

"I can't fathom you, Michèle," said Dominique. "This place is a hellhole, and we're stuck here for two years … two interminable years! How can you go around beaming as if this were heaven on earth? I can't step outside without feeling that I'm being looked at wherever I go. Foreigner! Whore! I can sense what the people are saying about me."

"Stop exaggerating, Domino. I'm sure the Moroccans have better things to do than to talk about you."

And more attractive women to look at, she added silently.

"I should never have come," pouted Dominique.

You're damn right, thought Michèle, and I was a fool to move in with you. But what's done is done. She supposed that Dominique might have found life easier if she had been given a post in Casablanca or Rabat or one of the other larger cities, but even there she would probably have had problems. Michèle realized that Dominique was one of those people who should never set foot out of their own country. Morocco, certainly, so different from France, was the last place she ought to have gone.

"I met Claudette at the Mondiale just now," said Michèle. "She's going to throw a party at the beginning of the Christmas break. She made it sound like quite an event."

Dominique looked up in interest, setting down the papers she was correcting and lighting a cigarette. "*Ah, oui?* Of course that's nearly two months away," she said. "Still, anything is better than rotting at home."

"Then why do you never go to the cinema? You missed that fabulous new Truffaut film last week."

"You know how terrible it was the one time I did go. All the Moroccan men just stood there and gaped at me as I entered the lobby."

"So? They look at me too," said Michèle. And have something a lot prettier to look at, she thought to herself. "You've only got to walk past them. Really, Domino, I think you create most of your own problems."

Just then, Aïsha entered the room carrying a glazed ceramic casserole which she set on the dining table. She left, returning a few seconds later with a large glass bowl of salad.

"It smells delicious, Aïsha," commented Michèle from the *banquette* where she sat. "You haven't actually made *Boeuf Bourguignonne*, have you?"

"*Oui, mademoiselle,*" answered Aïsha proudly in French. She had learned to speak it simply but with near fluency during her many years spent working for French *coöpérants* in Aïn El Qamar.

"I never believed when I came to Morocco that I'd be served French *haute cuisine* for lunch every day. You really are a wonder, Aïsha. But someday you must make us something typically Moroccan. Please."

"*Bien sûr, mademoiselle,*" replied the maid. "But Mademoiselle Dominique told me that she didn't care for Moroccan food."

"That's right," hissed Dominique. "You couldn't make me eat such slop!"

"Never mind Mademoiselle Dominique, Aïsha," reassured Michèle. "You can make something just for me one day."

"*Oui, mademoiselle*," said the maid, and left the room.

Turning to Dominique, Michèle said in annoyance, "Really, Domino. Don't you like anything here? Won't you even give this country a try?"

Dominique was finishing the correction of a test paper. She looked up. "*Pardon?*" she asked.

"Oh, never mind. Lunch is ready." The two women got up and moved to the other end of the spacious living room where they took their seats at the long cedar dining table.

Just then, a tall, dark-haired and quite good-looking young man with an athletic build appeared at the living room door, a somewhat smaller and younger but equally handsome Moroccan standing beside him. The Moroccan was buttoning his shirt.

"*Salut*, Michèle. *Merci*, Dominique," said American Peace Corps volunteer Dave Casalini in nearly unaccented French. "Lateef and I have been taking you up on your offer to lend us your rooftop for some sunrays."

Michèle recalled Dave's request of several weeks ago and her willing agreement to share their terrace with him. Dave lived in a first-floor house, whereas Michèle and Dominique's second-floor dwelling had access to a flat roof surrounded by a five-foot-high wall where clothes could be hung out to dry. Moroccan women also dried wheat on their rooftops, and Europeans were fond of sunning themselves there when the weather was pleasant.

"Hello, Dave," smiled Michèle. "*Salut*, Lateef. *Ça va aujourd'hui?*" Michèle recognized the student whom Dave had previously introduced to her as "Lateef Raffali, future statesman of Morocco." According to Dave, Lateef had been his top pupil since the previous year, and was already quite conversational in English. Dave's French itself was impeccable. He had studied a year in Tours, France.

"Don't let us interrupt your lunch," said Dave, adding, "We really enjoyed the use of your roof. It felt so good, I fell asleep there. I wish now that Kevin and I had taken a second-floor house instead of one on the ground floor."

"Well, you're welcome to use ours whenever you get the urge," said Michèle. "But didn't you have class this morning?"

"We both finished at eleven. We were only on your roof for an hour or so."

"That's long enough," said Dominique under her breath, and Michèle wondered what she could possibly be thinking. Luckily, Dave appeared not to have heard.

"Well, see you both later. You're invited to drop by Kevin's and my place any time. We'd enjoy seeing you. *A bientôt.*"

"*Au revoir, mesdemoiselles,*" said the young Moroccan, without the heavily trilled "r" of many of the students.

"*Au revoir,*" replied the women.

"Now what on earth was that remark about?" asked Michèle after Dave and Lateef had left.

"Isn't it obvious, Michèle?" said Dominique. "What other teacher in Aïn El Qamar has a student as a best friend? There's obviously something going on between the two of them."

"Nonsense, Domino," insisted Michèle, who knew from her experiences in the States that student-teacher friendships were not uncommon there. "You're imagining things."

"Oh, I don't know. You may be right," conceded Dominique. "All you have to do is take one look at Dave to know that he's no fag."

"Oh, eat your lunch before it gets cold!" snapped Michèle, finally at the end of her patience. "I've had quite enough of your sarcasm for one morning!"

CHAPTER 3

▼

Aïn El Qamar was not one of the great, legendary cities of Morocco which tourists spent days exploring. Unlike Fez and Marrakesh, there was no ancient walled city, or *medina*. It did not have the skyscrapers of Casablanca. There were not the sandy beaches or *kasbah* that could be found in Tangier or Rabat. It was, however, centrally located and thus had become a convenient stopping off point for travelers driving through Morocco or taking guided bus tours. For this reason, a large three-story hotel had been built on the outskirts of town where tourists could rest over a leisurely lunch or even spend the night. The French and upper-class Moroccans found its construction a godsend as they now had a place to go for an elegant meal, and its pool and tennis courts were popular during the warm months. In addition, it offered spectacular views of the Atlas Mountains from nearly every vantage point.

Today, as usual, there were a number of people sitting around the pool. Several middle-aged Moroccan men wearing expensive *jellabas* were seated at one table sipping mint tea. A group of younger men sat at another table drinking beer with a trio of Moroccan girls dressed in modern garb, doubtless travelers from one of the big cities, considering their way of dress and the fact that their Arabic was heavily sprinkled with French. A third table was occupied by a youngish French couple impatiently waiting to order *pastis*, the anise flavored aperitif popular in the South of France.

"*Merde!*" swore the Frenchwoman, whose name was Christiane Koenigsmarck. "There's no fucking service in this place."

"That *salaud* of a waiter must think we're invisible," grumbled her husband Laurent.

"Put your hat on, *petite tomate*," ordered Christiane. Her short plump husband had pale skin that burned easily. "Put on your hat!" she repeated. "*Tout de suite!*"

Laurent obeyed his wife, placing a visor-cap atop his prematurely bald head.

"Why can't you be more of a man?" complained Christiane. "It's your fault the waiter's not here, you little round tomato," and she snapped her fingers loudly, the waiter finally turning in their direction.

"I could have gotten his attention," whined Laurent.

"But you didn't!"

Christiane Koenigsmarck stood a good head taller than her husband. Today, as usual, she had overly teased her blond-streaked hair and been unnecessarily generous with her mascara, eye-liner, and iridescent blue eye shadow. Laurent and Christiane came from a small town in the French Midi. Though Laurent was hardly her Prince Charming, she had married him in the hopes that he would one day make his fortune. He had sold her on his dreams of amassing an easy bundle in Morocco, and so five years ago they had come to Aïn El Qamar. Neither was trained to be a teacher, and they did little lesson planning or test correction, preferring instead to come to the Hotel El Qamar or to spend their evenings drinking. Laurent's fortune remained years away, but Christiane still cherished the dream that one day they would be rich enough to retire to a small villa on the Rivera. Until then, they were content to receive a pair of salaries that they could never have earned in France.

"Isn't that Miss Claudette coming this way?" asked Laurent after they had finally ordered their drinks.

"It looks like she's been over on the tennis courts," agreed his wife. "That's the new tennis pro with her, isn't it?"

Il peut me baiser n'importe quand, thought Christiane. He can fuck me anytime. But aloud she said, "You're right, that's Fareed."

"I didn't think Miss Claudette needed tennis lessons," commented Laurent.

"Maybe she just wanted someone good to practice with," suggested his wife.

"Or someone's dick to suck."

"Laurent, you are such a pig," exclaimed Christiane. "You know that Claudette Verlaine never fucks Moroccans in Aïn El Qamar."

"There's a first time for everything," said Laurent. Then he added, "Could you try and find that waiter, *mon bébé*? He still hasn't brought our drinks."

"What a workout!" exclaimed Claudette Verlaine as she took a seat at a table on the other side of the swimming pool from where the Koenigsmarcks were sitting. "You never for a moment let me stand still on the court, Fareed. I shall have to find a way to pay you back."

"And what exactly do you have in mind?" asked Fareed, sitting down opposite her.

"You'll find out," replied Claudette mysteriously. Fareed pulled off his sweat-stained tennis shirt to reveal a hard muscled torso. *Mon Dieu*, thought Claudette. He's going to make me come right here and now.

With outward calm, she said, "I had no idea that Moroccans were such sun worshipers."

Fareed leaned back, his hands behind his head, his eyes closed against the sun, the black hair in his armpits dripping with moisture. Claudette thought she had never seen such animal grace and strength. His every movement, every detail of his body excited her.

"You're talking about my parents' generation," answered Fareed languidly. "For them, being dark was a sign of poverty. Only people who had to work in the fields got brown from the sun's rays. But I live in a different world. I love the heat of the sun on my skin."

And what delicious skin that is, thought Claudette, as her gaze wandered down from his finely-chiseled bronze chest to the line of hair that ran down his washboard stomach and finally to the prominent bulge in his tennis shorts. Like a stallion, she had told Michèle Perrault. Like a bull, she added to herself now, already feeling the wetness between her legs.

"Would you care for anything to drink?" asked a voice beside them. Claudette turned to face the often hard-to-find waiter.

"Mademoiselle Verlaine?" the waiter asked expectantly. It was one thing to keep the Koenigsmarcks waiting and quite another to do so to tennis champion and generous tipper Miss Claudette.

"Fareed, *chéri?*" asked the Frenchwoman.

"A Flag Pils for me," replied the tennis pro lazily, still reclining with his eyes closed to the sun's rays. Fareed obviously knew that even though Moroccan, he would have no trouble being served beer at this luxury tourist hotel where laws were bent to please its exclusive clientele.

"*Deux Flags,*" said Claudette with the poise and detachment that had always been characteristic of her dealings with Moroccans in Aïn El Qamar. Characteristic, that is, until the day last month when she had returned to the Hotel El Qamar for the first time since her summer holidays in Greece and Italy to find a new tennis pro giving a lesson to Dave Casalini. She had taken one look at his strong muscular body moving across the court like a panther and had known suddenly that her life was about to change.

As Dave stood talking with the tennis pro at the end of their lesson, she had gone over to greet the tall good-looking American, whom she would willingly have bedded had he not let her know that he preferred sleeping with men. How sad for me, she had thought at that time. Now, however, her interest was in the Moroccan with whom Dave was enjoying a friendly post-game chat.

"Dave, *chéri*," she exclaimed. "It's so wonderful to see you back for a second year in Aïn El Qamar. How were your holidays?"

"We had a ball, Claudette. Kevin and I spent all the money we'd saved up during the year traveling along the south coast of Spain."

"And did you find romance with the right … someone?" she asked with a wink.

"I became quite a fan of the bullfights," replied Dave, winking back.

"And this is …?" Claudette changed the subject by glancing in the direction of Dave's Moroccan companion.

"This is Mohamed Fareed, the new tennis pro. And Fareed, this is the famous Miss Claudette Verlaine of Aïn El Qamar that I was telling you about. Fareed's been dying to make your acquaintance, haven't you Fareed?"

"I've been waiting for this meeting," said the Moroccan, shaking her extended hand. "I've heard so much about your skills on the tennis courts."

"What beautiful … French," commented Claudette, who had been thinking something else.

"Fareed's been working at one of the hotels in Marrakesh for the past few years," said Dave.

"Then why come to Aïn El Qamar?" asked Claudette.

"My parents sent for me. My father is getting on in years and they wanted their eldest son to come back home."

"The dutiful son returns?" asked a surprised Claudette.

"For a while only. Small towns bore me."

"But you're from here? Why have I never seen you around town? I've lived in Aïn El Qamar for ten years, after all."

"I went to high school in Casablanca," explained Fareed. "Then I drifted down to Marrakesh and became a tennis pro."

"*Très intéressant*," commented Claudette. "And how did you come to learn tennis?"

"From tourists and French *coöpérants*. For some reason or other, they seemed to gravitate towards me. They were friendly and extremely generous. They often used to invite me to their hotels and tennis clubs, so I got to know French people, especially French women, intimately, you might say."

A month had passed since that first meeting, and today as Claudette sat drinking her beer, unable to keep her eyes off Fareed's sinewy body, she wondered what it would be like to be known intimately by Mohamed Fareed.

Arrête, Claudette, she told herself sharply. Stop this at once! Even a brief involvement with a Moroccan in this small town would put her carefully maintained reputation in danger, and Claudette knew that a one-night adventure with Fareed would never be enough. Since the first day she had laid eyes on him, he had been her obsession. She could not stop thinking of him, even for a moment.

More and more these days, Claudette felt tempted to throw caution to the wind. But could she, after the years she had spent building an image for herself in Aïn El Qamar? Dared she let that image be destroyed? Claudette knew that people considered her wild, eccentric, and even promiscuous, but she had made it a point to keep her relationships with Moroccan males in Aïn El Qamar strictly businesslike. These men understood that she had established a hands-off policy and that she only associated with those who accepted this. Claudette had known many lovers after Jean-Richard Moreau, and there had been Moroccans among them, quite a number of them in fact, but always on weekends in Casablanca or Marrakesh, never in her own town. Not that she limited herself to Arabs. She had bedded men from all over Europe during her ten years in Morocco, and from other continents as well, but she had to admit that she preferred Moroccans. No other men could equal the hard macho virility of her Moroccan lovers.

Was it because Fareed was the epitome of this virile masculinity that she found him so exciting? Or was there something more to her passion for him?

Claudette had stopped counting her birthdays when she hit forty a few years ago, and though she was still able to maintain the facade of youth, she knew that this could not last forever. Already her curvaceous body was losing its firmness, despite the regular exercise she gave it, and her auburn hair seemed less lustrous. Perhaps soon, the green fire that burned in her eyes would begin to dim. And then, without her youth and beauty, where would she be? She could already feel changes taking place, and her mirror was beginning to become her enemy. So far the changes could be hidden with skillfully applied make-up and expensive moisturizing creams, but they would not remain so forever.

Was Fareed a last desperate attempt to cling to her youth? Claudette knew that she found the nights spent alone between weekends and holidays more and more difficult to bear. Was she beginning to need a full-time lover's reassurance that she was still desirable? Was this what was urging her towards a dangerous liaison with the Moroccan tennis pro?

"What a morning!" exclaimed Fareed now, and Claudette was brought back from her reverie into the present.

"You must be exhausted," she said, smiling sympathetically at him as he finished his Flag Pils. "Playing tennis for enjoyment is one thing but spending the whole day doing it can't help but wear you out."

"It's not so much the playing as the teaching," answered Fareed. "Some of my pupils are not … gifted. This morning was particularly tiring. I really needed this beer."

"And how would you feel about a good home-cooked meal? You must be famished. Jean-Richard told me yesterday that he wouldn't be back from Rabat until early afternoon, and I'm sure Saadia has made enough for us both. She's a marvelous cook."

Claudette could scarcely believe what she had just done. It was insanity for her to invite a Moroccan bachelor to her house, especially when Jean-Richard was out of town. What if people should find out? What if being alone with Fareed should lead to …? Was she losing her mind?

"Sounds wonderful," he answered. "I don't have another lesson until late this afternoon."

"And I don't teach again until four," said Claudette. *Mon Dieu*, she was actually going through with it.

"Then we can have a long leisurely lunch," said Fareed. "What have you got planned for me?"

"Planned?" But she hadn't planned this! It had been a sudden impulse, a sudden uncontrollable impulse. She could still find an excuse to withdraw the invitation if she wanted to.

"Yes. What's on the menu?" Fareed seemed puzzled by her confusion.

"That will be Saadia's surprise," answered Claudette. "I'm sure it will be luscious, though." So she had made her decision. Right or wrong, there was no turning back. Her need for Fareed had overpowered her. Perhaps she had known all along that it eventually would.

"Shall we be on our way?" asked Fareed.

"Just as soon as I've paid our bill and changed into my street clothes. You go shower too, Fareed. I'll meet you … in … in the parking lot by my car."

"*D'accord*. I'll see you there as soon as I've changed."

Claudette summoned the waiter, who came running over with the check. She signed her name to it, leaving him a hefty tip, then headed towards the women's dressing room, grateful to Fareed for not having questioned her desire to meet him away from the pool. Those insufferable Koenigsmarcks were still sitting poolside, doubtless gossiping about her and Fareed. If they saw her leave with the tennis pro, the news would be public knowledge by evening.

Ten minutes later, Claudette emerged from the dressing room, once again wearing her sexy green blouse and white slacks. She was on her way towards the parking lot when she heard Christiane Koenigsmarck calling to her from where she and her husband sat. *Merde*! thought Claudette. What could that common vulgar hick possibly want? She forced herself to head in Christiane and Laurent's direction.

"Miss Claudette!" exclaimed Christiane. "Tell us your secret for getting that lazy waiter's attention. We absolutely refuse to tip him. He's never around when we need him." Claudette winced at the thick southern French accent. It seemed inconceivable that Christiane and Laurent should actually be teaching elementary French as Claudette herself did, but apparently they had the required high school diploma. Still, Claudette recoiled every time she heard them slaughter the language of Molière and Racine.

"One of these days I want to get your advice on how you get the little pricks to study," said Laurent in his unpleasant nasal voice.

"*Moi aussi*," agreed Christiane loudly. "Mine never stop screaming. Little assholes, if you ask me. *Petits cons*."

Claudette had always found the young pupils she taught enchanting, if a bit rambunctious. Doubtless they were so in awe of her that they did not dare to be too disruptive.

"Yes, one of these days …" hemmed Claudette, thinking: Never will be too soon.

"We'll be over for aperitifs this evening after our five o'clock classes," announced Christiane.

Claudette realized that it would be futile to make excuses, aware that the entire French community knew that her home was always open to friends during the cocktail hour. The groups of guests might change from day to day, but her house was invariably the center of the French community's social life.

"Delightful," said Claudette unenthusiastically, but the sarcasm seemed lost on the Koenigsmarcks. "And now I really must be going," she added. "*A toute à l'heure*."

As the statuesque Frenchwoman walked away, Christiane caught her husband's eyes straying after her. "Laurent!" she barked.

"*Pardon, ma grande,*" Laurent excused himself. "I was just wondering how Claudette Verlaine has stood living in this hellhole for ten years."

"The same reason we have," responded Christiane. "*Le fric.* The money."

"That's not all she likes in Morocco," leered Laurent. "Did you get a load of how Claudette was staring down at that tennis pro's crotch when they were sitting over there. She couldn't take her eyes off it."

And neither could I, thought Christiane. Aloud, she said, "Do you think there's something going on between them?"

"If they haven't already fucked," replied Laurent, "they're going to do it soon. You can bet on it."

"So you find it odd that I should be living in Aïn El Qamar?" remarked Claudette as she and Fareed waited for Saadia, Claudette's long-time maid, to serve lunch.

"Yes, it is rather strange. I can't understand why such a beautiful woman would want to hide from the world in a small Moroccan town."

Claudette looked down at her décolletage. "You think I am hiding?" He had called her beautiful!

"You know what I mean," said Fareed.

"Yes, I suppose I do. But you must understand that France stifled me. Wherever I went, there was always someone to report to *Papa* and *Maman* on my behavior. And to tell the truth, I have been quite a naughty girl at times. Other people may have their antiquated standards, but I will never conform to them. Living here in Aïn El Qamar, I have created my own world, a world in which I am unique, in which I am liked, admired, envied. Believe me Fareed, the feeling is good. I could never be happy in a place where I was just another woman. Besides, I make excellent money here, and I must admit to having amassed quite a substantial bank account back in France. I ski, I ride horseback, I sail, I travel the world whenever I get the whim. I've eaten in the best restaurants and slept in the best hotels. I've led the kind of life most women can only dream of."

"You are a fascinating, remarkable woman, Claudette," said Fareed, admiration in his eyes. "I've never met anyone quite like you."

"You make me blush," sighed Claudette, thinking: This is indeed the man for whom I have been waiting so many years. "Or perhaps it is just hunger …" She paused. "… for food. Let me see what's keeping our lunch." Claudette rose from the *banquette* where she had been sitting opposite the tennis pro and went to the kitchen. There, she found her maid removing a roast from the oven. "Saadia," she admonished the rotund dark-skinned woman. "Where is our *déjeuner?*"

"*Pardon, mademoiselle,*" answered Saadia, "but I thought that you and that Moslem might want to be alone. It's not my place to interrupt." Like many Moroccans, Saadia considered the words Moslem and Moroccan to be synonymous, just as were the Arabic words for Christian and foreigner.

"Do I sense a critical note in your voice, Saadia?" asked Claudette.

"I never criticize you, *mademoiselle.* But I can't help feeling the way I feel. What you need is a good husband, like Monsieur Jean-Richard or Monsieur Miguel. Not that Moslem out there. I don't like him. I don't like him at all."

Usually Claudette found Saadia's motherly instincts charming, and even comforting at times. Certainly she was grateful for her loyalty and dependability. Today, however, she was irritated at the woman's impertinence.

"What I do is my business alone, and don't you forget it! If you want to continue working here, you'll remember to keep your mouth shut. And that means not another word about Fareed's visit, not to me, not to Jean-Richard, not to anyone."

Saadia knew that Claudette would never fire her, but she said placatingly, "*Oui, mademoiselle.* If anyone finds out what's going on in this house, it won't be from my lips." And this was true. In her years of service, the maid had never spread stories about her employer, whom she thought of as a somewhat wayward sister. She had in fact done her best to quell the gossip she sometimes heard.

"Well, don't just stand there," snapped Claudette. "Get that roast on the table. It's been a long morning and I'm ravenous."

"You were right about your maid's cooking," said Fareed as he sipped from the cup of coffee Saadia had brought in after lunch.

"She's a treasure," agreed Claudette, thinking: Will that woman ever leave?

Just then, Saadia poked her head into the living room. "Will there be anything else, *mademoiselle?*"

"Have you finished washing the dishes?" asked Claudette.

"Everything but the coffee service."

"Never mind about that. I'll take care of it later. Now, why don't you run along? You have your family to look after."

"*Oui, mademoiselle,*" said the maid, and Claudette felt that she could read the expression in the woman's eyes. Behave yourself, it said.

"*Au revoir*, Saadia," said Claudette pointedly.

"*Au revoir, mademoiselle,*" replied Saadia, and hearing the front door shut, Claudette finally breathed a sigh of relief. It's now or never, she told herself as she picked up her cup of coffee, then let it fall from her hand onto Fareed's lap. "*Mon Dieu*," exclaimed Claudette. "Did I burn you? I'm such a clumsy girl."

"Accidents happen," remarked Fareed.

"You must get those slacks off at once so that I can soak them. Run into my bedroom and take them off. You'll find a robe there you can put on."

"I don't know where the room is," said Fareed.

"What a silly girl I am. Of course you don't. Let me show you the way." She rose and Fareed followed her across the entry hall into a room whose walls were covered with florescent Peter Maxx posters. "*Très psychadélique*, don't you think?" asked Claudette. "And do you like the carpet? I bought it in Marrakesh. It cost an arm and a leg, but it was worth it. I find the design quite unique, don't you? It's so ..." Claudette could hear herself babbling on making inane small talk.

"You wanted my pants," Fareed reminded her.

Relieved to be brought back to the matter at hand, Claudette said, "Yes, and your shirt too. I think I spilled a little coffee on it as well. Now don't be embarrassed. I won't peek."

Claudette turned demurely to face the door. A minute later, Fareed came up behind her and handed her his clothes. She took them in her hands, then turned boldly around. "I peeked," she admitted, pretending to blush. Then, stepping back, she gazed in awe at Fareed's superlative body, his muscular chest with its firm dark nipples, his long athletic legs.

"*Comme tu es beau!*" she exclaimed breathlessly. "How beautiful you are."

Dropping his clothes to the floor, she knelt down in front of him and, slowly and deliberately, pulled his briefs to his knees.

"You are truly the most beautiful man," she whispered, admiring his thick circumcised cock. She buried her face in his pubic hair and inhaled his maleness.

And then, all at once, he was kneeling in front of her, his mouth pressed against hers, his tongue forcing its way in, passionate, demanding.

He nearly ripped off her tight green blouse. "Le ... let me help you," panted Claudette, and she removed her blouse, boots, and slacks. Then she lay back on the carpet, Fareed's mouth on her breasts, his tongue making wet circles around her nipples.

Claudette wrapped her arms around Fareed, moving her fingers up and down his spine and exploring the warm moist crease between his buttocks.

She moaned in ecstasy as Fareed massaged her supple breasts, then bit her erect nipples. Soon she felt his lips descending lower, his tongue licking her belly. Sliding her black lace panties down her legs, he opened his mouth wide to shoot his tongue in and out of her pussy.

"Don't stop!" she moaned. "Don't ever stop!"

His mouth seemed to stay an eternity at her sex, yet she never wanted this exquisite fulfillment to end.

And then, finally, his hard cock could resist its goal no longer. She felt a moment of divine pain as he entered her, plunging deeper and deeper, filling her innermost recesses with his very being.

"*Je t'aime* Fareed," she screamed. "I love you! Oh God how I love you!"

CHAPTER 4

▼

Dave Casalini's student Lateef was in Dave's kitchen washing the dishes left from their lunch. It was typical of Lateef to volunteer to do the dirty work, thought Dave, and smiled. From the first week of classes last year, Lateef Raffali had stood out from among the crowd of other students. He was quicker; his instincts were sharper. When Dave was teaching a difficult point, Lateef always seemed to catch on even before Dave finished explaining. He participated eagerly in the classroom dialog; other students listened when he talked. It was no surprise that he had been his class's elected representative on the student council both last year and this. It was students like Lateef who made teaching a joy, though in fact there really was no other student like Lateef.

Dave could hear the nineteen-year-old putting away the dishes as he sat back on a *banquette* sipping at a cup of coffee. Watching the steam rise from the cup, he wondered how Lateef would react to the proposition he was about to make to him. He hoped the young Moroccan would be excited and happy, but Lateef was not always predictable, which was part of his allure. I've got to tell him right away what's on my mind, thought Dave, or I'm going to burst.

"Dishes are done!"

Dave set down his coffee and looked towards the living room door where Lateef stood, slender but muscled, dark-haired and heartbreakingly handsome, wiping his hands with a dishtowel. He smiled his dazzling smile.

"I don't believe you," said Dave in English, which he used almost exclusively with Lateef, who was now in his third year of studying the language. "You spend all morning in class, then you cook lunch for the two of us, you wash the dishes, and now you show up bright-eyed and eager as if you've spent the whole morning relaxing."

"First of all," answered Lateef, also in English and almost without accent, "I didn't spend 'the whole morning' in class. It was only two hours. And when you and I finished at eleven, we went over to Miss Perrault's house and I took a nap on the roof. Besides, cooking for two's no problem. It's not as if I prepared the kind of meal Kevin's probably being served at Mr. Hajiri's house right now."

"I still say you work too hard," said Dave.

"That's a change," answered Lateef. "You usually tell me I spend too much time flaking off!"

This was hardly the truth, but still Dave couldn't help beaming with pride at hearing Lateef sound so much like a native speaker after just over two years of study. He knew, however, that he could only take partial credit for the Moroccan's speedy progress, for Lateef spent hours studying on his own, in addition to the time spent here with Dave and Kevin.

Just then, the doorbell rang. "I'll get it," said Lateef, and ran to the door. Dave smiled as he savored the recalled image of Lateef, standing there with the towel in his hand, his sleeves rolled up to reveal his tightly muscled arms, his shirt unbuttoned to his thorax. Even after a year of knowing Lateef, just looking at him still made Dave's heart melt.

Voices speaking Arabic could be heard as Lateef opened the front door and then ushered a group of three of his classmates into the living room. Dave stood up and shook hands with each of them as was the custom in Morocco at every meeting and leave-taking. After each handshake, he touched his hand to his heart as a gesture of friendship.

The students took seats on the *banquettes* facing their teacher, two of them lighting cigarettes. They obviously felt comfortable in Dave's presence, and although he did not always see things their way, they knew that they could count on him to be a thoughtful and intelligent listener. Right now, Dave could see that they were upset about something.

"May we speak in French, Mr. Casalini?" asked one of them in English.

"*Allez-y*," said Dave, knowing that Lateef's near fluent English was the exception rather than the rule. Although Dave tried to use English as often as possible with his students outside of class, he switched when necessary to the language he had learned in high school and college, and perfected during his junior year in France. "*De quoi s'agit-il?*" he asked.

"*C'est le proviseur!*" said one of them.

"*Espèce de salaud!*" added another.

"What's Monsieur Rhazwani done now?" asked Dave in exasperation. He had decided from his several earlier meetings with the man that there were sure to be problems with the new *proviseur* this year.

"He's disbanded the student council!" said one angry student.

"*Mais c'est impossible!*" exclaimed Lateef. "He can't do that! The classes need representation!"

Lateef was referring to Lycée Mohamed Cinq's thirty *classes*, in each of which thirty-five or so students studied all their subjects together for an entire academic year. After the strikes which had shut down most of the schools in the country in 1972, Monsieur Mahraoui, the former *proviseur*, had organized a student council with the approval of the Aïn El Qamar school board in order to give each class a greater voice in the *lycée*'s activities. The students had no real power, but they felt at least that their opinions were being heard. Now, it seemed, this new tradition was to be short-lived.

"When did you find this out?" asked Dave.

"It was announced in the cafeteria at the beginning of lunch," said Mustapha Najeed, the student who had spoken first.

"*Ah, c'est vrai,*" commented Dave. "You're all *internes*, aren't you?" *Internes* were boarding students; day students like Lateef were called *externes*.

Mustapha nodded in agreement. "That man is a tyrant!" he continued, his voice seething with anger. "You know that he already confiscated our transistor radios, saying that they kept us from studying!"

"Unfortunately," explained Dave, "there is a school regulation prohibiting students from having portable radios. Why on earth I have no idea, but …"

"The music didn't bother anyone. It helped us to relax. You know how tired we get, Mr. Casalini. Most of us have more than thirty hours of class a week. Our transistor radios helped us study better."

"I'm on your side," Dave insisted. "But sometimes it's less hassle just to follow the rules, and save your protests for something really serious."

"But disbanding the student council is serious!" insisted Mustapha.

"Yeah," added another irate student. "We won't take it lying down!"

"So, what are you going to do about it?" asked Dave.

"Strike!" announced his three visitors in unison.

"Are you sure that's such a good idea?" asked Dave, who had heard tales of violent student-police confrontations during the year of the anti-government strikes. The departing Peace Corps volunteers whom he and Kevin had replaced had told them horrific stories of broken arms and bloodied heads and even of several deaths. In the end, the government had won, most students had failed the classes that had been interrupted mid-year, and the majority had had to repeat the entire school year. Most of their demands for reforms in the national educational system had gone unheeded, although a student council had been instituted at Lycée Mohamed Cinq. Now, it appeared that Monsieur Rhazwani wanted to eliminate one of the few positive changes that had taken place.

"The whole country was on strike four years ago," continued Dave, "and look where that got you. Nowhere."

"But if we don't strike, what else can we do?" asked Mustapha.

"Use your heads. This time, why not try being a bit more strategic?"

"What do you mean?" asked one of the students.

"It was the school board that ruled to initiate the student council after Monsieur Mahraoui made his recommendation to them. I don't know that Monsieur Rhazwani can disband it without the school board's agreement. So, instead of just making a lot of noise and maybe ending up in the hospital, why don't you get the student council together and go as a group to speak to the *délégué*? This was the official title of the school board chairman. "From what I've been told, he's pretty open-minded and progressive. I believe he'll listen to your complaints, if you just remember to express yourselves calmly and clearly."

The students had been listening attentively to Dave's words. Now Mustapha spoke up. "Well, what do you guys think?" The three students who had arrived together began arguing in rapid Arabic. Dave had difficulty following what they were saying.

"Dave *a raison*!" interrupted Lateef in French, silencing the other students. "We need to listen to Dave. We will speak to the *délégué* about this problem."

Once again, Dave was impressed at Lateef's quiet leadership. He knew now, more than ever, that he could no longer postpone talking with the young man about his future.

"*D'accord*," said Mustapha, after conferring briefly with his classmates. "At least it's worth a try. We'll do as you suggest, Mr. Casalini."

"Great!" said Dave approvingly.

"And now we have to go," said Mustapha. "We're not really supposed to leave the school grounds during the lunch recess from noon to two o'clock, but the gate-keeper is on our side, and he said that we could go out if we didn't stay too long."

"Then you'd better be getting back," agreed Dave. "I don't want you into any trouble, especially not now. Thanks for the visit. And good luck. You know that I'm behind you on this one hundred percent." The three students got up and

Dave escorted them to the front door. "I'll see you in class this afternoon. We meet at four today, *n'est-ce pas?*"

"See you in class, Mr. Casalini," said Mustapha, and the two others echoed his good-bye.

Dave waved to the departing figures, then returned to the living room which, like Janna's, was furnished Moroccan-style with *banquettes* arranged traditionally around a wooden coffee table. On the tile floor was a colorful hand-woven rug which Dave and Kevin had bought at the Aïn El Qamar *souk*. As Dave re-entered the room, he found Lateef sitting on the rug, his back against one of the *banquettes*. He was reading a book, of course. This time it was *The Graduate*. He seemed to be nearly at the end of it. Dave crossed the room and sat down on the rug beside him.

"You never cease to amaze me, Lateef," he said in English.

"What does that mean?"

"It means that you're always doing something surprising," explained the American, knowing that Lateef would now memorize the expression. "Didn't you borrow that book just yesterday?"

"It's a short book," said Lateef modestly. "And I saw the movie starring Dustin Hoffman at the Cinéclub last month."

"But still, that's a pretty hard novel."

"Aw, reading's a snap," announced Lateef, using an idiom which Dave had recently taught him.

"But with so many people in your house, how can you concentrate?" Lateef's parents had been killed in an accident when he was a young boy, and he had lived since then with the family of his father's elder sister, who had five children of her own. Dave knew that Lateef had always felt like an outsider in his relatives' home, and a burden on them as well. The family had little money, and though Lateef had greater freedom than the *internes* who boarded at school, his study conditions were less favorable. Perhaps that was why he had willingly accepted Dave's early invitations to study at his and Kevin's house, that and the fact that in the Americans' home he had found the warmth and affection that had so long been lacking in his life.

Lateef closed the book and placed it on the *banquette* behind him. He turned to look at Dave, his dark eyes large and long-lashed. "You said before lunch that you had something important to tell me," he reminded the American.

"That's right," said Dave. He felt his heart begin to pound, and wished for a moment that he were a smoker. If he had been a Moroccan, he would doubtless have lit a cigarette to calm his nerves, but Dave had never picked up the habit and had, in fact, even convinced Lateef to quit soon after they had become friends.

"So, what is it?" asked Lateef expectantly.

"What are your plans for the future?"

"The future?" Lateef seemed at a loss for words. "You mean after the *bac*?"

As a high school senior, Lateef faced the formidable obstacle of passing the dreaded *baccalauréat* exam in June. Dave knew he was worried about passing, although he himself was confident that his star pupil would have no difficulty breezing through the test. It was what would happen once Lateef had passed the exam that had Dave worried.

"Yes, after the *bac*," repeated Dave.

"We've been over this before. You know I'd like to go to the university, Dave. But I don't see how I can. Even if I do get in, very few students actually graduate. I've been a burden on my relatives long enough. It's time I started earning my own living."

"You're only nineteen, Lateef," protested Dave. "You've got your whole life ahead of you."

"I don't see what else I can do," said Lateef resignedly. "Anyway, you'll be back in the States when this school year is over. So you don't have to worry about it."

"I do worry," exclaimed Dave. "I can't not worry. And that's why …" Dave hesitated. What he was about to propose would change Lateef's life forever. The words Dave was about to utter might be the most momentous words Lateef would ever hear. So just say them, damn it, and get it over with, Dave ordered himself.

"I want you to come to the United States with me when I leave Morocco in June." There, it was out!

"You what?" Lateef seemed not to have understood.

"I said I want to take you back to the States with me."

The words seemed to be taking forever to sink into Lateef's consciousness. Then, all of a sudden, his arms were around the American, and Dave could feel Lateef's tears on his cheek. He wanted so desperately kiss them dry, but he restrained himself, as he always did.

"I'm so happy! I'm so happy!" wept Lateef.

"Does that mean the answer is yes?"

"Of course it is!" shouted Lateef, jumping up, pulling Dave with him. Hugging the tall American once again, he looked into his eyes and cried, "Thank you! Thank you!"

Then, without warning, he pulled away, a look of near despair shadowing his face. He turned and moved slowly towards the window, staring out into space.

Bewildered by this sudden change, Dave walked over to him, put his hand on Lateef's shoulder, and turned him around so that they were face to face. "Lateef. What's wrong? A minute ago you were happier than I've ever seen you."

"I was, until … until I realized … Dave! They'll never let me leave the country!"

"Who are 'they'?" asked Dave. "Your relatives?"

"No, of course not. To them, I'm just another mouth to feed."

"Then who are you talking about?"

"Do you have any idea how hard it is to get a passport to leave Morocco? Especially when you're poor like I am. And even more so for the United States? It is possible for students to get visas to study in France, but that's only if they're on full scholarship. I still don't know enough English to even get into an American university."

"Your English is excellent," reassured Dave. "You should hear yourself talking now! Besides, I've already thought of that. You know I recently applied for grad school at my alma mater, Chicago State University. Anyway, Chicago State has a great English language program for foreign students. After you've studied there for a few months, it'll be a piece of cake for you to get into college. As far as money is concerned, don't worry about it. We'll find a way."

"You really think it's possible, Dave? I want to believe you, but …"

"Leave it up to me, young man. I promise you that this is one dream that's going to come true … for both of us."

"I can hardly believe it!" exclaimed Lateef. He walked over to one of the *banquettes* and sat down. "It's just too wonderful!" he added, and broke into tears once again.

Dave moved over to sit next to him. He put his arms around Lateef and let him cry on his shoulder.

At first it seemed that Lateef's tears of joy would never end, but eventually he regained his composure and Dave said to him, "We'll have lots of time for making plans. And I promise to get to work on your passport right away." After a moment's pause, he added, "And now Mr. Raffali, if I'm not mistaken, hadn't you better be getting yourself ready for your afternoon classes? As for me, I've got a lesson to plan."

The two got up from the *banquette*, Dave reaching down to the coffee table for a tissue with which he dried Lateef's swollen eyes. "Wash your face before class, or your friends will think something terrible's happened to you."

"But I'll just tell them the truth," suggested Lateef.

"I'd rather you didn't," said Dave, "at least not for now. Let's not tell anyone about our plans until we've started getting some positive results."

"Couldn't I even tell Naï …?"

"No one!"

"All right," said Lateef grudgingly. "And thank you!" he added, looking up to kiss Dave on both cheeks, as was the Moroccan custom between close friends. What a difference a few inches make, thought Dave ruefully. But he kept his thoughts to himself. "Off to school with you," he ordered.

Lateef picked up his books from the *banquette*. Then, giving his teacher and friend a last smile, he left the room. A moment later, Dave heard the front door shut.

"Am I doing the right thing?" he asked himself for the umpteenth time. Dave recalled the name that Lateef had been about to say before he had interrupted him. Naïma. That was who he wished to tell of his good fortune. Naïma, the pretty teenaged girl that Lateef had known since childhood and whom he referred to as his girlfriend. Naïma!

Dave had only seen the girl once or twice, and yet he hated her, could not hear her name without wanting to scream. For it was Naïma who was Lateef's girlfriend. It was Naïma whom he willingly kissed and held, and not Dave. Doubtless Naïma's Moslem code of morality had prevented her from letting Lateef go any further than that in their lovemaking. Still, the mere thought of the two of them alone together in the olive groves was enough to make Dave nearly explode with jealousy.

For Lateef had let him know in no uncertain terms that he could never kiss a man, could never allow a man to make love to his body, and this was precisely what Dave yearned for with all his heart and soul.

Dave glanced at his watch. Half past two. Only half an hour until he had to be in class, yet he still had no idea what he would be teaching or how he would teach it. As he sat at his desk, pen in hand, a notebook before him open to a blank page, several textbooks and grammar manuals strewn across the desk top, Dave found himself unable to concentrate on his work. His mind kept wandering back to Lateef, reviewing the time they had spent together. Now, as always, he sensed his friend's absence. Never before had he felt such a constant need to be near another human being. Never before had he loved another human being so deeply, not even Ethan, with whom he had lived for nearly a year in college. Last summer in Spain had been spoiled by Lateef's absence, though at first he had thought it would be good to get away for a while to better evaluate his feelings, and Lateef's lack of a passport had seemed to offer him the perfect excuse to put some distance between them. He had even had a brief fling with an apprentice bullfighter, as he had hinted to Claudette. But it hadn't been enough. Dave had thought of Lateef constantly while in Spain, and the pain of his loneliness and longing had been nearly unbearable.

And yet, was it any easier being around Lateef, knowing that they could not be lovers?

Once he had thought that Lateef was the answer to his prayers. Once he had had such beautiful dreams of a love that he knew now was impossible. Once his life had been so much less complicated than it was today.

*   *   *   *

It was late June, the end of his first year in Morocco. The burning summer heat had finally arrived. Days were long and dry and the temperature was often over one hundred degrees at noon. People kept their windows and shutters closed so that their houses would stay cool against the heat, opening them at night to let in the evening air which was only slightly less sweltering. The streets were deserted during midday. In the late afternoon, workers in un-air-conditioned offices wondered if the day would ever end. Finally, reluctantly, caftaned women emerged from their houses with buckets of water which they splashed on the parched earthen sidewalks. As the sun set, the promenades began. People were everywhere in the streets, greeting each other after long hours spent indoors. Men sat in cafés, drinking Coca-Cola or mint tea. Women congregated in groups before front doors and gossiped. No one went to bed early. It was too hot to sleep comfortably.

Dave lay on a *banquette* in his living room, all the windows wide open in the vain hope that an evening breeze might enter. The room was lit only by candles. He was alone, Kevin having left that morning for Rabat where he was to help in the tabulation of *baccalauréat* exam results. As Dave lay listening to a Barry White cassette he had brought over from the States, hearing the strings interweave through the sensuous romantic melody, images kept appearing before his eyes, images of Lateef, as Dave wished him to be, naked and in Dave's arms, Dave inside Lateef, Lateef inside Dave. Releasing himself to his fantasy, Dave imagined what it would be like to finally make love to Lateef, at last, after all these months of growing desire.

Then the tape clicked to a stop, silence filled the room, and the images faded, leaving Dave to face cold reality. It was undeniable that Lateef had become a frequent visitor to Dave and Kevin's house, eating with them, studying endlessly, having long conversations about music, books, and politics. But it was equally undeniable that he was Dave's student, and while school was still in session, that was one line that Dave had forbidden himself to cross.

It's unprofessional, Dave insisted to himself, although there were times that he was sure he caught in Lateef's gaze the look of desire that he had come to recognize during his university years. If only he could just come out to Lateef, as he had done to Janna, things might be simpler. But he had no way of knowing how Lateef would react, and there was the risk that such a revelation might get spread around school. There was, after all, no gay liberation movement in Morocco. Quite the contrary, homosexuality was forbidden by the Koran, and therefore illegal, though the law was rarely enforced.

School had ended several weeks ago, but still Dave hesitated to make a move that might possibly lead to rejection and the end of the most meaningful relationship, albeit chaste, of his life.

Dave got up to turn over the tape, and as he was pushing the recorder's play button, there was a knock at the door. Dave recognized the three quick taps.

Running to the door, he threw it open to find Lateef standing there in his thin blue *foqia*, the sleeveless ankle-length cotton robe that Moroccan men often wore during the summer months. It was possible to wear only briefs beneath a *foqia* and thus be cool and modest at the same time. Knowing that Lateef was nearly naked under his *foqia* gave Dave an almost immediate hard-on.

"Come in," he exclaimed, and kissed Lateef on both cheeks. "Go on into the living room," he continued. "I'll be right in. I just want to pour myself a glass of wine in the kitchen."

"Pour me one too, okay," asked Lateef. It was not the first time he and Dave had drunk wine together, despite Islam's prohibition of spirits. What the hell, thought Dave, he'll be nineteen in a few weeks.

"Sure thing," he said. In the kitchen, he filled two glasses with chilled rosé wine. Dave and Kevin had recently pooled their savings to invest in a small refrigerator which a departing French teacher had wished to sell. He was grateful that they had on hot summer evenings like this.

Returning to the living room with the bottle and the two glasses on a tray, he set the tray on the coffee table and sat by Lateef on the rug, the two of them leaning back against one of the *banquettes*. He handed one glass to Lateef, took the other one, and clicking his glass against Lateef's, said "Cheers."

"Cheers," repeated Lateef, and sipped at the wine. "It's cold!" he exclaimed with pleasure.

56   Moroccan Roll

"Boulaouane," said Dave. This was the famous Moroccan "gray" wine.

"Barry White," said Lateef, who had become an encyclopedia of pop music since getting to know Dave and Kevin. "My favorite."

As the two of them sat drinking the wine in silence, Dave could feel Lateef's body dangerously and invitingly near his, the thin cotton *foqia* hugging the compact muscles of his body. One of Lateef's arms was reclining on the *banquette*, revealing his soft black underarm hair. Dave felt himself becoming erect again, wanting to lean over and lick that delicious spot. You and your armpit fetish, he thought. Control yourself!

But Lateef was looking at Dave now too—in that special suggestive way of his. And suddenly Dave felt that the time had come to explore Lateef's potential as a lover. The school year was over, after all, wasn't it?

Dave reached up to touch Lateef's cheek, and the young Moroccan did not recoil at Dave's touch. In fact, he began to smile, reaching up with his own hand to run his fingers through Dave's hair. Dave took this as a sign to continue.

"Lateef," whispered Dave. "You don't know how long I've wanted this." He leaned his face closer to Lateef's, and brushed his lips against the young man's. Opening his mouth slightly, Dave let his tongue glide back and forth along Lateef's teeth. He was about to shoot it in farther when he felt hands pushing him gently away, reaching down to unbutton his fly and lower the zipper. Lateef pulled Dave's shorts and underpants down to his knees, and Dave's erect cock jumped to attention. At first, Dave thought that Lateef was going to go down on him, but the young Moroccan apparently had other plans.

"Lie down on the *banquette*," said Lateef. "Lie down on your stomach."

Dave knew that this was happening too quickly, but it was their first time after all, and he would have ample opportunities to show Lateef the proper way to make love in the months ahead, so he did as Lateef instructed. Then the thought occurred to him that he had better go get some kind of lubricant.

Before he could suggest this, however, he felt a stab of pain as Lateef entered him. God, he was bigger than Dave had expected, maybe even bigger than Dave himself! But I wasn't ready yet, Dave's inner voice screamed as he felt Lateef inside him, piercing him, tearing at him, ripping him apart. There was pleasure to accompany the pain, but at the same time the horrible realization that this was not what he had been anticipating.

And then, almost as soon as it had started, it was over. Lateef rose from the *banquette*, pulled his briefs back up, and lowered his *foqia*.

Slowly, Dave lifted himself to a seated position, his shorts still down to his knees. "What about me?" he asked Lateef, gesturing to his still hard cock.

"What do you mean?" asked Lateef, uncomprehendingly. "I did what I knew you wanted me to do. I thought that would make you happy."

"You fucked me. That's all."

"Yes."

"So, that's not enough," exclaimed Dave. "What about kissing? What about touching? What about letting me touch you, fuck you? I love you, Lateef. How am I supposed to show you my love?"

"You want to fuck me?" gasped Lateef. "But I'm not gay!"

"You just stuck your dick in me! How can you say you're not gay!"

"Because I'm not. I know that you are, and that doesn't bother me, but I'm not."

As Dave heard Lateef's words, he thought to himself: We're both speaking English, but we're using different languages. The words we're using have different meanings.

Suddenly Dave could take it no more. Pulling up his shorts and rebuttoning them, he stood and faced Lateef. "I think you'd better be going. I need to be alone."

"Of course, Dave. If that's what you want …," said Lateef, but his expression showed that he did not understand what Dave was telling him. "I thought I was making you happy. I love you too, Dave. It's just, I'm not gay."

"Go home, Lateef. Just go home," insisted Dave, and the young man turned to exit.

"I'm sorry, Dave. Please don't be angry," Lateef said as he went out into the hot summer night.

The following morning, Dave woke early and took a bus to Rabat. Upon his arrival, he paid a visit to Ali Sadiq, one of his Arabic teachers during last summer's Peace Corps training program. He and Ali had had a brief and casual but sexually satisfying affair during training, and he wanted to ask Ali about what had happened with Lateef and about Lateef's insistence that he was not gay, despite the fact that he had willingly had sex with Dave.

"In Morocco, we only have the word *zamal*," Ali began, and when Dave's expression showed that he was unfamiliar with the term, he explained. "*Zamal*'s a guy who enjoys getting fucked in the ass."

"What about the guy who's doing the fucking?" asked Dave. "What's he called?"

"Oh, we don't have a word for that," said Ali.

And Dave realized that he and Lateef had indeed been speaking different cultural languages. In this country, where girls were off-limits before marriage, many basically straight guys apparently turned to members of their own gender as a temporary substitute for women until their wedding day. Some of them might actually be gay, but not all. And Dave had been so sure that Lateef's desire for him had meant that he was gay in the American sense of the word.

Returning to Aïn El Qamar, Dave was met by a still distraught Lateef. "I'm so sorry, Dave," the young man wept. "I didn't mean to hurt you. You know I love you more than anyone in this world."

Looking into Lateef's tear-filled eyes, so full of sincere remorse, Dave had no choice but to forgive him. After all, loving Lateef unconditionally meant accepting him on his own terms.

Still, from now on, any sexual activity between the two of them was out of the question. Dave could not accept a physical relationship which did not include kissing, caressing, and other expressions of intimacy that felt so natural to him. He was not nor could he ever be simply Lateef's sex toy.

Their friendship must remain strictly platonic, Dave told Lateef, and the young man, relieved not to lose Dave as his friend, agreed.

That was four months ago.

∗   ∗   ∗   ∗

In the four months which had passed since his misunderstanding with Lateef, Dave had visited Spain with Kevin, found a new Moroccan fuck-buddy at the Hotel El Qamar, and been assigned to teach Lateef's class again. Lateef's daily visits had continued, the young man's English level skyrocketing due to his frequent contact with his two American friends. And Dave had conceived his plan to guarantee Lateef a better future in the United States, and in so doing, to keep him a part of his life. After all, even a non-sexual relationship with Lateef was better than no relationship at all.

Still, on days like this, when they had lain in their undershorts on Michèle Perrault's roof, it was nearly impossible to think of Lateef as just a friend. His longing for him today had been almost unbearable. And Dave still could not help wondering about Lateef's sexuality. He had been so turned on by Dave that night back in June, there had been such passion in his eyes! Was what Ali had told Dave really true, that Lateef was essentially straight, or did his feelings for Dave run deeper? If Dave gave him enough time, wouldn't Lateef eventually come to realize that he was as much in love with Dave as Dave was with him?

Or was Dave just being an overly optimistic fool?

Well, thought Dave, if my plans for Lateef's future come true, there will be plenty of time for us to explore our feelings for each other. In the meantime, I have more difficult things to worry about. Like getting Lateef a passport and student visa from the Moroccan government. If what Lateef had said was true, that was not going to be easy.

Dear God, Dave told himself. There's just got to be a way to bring Lateef back to the States with me. There's just got to be!

CHAPTER 5

▼

The Atlas Mountains loomed larger and larger on the horizon as the driver of the white Fiat sports coupe approached Aïn El Qamar. Less than three hours earlier he had been in Rabat, the seaside capital of Morocco, with its bustling streets, gleaming white villas, purple bougainvillea, and cosmopolitan air. Now he was truly in another world. Around him as he sped along the two lane highway were tiny farms where chickens and goats intermingled outside modest box-shaped earthen dwellings. *Jellaba*-clad men pushed wooden plows drawn by donkeys. Women were invisible, doubtless indoors as was their custom. Occasionally, the driver could see flocks of sheep tended by small boys. At times he whizzed past older children holding up a scrawny chicken or rabbit for sale. He did not stop. He saw these things, but paid little attention. In his ten years in Aïn El Qamar, similar sights had become commonplace. They were not part of his own private world which consisted of the school where he taught, his French friends, the tennis court of the Hotel El Qamar, long weekends out of town in four-star hotels, and countless brief affairs with beautiful women, French, Italian, Spanish ... that is to say whoever was desirable, available, and willing.

I hardly know Morocco, thought Jean-Richard Moreau. Not its people. Not its customs. I'm really nothing but an intruder here, and if at times the Moroccans seem unwelcoming and even hostile, then who really is at fault?

People like Laurent and Christiane Koenigsmarck would not hesitate to blame the "natives," Jean-Richard knew. Their kind obviously felt that they had the right to claim whatever they desired in Morocco as their own and that the Moroccans were born to serve them.

Jean-Richard did not share this racist attitude, though he understood it. Prejudice allowed the Koenigsmarcks and others like them to forget their own inferiority, and ironically, despite their frequent complaints, they were probably happier here than they could ever have been in France. Still, there were times when Jean-Richard could hardly prevent himself from telling them how much he despised them. But he never said a word. One did not publicly criticize one's own kind, and the facts were plain. Jean-Richard had remained in Morocco for ten years, and like the Koenigsmarcks, he had no intention of leaving. From the beginning, Morocco had offered him asylum, not merely from his own country, but from memories that haunted him, that denied him and would always deny him the happiness that he had once believed possible.

Happiness! Jean-Richard laughed bitterly at the word as he drove past a tired elderly couple hoping for a free ride. He had not deliberately snubbed them. They were merely part of the scenery and his thoughts were elsewhere.

"Happiness!" he repeated aloud. Did such a thing as happiness even exist? He thought he had known happiness those years ago in Paris. Happiness had meant being twenty-two, twenty-three, twenty-four, feeling that each new day would bring you joy upon joy, loving, and the security of being loved.

What idiocy! You did not stay young forever and each lonely day only destroyed you more. You dared not love for fear of being hurt, and the love others professed to give you was a sham, a dirty painful farce.

The French in Aïn El Qamar thought of Jean-Richard as a carefree, fun-loving playboy, but that was because they did not see his moments of despair, did not sense the hollowness of his life. These he hid with smiles and charming remarks and a gallant manner. His friends knew only the exterior, the wavy golden blond hair, the sun-bronzed skin, the deep brown eyes, the lithe athletic body, the impeccably tailored clothes. They did not see the ashes where once his heart had beat.

Only Claudette Verlaine knew of the conflicts within Jean-Richard, and though she sympathized with his private agonies, she was unable to understand them fully. She was in reality what Jean-Richard only pretended to be, a lover of fun and excitement and adventure. She relished these things, while for Jean-Richard they were only a way to fill up the empty hours and to stave off boredom. Claudette knew the real Jean-Richard, and considered him her dearest friend, but she realized that she was powerless to help him, and had long ago stopped trying.

Jean-Richard still wondered what had prompted him to bare his soul to her that day ten years ago in Casablanca. Neither had been in Morocco for more than twenty-four hours when, totally by chance, they had made each other's acquaintance in a popular Italian restaurant. In the course of conversation, they had discovered to their amazement that they were both heading for Aïn El Qamar.

"Live with me," Claudette had said boldly and unexpectedly.

"*Quoi?*" asked a stupefied Jean-Richard.

"Live with me," she replied. "I do not wish to be alone in a small town. It does not suit me to share a house with another woman. You are single. I am as well. We shall live together. Nothing could be simpler."

Jean-Richard admired her boldness, but had hesitated to agree to her request.

"What is the matter, *chéri?*" Claudette had asked.

And then, surprising even himself, Jean-Richard had found himself taking her question literally and telling her exactly what the matter was. Perhaps it was because she was a stranger. Perhaps it was because this beautiful woman seemed to have lived and experienced many things in her thirty-five-odd years. Whatever the reason, Jean-Richard was soon revealing to her all of his secret anguish, telling her every humiliating detail of the memories which had rendered his life meaningless.

"*Pauvre garçon,*" said Claudette sympathetically when he had finished. "What a horrendous thing to have happened to you!" Then her face had brightened and she had said, "But now is the time to start anew. I want someone to live with, a friend, a confidant, a protector. Should we become lovers, so much the better. *Mais ce n'est pas nécessaire.*"

Jean-Richard could scarcely believe what he was hearing, but Claudette had been insistent.

"*Alors*, will you share a house with me?"

And Jean-Richard had impulsively decided to take the plunge. "Yes. I will," he had replied. "You've made me realize that I don't want to live alone either. It's a great idea, in fact. *D'accord*, Claudette. We'll greet Aïn El Qamar as a team."

Jean-Richard caught a distant glimpse of Aïn El Qamar now, cradled at the foot of the Atlas Mountains on this October afternoon ten years later. He was thirty-four years old. And the town where he lived was, if not home, then at least a comfortable and non-threatening place for Jean-Richard to hide.

Aïn El Qamar was growing larger by the minute as he neared it. He could perceive the minarets of its many mosques beginning to distinguish themselves from the rest of the town. Then, as he approached the turnoff from the main highway, the olive groves which surrounded Aïn El Qamar blocked his view of it.

Not yet, he thought. I can't drive in yet. I need more time to myself. He slowed down, pulled his Fiat over to the side of the road, and got out. The olive groves were deserted at the moment. Locking the car, he walked across the wild grass which covered the ground and sat in the shade of an olive tree.

Jean-Richard glanced at his watch and saw that there was still another hour before his first class. He had prepared it yesterday after his morning lessons. Then, just before twelve, he had left for Rabat, having no classes either that afternoon or this morning. It was a business trip. Somehow or other there had been a foul-up in his accounts, and his last statement had shown too much money being transferred into French francs, leaving him not enough Moroccan *dirhams* for his daily expenses. Knowing that a phone call would be futile, he had decided to make the trip by car. The hours waiting for the Moroccan bureaucracy to attend to him had seemed endless, but finally yesterday evening he had finished his business. Having already checked into a comfortable downtown hotel, he had gone directly to a restaurant he did not know personally, but which a friend had recommended to him. And yet another of his romantic adventures had begun.

"Chez Mikos" it was called, and was popular in Rabat for its Greek cuisine. Jean-Richard sat alone at a corner table, listening to the recorded bouzouki music in the background. The meal had been delicious, the *mousaka* hot and spicy, the *ouzo* warming. He was having an after-dinner *digéstif* when he heard a woman's voice.

"Did you enjoy your *dîner*?" The voice was soft and sweet, the French ever so slightly accented.

"*Beaucoup*," he replied, looking up to see a delicate face, large hazel eyes, and long soft brown hair.

"*Je m'appelle* Helena. This is my parents' restaurant. My father is Mikos. I'm so glad you enjoyed the meal."

God, she is beautiful, thought Jean-Richard, sultry and sensuous with the look of the Mediterranean, and certainly not a day over twenty.

"Would you like to sit down?" he asked.

"*D'accord*," replied the girl, and sat opposite him. "Are you a tourist?" she asked, lighting a Gauloise.

Jean-Richard introduced himself and briefly explained his presence in Morocco.

"I have no teachers so handsome as you," said Helena flirtatiously.

"Do you study here in the university?" asked Jean-Richard.

"No, I go to the Lycée Français in Marrakesh, but I am here this week during my parents' absence."

A high school girl, thought Jean-Richard. She's even younger than I imagined.

"But Rabat is so dull," Helena pouted. "In Marrakesh I have many friends. We go out often. *Les discos, les boîtes* ... But here I am alone. The only people I know are my parents' age, and they bore me. *Je suis triste et seule.*"

Jean-Richard nodded in sympathy. The girl was lovely, really, and he enjoyed her company. No longer did he feel the desire to be by himself.

She smiled at him. "Perhaps you would like to do something, go somewhere?" she suggested. "I hear there is a new *discothèque* opened by the beach. Shall we go dancing together?"

"I'd enjoy that," replied Jean-Richard. "Yes, Helena, I'd enjoy that very much."

They drove to the seaside disco. Though it was nearly empty when they arrived, crowds soon started entering, and as the music blared out of countless speakers and as he danced with this charming beautiful Greek girl, Jean-Richard felt past memories numbing as they always did when he was dancing or making love. And he knew tonight that the first would inevitably lead to the second.

It was past two in the morning when they finally left the *discothèque*. Jean-Richard did not refuse Helena's invitation for a nightcap at the villa she shared with her parents when she was not in Marrakesh. "They have left me here alone for the entire week," the girl pouted, "and I am so bored when I am by myself."

The villa was located in Aguedal, one of the wealthy suburbs of Rabat, and the Mediterranean influence characteristic of much of the French-built capital was evident in its design. Bougainvillea climbed the white wall which surrounded it. Flowers grew in profusion in the front garden. In the moonlight, it was worlds away from Aïn El Qamar.

Jean-Richard let himself be ushered into an elegant living room and sat down on an exquisitely upholstered sofa. It was clear from the expensive furnishings that these Greeks had lived in Morocco for many years and that their restaurant had brought them success. Helena took two brandy snifters from the antique sideboard and filled them with French cognac. She moved with feline grace across the room and sat on the sofa beside Jean-Richard.

"A toast, *à l'aventure*," she said breathily.

"To adventure," repeated Jean-Richard, and sipped the cognac. It sent a wave of warmth throughout his body. He was physically tired from his long drive, the endless waiting in government offices, and the frenetic dancing at the *discothèque*. But the cognac and the girl's provocative presence awakened him, excited him.

"To adventure," said Helena again, and as she pressed her lips against Jean-Richard's, the kittenlike softness disappeared and she became a tigress. She explored his mouth with rapid darting movements of her tongue, then sucked on his earlobes as she reached inside his shirt to play with the blond hair of his chest.

Jean-Richard surrendered himself to her passionate nibbling and fondling, his head spinning from her caresses, his whole body responding to her touch.

"Come to the bedroom," she whispered, and Jean-Richard followed her in a daze. Usually he was in control, but not tonight.

He soon found himself in a large double bed on clean fresh sheets. Looking up, he saw Helena naked, standing over him like an erotic statue. Her long dark hair hung down past her shoulders. Her full breasts were firm and proud, the nipples hard and pointed. Jean-Richard let his eyes drink in the smooth skin of her belly and below it the triangular mound of her dark pubic hair. He pulled her towards him, and she knelt astride his face, moaning as he shot his tongue inside her, exploring her sex.

As the minutes flew by, Jean-Richard was invited to discover, to caress, to lick every inch of her body, as she herself played with his balls and moved her moist tongue in circles around his throbbing cock, taking it at times fully in her mouth but always holding back when she sensed that he was at the point of orgasm.

Finally, when Jean-Richard felt sure that he was about to die, she moved her body lengthwise atop his and cried out, "Now! Take me now!" Jean-Richard pulled her down on top of him, his hands cupping the twin moons of her buttocks. She rose and fell on his manhood, he felt himself burst into a million pieces, and for that moment he was able to forget the past.

Now, as Jean-Richard sat under an olive tree at the entrance to Aïn El Qamar, he inscribed her name mentally on the long list of his conquests since his arrival in Morocco, though in fact there had been so many that he had forgotten most of their names, and their faces and bodies he only dimly remembered.

His first liaison had, inevitably he supposed, been with Claudette. It had been a casual one, neither of them wishing to become involved emotionally, but it had allowed Jean-Richard temporary release from his memories. Then, one day, it had ended as he had known it would. Claudette, who had become restless for more excitement, had begun seeing a handsome young Romanian engineer who was spending several months in Aïn El Qamar on a government project. And Jean-Richard had wished her luck in her new romance, grateful for the good times they had shared, but relieved to see the glamorous pleasure-relishing Frenchwoman, ten years his senior, converted from lover to best friend. They had decided to continue sharing the same house, for they enjoyed each other's company and found the living arrangement convenient and practical. Never again had they shared the same bed, though their lives had remained closely inter-twined ever since.

In the distance, Jean-Richard could make out a group of elderly country women walking through the olive groves in his direction. He looked at his watch. Only forty minutes till he had to be in class. He stood up reluctantly and walked over to his car, unlocked the door, got in, and drove on into Aïn El Qamar.

Jean-Richard pulled up and parked in front of the house where he and Clau-dette lived in Cité Jamila. He was about to get out when he saw the front door open and a tall, strongly-built Moroccan emerge. The man wore a navy blue striped Lacoste shirt and beige slacks. His face looked familiar. So did his outfit. My God, it was the new tennis pro from the Hotel El Qamar and he was wearing Jean-Richard's clothes! The Moroccan shut the door behind him, then sauntered off in the direction of downtown Aïn El Qamar, a satisfied smirk on his face. The tennis pro's smug smile and his presence here wearing Jean-Richard's shirt and slacks could mean only one thing—Claudette had taken leave of her senses and broken her rule about never entertaining Moroccans in the town where she lived.

Jean-Richard waited until the man was some distance away before leaving his Fiat, getting his suitcase from the trunk, and heading towards the front door. He unlocked it and walked inside. The house he and Claudette shared was a two-story dwelling, and Jean-Richard's bedroom and bath were upstairs. As he was about to go up, Claudette emerged from her downstairs bedroom wearing a diaphanous red silk dressing gown and obviously nothing else. Looking up at him in surprise, she said, "I didn't hear you come in. How was Rabat?"

"Evidently not as interesting as things have been here in Aïn El Qamar," replied Jean-Richard. He set down his suitcase at the foot of the stairs and walked into the living room where he poured himself a glass of Martini Rouge.

Claudette followed him in, and as she did so, he noticed that her auburn hair was disheveled and her make-up smeared.

"I can see you've had quite a lunch break," he said icily.

Claudette glared at him. "That's the second snide remark you've made since you came in. What exactly are you getting at, Jean-Richard?"

"Come off it, Claudette! It's not every day I find you fresh from a romp in the hay with a Moroccan. What happened to your vow to keep your lovers discreetly out of town? And where did you get off letting him wear my clothes?"

"I had no choice," declared Claudette. "His got stained. And anyway, I *am* being discreet." She turned and walked away from Jean-Richard over to a mod-ernistic black end table at the opposite corner of the room where she reached for a cigarette. Lighting it, she took several puffs and said, looking out the window, "We came straight from the tennis court. No one saw us on the way. Saadia knows damn well she'd better keep her mouth shut, and Fareed *swore* to me that he won't say a word."

"I wouldn't count on it," cautioned Jean-Richard. "He's probably bragging to all his buddies right now how he was the first Moroccan stud to lay Miss Claudette Verlaine right in the heart of Aïn El Qamar."

"*Cochon!*" spat out Claudette. "You're a pig, Jean-Richard. You have no right to say such things to me." But she still faced out the window, not daring to meet Jean-Richard's eyes. "I thought you were the one who claimed to be above prejudice. Now who is it who's making racist statements!"

"*Je ne suis pas raciste,*" insisted Jean-Richard. "I've seen that guy. I've talked to him. We've played tennis together. He's been around, and he's out for whatever he can get from people. He'll take you for every *centîme* you have. Is that what you want?"

"Damn it, Jean-Richard, I don't know what I want!" cried Claudette, turning at last to face the Frenchman but remaining at the other end of the room. "I just want … I just want … someone! I'm so … damn … tired of being alone all the time! *Je n'y peux plus!*"

Jean-Richard walked over to Claudette, put his arms out and held her gently. "I've never heard you talk this way before. What happened to the fun-loving carefree Miss Claudette who only wanted to have a good time?"

"I do want a good time, Jean-Richard. It's just not enough anymore. It's just not enough."

Jean-Richard pulled back and looked Claudette squarely in the eye. "*Ecoute, ma chère,* I know it's your own life and that I have no right to tell you how to live it. But please, promise me that you'll think seriously before getting involved with this man. I don't want to see you get hurt."

Suddenly, Claudette's moment of self-revelation was over. She removed herself from Jean-Richard's arms and smiled. "You know me, silly boy. I am indestructible. So don't worry about me, Jean-Richard. I'm a grown woman and I can take care of myself." She paused, then said brightly, "And now, hadn't Monsieur Moreau better be on his way to school. It's nearly three."

"*Ah, mon Dieu!*" exclaimed Jean-Richard, looking over at the wall clock. "I can see I won't have time to change. I'll just fetch my school things and run."

On his way out of the living room, Jean-Richard stopped and looked seriously at Claudette. "I hope you're right about being indestructible. I hope I never have to say 'I told you so.'"

"Run along now, or you'll be late. No doubt I'll see you at four o'clock in the *salle des profs.*"

Jean-Richard hurried upstairs, collected his teaching materials which he had laid out the previous day, splashed on some Eau Sauvage cologne—it'll have to take the place of a shower for now, he thought—and minutes later he was driving into the parking lot of Lycée Mohamed Cinq.

As he was getting out of his car, he noticed Dave Casalini walking in towards the main gate. Jean-Richard liked the tall out-going American, admired his athletic prowess, and his nearly unaccented French. He respected his openness as well. Knowing Dave had made Jean-Richard see gay men in a new light.

"*Salut, l'Amérique!*" Jean-Richard said smilingly.

"*Salut, la France!*" replied Dave, and they shook hands.

A middle-aged Moroccan wearing a blue work coat sat by the entrance to the school courtyard, which it was his duty to guard. "*Bonjour, messieurs,*" he said as the two teachers passed him.

"*Salem u alikum,*" responded Dave in Arabic.

"*U alikum salem,*" said the gate-keeper.

"*Quel exhibitioniste!*" joked Jean-Richard.

"*Moi?*" asked Dave. "My Arabic is probably the worst of all the Aïn El Qamar Americans. Kevin's is a whole lot better than mine, and Janna's is by far the best, though she doesn't know much French."

"And the new girl?" asked Jean-Richard as they walked across the now empty courtyard. He was surprised to hear the curiosity in his voice.

"Marcie? Marcie Nelson?" asked Dave. "Well, her French is pretty good. I think she majored in it. But this is her first time out of Wisconsin, so she hasn't had much practice yet. She had three months of Arabic during training like the rest of us, but I've never really heard her talk."

The two men entered the *salle des profs*, where there were several groups of teachers waiting to begin their afternoon's work. Others were already in class, having started at two o'clock. Most of the Moroccan teachers present were dressed in dark suits and ties. Jean-Richard and Dave, on the other hand, wore short-sleeved shirts and casual slacks as did most of the foreign faculty. Jean-Richard saw Michèle Perrault and Janna Gallagher talking together. He and Dave walked over to them.

"'ello to zee Americans," said Jean-Richard in his thickly accented high school English.

"*Ne sois pas ridicule*, Jean-Richard," said Michèle, sharp with the Frenchman as usual. "Don't be ridiculous." Here was one woman who was proving a challenge to seduce, and Jean-Richard was beginning to doubt the outcome of his attempts.

Dave and Janna started chattering away in rapid American English and when Michèle joined in, Jean-Richard wandered away. Kevin Kensington, racing into the teachers' room, nearly bumped into him.

"*Salut*, Jean-Richard," greeted the sandy-haired American. Kevin was of medium height, fair-skinned, self-effacing but warm and friendly. Jean-Richard enjoyed his enthusiasm.

"*Pourquoi si pressé?*" asked Jean-Richard. "Why the hurry?"

"I've just come from the most delectable Moroccan meal," he exclaimed in French, "and I was afraid I'd be late for class."

"Well, you've got …"—Jean-Richard looked at his watch—"exactly three minutes until the first bell, if it's on schedule."

Just then the bell rang.

"Wrong again!" laughed Jean-Richard.

"Who?" asked Kevin. "You, or the little old bell-ringer?"

"I wouldn't presume to say," replied Jean-Richard with a twinkle. Through the windows of the *salle des profs* he could see classes being dismissed. Students left their classrooms, chatting in groups, a few boys taking advantage of the relative freedom the school grounds offered to flirt with girl students. Teachers too emerged, rushing to the faculty room for a quick smoke. Dominique Moulin was walking in now, plain and sour-faced as usual. Oh God, thought Jean-Richard. Going to bed with her had been a silly, impulsive mistake. She ignored him and went to talk with several of her French colleagues, no doubt to complain about Aïn El Qamar as was her habit.

"Hello, Kevin. *Salut*, Jean-Richard." Jean-Richard heard the sweet, American-accented voice before he saw the honey blond shoulder-length hair and the rosy cheeks of Marcie Nelson, the new American girl. I've never seen such perfect skin, thought Jean-Richard, always the connoisseur of feminine beauty. The quintessential small-town girl, he thought.

"Only one more hour," she said in French, her face lit by a smile. "I'm exhausted. But I love the work. I don't know how I could have stayed in Wisconsin for so many years. Every day here I seem to discover something new, fascinating … I don't know … *C'est merveilleux!*"

Jean-Richard found himself at a loss for words. He didn't usually lose his cool, but on the few occasions he had met Marcie, she had had this effect on him.

Finally he found his voice. "Marcie, Kevin," he said, "why don't you drop over to Claudette's and my place tonight for aperitifs? You've been by before,

Kevin, but it'll be a first for Marcie. She might enjoy meeting some of the other French *cöopérants* socially."

"*Bien sûr!*" answered Kevin. "Sounds great. *Et toi, Marcie?*"

"I'd love to," replied the American girl eagerly.

"Wonderful!" exclaimed Jean-Richard. "We'll expect you around seven. And now, if you'll both excuse me, I'd like to get to class early and make sure that my lab assistant has set up today's experiments. *A ce soir alors.*"

"See you this evening," replied Kevin and Marcie.

Jean-Richard left the *salle des profs*, amazed to find as he walked among the groups of students that he was humming a tune. He smiled and said hello when several of them greeted him.

Jean-Richard was one of five teachers of *sciences naturelles* at Lycée Mohamed Cinq, and certainly the best-liked and most highly respected. Science had always been his favorite subject, and he enjoyed teaching it to his young Moroccan pupils. Although few were truly gifted, they were almost without exception intelligent and eager to learn. Initially he had found them slow to understand, however since learning to gear his lessons to their rural background, he had changed his mind.

Now, as Jean-Richard headed towards the science building which had been constructed during his seventh year in Aïn El Qamar, he thought to himself how lucky he was to have the most up-to-date facilities in Lycée Mohamed Cinq. Or at least how lucky he had been. Under Monsieur Mahraoui the laboratories had been well supplied and staffed. Things had been going downhill, however, since Monsieur Rhazwani had taken over the school reins. Still, Jean-Richard was unprepared for the disarray he found today upon entering the modern laboratory where he was to give his lesson. Microscopes which should have been arranged neatly, two per desk, were strewn haphazardly around the room and the unwashed counter top was covered with fingerprint-smudged slides, some of them broken. The room had a strange, sweet smell, as if someone had been smoking *keef* or hashish. And the lab assistant was nowhere to be found.

"Sameer! Sameer!" shouted Jean-Richard. He could not believe that the assistant, who was usually so scrupulous in following instructions, could be capable of such untidiness.

Just then the storeroom door opened and a stocky unshaven Moroccan wearing a dirty white lab coat and a glazed expression entered.

"Sameer's not working here anymore," he said nonchalantly. "I'm his replacement."

"His replacement?" asked an uncomprehending Jean-Richard. "What happened to Sameer?"

"How should I know?" said the new assistant.

Jean-Richard was livid. "Who trained you?" he asked, his voice seething. "How could you make such a mess? This is unforgivable."

"I was going to clean up the counter, until you started yelling at me. It's not my fault Sameer was fired."

"Fired?" Jean-Richard thought he must be hearing things. "Fired?"

Just then, there was a knock at the door and Jean-Richard turned to see one of his students peer in. "*On peut entrer, monsieur?*" he asked.

"Yes, come in," replied Jean-Richard. Then, turning to the sly-looking new lab assistant, he said, "I'll see the *proviseur* about this as soon as class is over."

The lab assistant only grinned.

The five o'clock bell had finally rung after Jean-Richard had thought that his two hours with the class would never end. Ordinarily, he might have been able to control his exasperation at the disorder in which he had found the laboratory, but he had hardly slept in the past thirty-six hours. It had not been easy to calmly ask the students to help set up the equipment properly, saying nothing about the reason for the mess. Throughout the lesson, the ill-mannered and possibly stoned lab assistant had been nowhere in sight. Doubtless the students had noticed Jean-Richard's peculiar irritation, though he had tried to keep it under control. When the lesson was nearing its end, he had asked his students to return the equipment to its proper shelves and drawers. He certainly was not going to leave the task to his inept and disrespectful new helper.

Now, with the ringing of the bell, Jean-Richard quickly gathered his materials and dashed out of the classroom without even pausing to sign the absence list or to answer the usual questions. He pushed his way through groups of students emerging from other classrooms, not seeing them, disregarding their hellos.

Reaching the administrative wing, he paid no attention to Monsieur Rhazwani's veiled secretary but stormed directly into the *proviseur*'s office.

The large man was jabbering on the phone to someone in Arabic. Jean-Richard stood there impatiently waiting for Monsieur Rhazwani to finish.

"What is the meaning of this!" roared the heavy-set Moroccan when he had at last hung up.

Jean-Richard did not beat around the bush. "Why was Sameer fired!" he exclaimed. "And why was an incompetent hired to take his place!"

"My nephew, incompetent?!" The *proviseur* was indignant.

A flabbergasted Jean-Richard found himself at a loss for words. "Your … your what?" he stammered.

"Moulay Khalil is my nephew, and he has assured me that he is completely qualified for his new position. Let me remind you, Monsieur Moreau, you are not in charge of who is hired as your lab assistant. That is an administrative decision."

"I won't work if he stays," protested Jean-Richard impulsively.

"Don't be a child," replied the *proviseur* so patronizingly that Jean-Richard wanted to strike the man. "You are under contract, or have you forgotten? You know that any unjustified absence will cause you a severe financial penalty and leave a black mark on your record as well. Think about your future in the teaching profession, and I'm sure that you will be able to accustom yourself to Moulay Khalil's way of doing things. And now, if you're through wasting my time, I have more important matters to attend to than a peevish science instructor."

So I'm dismissed, just like that? thought Jean-Richard angrily. But he said nothing. The *proviseur*'s remarks about job security had hit home.

Not knowing what else to say, Jean-Richard stood up and stalked out of the office.

Outside, Jean-Richard felt the sudden need for tobacco, although he smoked only occasionally. "Have you got a cigarette?" he asked the person nearest him, a handsome young Moroccan teacher.

"This is my last pack," replied the Moroccan. "I'm supposed to be giving up the habit tomorrow." A twinkle in his eye, he offered Jean-Richard a cigarette.

"Oh, never mind," replied Jean-Richard, suddenly feeling less angry in the presence of this pleasant young man. He was curious to know who he was. "I don't believe we've met. I'm Jean-Richard Moreau, *science naturelles*."

"Kacem Hajiri, *prof de physique*," replied the Moroccan, extending his hand. "Very new physics teacher. It's my first year." The young man's manner was naturally ingratiating.

"You won't be so perky after you've been here for ten, as I have," remarked Jean-Richard.

"You must have been in speaking with the *proviseur*."

"Unfortunately, yes," answered Jean-Richard and briefly outlined his run-in with the man.

"*Salaud! Con!*" exclaimed Kacem. "That bastard never changes."

"You sound like you know him well."

"You're damn right. He was the *directeur* of my elementary school. After that he was transferred to another post, and no one ever heard from him again. But even back then he was a sadistic, self-centered, greedy, corrupt son of a bitch. And unfortunately no idiot either. That man is cleverer than a fox."

"What bad luck for you to start working at Lycée Mohamed Cinq just when he takes over," commiserated Jean-Richard.

"Yes," agreed Kacem, "and especially after I'd fought so hard to be posted back in Aïn El Qamar in order to be with my family. We'd been separated since I went to France for my high school and eventually my university studies."

"So, what's your advice about Rhazwani?" asked Jean-Richard. "You seem to have had more experience with him than anyone else."

"Just give him time. At this rate, the entire school will be against him by the end of the year. We'll see what happens then."

"You know him better than I do, Monsieur Hajiri," said Jean-Richard. "I'll just have to take your word on it."

"Please call me Kacem."

"And I'm Jean-Richard."

"I'd love to talk more, Jean-Richard," said the Moroccan teacher, "but I'm on my way to run some errands for my mother. It was really very nice meeting you."

"A pleasure to meet you too," said the Frenchman as Kacem Hajiri crossed the deserted courtyard.

So, things are finally changing, thought Jean-Richard. Once, only French *coöpérants* taught physics at Lycée Mohamed Cinq. Now there was Kacem Hajiri, and unless appearances were deceiving, the man was probably quite good at his work. To think that he was a native of Aïn El Qamar. It was definitely an encouraging sign.

Then Jean-Richard corrected himself. How could anything be encouraging when each new day at Lycée Mohamed Cinq brought fresh evidence of Monsieur Rhazwani's arrogant and corrupt administration?

What in God's name will he think of to do next? Jean-Richard asked himself as he headed for the parking lot, worn out after nearly a day and a half without sleep.

Then, as he drove away from school, he spotted Kevin and Marcie walking home. He suddenly remembered that the pretty, sunny American girl was coming by for aperitifs that evening, and he found that he was tired no longer.

CHAPTER 6

▼

Kevin Kensington was disappointed when he heard the bell ring at ten to five signaling the end of class. He had been enjoying himself in spite of the late hour. His lesson was absorbing and the students were responding eagerly. Some days they would begin putting away their notebooks before class was over, but today, Kevin thought, even they had been taken by surprise when the bell rang.

As Kevin was putting his teaching materials back into his briefcase, a group of students gathered around his desk. Some asked about the lesson, others about grades, still others wanted to know more about America or about Kevin personally. Kevin adored the attention, soaked it up like a sponge. Sometimes he felt that teachers were like actors who could never get enough applause. Kevin's students were his audience, and in teaching them every day he was also seeking their approval and their affection.

Kevin's housemate Dave often criticized his friend's devotion to his job. "You've got to stop living for your moments in class, Kev. You come home depressed because a lesson didn't work and you brood about every little thing that's gone wrong. A good lesson gets you too high, and a bad one gets you too low. You need to find some kind of equilibrium in your life."

Kevin knew that his friend was right, yet since he had been in Aïn Qamar, teaching had been like a drug, numbing the painful memories of his devastating trip to New York a year and a half before, allowing him to forget for an hour that he had once wanted so desperately to die.

However, could it possibly be that his life was about to change? After today, did he dare to hope for happiness?

Kevin was sure that his students had noticed how bright and cheerful he felt this afternoon. Maybe that was why the lesson had been such a success. *I haven't felt this good since … since …*

As Kevin answered his students' eager questions, he caught sight of Marcie Nelson walking past his classroom. She saw him and stuck her head in through the door.

"*Sa-fi!*" she exclaimed, and Kevin's students chuckled at her use of the Moroccan expression meaning, "I'm finished."

"Me too," said Kevin.

"Meet you in the *salle des profs?*" she suggested.

"In just a minute."

As Marcie walked away, one of Kevin's students asked with a giggle, "Is she your girlfriend, Mr. Kensington?"

"No, she's just a friend," said Kevin, and the students snickered knowingly. In Aïn El Qamar, there was no such thing as a girl who was "just a friend."

"You have dirty minds," said Kevin.

"We will wash them!" responded one of his cleverest students, and Kevin nearly burst with pride at the knowledge that they owed so much of their English ability to his teaching.

"I'll see you tomorrow," he said, and left the classroom to head towards the *salle des profs.*

"Good-bye Mr. Kensington," called out a chorus of voices behind him. "Have a nice dinner. Have a nice evening. Have a nice night!"

God, they're wonderful! thought Kevin. *And what a day this had been!*

He found Marcie waiting for him in the faculty room, where a few other teachers had congregated. As usual, she looked fresh and wholesome, quite like a sister of Kevin's would have looked had he had one. Kevin was not the only person to wonder why Marcie, away from Wisconsin and her family for the first time, was having little or no trouble adapting to life in Aïn El Qamar. She could walk past groups of local men oblivious to their remarks, but more often than not they were silent. Probably Marcie reminded them of a younger sister too.

Her life had been made easier by the fact that she had moved in just down the street from Dave and Kevin. Everyone had been surprised when this obviously sheltered new girl had insisted upon living alone, but she had been adamant, maintaining that the time had come for her to try independence. Luckily a small house on Dave and Kevin's block had been available, and this had seemed the ideal solution.

Dave considered Marcie "too perfect to be true," and to Kevin's relief, he had not insisted on telling her that her two American neighbors were gay. Kevin still wished Dave had not been quite so open to Janna, Claudette, and Jean-Richard. But Dave believed in being "out." Kevin was still less sure of himself, and Marcie's not knowing about his sexuality made it possible for him to feel at ease with her, though Dave insisted that just the opposite ought to be true. In any case, Kevin and Marcie had become buddies at once, and he felt a closeness to her that he had never felt with Janna. Marcie truly saw the good in everyone, and Kevin respected and admired her for that.

As Kevin entered the *salle des profs*, Marcie smiled and said, "You look like you're about ten stories high."

"It was a fabulous lesson," replied Kevin. "In fact, it's been an altogether fabulous day!"

"That's right. I was going to ask you about your Moroccan meal. I'll bet it was super!"

"The whole thing was like a dream," exclaimed Kevin.

"I envy you so much. You know, I've been in Aïn El Qamar for a month now and I still haven't been invited into a Moroccan home."

"Just be patient, Marcie," reassured Kevin. "Your chance will come."

At that moment, the bell rang and Kevin saw those students who still had one more hour of class start trudging reluctantly towards their classrooms.

"There's Dave outside," said Marcie. "Don't tell me he's got a five o'clock class today."

"Yes, and you know what? I almost wish I did too," declared Kevin. "I love teaching that much."

"I love it too," said Marcie, "but I'm glad it's over for today. We've got to go get ready for aperitifs at Claudette and Jean-Richard's."

"You're right. Let's be on our way!"

The two Americans left the *salle des profs* together, just as Jean-Richard stormed out of the *proviseur*'s office.

"He looks upset about something," said Marcie, glancing in the Frenchman's direction. "I wonder what it is. He usually looks so cheerful, so ... so full of life."

Kevin heard something in Marcie's voice that made him wonder if she too, like so many before her, was falling under Jean-Richard's spell. Earlier, in the *salle des profs*, he had noticed that she had not been able to take her eyes off him. Poor Marcie, he thought, fresh from the farm and all too vulnerable. He hoped that she was not letting herself in for a broken heart.

"Who's that he's talking with?" asked Marcie. "He looks Moroccan, but he's dressed like one of us."

Kevin felt his heartbeat quicken as he recognized the other man. "That's … that's Kacem Hajiri, a new physics teacher. He's the one whose family's house I ate at today."

"I've never noticed him before," commented Marcie.

Are you blind? thought Kevin. Who could help but notice the most gorgeous man in Lycée Mohamed Cinq? Aloud he said, "He … he just graduated from the university in France." Kevin hoped that Marcie could not hear the quiver in his voice.

"I'd like to meet him," said Marcie. "But maybe now's not the best time. He and Jean-Richard seem to be having a pretty serious discussion. I wonder what's unsettled Jean-Richard so."

"You can ask him about it this evening," suggested Kevin.

"That's right. You and I are visiting 'la France' tonight." Marcie's face brightened at the thought. "And now, Kevin, I want you to tell me about your Moroccan lunch."

As the two Americans left school and headed towards their neighborhood, about halfway between Janna's house and the French *quartier*, Kevin described in detail the delicious and lavish meal he had been served at Kacem Hajiri's house that afternoon.

The men sat on *banquettes* around a knee-high silver platter more than a yard in diameter. There was Kacem Hajiri, his father—a tiny *jellaba*-clad man who looked older than his fifty-three years, Kacem's two adolescent brothers, and a visiting cousin from Fez. No women were present. They ate in another room, isolated by custom. Madame Hajiri, of course, was busy in the kitchen, and tempting aromas wafted in from it to the living room.

A small boy entered shyly and Kacem explained that this was his youngest brother Abdenbi. The boy carried a kettle of warm water in one hand and in another a large metal pot, the lid of which resembled a shallow colander. A small metal dish was attached to the center of the lid, and in it lay a bar of soap. There was a dishtowel over the boy's left shoulder.

Kevin had participated in this hand-washing ceremony before so he knew how to proceed. He took the bar of soap and held both hands over the colander-like lid. Abdenbi poured warm water over Kevin's hands. When they were covered with lather, the boy poured more water over them to rinse them. The water dripped through the holes in the lid to the pot below. Kevin cupped his hands and, filling them with more water, rinsed his mouth as he had often seen Moroccans do. Then he spat the water into the container. Finally, taking the towel from the boy's shoulder, he dried his hands. Kacem, next to him, repeated the same actions, and when he was through, accepted the towel from Kevin. When all the men had washed up, the little boy exited quietly.

He returned seconds later carrying a wide shallow straw basket on which reposed four or five steaming round loaves of homemade *khobs*, Moroccan bread fresh from the public oven. He set the basket down and handed the loaves one by one to Kacem's father, who sliced each into six triangular sections, then gave several pieces to each of those present.

Little Abdenbi went to stand by the door. Soon, a pair of hands reached into the room with a platter of small bowls of salad. It was doubtless one of the women serving from the kitchen, whose modesty prevented her from coming into the room. Abdenbi took the platter and placed the bowls around the table. Some contained a mixture of finely chopped tomatoes, onions, and green peppers. In others there were toothpick-sized carrot slivers combined with raisins and a cinnamon topping. "*Bsmillah*," said the men, "In the name of God," and began breaking off small morsels of *khobs* which they used to eat the salads. They ate with the right hand only, as the left hand was reserved by ritual for washing oneself before prayer.

Ten minutes later, the mysterious pair of hands offered Abdenbi the next course from the kitchen. It was *tajine*, Moroccan stew. The name referred to both the food itself and to the large glazed brown clay dish with its cone-shaped lid in which the *tajine* was cooked and from which it was eaten. Abdenbi set the dish down on the center of the table, and cleared away the salad bowls. His father lifted the conical lid, giving it to his youngest son, and Kevin saw piping hot potatoes, peas, and carrots forming a high mound in the center of the *tajine*. Under them, but invisible now, were chunks of lamb which were slowly cooked over low heat for hours until they were as tender as filet mignon. All this swam in a saffron-colored sauce made of olive oil, the juices from the meat, and various pungent spices such as cumin, ginger, paprika, and cilantro.

The *tajine* too was eaten with the right hand. One first drenched pieces of bread with the flavorful sauce and enjoyed the luscious taste. Later, one sampled the vegetables which had absorbed from the steam the fine mixture of seasonings. Finally, the meat was revealed, and savored. It was so tender that it fell apart as soon as it touched one's tongue.

As the men seated around the table enjoyed the *tajine*, Abdenbi filled small glasses with Coca-Cola and Orange Fanta. No wine was served in this traditional Moslem home.

Kevin felt sure he could eat no more, but when Abdenbi had cleared the table once again and refilled their glasses, he took from the same two bodiless hands a large tray piled high with *couscous*. Kevin and originally thought that this must be some sort of tiny round golden-colored rice, but he later learned that it was semolina, a part of the wheat not used in making flour. Moroccan women made their own flour and *couscous*, although it was possible to buy both in grocery stores. Today, the pyramid of *couscous* was topped with raisins and cinnamon and a delectable sugary sauce. The younger men at the table ate the *couscous* with soup spoons, but Kacem's father filled his cupped right hand with the tiny grains, rolled them into firm round balls, and popped them into his mouth. Rolling *couscous* balls was becoming a lost art. Kevin had tried once but had found the *couscous* sticking to his hands and falling through his fingers.

Kevin ate several half-spoonfuls out of politeness. It was delicious, but he knew he should have anticipated it and eaten less *tajine*. The difficulty was that at a Moroccan meal, from start to finish, the host would incite his guests to "*Kull! Kull!*"—Eat! Eat!—and Kevin had not yet found a polite way to refuse.

The partially eaten *couscous* disappeared and—oh no!—there was still more to come.

Abdenbi now placed a tray of apples, oranges, and bananas on the table. "*Kull!*" said Kacem's father, and Kevin reluctantly took a banana. He peeled it as slowly as etiquette permitted, and took tiny nibbles, trying to look as though he was not about to explode. Finally, he put down the half-eaten fruit. "*Kull!*" repeated Kacem's father. "*Shebaat!*" said Kevin. "I'm full!" The man smiled and his little boy took away the remaining fruit.

Returning with a plastic tray and a sponge, he wiped the table clean of peels, left-over slices of bread, spilled bits of vegetables, and scattered grains of *couscous*. Then he added the soda glasses to the tray and left the room.

All that remained now was the drinking of *atay b'nanaa*, mint tea, the unofficial national beverage of Morocco.

Abdenbi reentered carrying a kettle of boiling hot water which he set down on the table. Next to it he placed a silver tray on which reposed a half-dozen four-inch high tea glasses, two engraved silver-plated boxes, an elegant bell-shaped teapot, and a bunch of fresh mint. Kacem's father opened the smaller of the two boxes, measured the proper quantity of tea in his hand, and after putting it in the teapot, added a small amount of boiling water which he swirled around the pot. He then poured this into one of the empty glasses and set it aside. Into the pot he now placed the sprigs of mint. He opened the larger box and from it removed several hefty chunks of sugar which he added to the pot until he had nearly filled it. On top of this he poured boiling water until the pot was full. After covering the teapot, he waited about thirty seconds, then, holding the pot perhaps a foot and a half above the glass and with perfect aim, he filled a glass with tea, then returned it to the pot to strengthen the brew. This action he repeated several times until the tea was what he considered to be the ideal strength. He was then able to serve his guests. One glass of mint tea was never enough, though, and Kevin could hardly prevent his host from refilling his glass a third time.

"Was it really that difficult to refuse?" asked Marcie, who had been listening attentively to Kevin's recital as they had walked from school to their neighborhood. They were now standing outside Kevin's front door. Children returning from school walked past them, sometimes glancing curiously at the two blond foreigners. Marcie smiled at them and they returned her infectious smile.

"It's nearly impossible to turn anything down at a Moroccan meal," explained Kevin. "There are times when you feel you can't eat another bite, but you know if you told your hosts you'd had enough, they'd be offended. Sometimes it's almost embarrassing to realize how much money they've spent on you, when you know that they can't possibly afford to eat so well on a day-to-day basis."

"I'll never understand people who put down Moroccans," said Marcie, sitting down on the front step, Kevin taking a seat beside her. "They are probably the most generous hospitable people I've ever met. Of course, there may be exceptions, but … Finish telling me about your meal, Kevin. Did they serve you anything else after the tea?"

"No, thank God," replied Kevin. "Little Abdenbi brought the washing equipment back in again and we all got the grease off our hands. Then we just sat talking for another half hour or so. They all wanted to know about America, and how I'd learned Arabic and French. Kacem and one of his brothers know some English, so we ended up speaking this crazy mishmash of three languages."

"I can imagine," commented Marcie. "I sometimes wonder how I got along just using English before I came to Morocco."

"Anyway," continued Kevin, "before I knew it, my watch said nearly ten of three, so I literally had to run to school in order not to arrive late. Thank goodness Kacem's family lives near the *lycée*."

They sat in silence for a moment, Marcie staring into space, her thoughts seemingly miles away. Then suddenly her face lightened.

"I'm so excited about this evening!" she exclaimed. "I've never been invited into a French home before. I just know it'll be wonderful! We really are spoiled here in Aïn El Qamar having the Moroccan world to explore and at the same time living in a place where the French have created their own little world apart. It may not be the healthiest thing for Morocco, but for me it's like a dream. Claudette Verlaine reminds me of a famous film star, and Jean-Richard … well …"

Once again, Kevin wondered whether Marcie was becoming infatuated by the French bachelor. If so, she was asking for trouble. Although Jean-Richard was one of Kevin's favorites among the French in Aïn El Qamar—he had style and class and always made you feel special—Kevin knew he was all wrong for Marcie. Jean-Richard would never get serious about a woman, and Marcie was not the type of girl who would settle for a one-night romance.

"I hate to interrupt our conversation, Kevin," said Marcie, "but I've got forty papers to correct before we go to visit *la France*. Why don't you knock at my door at about a quarter to seven? I'll be ready and waiting with bells on!"

"Sure thing," said Kevin. They both got up from the doorstep and he watched as Marcie nearly skipped down the street to her nearby house. She *was* excited about tonight, Kevin thought amusedly.

Once inside his own house, Kevin headed towards his bedroom. It was a rather sparsely furnished room, containing only a single bed covered with a heavy red and brown striped wool blanket he had bought at the Aïn El Qamar *souk* and which served as a bedspread, a small round night table, an inexpensive wooden desk and chair, and a few souvenirs from his travels in Morocco and Spain. Since he and Dave spent most of their time in the living room and kitchen, he hadn't felt the need for much furniture here.

Kevin shut the door behind him, then crossed over to the window and reached out to pull the shutters closed. The room was now in near darkness. He set his things on the bedside table and lay down supine on the mattress.

Staring up at the darkened ceiling, Kevin recalled Kacem Hajiri's flawlessly handsome face as it had been during the meal at his house. He could once again feel the heat of the man's hard strong body next to his own. He could see Kacem's virile bronzed arms extending from his lightweight short-sleeved shirt, so near he could hardly resist touching them. He could smell Kacem's manly scent.

As Kevin lay on his bed, he felt his heart begin to pound, his cock growing larger and harder, straining against his pants, begging for release. Reaching down, he unzipped his fly, lowered his undershorts to his knees, and pulled up his shirt. With his right hand, he encircled his erection and began to massage it.

He tried to imagine how Kacem would look without his shirt on. Would his chest be smooth or hairy? Were his nipples small like dimes or full and round like Hershey's kisses? Did he have a washboard stomach? And what about the private regions? What about the shape of Kacem's ass under his briefs? How beautiful his cock must be, and how exquisite it would feel to have Kacem inside him!

Kevin surrendered himself to the sensations he felt in his groin, reveling in his sexual fantasy, his body jerking in ecstasy at the powerful erotic images he had created, and finally exploding as he experienced a moment of climactic rapture.

Later, in the living room, Kevin inserted a Barry Manilow cassette in the tape player. As he listened to the words of "Could It Be Magic?" Kevin couldn't help thinking how magical it would indeed be once his dreams of Kacem were realized.

Those dreams had to come true. Kevin was due for happiness. It was his turn to find fulfillment. He was sure of it!

If only Dave would get back from school! Kevin needed to talk to someone about his feelings for Kacem, about his certainty that Kacem was the answer to his prayers. Dave would understand. Dave was his closest friend. Dave was like a brother. Back then those many months ago when they had both been trainees in Rabat, Dave had saved his life.

✳   ✳   ✳   ✳

They were among the few trainees remaining in Rabat that weekend in late August of last year. Most of their fifty-odd colleagues had left the training site to explore various destinations in Morocco—Tangier, Fez, Marrakesh—or to visit those Peace Corps volunteers who had remained in country despite this being the hottest month of the summer. Dave was recovering from the flu; otherwise he would certainly have left the high school dormitory where they were staying for a more entertaining destination. Kevin, on the other hand, had not wanted to travel anywhere despite being in perfect health. For the past several weeks, in fact, he had scarcely wanted to leave the training site, even to go to a restaurant for dinner.

Kevin occupied the cubicle next to Dave's. It was for this reason that Dave overheard Kevin's tears that August evening. Even so, he hesitated at first to interrupt Kevin's pain. Kevin had been a loner during the first six weeks of training and Dave had felt that any intrusion upon Kevin's privacy would have been just that, an intrusion. And so he had held back, until today.

But the tears Dave heard seemed to hold such desperation that they were finally impossible to ignore. Rising up from the bunk where he lay attempting to read a French novel, Dave went out and stood for a moment next to Kevin's adjoining cubicle. Then, pulling back the curtain which gave a modicum of privacy, he entered.

"Get out of here!" Kevin cried out from the bunk where he lay. "Can't you see I want to be alone!"

Ignoring Kevin's anger, Dave went over and sat next to him. "What's wrong?" he asked sympathetically. "I know something's been bothering you. You've seemed really depressed these past few weeks, and it's not getting any better. Why don't you talk about it?"

"What good will talking do!" exclaimed Kevin. "Talking won't bring him back to me! Nothing ever will! I ... I wish I were dead!"

"Won't bring who back to you? Who are you talking about, Kevin?" Dave paused. "An ex-boyfriend?"

At first Kevin couldn't believe his ears. He had been so careful not to let on to anyone in his training program that he was different. How in God's name had Dave figured out his secret?

"You can talk to me about it, you know. I promise you I'll understand."

Incredibly, Kevin could hear sympathy in Dave's voice. But how could that be? Dave was so normal. He must have dated dozens of girls back in the States. How could he possibly understand Kevin's feelings for another man? And yet here he was looking at him compassionately and saying, "You can tell me about it, you know. I know what it's like to lose a boyfriend."

"What?" Kevin thought he must be hearing things.

"That's right, Kevin," said Dave. "I came to Morocco because the guy I shared my bed with wouldn't live openly with me as my boyfriend. Leaving Ethan was the saddest thing I ever had to do, but I couldn't go on living a lie, and once it was over between us, I needed to get away, far away. That's why I came to Morocco. To escape. So tell me, what brought you here?"

"You're ... you're ...," Kevin stammered.

"I think the word you're looking for is gay," completed Dave.

"But you're so ... I mean, you're not ..."

"I don't act gay?" asked Dave. "What does acting gay mean? Stop thinking in stereotypes, Kevin. You're no more stereotypical than I am."

"How come you never said anything before?"

"You weren't ready to hear it. But I've come out to four of the other trainees," admitted Dave. "Or shall I say, we've come out to each other."

"You mean …?"

"There're at least five of us in this training program. Five that I'm sure of. And now you make it an even half-dozen. They came for the same reason I did. Moroccan men are hot. I had a Moroccan boyfriend when I was studying in France. That's why I'm here. And you, Kevin? Why are you in Morocco? Or more to the point, what are you running away from? What happened between you and your boyfriend? What was his name by the way?"

"Jamey. Jamey Morales" said Kevin. "And he was my college roommate, not my boyfriend."

"But you wanted him to be?"

"Yes, I wanted him to be!"

Kevin once again burst into sobs and Dave pulled him close and let Kevin's tears fall on his shoulder, all the while holding him in his arms and saying over and over again, "It's all right, Kevin. It's all right."

Finally Kevin's tears subsided, and he removed himself from Dave's embrace. "I honestly can talk to you about it?" he asked disbelievingly.

"Yes, Kevin, you can."

Was it actually true? Could it be that Dave was really gay? And not only Dave but others of his fellow trainees as well? What a relief already to know that he was not alone!

And so Kevin began to unburden himself of the pain which had been getting steadily more unbearable until today he had thought seriously about taking his own life. For it was three months ago today that …

"It was my last year at Penn State," Kevin began softly. "I was rooming with two other guys, Chet Carmichael and Jamey Morales. We'd been together since September and I guess you could say we got along as well as roommates usually do. Still, there were times when I felt that I just didn't belong. Chet and Jamey used to talk about the girls they were dating and, you know, exchange stories about what this girl did or what she didn't do, and how they'd rate them on a scale of one to ten, and things like that. I used to join in, but it was all a farce to me, a dumb ugly farce. I felt guilty lying to them, but I didn't want them to think I was some kind of freak. You see, I'd … I'd never slept with a girl, never even wanted to. Sure, I'd go out on a date once in a while. Sometimes I'd kiss the girl goodnight, hoping to have some kind of reaction, but all I ever felt was sick to my stomach.

"Anyway, that last year I started rooming with Chet and Jamey. Chet was nice enough. I mean, we didn't get on each other's nerves or anything. But Jamey … I thought the sun rose and set by him. He was everything I wanted to be, warm, funny, clever, good-looking, smooth, in control. He had this long straight black hair, and this beautiful tan skin, the kind that I could never achieve in a million years, and the body of a swimmer. He was the kind of guy that girls call a hunk."

"Sounds like the kind of guy I'd call a hunk too," smiled Dave. "Sorry for interrupting. Go on."

"I tried to convince myself that he was just a good friend," continued Kevin, "but … but I knew that I wasn't reacting to him in the right way. I mean, you aren't supposed to feel like the world is ending because your best friend has gone away for a weekend, and you aren't supposed to feel like everything is perfect just because he's walked into a room.

"God I was so confused. I wanted to be like everyone else, but when I'd see him half undressed … I just wanted to grab him in my arms and kiss him and hold him and tell him how much he meant to me. But of course I didn't. How could I? Jamey was straight!

"Then last April when classes let out for spring break, Jamey suggested that the two of us spend the week in New York. I was floating when he said that, I mean really floating. To think that he liked me enough to want to spend the week in New York with me, it was more than I'd ever hoped for. The day we left, I'd never felt so happy and excited in all my life. And scared … scared of what might happen.

"When we arrived in New York City, we went to this inexpensive hotel which someone had recommended to Jamey. Jamey asked for the cheapest room, and when the desk clerk said that that was one with a double bed, Jamey said, 'No problem. No problem, huh, Kev?'

"I was so terrified. I couldn't sleep in the same bed with him! If I did, he'd see right away how excited I was. He'd be disgusted, he'd laugh at me, he'd hate me.

"But I said nothing. I just made myself promise that I'd control myself, no matter what.

"We got to the room and unpacked, and I decided to take a shower. I was feeling hot and sweaty from the long trip, and I wanted to … The fact is I decided to beat off, just to make sure that I wouldn't have a hard-on once we got into bed together. And Jamey said that he was going to run out and get us some beers. So anyway he left the hotel room, and I … well I did like I said. And then I dried off and got dressed and waited for Jamey to return. And I waited. And I waited. And then I really started to get worried. What if something had happened to him? What if …?

"Then there was a knock at the door. I knew it couldn't be Jamey. He'd taken the key with him. I got up and walked over to the door, and when I opened it there was a policeman standing there. They'd found Jamey's hotel key on his body. He'd been mugged, stabbed to death, and all for a lousy twenty dollars he was carrying. The rest of his money was in his suitcase! In his suitcase!"

Once more Kevin was sobbing in Dave's arms, feeling that his tears would never end. Finally Dave reached for a tissue and handing it to Kevin, asked him to finish his story.

"I had to pack up his things and take them back to school with me. It was while I was going through his stuff that I found a date book. I opened it and looked at the entry for that date, and it said, with three big exclamation points, 'Kevin and Jamey do it at last!!!' And that's when I knew, that's when I knew that he'd felt about me just as I did about him, and that the trip to New York City had been his plan to get us away from that idiot Chet and into a setting where we didn't have to lie about our feelings anymore.

"I wonder every day about what would have happened if he'd lived. And I know now that I can never tell him how much I loved him and how much I still love him and always will. Oh Jamey … Jamey … I love you … I love you."

Once again Kevin was in tears, Dave holding him tightly in his arms. After a while, he told Kevin his own story. The story of a popular college athlete. President of his class. Girls chasing him wherever he went. He'd gone out with them, even tried sleeping with a few. But he had known all along that he was gay. Throughout his freshman and sophomore years, he'd led a double life, dating girls in public and sleeping with men clandestinely. Then had come his junior year in France, and several semi-serious love affairs that had convinced him to stop leading a double life. Back in the States for his senior year, he'd met fellow varsity letterman Ethan O'Connor. And fallen in love. And been fallen in love with. They'd started rooming together almost immediately. Dave loved living with Ethan, loved sharing his life with him, and more and more he felt the desire to come out about their relationship. There were other openly gay couples at their university. Why not the two of them? But Ethan would hear nothing of it! As far as the world was concerned, he and Dave were best friends, and nothing more. They began to argue, and then to fight, neither one willing to give an inch. And finally Dave could stand it no more. He'd moved out of the apartment they shared, and when a month later the opportunity to go to Morocco had come up,

Dave, who had fond memories of one very special Moroccan lover he had known in France, had jumped at the chance to get away, far away from Ethan.

"So that's why I'm here," Dave said now. "I'm looking for the same thing you are, Kevin. Just because we're gay doesn't mean we don't want to be in love. So many people think gay guys' whole lives are about fucking. But I'm as romantic as the next person. I just happen to fall in love with men. I'd really like to be your friend Kevin, if you'll let me …"

And so, over the next few weeks, a real friendship grew between Dave and Kevin. They studied Arabic together, planned lessons together for their practice teaching, traveled together on weekends, and when they learned that there were three posts to be filled in Aïn El Qamar, they requested to be sent there together, Janna completing the trio.

In the ensuing months, Dave found several of what he referred to as his "fuck-buddies," but Kevin, who was still insisting on the kind of romantic love that he had felt for Jamey Morales, chose to remain a virgin, though he frequently found himself indulging in masturbatory fantasies when his sexual urges became too great to control.

Now, however, for the first time since Jamey's murder, Kevin had begun to feel that same romantic passion that he had felt for Jamey, only now it was for Kacem Hajiri that his heart beat faster. Not only that, but there were unmistakable signs that the Moroccan shared his feelings.

At lunch today, for example, Kacem had been so friendly, so attentive. At times, Kevin had been positive that he recognized in Kacem's eyes the same look of love and desire that he now knew had been in Jamey's, if only he had not been too blind to see.

I'm finally starting to live again, thought Kevin to himself now as he sat waiting for Dave to return from school. I was so sure that everything had ended when Jamey died. I was so sure that I'd never fall in love again. But I was wrong. Thank God, I was wrong. Now there's Kacem, and my life isn't over. It's just beginning!

CHAPTER 7

▼

Marcie Nelson was examining her face in her bathroom mirror. Darn! she thought disgustedly. No face could be more out of its element than mine is in Aïn El Qamar. Why can't my skin be a little less pale, or my cheeks just a little less pink, or my eyes a shade less blue? Maybe I should dye my hair black, she fantasized.

Marcie giggled as she imagined herself with black hair. That would probably make her look like "Morticia Addams" or something equally horrifying. No, she would just have to face the fact that she was going to stand out in whatever crowd she might find herself here in Aïn El Qamar. And that meant among the French as well as among Moroccans.

She wished she could master the art of dressing stylishly. It was true, of course, that not all the Frenchwomen in Aïn El Qamar were clothed like something out of *Vogue*. Claudette wore her flamboyant sexy tight things, Michèle looked like a left-over flower child from the late sixties, and then there was Christiane Koenigsmarck who might easily have bought her clothes at K-Mart. But there were others, Madame Lemont, and Madame Marchand, and Madame Arrier, women Marcie hardly knew but whose style and sophistication she admired. Unfortunately, their clothes would no doubt look as foolish on her as would black hair or heavy eye make-up. She'd only look like a small town girl making believe she was someone else and fooling nobody. Face the facts, kiddo, she told herself. You are what you are and only time and experience—if you're lucky—are going to change that.

She ran a brush through her thick honey blond hair, rinsed her mouth, dabbed on some cologne she had received as a going-away present, and walked into her living room to wait for Kevin to arrive. She sat down on the lone *banquette*. It was the only seat available, because after just a bit more than a month in Aïn El Qamar, she had not yet bought much furniture, only the *banquette*, and the coffee table on which she ate and prepared lessons, one lonely plant by the living room door, her bed, and some kitchen supplies. On Kevin's advice, she had decided to accumulate things slowly, and get only what pleased her, instead of buying a lot of furniture on credit right away as did some volunteers who then ended up with a ton of junk which they didn't really like, and a mountain of debts.

Marcie already found herself thinking of a third year in Aïn El Qamar after she had completed her two-year stint. This mixture of Arab and European worlds never ceased to fascinate her. In fact, she couldn't imagine wanting to be anywhere else. As far as furnishing her house was concerned, she could probably pick up some nice things from teachers who were planning to leave at the end of the school year.

Looking around the nearly bare living room now, Marcie thought to herself: It certainly isn't a home yet, but in time it will be. In time …

Involuntarily she looked down at the airmail envelope on the table before her. Time … How could she think of time here when there was Eddy to consider? Eddy, who had been so hesitant to let her leave. Eddy, who still wrote her constantly, trying to get her to change her mind and come back home.

She had known Eddy Gustafson since they were kids. They'd been best friends in grammar school, steadies in high school, and they'd continued their relationship by mail throughout college. Marcie had stayed at home and attended the University of Wisconsin at River Falls, just a few miles from where she and her family lived. Eddy had gone to the University of Chicago. They'd seen each other during vacations, though, and when graduation had approached, he'd asked her to marry him.

I always knew he would, she told herself now in Aïn El Qamar, and I always knew I'd say yes. So why then am I here, thousands of miles away from Eddy? And why is his ring hanging from a chain around my neck, and not on my finger?

Eddy hadn't understood her hesitation to marry him right away. She'd told him she wanted to see more of the world. She'd told him not to worry, they'd known each other for so long, two more years apart wouldn't make a difference. He could come over during the summer, or she could go home. She had done her best to be persuasive, and finally he had agreed, however reluctantly, to let her go.

Another letter had arrived from Eddy today. Come home. Please. I need you. I want you. I love you.

Marcie loved him too. But she was beginning to come to the awful realization that she didn't really need him. She had taken to life in Aïn el Qamar like the proverbial fish to water, and though she wrote Eddy regularly, it was more out of excitement over her new and thrilling experiences in Morocco than out of a need to feel closer to the man she loved.

And did she really want him as he wanted her? If so, how was it possible that they had never slept together? Was it true, as she had told him, that her religious and moral values forbade her to have sex with a man before marriage? Or was she merely fooling herself? Was the answer much less complicated? Could it be simply that Eddy did not excite her? Would she, for example, have turned down a man like Jean-Richard?

The thought of the Frenchman jerked Marcie back to reality. Now what on earth had made her think of him? She hardly knew the man. Not only that, but she had already heard enough stories about him to make her realize that he was not the sort of person she wanted to become involved with. She had too much self-respect to let herself be seduced by someone whose reputation for one night stands was legend in Aïn El Qamar.

Still, she could not deny that she felt a shiver of excitement whenever she saw his wavy golden hair and sun-tanned face. Just the sound of his voice speaking French almost made her heart stop beating. And like it or not, she had lately begun thinking of the man much too often for her own good.

Marcie had tried to tell herself that this was because he was foreign, because he was French. She had majored in *la langue française* at U.W. and was enchanted by its sounds and the feeling of romance she got whenever she heard or spoke it. That was one of the reasons she had chosen to come to Morocco. For the first time in her life now, she found herself in a place where she could hear and speak French whenever she wished. Was it merely that Jean-Richard was the first Frenchman that she had ever really known? Was that the reason she reacted to him in a way that threatened the stability of her relationship with Eddy?

Or was there more? Could it be that she sensed in Jean-Richard some deeply hidden pain that cried out to her? No, she was being foolish and fanciful! All the same, there were moments at school when she would catch a glimpse of him with a look of emptiness in his eyes even as there was a smile on his lips. Or was that merely her overactive imagination reacting to life in a strange and exotic world?

What a lot of questions without answers, Marcie told herself now as she looked down at Eddy's letter. She knew that she ought to answer it tonight, but tonight she was invited to Jean-Richard's, and after that she had to plan a lesson for an eight o'clock class tomorrow morning. I'll write you tomorrow afternoon, Eddy, she promised.

Just then the doorbell rang. Marcie rushed back into the bathroom for a last quick look in the mirror. There's nothing you can do about that face, she groaned. Maybe someday you'll have glamour, maturity, and sophistication, but for now you're just a small-town Wisconsin hick.

She ran to the door where Kevin was waiting, looking very American himself in a plaid shirt and khakis.

"Ready?" he asked."

"As ready as I'll ever be," replied Marcie with some trepidation.

"Then we're off," he exclaimed.

"Are you sure I don't look too plain in this outfit, Kevin?" she asked. She had chosen a pale blue summer dress and a lightweight off-white sweater. The outfit had seemed wholly appropriate in River Falls, but here in Aïn El Qamar she wasn't sure.

"You look fine!" insisted Kevin. "You'll be like a breath of fresh air in that house."

"Yech!" said Marcie, and laughed.

"The days are getting shorter," remarked Kevin as they left her house. It was twilight already.

"It'll be sad to say good-bye to this lovely fall weather," said Marcie. "It's been so beautiful here since the summer heat finally ended."

In the distance they could hear the chanting of the muezzin from the minaret of a nearby mosque calling the faithful to prayer. As Marcie walked beside Kevin in the fading light, she spotted an old man in the olive groves beyond. He had knelt down to pray, raising and lowering his head from the ground, his arms outstretched before him.

"He didn't have time to get home," commented Kevin.

Marcie nodded. "Doesn't it seem incredible to you, Kevin, that in just a few minutes we'll be in a house where everyone will be speaking French and drinking Pernaud and Martini Rouge and thinking and acting as though they were in France, and yet here, and now, wherever you look, you see men and women dressed like something out of the Bible with their own culture which has remained steadfast for centuries and centuries?"

"It seems normal to me now," said Kevin, "which shows just how far away from the United States I've gotten in the past year. I'm not sure I even want to go back. It'd mean giving up so many things."

"So you still haven't decided whether you're leaving in July?" asked Marcie.

"Not yet. I wish it could be as easy for me to come to a decision as it was for Dave."

"Just between the two of us, which way are you leaning?"

"Until today, I was pretty sure that I was going back to the States too," answered Kevin. "But I think now that I might have a good reason for staying at least one more year."

"Really?" Marcie waited for Kevin to elaborate, but when he seemed disinclined to do so, she said, "It'd be nice to still have you around. Who else would accompany me for *apéritifs en France*?"

It was a fifteen minute walk to the French *quartier* where Jean-Richard and Claudette lived. As Kevin and Marcie approached the couple's house, they could hear the music of Serge Reggiani floating out from inside.

"His songs are so romantic," commented Marcie.

"*N'est-ce pas?*" agreed Kevin.

They rang the doorbell and waited. Marcie smiled nervously at Kevin. "I'm so excited," she said unnecessarily.

Suddenly the door was thrown open and there stood Claudette, her auburn hair piled high atop her head. "Do you like my new coiffure?" she asked. "And my caftan?" She was wearing an elegant royal blue brocaded gown with buttons which descended to the floor. She had left it unfastened almost to her navel and she was wearing no bra. Marcie felt herself blush as she replied, "*Tu es belle comme toujours!*" And I look more than ever like a silly country girl, she added silently.

"*Entrez!*" commanded Claudette. "We are already quite a few."

Miss Claudette's living room was lit this night by candles, and in the flickering light Marcie could see several French couples. She recognized the sophisticated Arriers, and once again wished that she possessed the elegance of Madame Arrier. (Marcie didn't know her first name, would be afraid to use it even if she did.) Also invited were the Koenigsmarcks, Laurent and Christiane. They must be of Germanic background, with a name like that. Certainly they were worlds removed from the Arriers. Miss Claudette had mentioned at school that she considered them common and vulgar, so Marcie was surprised to find them here this evening. They were an almost comic couple, he so small and round, she so tall and big-boned. Marcie was forced to remind herself that assuming things or people to be elegant and stylish simply because they were French was a bit of an overgeneralization. Certainly neither Laurent nor Christiane was elegant or stylish. She could hear Christiane's shrill voice complaining, "*Putains de voleurs!* Damn robbers! They wanted eighty *dirhams* for that bracelet. *Ils veulent tous nous baiser.*

They want to fuck us all!" Marcie felt sorry for the Arriers who were forced to listen to Christiane's wrath.

"*Quelle garce*," whispered Claudette to Marcie and Kevin. "She's nothing but a tramp! And her husband is *très vulgaire aussi*! They had the nerve to invite themselves here tonight when we crossed paths at the Hotel El Qamar this afternoon. Those two have no concept whatsoever of the word class."

"They're not very polite," agreed Marcie.

"*Alors* … what can I get you to drink?" asked Claudette.

"Martini Rouge?" said Marcie.

"*Moi aussi*," said Kevin.

The two Americans walked over to greet the other guests, then took seats on *banquettes* some distance away.

"I thought you wanted to converse with *la France*," said Kevin.

"Unfortunately I don't really like the Koenigsmarcks that much, and the Arriers intimidate me. I wonder where Jean-Richard is."

"Did I hear you mention Jean-Richard's name?" asked Claudette as she brought over their drinks. "You wanted these on the rocks, *n'est-ce pas?*"

Marcie and Kevin nodded as they accepted the Martini aperitif wine.

"Jean-Richard is upstairs changing. He had a bad day at school. It seems the *proviseur* replaced the science laboratory assistant with his own incompetent nephew."

"That explains why Jean-Richard looked so upset when we saw him at the *lycée* this afternoon," commented Marcie.

"I was able to calm him down," said Claudette, kneeling before them, "but he's still rather depressed." She lowered her voice. "I think I hear him coming now. I suggest you don't mention anything about work. We don't want Jean-Richard's troubles to spoil the evening. That is if they"—she glanced towards the Koenigsmarcks—"don't spoil it first."

Just then Jean-Richard entered the room. Marcie looked up at him, felt her palms become moist.

"*Bonsoir* Mademoiselle Marcie," he said to her.

"*Bonsoir* Jean-Richard," said Marcie, and hoped he did not notice the shakiness in her voice. "I'm … I'm happy to see you."

The entire roam was in hysterics.

Miguel Berthaud had arrived and as usual he was the center of attention with his outrageous remarks and near-perfect impressions of various residents of Aïn El Qamar.

He even looks funny, thought Marcie, with his bulging round eyes and that large angular nose. He's so tall and skinny and his arms and legs seem to be made of rubber, she thought.

At the moment he was telling the story of one of his classroom antics.

"*Ecoutez*. I know this is Morocco, but who's to say one cannot amuse oneself while teaching. So … I decided to hold a 'Miss Aïn El Qamar' contest in class. Only the contestants were all boys. You should have seen them pretending to be walking down the runway in their imaginary swimsuits."

"Miguel, you're incorrigible!" cried Claudette.

"But the best part was the talent competition," continued Miguel. "The biggest, toughest guy in class was set on winning the title, and he chose to sing 'I Enjoy Being a Girl,' with all the proper gestures."

"And what about the real young ladies in class?" asked Monsieur Arrier.

"They were the judges, of course! *Vous savez*, Aïn El Qamar is not nearly as traditional as you think! Times are changing."

Marcie was delighted by Miguel's tale, though she couldn't help wondering how he had managed to get away with such a stunt. And yet dear sweet Miguel seemed to be able to get away with almost anything because of his genuine sense of humor, just as Claudette managed to dress and act the way she did because of her innate classiness.

Now Miguel was impersonating Monsieur Rhazwani, and he seemed to swell to twice his size as he took on the characteristics of the pompous arrogant man.

For a moment, Jean-Richard, who was sitting next to Marcie, seemed to withdraw, and she recalled how disturbed he had looked that afternoon at school. Then, he too was overcome with laughter. "That's him exactly!" he screamed. Pointing his finger at Miguel, he pretended to pull the trigger of a make-believe gun. "They got me," gasped Miguel, and fell to the floor in a comic exaggeration of the throes of death. Finally he lay still. The room cheered, and he rose to take a bow.

Marcie watched him take a seat beside the Arriers and begin to chat with them. The French couple, usually so reserved, had joined in enthusiastically with the others in the laughter. Miguel had the gift of putting people at their ease, and Marcie wondered if the Arriers might possibly be more approachable than she had imagined.

Kevin and Claudette were deep in conversation in another corner of the room. Marcie wondered if she might perhaps be telling him of her latest romantic adventure.

The Koenigsmarcks were sitting alone, left in each other's company and looking bored.

And I'm here with Jean-Richard, thought Marcie in wonder. It's like a dream, like a scene from some romantic French movie.

Jean-Richard was asking her about Morocco, about how she was adjusting.

She answered slowly, wanting to make as few grammatical errors as possible in French. Jean-Richard corrected her occasionally, but so gently that she hardly noticed. She found herself telling him about her training program, and was surprised at the realization that he was listening intently. She reminded herself that this might be one of his famed seduction techniques, but somehow she felt that he was sincerely interested in her experiences.

"I'll never forget the morning our plane landed in Casablanca," said Marcie. "It was gray and overcast and we'd been flying all night from New York. It was only seven a.m. when we arrived. I remember scanning the airport for signs that I was in a foreign land, and they were inescapable. Women in dark wool *jellabas* and veils, signs written in Arabic and French, a strange mournful kind of music coming from someone's radio … I learned later that it was the Egyptian singer, Oum Kalthoum, but then, naturally, I had no idea how famous she is. They were nice to us in customs, didn't even ask to open our bags, and I'd been so afraid they'd search mine, not that I had anything to hide, but I was afraid that the strangeness and the newness of the surroundings would make me look nervous, and they'd think I was transporting drugs or contraband or something."

"Never in a million years could you be mistaken for a smuggler," smiled Jean-Richard. "You haven't the face."

"I know," groaned Marcie. I wish … I mean … well …"

"Go on, tell me more!" urged Jean-Richard, and Marcie thought, How kind, to pretend to not to have noticed my embarrassment.

"Well, they loaded us into these big Ford wagons called 'greenies,' because they're all painted green, and off we went to downtown Casablanca. All along the way during that half hour drive I couldn't stop staring at the farms and the donkeys and the rickety old wagons and the sheep and … and then suddenly we were coming into Casa. American traffic is bad, but I thought we were going to be run into for sure, or that we'd knock down some motorbike rider. They were everywhere. And busses, with huge clouds of black smoke pouring from the exhaust. And bicycles swerving in and out of the traffic. And horns honking."

"I've been there," chuckled Jean-Richard.

"The funny thing was," Marcie continued, "that everyone seemed to be accepting this chaos as normal."

"It is, in Morocco," said Jean-Richard.

"It was such a contrast from the fields that I'd seen stretching endlessly from the airport in all directions. Of course I knew that Casa was the biggest city in Morocco, but still I wasn't prepared for the skyscrapers and the modern hotels and those trendy boutiques. At times it seemed so European, and yet there were always the veiled women in their *jellabas*. They scared me at first, the way they always seemed to be hiding something mysterious. Of course now I laugh at my misgivings.

"We could have bypassed Casa, but I was glad they let us see it. Then we were off to Rabat, on that new two-lane highway. The traffic was heavy, and yet speeding cars would suddenly pass slow-moving trucks without even being able to see whether anything was coming in the opposite direction. I was sure there would be some terrible bloody accident. Every so often I'd just squeeze my eyes shut and pray that Rabat was around the next bend.

"I really loved Rabat. Though we studied Arabic six hours a day, we still had enough free time to explore the city, and I visited the Roman ruins at the Chellah, and the Royal Palace where King Hassan II lives, and the *kasbah* overlooking the Atlantic.

"I fell in love with Aïn El Qamar the first time I saw it, in spite of the summer heat and dust which was nearly unbearable. I was really happy when I learned that I'd be posted here. I enjoyed the big city, but I wanted to discover the real Morocco, and Aïn El Qamar has been ideal."

"Did you spend all your time in training studying Arabic?" asked Jean-Richard.

"No, there were lectures on Moroccan culture, which were helpful, but I think I've learned more in the past month just by being here in Aïn El Qamar than I ever did in training.

"We also did practice teaching for a month. The first day I thought I was going to make a fool of myself and I was sure the students could see my knees knocking. But after a few days I started to calm down, and eventually I found myself loving every minute of it."

Jean-Richard had a distracted look on his face.

"I must be boring you," apologized Marcie. "I have a tendency to run on when I get on the subject of Morocco."

"*Pas du tout*," said Jean-Richard. "I was just thinking how long it's been since I've felt your excitement. And about how fortunate you Americans are to be so well trained. I'm sure that we French would do better here if we had the same preparation."

"How long is it that you've been here, Jean-Richard?"

"*Dix ans*," he answered.

"Ten years!" exclaimed Marcie. "Don't you ever think of going back to France to settle down?"

Jean-Richard's expression turned suddenly cold. "I have no intention of ever returning to France," he said curtly. "Let me freshen your drink."

Now what did I say? Marcie asked herself. She realized that from now on with Jean-Richard, the subject of France was taboo.

"Are you having a good time?" asked a voice speaking English, and Marcie looked up to see Kevin.

"Wonderful," she said, putting Jean-Richard's sudden mood swing out of her mind.

"You'd hardly know we're in Aïn El Qamar, would you?"

"I don't even feel like I'm in Morocco," agreed Marcie. "It's truly another world here."

Jean-Richard returned with Marcie's drink, and she was relieved to find that he was back to being his usual cheerful self. "You were having quite a *tête-à-tête* with Miss Claudette," he said to Kevin.

"*Elle est fascinante!*" Kevin replied enigmatically, and Marcie wondered again what "fascinating" conversation he and Claudette had been having.

"I see that the Arriers are leaving," commented Kevin now.

"Perhaps we'd better be moving along too," suggested Marcie.

"Let me drive you both home," offered Jean-Richard. "It's dark outside and you shouldn't be wandering around alone."

"Don't you think I can protect Marcie?" smiled Kevin.

"*Ce n'est pas ça*," said Jean-Richard. "Really, it would be my pleasure to escort you back to your *petite Amérique*."

"Shall we take him up on his offer?" Kevin asked Marcie.

"*Bien sûr!* I only wish that I didn't have to return to reality too soon."

"Then I'll just have to see to it that you don't," replied Jean-Richard.

She was showing him her house and apologizing for its lack of furniture. They had left Kevin off at his house just down the street; he'd said he had something important to discuss with Dave. Jean-Richard had asked Marcie if he might borrow an English-language novel, an easy one, he said, to refresh his memory, so she had invited him in while she looked for something. Marcie didn't think he would actually read the book she found for him, but she was pleased to prolong her encounter with the man.

"I think you're wise to wait to buy nice pieces of furniture," Jean-Richard was saying, "instead of the trash some people have. I can see you have good taste. The fabric on that *banquette* is *très chic*."

He walked over to it, sat down, and rubbed his hand over the burgundy brocade. Marcie moved to stand in front of him. His golden hair shone in the light from the ceiling lamp. He looked up at her, and she found herself gazing into his deep brown eyes.

"You are an enchanting young woman, *mademoiselle*," he whispered. "I have thought so since the first time I saw you. You were walking down Avenue Hassan Deux and the light of the day seemed to be radiating from you and not from the sun."

Marcie felt herself trembling under his spell. He was truly unlike anyone she had ever met. He was handsome, he was debonair, he was fascinating, he was … Hold on, she warned herself. What he was was the most infamous playboy of Aïn El Qamar and she was certainly not interested in becoming just another one of his brief conquests. She liked him too much already to put herself in a position where she would only end up despising him later.

Detaching her gaze from his, she said lightly, "Be careful, Monsieur Moreau, or you'll have me believing you and deciding I can do without electricity in this house."

The spell was broken. Marcie could feel Jean-Richard withdraw from her, and once again she sensed that there was something innately sad about the man. He needed something, but she doubted that it was Marcie Nelson of River Falls, Wisconsin, U.S.A.

"Claudette is probably fuming now, waiting for you to get back for dinner," she said. "And I have lesson plans to do and a letter to write to my fiancé."

Darn! she said to herself. Why had she mentioned Eddy, especially when she knew perfectly well that she wouldn't have time to write to him tonight?

"I … I didn't know you were engaged," said Jean-Richard, standing up. He seemed genuinely flustered.

"Well, sort of," stammered Marcie. "I mean, he did give me a ring, but if we ever do get married, it won't be for quite a few years yet, so I suppose I really shouldn't call him my fiancé even if he thinks he is …" Marcie could her herself blathering on like an idiot, and wished for an earthquake to stop her inane chatter. Jean-Richard must surely think her a fool.

"I see," said Jean-Richard as she accompanied him to the door.

No, you don't see, she replied inwardly. I'm not even sure I do.

"Thank you again for coming by this evening," he said, warmth returning to his voice. "Please visit again. *Vraiment.* Anytime at all. *Je t'en prie.*"

Marcie was touched by the ring of sincerity in Jean-Richard's words. He seemed almost to be pleading. Or was she letting her imagination get the better of her once more?

"*Bien sûr*, Jean-Richard," she promised. "Of course I'll drop by again. I had a marvelous evening. *Bonne nuit.*"

Jean-Richard kissed her lightly on the cheek. "*Bonne nuit,* Marcie. *Fais de beaux rêves.*"

And then, having wished her beautiful dreams, he was gone into the Moroccan night.

Later that evening, as Marcie sat staring at the letter she had received from Eddy, she found herself thinking not of him but of Jean-Richard, and of the strange look of sadness and emptiness in his eyes, and of the softness of his lips on her cheek.

CHAPTER 8

▼

Of the guests who had gathered at Claudette's house for aperitifs, only Miguel Berthaud remained. "Be a dear, Miguel, and help me clean up this mess," Claudette had asked, and as usual Miguel had obeyed. So now, here he was emptying ashtrays, returning half-empty bottles to the liquor cabinet, and sweeping up fallen ashes and crumbs.

"*Tu es un ange!*" exclaimed Claudette as she came into the living room from the kitchen where she had left the dirty dishes and glasses in the sink for Saadia to clean the next morning. "I don't know what I'd do without you, my angel!" she added, and squeezed the man's hand affectionately. "Stay for dinner, Miguel *chéri*. Jean-Richard and I had a bit of a tiff today and there's a slight chill in this house at the moment. Your being here will do wonders to ease the tension between us. Will you stay? Please?"

"*Bien sûr*, Claudette," replied the tall skinny man.

"You've saved my life," she exclaimed. "And now, if you'll excuse me for a moment, I'm going to change out of this caftan and into something a bit less … flashy."

As Claudette left the room, Miguel felt the same void that invariably accompanied her departures. He sank down onto one of the *banquettes* and lit a cigarette. Why did Claudette have this effect on him? Why was he unable to resist an attraction that brought him only pain? Why was his life as miserable when he was with her as when the two of them were apart?

Miguel laughed, a bitter laugh, at the thought of what others would say were they to know how much he suffered because of Claudette. *Toi*, Miguel? *Tu souffres*? No, Miguel Berthaud did not suffer. Miguel Berthaud did not cry. He was the clown, the buffoon, the man who brought joy and laughter into the lives of others. It was unthinkable that his own life should be empty of laughter or joy.

Loneliness. That was the disease Miguel suffered from. Despite his friends in Aïn El Qamar, and there were a multitude of them, he was unable to stop feeling desperately and agonizingly alone.

Miguel had read once that few clowns were truly happy, and he knew that at least in his own case this was true. You told jokes and acted the *farceur* in order to hide your aching from others, and maybe if you were lucky, from yourself. But your buffoonery only served to make you lonelier, because no one could see you as anything other than the jester. They saw only the outward mask and never what was behind it. Maybe they were afraid to look within, afraid that the reality of your solitude would put an end to the laughter they so desperately craved. Or maybe they were just too lazy or insensitive to look.

Miguel was well aware that Claudette considered him among her dearest friends. He was one of her most frequent guests for aperitifs, and she could never throw a party without first checking on Miguel's availability. He received invitations to any major gathering which involved Claudette, for people knew how much she enjoyed his company and that with Miguel Berthaud present, no party could ever be dull.

Miguel Berthaud. What a strange combination of names, people would say, and ask if he were perhaps a mixture of Spanish and French.

In fact, there was no Spanish blood in him, but due to his black hair and olive skin, the legacy of an Italian *grandmère*, Claudette, who had just returned from a trip across the Iberian Peninsula, had dubbed him Miguel in place of Michel. The name had stuck. A comic blend which made people laugh as did the man who bore the name.

Miguel heard the door to Claudette's bedroom shut, and cursed himself for being maudlin. Nobody wanted a self-pitying clown, least of all Claudette.

"I feel at last that I can relax," she said as she entered wearing a silver and black dressing gown. Even out of the public spotlight, Claudette could not help but be glamorous. "Would I be imposing if I asked you to set the table for dinner?" she coaxed. "It has been an exhausting day. Class in the morning, then several sets of tennis, and I taught again this afternoon until six. Please, Miguel? I am *so* tired." She took a seat on one of the *banquettes* and reclined against the wall, stuffing several cushions behind her back.

Was there any need to ask? thought Miguel, and went into the kitchen to get plates, glasses, and silverware for three. He knew where everything was kept. He had done this countless times before.

"There's a pot in the refrigerator left over from lunch yesterday," she called out from the living room. "Will you be a sweetheart and put it on the stove to heat? And get a bottle of Vieux Papes and the corkscrew, *s'il te plaît?*"

Sometimes, as now, Miguel was tempted to shout back, "I've had a long day too, Claudette. You're not the only one who's exhausted. So stop ordering me about as though I were your slave!" But of course he said nothing. He never would. There was nothing he would ever refuse Claudette. He would be her clown. He would be her servant. He would be her admirer. But the one thing he wished for more than anything else, that he would never be, not in a million years.

Dave couldn't help smiling as he strolled down the brightly lit main street of Aïn El Qamar this evening. As always, it was full of movement and life. Men sat outside in cafés drinking mint tea or coffee or soda, smoking unfiltered cigarettes, and watching passers-by. Others were inside the cafés, their eyes glued to a tele-vised soccer match. Barbers stood waiting for customers outside their shops, which would stay open long into the night. A bus was pulling into the station arriving from Marrakesh, its roof piled high with luggage, mattresses, bicycles, and even chickens.

Dave was smiling partly because of the colorful spectacle which presented itself before his eyes and which was so different from anything he had known before Morocco, but mostly because he had just come from an extraordinary sex-ual encounter.

It had been a pleasant surprise to find Mohamed Fareed, the tennis pro, at his door after school today at six. The Moroccan had been carrying a string bag in which Dave could see a towel, a bottle of shampoo, and a bar of soap.

"Want to go to Douche El Atlassi?" Fareed had asked.

"*Super idée,*" Dave had replied.

Douche El Atlassi was one of several public showers in Aïn El Qamar. Kevin and Dave had started going to it about a month ago when their hot water heater had suddenly gone on the blink. The landlord was still promising to fix it, so Kevin and Dave were still showering at the El Atlassi.

They preferred this to the *hemmam*, or public bath, which was the choice of most Moroccans. In a *hemmam*, bathers would sit around a large steamy room with buckets of hot water which they would pour over themselves and each other for hours on end until they finally felt clean. In a public shower, on the other hand, you could have all the hot water you wanted for half an hour in your own private stall. It cost only a *dirham*, about a quarter in American money, the showers were clean, and because each stall was protected by a solid wooden door, one's privacy was total.

Dave remembered the first time a few weeks ago when Fareed had tapped on his shower door and invited himself in. The attendant was far away in the dressing area, so no one had seen the Moroccan enter. That shower, and the several since, had been unforgettable erotic experiences, but tonight's had topped them all.

Walking down the main street of Aïn El Qamar this evening, Dave could vividly recall the images and sensations he had seen and felt:

Touching Fareed's muscular slippery body with his own, strong and hairy …

Feeling their hungry mouths meet and tasting the blend of Fareed's saliva and the soapy water which ran down their faces …

Caressing Fareed's lather-covered groin, then reaching between his legs to probe his ass …

Taking Fareed's cock in his mouth and sucking until he felt Fareed's cum shoot down his throat …

Finally, rising to stand behind Fareed, entering him with his own throbbing organ, slick with soapy water, his arms tightly encircling the other's hard belly, feeling himself climax explosively within his partner, as the scalding water poured down upon their naked bodies.

You can fuck me next time, he promised Fareed mentally, recalling how quickly the Moroccan had propositioned him after their first tennis lesson a month ago.

"I do it with women," Fareed had declared, "but that's mostly for the money and gifts. There'd be no charge with a stud like you."

Dave could not remember the French word which Fareed had used for "stud," but he had understood its meaning immediately, and been flattered. It was not for nothing that he had been a varsity athlete in college.

There was no pretense of love between Dave and Fareed. Fareed claimed, even boasted, that he was incapable of love. And Dave had accepted what Fareed offered him, sex without love, sex without commitment, great sex at that, but a substitute for what he really craved, if only Lateef were willing to give it to him.

Oh, well, what was the point of rehashing his imperfect love life? Things were what they were, and Dave supposed that there were people worse off than he was. Certainly Kevin, with his insane crush on Kacem Hajiri was asking for nothing but grief.

Not everyone's gay, Kev, Dave thought to himself now. And I'd be willing to bet you that Kacem's as straight as an arrow. Which means that you, my friend, are heading for trouble.

Big big trouble.

Kevin was changing into jeans and a tee-shirt when he heard Dave enter the house. "I'm in my room," he called. "Be right out!"

"I stopped and got us some pasta and tomato paste on the way home," called back Dave. "I thought I'd make up some spaghetti."

That's all I need after my lunch, thought Kevin as he put on his pointed white leather Moroccan slippers called *baboosh*, then joined Dave in the kitchen.

"I'm still stuffed from lunch," he said, "so don't make too much for me."

"No *mushkila*," said Dave. (*Mushkila* was Moroccan for problem.) "Where'd you put the olive oil?"

"It's on that shelf next to the corn flakes."

"Corn flakes," repeated Dave, smiling. "Weren't we surprised to find Kellogg's corn flakes for sale at the Mondiale!" He reached for the bottle of oil. "In Aïn El Qamar, of all places."

"International city!" joked Kevin. As he watched Dave mix tomato paste, oil, spices, and water in the saucepan and put it on the three-burner countertop stove to heat, Kevin began talking to his friend about the lunch at Kacem Hajiri's house, telling him of Kacem's warmth and kindness, and about his certainty that the Moroccan shared his feelings.

Dave filled a second saucepan with water and set it on the fire to boil. "Are you sure this isn't just wishful thinking? I'd hate to see you get hurt again."

"I lost Jamey because I didn't have the guts to tell him how I felt about him," Kevin said. "I'm not going to have the same thing happen again."

"I understand, Kev. I'm just saying to take it slow. What happened to Jamey was tragic, but you can't go on thinking that you're going to lose everyone you love. It doesn't make sense. Don't go pushing your friendship with Kacem."

"You were certainly in enough of a hurry with Fareed," Kevin reminded him.

"Fareed and Kacem aren't the same, and you know it," said Dave. "Fareed's an animal, and from the first time we met, the signals were loud and clear. God, he nearly fucked me right there on the tennis court."

"All right, I know things won't be that easy with Kacem," admitted Kevin. "But that's why I love him the way I do. He's somebody worth waiting for."

"So …" Dave was eager to change the subject. "Tell me about your evening at Claudette and Jean-Richard's."

"It was fun. Miguel Berthaud was there with his impressions. He did one of Monsieur Rhazwani that had us all nearly on the floor. Then there was Aïn El Qamar's odd couple."

"You mean Laurent and Christiane?" laughed Dave, and Kevin nodded. "So, how'd she look tonight? Cheap … or trashy?"

"She might as well have been tricking on Times Square," said Kevin, "the way she was dressed."

"What about Marcie?" asked Dave. "Did she have fun?"

"Our Miss Nelson was having the time of her life—with Jean-Richard. Talk about crushes! Marcie's got it bad. Do you think I should warn her about the Don Juan of Aïn El Qamar?"

"You honestly think she still hasn't heard about his reputation? Come on, Kevin. Marcie's over twenty-one. She's going to have to learn how to handle herself someday." Kevin nodded. "And how is the famous Miss Claudette?"

"In love, she says," revealed Kevin.

"No kidding. So what else is new?" As Dave drained the spaghetti, Kevin took two plates and placed them on the counter beside the stove.

"No, I mean, this time she's really in love," said Kevin as Dave dished out one ample and one smaller portion of pasta and poured sauce over them. Kevin filled two glasses with wine, grabbed a pair of forks, and the two Americans took their dinners into the living room. They sat on the *banquettes*, Moroccan style, and sipped their wine.

"So, who's the lucky victim?" asked Dave.

"What?"

"Who's Claudette in love with now?"

Kevin almost gagged on his wine. "You're not going to believe this. Or then again maybe you are. Three guesses as to which Moroccan hustler is now the man of Miss Claudette's dreams."

"Not …?" Dave mimicked a tennis swing, and Kevin nodded.

"That little sex fiend. We were fucking just half an hour ago, and he didn't tell me a thing!"

"Dave, this isn't funny," protested Kevin. "Isn't there any way we can warn Claudette?"

"Yeah, sure. We'll just tell her he's my fuck-buddy and that's how we know what he's really up to."

"Well, you're the one who's always talking about being open with everyone," Kevin reminded him.

"There are limits, Kev."

"Well all I can say is, poor Claudette!" said Kevin.

"Poor Fareed, you mean," Dave corrected him. "He's the one who's going to have his hands full trying to satisfy the ever horny Miss Claudette!" Dave suddenly grinned. "Don't you just love living in Aïn El Qamar?"

Jean-Richard had retired early, but lying in bed now, he found himself unable to sleep. I must have passed the point of exhaustion, he told himself. The past day and a half he had hardly slept at all, except for a few hours at the home of the Greek girl last night, or rather this morning. The return drive from Rabat had been tiring, and the confrontations with the new lab assistant and then with Monsieur Rhazwani had left him emotionally drained. Only the conversation with Marcie had revived him. Still, even that had been disturbing.

What was it that he felt about Marcie that he hadn't felt in the presence of the Greek girl, that he didn't feel with any other woman, hadn't felt since ...

Arrête, Jean-Richard! he told himself. Don't let yourself get emotionally involved. Think of something else. Think of the Greek girl, of her breasts, of the taste of her mouth, of the warmth of her sex. Think of her long blond hair ... No, damn it! It was Marcie whose hair was blond. Think of the Greek girl with her blue eyes. No ... not blue eyes! The images of the two women, so different, became one in his fatigued brain. He was so mixed-up. Which was which? And then suddenly the two female bodies were entwined, and they were having sex together, and he remembered!

Janna inhaled the sweet strong smoke. Jesus, that felt good! Her whole body was weightless; she was floating on a cloud.

She passed the pipe to Michèle. "I think I've had enough, love," said the Frenchwoman, who had taken only two half-hearted tokes. "I've never been much on getting high." She handed the long engraved pipe with its tiny bowl of *keef* back to her friend.

They were at Janna's house, Michèle having stopped by to visit, unable to bear Dominique's complaining any longer, she had said.

Janna pouted. "Some people don't know how to have any fun."

"Some people don't need drugs to enjoy themselves," corrected Michèle. "I get the feeling you're trying to escape from something, Janna. Do you want to tell me what it is?"

"Why do you have to be so damn perceptive?" Janna looked at the slender young woman with the little girl figure and boyish mop of hair, thinking: This woman is my friend. If anyone will understand, she will. I need to talk to someone about Lahcen. If I don't open up about this tonight, I think I'll burst.

And so she began for the first time to unburden herself to Michèle, to tell of her love affair with Lahcen Cherqaoui. In the month she had known the Frenchwoman, she had wanted many times to reveal to her everything that had happened, but she had been afraid that Michèle would not understand what she had done. Suddenly, tonight, Janna knew that she had no reason to fear her friend's reaction.

She told Michèle about the Arabic lessons, about Lahcen's fear of the *baccalauréat* exam, about that moment of compassion mixed with desire that had led to love. She spoke of their summer together, of Lahcen's departure for the States, of the infrequency of his letters. She talked until there was nothing left to expose of the past.

"That letter you brought me today," she said to Michèle now. "It was from him."

"That's good," said Michèle, "isn't it? What did he have to say?"

"The usual things. What he was doing. The people he was meeting. Things that surprised him about the States. But it wasn't what he said so much as what he didn't say. He didn't apologize for not having written in two weeks. And he didn't tell me that he loved me. I mean, he signed it 'Love, Lahcen,' but I was expecting to read the words 'I love you, Janna,' and I didn't."

"That could just be an oversight," Michèle reminded her. "It's certainly not enough to put you in such a funk. So tell me, love. What is it that really has you worried?"

"I'm scared shitless that he's started meeting American girls his own age, girls who aren't cloistered like Moroccan girls, girls who'll sleep with him in an instant. And then where will I be? In Aïn El Qamar I was unique. I was different. I was special. How is Janna Gallagher going to stand up against all those high school cheerleaders, each one of whom is younger and prettier than I am, and more than willing to have sex with him? What am I supposed to do then, Michèle?"

"But Janna, you must have suspected that this would happen. Why on earth did you encourage him to leave Morocco? You apparently didn't even try to stop him."

"To the contrary," agreed Janna. "He never would have had the courage to leave if it hadn't been for me."

"So?" asked Michèle.

"So I was a fool. I knew what a fantastic opportunity this was for Lahcen. After a year in the States, he'd have so much more to contribute to Morocco. I only allowed myself to look at the positive side, when all along I should have thought about the risks, and about how much I'd miss him and how empty my life would be without him."

"Then why not go back to the States and be with him there?"

"As if I could," replied Janna sarcastically. "Michèle, I'm twenty-six years old and Lahcen doesn't celebrate his eighteenth birthday for another month yet. Can you imagine the scandal? Right away it would become public knowledge that the high school exchange student was seeing an older woman. I'm not worried about my own reputation, but think about his! Besides, how can I be sure that he'd even want me to join him? He certainly didn't sound like he would in his letter today."

"Then, I guess, love, that you're just going to have to do your best to be patient and understanding with him, and try not to lose whatever hope you still have. I don't know what else you can do."

Taking another deep toke from the *keef* pipe, Janna said sadly, "There's nothing else I can do, Michèle. Nothing at all."

The young Moroccan sat in his bedroom, a notebook open on the table before him. He wrote by candlelight so as not to awaken his parents. His Arabic script was an awkward, nearly illegible scrawl. He wrote:

"I spoke with Ms. Gallagher today. I offered to walk home with her. The whore! She turned me down! But she wanted me. I know it. I could see it in her eyes. She fucked Cherqaoui. She'll fuck anyone. Someday, she'll fuck me!"

He closed the notebook, and smiled.

DECEMBER 1976

CHAPTER 9

▼

What a glorious December day, thought Michèle as she stood on the rooftop terrace of her house in Aïn El Qamar. And such a change from last year in Southern California! In place of the ocean and palm trees she could see the snow-covered Atlas Mountains clearly outlined under an intensely blue sky. They seemed almost near enough to touch. Yesterday had been gray and cold and it had rained throughout the night. Now, with the arrival of a new morning came a cloudless sky and a sun which brought warmth to her chilled bones. Not only that, but tomorrow would mark both the Moroccan *Aïd El Kébir* holiday and the beginning of two much-needed weeks of vacation. Michèle could almost feel herself already lying on the beach at Agadir, the modern resort town located far south on Morocco's Atlantic coast. Well, the day after tomorrow she and Janna would be there. Only forty-eight more hours, she told herself excitedly.

Michèle took off her heavy woolen sweater, surprised to find herself almost perspiring. For the past week of cold and rain she had not ventured outside without a sweater or coat. In her house, of course, the gas heaters did their job, but the classrooms in Lycée Mohamed Cinq were usually colder than it was outdoors, and Michèle found herself moving around in the classroom almost as actively as her friend Janna did.

Or as she used to do, Michèle corrected herself.

What was happening to Janna lately? she wondered. She rarely smiled, and her enthusiasm for her work and liveliness in the classroom seemed things of the past. Michèle suspected that it was because Lahcen Cherqaoui had only written her once since that day in late October, and that had been but a post card, and weeks ago at that. "Snap out of it, Janna," she had told her friend. But to no avail. At times Janna seemed to be sleepwalking, hardly reacting to what went on around her. Michèle wondered how heavily she had gotten into smoking *keef*. What had been an occasional recreation seemed to have become a steady habit.

I hope this trip to Agadir will do her good, thought Michèle. Perhaps being away from Aïn El Qamar would help her, although Michèle was afraid that Janna might take her troubles along. You'd better not, she said silently. It took me long enough to convince you to go to Agadir with me. I won't have you spoiling my vacation.

Well, she'd just have to see what would happen. In the meantime, there was tomorrow night's eagerly awaited party at Claudette's. It seemed that the entire foreign population of Aïn El Qamar would be there, perhaps as many as sixty! Claudette could speak of nothing else, and assured all that it would be a night to remember.

Of course, that was tomorrow, and today was still a work day. Not that Michèle would be teaching. Classes had ended several days ago. The dormitory had closed early, some said in order to allow Monsieur Rhazwani to pocket the money which would have paid for food. In any case, the *internes* had already left for their homes. Their departure had brought about that of the *externes* as well, so for the past several days the classrooms had stood empty.

Actually there was still some remaining work to accomplish. At the end of every quarter there were meetings, called *conseils de classe*, where those teachers in charge of a single class of students—who remained together for all subjects— would discuss their students' progress. Those whose work was outstanding would receive *tableau d'honneur* and be inscribed on the honor roll. Those in danger of failure would receive an official warning, or *avertissement*. Michèle had had two *conseils* the day before yesterday, and there remained her third and last today. She enjoyed meeting with her fellow teachers and learning how her students were doing in their other subjects. Unfortunately, each *conseil* meant spending an hour with Monsieur Rhazwani in his office, and Michèle preferred to avoid encounters with the unpleasant man, who was becoming more and more offensive and obnoxious as each day brought new complaints from his latest faculty victims.

"Michèle!" called Dominique Moulin from inside their house. "You'd better get ready to leave. It's nearly ten-thirty."

"Damn," said Michèle. She had been enjoying the warmth of the sun and the beauty of the freshly fallen snow on the mountain peaks. "*J'arrive!*" she answered.

Michèle went down the stairs which led to the entry hall of their house, bolting the door behind her. Dominique was waiting for her in the living room, smoking a Marquise. She had begun to chain-smoke recently, claiming that it relieved the endless boredom. Poor Domino, thought Michèle. Things aren't improving for you, are they? But then you do nothing to help them improve.

Today, amazingly, the other Frenchwoman was smiling as Michèle entered the living room.

"What's made you so cheerful today, Domino?" she asked.

"Are you kidding?" replied Dominique. "It's the last fucking day of school. Tomorrow we're free! And the next day I'm back to civilization for a week. *Je retourne en France*! Why shouldn't I be smiling?"

"I still think it's silly of you not to do some traveling in Morocco," said Michèle. "You ought to be thankful for such beautiful weather in December, just in time for the start of vacation."

"The only vacation I want is out!" exclaimed Dominique.

"I was only suggesting," said Michèle.

"Well, get off my back!"

Touchy today, thought Michèle. I guess the cheer was only skin deep. Dominique needed something more than just a vacation in France, but Michèle had no idea what it was. "*Pardon*, Domino," she said.

Dominique lit another cigarette with the still burning end of the one she was finishing. "We'd better be leaving or we'll be late," she said, putting out the butt in the nearly overflowing ashtray in front of her. "I'll put on my coat and meet you in the car," she added.

Michèle grabbed her class grade book from the dining table where she had been checking it over earlier. Then she ran down the stairs and got into the driver's seat of her car. She and Dominique both had the same *conseil* at ten-thirty, Michèle as the class's English teacher and Dominique as their *prof de maths*. This was the only class they shared, and Michèle, who enjoyed them immensely, could not fathom Dominique's constant complaints. But then Dominique complained about all her classes.

Michèle looked out and saw Dominique coming towards the car. Reaching over, she unlocked the right-hand door. Dominique got in and lit another cigarette.

As Michèle drove down the main street, she could still see signs of the previous night's rains. There were puddles wherever she looked, and mud had formed on the unpaved side streets. Children were playing everywhere, obviously enjoying the vacation which for them had already started. Women sat on their doorsteps, holding their veiled faces up to the sun to soak in its rays and sharing neighborhood gossip. In a way, thought Michèle, she would be sorry to be leaving Aïn El

Qamar for even two weeks, but she knew that she would return with new enthusiasm and a feeling of being back in a place she could call home.

"I hope we're not late," she said to Dominique as she pulled into the school parking lot. There were already quite a few other cars there. She and Dominique hurried past the *shaoush* who guarded the gate and across the now muddy courtyard to the door of Monsieur Rhazwani's office. His secretary told them there was another *conseil* still in progress, but it would be out shortly. Dominique walked over to talk with several other waiting teachers, leaving Michèle alone.

It seems strange to see the school so empty, thought Michèle. She was used to the sight of busy classrooms or a courtyard filled with hundreds of dark-haired students, all of them …

"God am I pissed!" said an English-speaking voice behind her and Michèle turned to look at Dave Casalini. He had apparently just left the *proviseur's* office along with another group of teachers.

"What's wrong, Dave?" asked Michèle. She was surprised to find the usually easy-going American so upset.

"It's that bastard Rhazwani!" he exclaimed.

"Be careful about what you say. People will hear you," she cautioned.

"None of them speak English," said Dave. "And I'm damned if I'll keep my voice down."

Michèle's curiosity was piqued. "What did he do now?" she asked.

"You know that the student council members went to see the *délégué* about the council's being disbanded."

"Yes," answered Michèle. "The *délégué* supported them against the *proviseur*. I remember how ecstatic you were at the news."

"Well, that mother-fucker's gotten his revenge. In this last *conseil*, you know what he had the gall to do? The son of a bitch refused to put Lateef, who's the council president, on the honor roll!"

"That's terrible!" cried Michèle. "What possible reason did the *proviseur* give?"

"He called it an 'administrative decision,'" said Dave. "Naturally, I protested, and so did Kacem Hajiri, who's the class's physics teacher, but the *proviseur* refused to give in."

"I'm really sorry," said Michèle. "What a rotten way to punish him. You have good reason to be angry at the man."

"Are you talking about Rhazwani?" asked a voice behind them speaking in French.

"*Oui*, Kacem," said Dave to the young Moroccan physics teacher who had just come up.

"Someday that man is going to hang himself," said Kacem, "and I just pray that I'm around to see it happen."

As he was speaking, Monsieur Rhazwani's secretary came up to Michèle and said, "Mademoiselle Perrault, your *conseil* is about to start."

"I have this class too," said Kacem.

"I hope the two of you have better luck with this class than I did with mine," said Dave. "*A bientôt.*"

"*Au revoir,*" replied Michèle and Kacem, turning to follow Dominique and the other teachers into the *proviseur's* office where they sat in a half circle facing Monsieur Rhazwani's desk. There were eight of them in all, four Moroccans and four French. Michèle ended up sitting next to Kacem, and as always when she was around him, she found herself amazed that one man should be gifted with such perfect looks and an apparently charming personality as well. If only he weren't so shy around me, she thought. I'd really like to get to know him better.

The *proviseur* was calling the *conseil* to order and Michèle opened her grade book to the class in question. Monsieur Rhazwani read off each student's *moyenne générale*, or grade point average, and a short discussion among the teachers followed. It was then decided whether or not the student's name should be placed on the honor roll or if he or she should receive a warning.

Michèle was surprised after her conversation with Dave to find things going almost smoothly. Dominique, as expected, was critical of many of the students, but the *proviseur* had so far not made any objections to the teachers' decisions.

Then, as they were discussing the case of a female student named Malika Dahmani, Michèle was astounded to hear Monsieur Rhazwani announce forcefully, "*Avertissement de conduite.*" What! thought Michèle. A warning for poor conduct? Not for Malika! She was such a polite, well-behaved girl.

"*Je proteste!*" exclaimed Kacem Hajiri.

"*Moi aussi!*" joined in Michèle.

"*Décision administrative,*" said the *proviseur*. Another "administrative" decision.

"For what reason?" asked Kacem, clearly angry but attempting to retain his self-control.

"She has been seen walking alone and unchaperoned after sunset! Her conduct is a black mark on this school's reputation!"

"But *monsieur le proviseur,*" said Kacem. "Malika works evenings at the Clinique El Qamar as a nurse's helper. She isn't always able to find someone to accompany her home."

"A young girl should not behave scandalously for whatever reason!"

My God, thought Michèle, how can anyone be such a sexist bigot? And why were only she and Kacem Hajiri protesting? What about the other teachers, French and Moroccan? Were they all cowards?

"Monsieur Rhazwani," Kacem was saying. "Malika is a fine young girl who has a decent respectable after-school job. Please reconsider your decision!"

"We've got to be just!" agreed Michèle, thinking: Damn it, you others, speak up! Dominique was just sitting there, smoking as usual and looking bored.

Finally, Monsieur Francheaux, the history teacher, said, "I must agree with my two colleagues. The girl should not be punished for having to work outside school."

Thank God someone else has some courage, thought Michèle, and then several other teachers said that they too supported Kacem's protest. Dominique remained silent.

"I can see that the honor of Lycée Mohamed Cinq means nothing to any of you," declared Monsieur Rhazwani, "but I have better things to do with my time than to waste it arguing with you. There will be no *avertissement ...*" Michèle smiled at Kacem who returned her smile.

"... but I intend to speak to the girl privately about her indecency."

The smiles on their two faces faded.

Hypocrite, thought Michèle. You probably intended from the start to give in, just so that you could have an excuse to be alone with her!

Luckily, the rest of the *conseil* proceeded calmly and without incident and when, at last, it was over, the teachers who did not have the class next under discussion filed out of the *proviseur's* office. Michèle told Dominique, who had to stay, that she would wait for her, then headed towards the *salle des profs* with Kacem Hajiri beside her.

"Thank you for your support," he said.

"Thank *you* for speaking up in the first place," Michèle corrected him. "If it hadn't been for you, none of us would have had the courage to say anything."

Arriving at the teacher's room, Michèle walked over to the large table on which lay a pile of mail. "Nothing for me," she said disappointedly, "but here's a letter for you." She handed Kacem an envelope. He sat down on the table and read it.

"It's from Armand Rochefort, my closest friend at the university in Lyon. He's making his first visit to Morocco three days from now, so naturally I'm looking forward to showing him around."

"Janna mentioned that you'd spent a good deal of time in France," remembered Michèle.

"Yes, from high school on," said Kacem, "but I'm glad to be back in Aïn El Qamar. I was born and raised here."

"Really?" Michèle was surprised. He looked so different from the other Moroccan teachers at the school. His dress was stylish and casual, like Jean-Richard's, for example. Today he was wearing a gray and blue plaid sports jacket over a light blue turtleneck with gray slacks completing the ensemble. But it wasn't only his choice of clothes that distinguished him. He seemed more modern, more aware, more enlightened. Of course this might be nothing more than a facade, with a core of traditionalism underneath. All the same, Michèle was definitely impressed.

She asked Kacem how it was to be back home after so many years in France, and as he answered, she found herself drawn to him in a way that startled her. She felt at ease with him, as he seemed to be with her, which after several months of considering him shy and reserved came as quite a revelation. The *conseil* had obviously brought them closer together and Michèle realized that she was hoping to see more of this handsome young man after vacation. Still, at the same time, she hesitated to become involved. After all, he was a Moroccan, and several years younger than she. Not only that, but Michèle enjoyed her freedom. She didn't want ...

Arrête, Michèle! she told herself. Get hold of yourself! You hardly know the man and already you're worrying about getting too involved with him. You really do need a vacation.

Even so, as she listened to his quiet impeccable French and watched his face break into a brilliant smile as he recalled things which had amused him during his first weeks of teaching, Michèle could not help but find him attractive.

Kacem was asking her about her reactions to life in Aïn El Qamar when Dominique suddenly entered the *salle des profs*. That's odd, thought Michèle. The *conseil* can't possibly be over yet, can it?

"Have you any idea where that Janna Gallagher is?" scowled Dominique. "She's hasn't shown up for the meeting yet. *Quelle irresponsabilité!*"

"*Mais c'est impossible!*" exclaimed Michèle, who knew that attendance at *conseils* was mandatory. She was aware that Janna had been depressed recently. Still, it was unlike her to miss such an important meeting.

"Do me a very big favor, Dominique," Michèle pleaded. "Ask, no *beg* Monsieur Rhazwani to wait just five minutes more. I'll rush over to Janna's house and see what's keeping her. Please, Domino. I'll make it up to you, I swear!"

Dominique looked peeved and did not reply.

"I'll speak to him," offered Kacem. "You hurry over and get Janna. Hurry!"

"Thank you!" exclaimed Michèle, and without further pause, ran out of the *salle des profs* towards the adjoining parking lot. What a remarkable man Kacem Hajiri was!

As she pulled out of the parking lot, her thoughts turned to Janna. What was causing her to be late for the *conseil*, or perhaps to have forgotten about it entirely? Had she let Lahcen's silence affect her so deeply that she was losing track of time?

As Michèle approached Janna's nearby house, she noticed that the shutters were closed. That's strange, she thought. Janna always opened them as soon as she got up in order to let in the morning light. Michèle pulled up in front of the door. Not even bothering to lock her car, she hurried over to ring the bell, but there was no answer. She rang again. Still no answer. She tried a third time.

Finally, the door opened and there stood Janna in her robe, her hair uncombed, her eyes strangely glazed. She seemed hardly to see the French-woman.

"Janna!" gasped Michèle. "What on earth's the matter with you?"

"Oh, it's you," she said tonelessly. "What is it?"

Without waiting for an invitation, Michèle marched in and shut the door behind her. She took Janna by the arm and led the unprotesting woman into the living room.

"It's freezing in here," said Michèle.

"I ran out of gas for the heater," replied Janna in the same monotone.

"Sit down on the *banquette* and let me get a blanket to wrap around you," said Michèle. God, but these Moroccan homes held the cold when they went without heat. It must be twenty degrees cooler inside than out.

Michèle returned carrying a heavy woolen blanket which she put around Janna's shoulders. Then she spotted the *keef* pipe on the coffee table. She sniffed. The smell of *keef* in the air was unmistakable.

"Oh God no," exclaimed Michèle. "Janna, it's not even noon yet. What's happening to you?"

"Nothing," replied the American woman, with a silly smile on her face. "Nothing," she repeated, "except that my life's falling apart." Now the smile had become bitter.

"Janna," said Michèle forcefully. "Listen to me. You've got a *conseil de classe* this morning."

"Oh?" said Janna languidly. "Then I'd better get dressed, hadn't I?"

"I mean right now," said Michèle. She looked at her spaced-out disheveled friend, then made a quick decision. "You're in no condition to leave this house. I'll have to take your place. Where's your grade book?"

Janna appeared not to have heard.

"Your grade book, damn it!" cried Michèle. "Where is it!"

"My grade book? Over there on the desk."

Michèle rushed across the room to get it. "Listen, Janna. I'm in a hurry. I'm going to see if they'll let me fill in for you at the *conseil*. I'll invent some story about your having the stomach flu, or something. But listen. Pull yourself together. Make yourself a strong cup of coffee and for God's sake, keep warm. I'll be back as soon as I can."

Michèle ran out of the house and drove the few blocks back to school as quickly as she could. Damn it! Things were much worse with Janna than she'd imagined. Michèle wondered if even two weeks away from Aïn El Qamar would be enough to bring her out of her depression.

The *conseil*, once she had arrived, seemed to drag on endlessly. Fortunately, the *proviseur* had accepted her story about Janna and allowed Michèle to take her place at the meeting, but Michèle wondered how long she could keep covering for her friend.

Finally, the *conseil* was adjourned. Dominique did not even bother to ask about Janna. Typical, thought Michèle, wishing that she could return to Janna's immediately. But she first had to drive Dominique back to their place. Hell, she thought. Why hadn't she and Domino driven separate cars?

As they walked towards the *salle des profs* on the way to the parking lot, Kacem Hajiri came out and headed in their direction. "How's Janna?" he asked in obvious concern. "I didn't want to go home until I was sure she was all right."

"It's just a bad case of the stomach flu," lied Michèle. "She'll be fine by tomorrow."

"That's a relief," said Kacem.

"Anyway, thanks a million for getting the *proviseur* to hold up the *conseil*. Janna really appreciates it, and so do I."

"I'm glad I could help," replied Kacem. "So … the two of you have a wonderful holiday!"

Michèle gave Kacem her warmest smile. Dominique merely snorted.

"Let me buy you lunch after vacation," Michèle offered. "To thank you for everything you did today."

"I'd enjoy that," replied Kacem. "But it'll be my treat. Your company will be thanks enough."

"Hurry up, Michèle!" snapped Dominique, already halfway to the parking lot.

"*J'arrive*," answered Michèle, turning back to give Kacem Hajiri a final smile and wave. I am definitely going to get to know this man better after vacation, she thought.

Michèle's hopes of a quick return to Janna's place were dashed by Dominique's insistence that they stop at the Mondiale on the way home. And after that, at the cleaners. Finally arriving at their house, Michèle invented a sudden errand. "Go ahead and eat without me," she told her housemate. "I may be a while."

Dominique looked suspicious, but she did not question Michèle's excuse. "*A toute à l'heure, alors,*" she said.

Michèle raced back into town in the direction of Janna's house. She almost ran over a sheep that was being taken somewhere by an old man dressed in a ragged *jellaba*, but she was hardly aware of their near collision. Just before arriving at Janna's house, she stopped at the nearest grocer's and asked the shopkeeper to bring over a large bottle of butane gas, referred to locally as *butagaz*, to Miss Janna's house as quickly as possible. She knew almost no Arabic and the shopkeeper very little French, but sign language helped her get the point across.

Michèle then walked the remaining half block to Janna's door. This time Janna answered it more quickly, and Michèle was relieved to see that her friend's eyes were not so glazed. Perhaps the *keef* was beginning to wear off.

"The first thing we're going to do is get you into bed and warm you up," ordered Michèle, and led an unresisting Janna into her room.

Naturally the bed was unmade, and looked as if it hadn't been for several days. Janna got in and Michèle, after putting several pillows behind her back, pulled the covers up over her.

"Did you make yourself any coffee?" asked Michèle.

"Didn't want any," answered Janna.

"I'm going to make you some whether you like it or not," said Michèle, "and you're going to drink it. No buts about it!" The Frenchwoman went into the kitchen to put a pot on the stove. What a mess! she thought as she entered. It obviously had been several days since the maid Halima's last visit. Michèle wondered how Janna had managed to make it to school the past few days. Then she recalled that Janna had not had any *conseils* yesterday. She had probably been smoking off and on since the evening before last.

Michèle had just put the coffee pot on the burner when the doorbell rang. It was the shopkeeper with the heavy metal *butagaz* bottle. He removed the empty from the large portable heater, then installed the new one. Michèle paid the man and thanked him in her few words of Arabic.

When the shopkeeper had left, Michèle rolled the heater into the kitchen where she found a match, and lit it. The warmth felt good in this damp chilly room. The water was boiling, so Michèle made two strong cups of Nescafé and put them on a tray. Then, setting the tray on top of the heater, she rolled it into Janna's room.

"Drink!" she commanded as she handed Janna a cup and then sat down on the edge of the bed facing her friend.

"I really blew it this time, didn't I?" said Janna after she'd taken a few sips. "Were they awfully upset at school?"

"I didn't tell them the truth, silly," said Michèle. "What kind of a friend do you think I am?"

"How was the *conseil*?" asked Janna. "Did Farhaoussi get *tableau d'honneur*?"

"Who's that?"

"He's just the best student in class," said Janna.

Michèle took the grade book from the bedside table where she had left it when she had put Janna to bed. "Farhaoussi," she said. "No, Janna. Dominique refused him honor roll. She said he was a numskull in math, or something in French to that order."

"Oh fuck," said Janna. "If I'd been there, I might have been able to convince her to change her mind. I really let Farhaoussi down. He's my top student, just like … like …"

Michèle knew that Janna was thinking of Lahcen.

"I understand," said the Frenchwoman. "I understand what you're feeling. And Janna, it could very well be that Lahcen will write again soon and that there's a logical explanation for the delay. But it's also possible that there isn't any. I don't want to hurt you, love, but I'm afraid you're going to have to face the possibility that what you told me a few months ago is true. The temptations of an American high school may just have been too much for him."

"But he said he loved me!"

"I know," sympathized Michèle. "And I'm sure he meant it at the time. But things change. And you've got to go on with your life. You are too valuable a person to waste your time suffering over someone who, quite frankly, doesn't seem to deserve someone as special as you."

"I appreciate the words, Michèle," said Janna. "I really do. But they don't take the pain away. Oh, damn it all! I'm a twenty-six year old woman. Why can't I behave like one?"

"I'm nearly thirty," said Michèle, "and who's to say I wouldn't feel just the same way you are in your situation." She took her friend's hand reassuringly.

Janna gave her another half smile. "I waited twenty-six years to screw up my life," she said. "All that time, in Berkeley, in Europe, in Washington, I never needed to feel anything more than a physical attraction to go to bed with someone. Why did I have to screw up everything this time by falling in love—and with a damned seventeen year old! I really do love him, Michèle. And though I can rationalize his maybe having found someone to replace me, that doesn't make it any less painful. I don't know if I can pull through this. It hurts too much!"

"I know it hurts," said Michèle. "But is getting stoned before lunch the answer?"

"I'll try to quit, Michèle. I promise." Janna's voice was no longer toneless as it had been on Michèle's arrival. She was pleading with her friend for love and support.

Michèle squeezed Janna's hand reassuringly. "I'm going to see if you have any food in that filthy kitchen of yours," she said lightly in an attempt to rid the room of its maudlin atmosphere. "And if there isn't anything to eat, I'll run out and pick something up. As for you, I want you to take a hot shower and wash your hair. Excuse me for saying so, but it looks filthy. Then put some clean clothes on and start thinking about something cheerful. Claudette's party tomorrow night, for example, and our next two weeks in the sun in Agadir. You can pull through this Janna. You just need to believe in yourself."

"I'll try," promised Janna, though her voice was shaky with doubt. "I will try. I only wish I had your confidence in me. The truth is, Michèle, I don't know if I can make it. I really don't."

CHAPTER 10

▼

The crumbling remains of a once majestic castle, or *qsar*, still stood on a hill high atop Aïn El Qamar. Centuries before, the *qsar* had been used as a vantage point to protect the town from warring tribes. Of the original four towers built surrounding a central courtyard, only two remained standing, and at places one could see the stone foundation where time and winds and temperature extremes had eroded the clay surface. More recently, young people on outings had begun to leave evidence of the twentieth century; graffiti was everywhere, in both French and Arabic script. Behind the *qsar* towered the Atlas Mountains, with their thick mantle of newly fallen snow. Below, like a sleeping man clad in a pearl-white *jellaba*, lay Aïn El Qamar.

This was Dave's special place for privacy and meditation. During the school week, it was mostly deserted, and he could come here to be alone, to contemplate the splendor of the mountains behind and the town below. The mountains in their grandeur reminded Dave that he was only human, and that his problems were insignificant compared to the vast panorama of nature. Seeing Aïn El Qamar from above made him aware of how small the town really was and helped him put his troubles in perspective. How could he let himself be tormented by things which occurred in a school or a house or an office building that was no bigger than a matchbox?

Today, especially, Dave felt the need for the solace that the *qsar* and its environs offered him. His day had started out badly with the *conseil* de class in which Lateef had been unjustly denied *tableau d'honneur*. Dave had already come to dislike the *proviseur* and to detest his arrogant hunger for power, but now he truly hated the man as he had never hated another human being in his life. And if that were not already enough, the *conseil* had been followed by a catastrophic interview with the provincial governor regarding Lateef's passport, after which Dave had stopped a tiny Fiat taxi and asked to be driven to the *qsar*.

Now, Dave sat silently trying to find some peace and consolation in his surroundings, grateful that despite the end of classes, no students had chosen to visit the ruins so far today. Aïn El Qamar looked so safe, so clean, so harmless from high above. There were no traces of poverty or dirt or human suffering. How could such a place be causing him so much pain and frustration?

Dave could see Lycée Mohamed Cinq, but if there were people in its courtyard now, they were too small to be perceived. Only a few hours ago, however, when he had been there, the walls of the school had been so oppressive that he had longed for escape.

God, he had been naive to think that logic and reason and restraint could be successful in combating Monsieur Rhazwani's tyranny and his lust for power. The man had gotten his revenge on Lateef for having led his fellow student council members at their meeting with the *délégué*. Dave recalled his joy and sense of victory when the council had been reinstated and elections for student body officers had been held, with Lateef the easy winner. The *délégué* had agreed with the students and supported them against the *proviseur*. He had even told Lateef how impressed he was with the maturity with which he had presented their case. Well, Lateef would see now where being sensible and mature got him. Nowhere!

Dave recalled indignantly another of the *proviseur*'s recent decisions. He had begun to enforce restrictions on weekend passes. Officially students who boarded at school on government scholarships could not leave the school grounds without a notarized letter from their parents. Since the parents were mostly poor farmers who lived outside Aïn El Qamar, such permission was nearly impossible to get on a regular basis. Always before, the rule had been virtually ignored, and students had been able to spend their weekends wherever they pleased and however they wanted. But those days of laxness were no more. Students who left without passes were not readmitted to class until they had brought a parent to school with them. This was such a costly and time-consuming inconvenience to their families that few students had dared to go against the *proviseur*. They talked of going on strike, but Dave sensed that they were truly frightened of Monsieur Rhazwani, of the ways in which he could ruthlessly use his power to destroy their futures.

The bastard! thought Dave. The evil bastard! These students had enough to worry about just passing their exams in order to stay in school, which in this land of high unemployment was their only hope for success. Now, even hard work might not be rewarded, as Monsieur Rhazwani had shown in the *conseil* today.

Dave had been staring bitterly at the school. Now his eyes drifted over to the large government building which housed the offices of the provincial governor and his staff. Today, after two long months of bureaucratic hassles, endless hours of running from office to office and waiting for hours on end just to complete the formal applications for Lateef's passport, today, finally, Dave had been granted a personal interview with the governor.

It was as Lateef had feared. No, said the governor. It was unlikely that a student would receive a passport merely to study in an American language institute. Too many Moroccans used student visas as means to emigrate permanently to foreign lands, in search not of an education but of jobs that were scarce or even unavailable in Morocco. Dave had insisted that Lateef would have no need to work, producing letters from several of his friends offering to help support Lateef financially during his stay in the United States. But the governor said that Dave would have to wait several months longer for the final results of Lateef's application, and he warned the American not to be optimistic. Finally, in desperation, Dave had taken out his wallet and said that he would be prepared to do anything in order for Lateef to get his passport, but the governor had simply laughed in his face. He obviously knew how little American Peace Corps volunteers earned.

What in God's name am I going to do? agonized Dave as he stared at the government building, so tiny, so insignificant. It looked small enough for him to grasp in his hand and crumble to bits. But this was only an illusion, as had been his dreams for the future.

Dave stood up from the rock where he had been sitting. Coming to the *qsar* to meditate had done him no good today. His problems were too insurmountable for peace to be found here. He began the half hour descent by foot into Aïn El Qamar. It was sad, thought Dave, that he could not appreciate the beauty of this bright December day which had followed so many that were dark and rainy. Today there were no clouds in the sky, but there were many in his heart, dense and black, which blocked his view of the sun.

Well, if there was little or no hope for the future, at least the next two weeks might be enjoyable. He and Lateef had planned a trip through the South of Morocco, to the fabled walled city of Taroudant, to the town of Tafraout with its rose-colored villas built by Berbers who had made their fortunes in the North, and then on to the desert, to Goulimine and Ourzazate and Zagora. They were going to travel by bus, as renting a car would be too costly. Lateef wanted to help with expenses, so he had been saving his money. Though he had accumulated little, he would be able to feel that he was contributing to the trip. Fortunately they were going to stay at the homes of other Peace Corps volunteers, some of whom would be in town, others of whom had promised to leave the house keys with neighbors. It would be hard for Dave to keep his hands off Lateef during two weeks of close daily proximity, but it would be harder still to leave him behind in Aïn El Qamar. In any case, Dave knew he had better get used to the fact that he and Lateef were not going to be lovers. Now was as good a time as any to begin.

Dave was approaching Aïn El Qamar when a car stopped beside him and he heard a voice call his name. He turned to see Michèle Perrault.

"Care for a lift home?" she asked.

"Are you sure I'm not taking you out of your way?"

"Nonsense," replied Michèle. "I've just been driving around enjoying the beautiful weather. Actually, Dave, I'm glad that I've run into you. There's something I wanted to discuss. Hop in."

As they drove towards Dave's house, Michèle told him of how she had found Janna that morning. "She was half stoned out of her mind," said Michèle. "I can't believe the change in her. Just two months ago, she was bubbling with life and energy. And now … Of course, a lot of it is the *keef*. She's using it as a crutch, to get through the bad days, but it's only making things worse."

Dave promised Michèle that he too would speak to Janna. "I'll talk to her on the way to Claudette's party tomorrow," he offered. "She's probably heard enough lecturing for today. Let's give her twenty-four hours to think things over."

"Perhaps you're right," said Michèle as she pulled up in front of Dave's house. Halima, the maid, was coming out carrying a trash bucket. She had thrown her *haïk* over her caftan rather than leave the house uncovered, but she evidently had not wanted to bother with putting on her veil, so she held the sheet between her teeth to partially hide her face.

As Dave got out of the car, Michèle waved at Halima and greeted her with several words of Arabic. Letting the *haïk* fall from her mouth, Halima responded with a long intricate sentence which Michèle clearly did not understand.

"Tell her I haven't the slightest idea what she's saying, but thanks anyway," smiled Michèle. "My students and Janna have been trying to teach me some Arabic, but my knowledge remains about nil."

Dave explained this to the maid. She gave a broad grin showing her perfect dentures, and nodded to Michèle that she understood. "*Rhadi ttaalemi*," she said, and Dave explained that she was telling Michèle that she would learn in time.

"*Insha'allah*," replied Michèle, "God-willing," and the maid exclaimed in Arabic, "See, she knows a little already!"

Michèle smiled and drove off. Halima once again gripped the edge of her *haïk* between her teeth to shield her face and crossed the street to take the trash bucket to the nearest dump.

Dave was about to go inside when he heard Marcie calling him from her door-step down the street. She looked fresh and wholesomely pretty in a light green pullover sweater and a darker green skirt.

Heading towards him, she exclaimed, "I've just been thinking about tomorrow evening. The party at Claudette and Jean-Richard's is going to be so much fun!"

Dave agreed with her, and said so, though he knew that his troubles with Lateef's passport would cloud the evening for him.

"Halima's invited me to her house to watch the sacrifice tomorrow morning," said Marcie excitedly, "and I'll be going to Claudette and Jean-Richard's in the evening. Not only that, but Halima's taking me to the *souk* in about an hour to help her pick out a sheep! I think I'm the luckiest of us all—to be invited to a Moroccan home for the *Aïd* and then to be going to a French party afterward!"

"Well, I'll see you there," said Dave, who was getting hungry for whatever Halima had made for lunch.

Entering his house, Dave was greeted by a tempting aroma wafting out from the kitchen. Halima's cleaning days always meant a tasty Moroccan *tajine* or sometimes *couscous*. Dave left his things in his bedroom, then went into the living room. Lateef was there, sitting on one of the *banquettes*, reading.

"How was the *conseil*, Dave?" he asked. "And your meeting with the governor?"

"Let's wait till after lunch, okay?" said Dave.

"It can't be good news," said Lateef dejectedly.

"It's not, but let's wait till we've eaten, and till Halima's left."

Just then, the maid came into the room carrying two bowls of *harira*, spicy hot Moroccan vegetable and lentil soup. She set them on the coffee table in front of Dave and Lateef.

"*Barakallahoufik*, Halima," thanked Dave. "It smells delicious."

"For you and Mr. Kevin, anything," said the maid. "You are my sons."

Halima withdrew from the room, and Dave felt a surge of affection for the kind-hearted woman who had spent the last seven or eight years working for American Peace Corps volunteers and seeing each of her "children" eventually leave her. It would be sad to say good-bye to her in July. She really did mother her employers.

Dave and Lateef were just finishing their *harira* when Kevin arrived back from a noon *conseil* at school. He set down the notebook he was carrying and went over to join them on the *banquettes*.

Halima entered the living room with a *tajine* which she put down on the table before them. She had made a beef *tajine* today with fried potato strips piled high atop the meat. She exited briefly, then returned with a *komira*—a long loaf of French bread which she had bought at a local *hanoot*, a bowl of *harira* for Kevin, and a small bottle of red wine.

"*Barakallahoufik*, Halima," thanked Dave.

As usual, Halima had proved herself a marvelous cook. The spices in the sauce were blended expertly, and the potatoes, which had been cooked separately, were crisp and salty. Dave and Lateef dug in voraciously. Kevin, however, seemed to be picking at his meal.

"No appetite?" asked Dave, savoring a tender piece of beef.

"I'm too excited about tomorrow to even feel like eating," exclaimed Kevin, who had been invited to spend the *Aïd El Kébir* holiday at Kacem Hajiri's family farm outside Aïn El Qamar. Kevin had been gung ho over Kacem since the day of the Moroccan meal he had been served at the physics teacher's home last October. Now, Dave was worried that Kevin's pushiness might be turning Kacem off before the two of them really became friends.

"I'm going to tell Kacem tomorrow," said Kevin.

"What are you talking about?"

"I'm going to tell him how I feel."

"You're what!" Dave could hardly believe his ears. "Could you excuse us Lateef?" he said. Grasping Kevin by the arm, he pulled him up and dragged him out of the living room and into Dave's bedroom. He closed the door.

"Are you out of your fucking mind?"

"I'm perfectly sane," insisted Kevin.

"Sanity like this will get you committed!" exclaimed Dave.

"Damn it, Dave, I've had it with patience! I waited too long once before and you know what happened. I'm not going to repeat the same mistake again. Jamey used to look at me the way Kacem does, only I was too blind to see how much he loved me. This time I'm going to do what I should have done with Jamey. I'm going to make the first move tomorrow night. And I know exactly what Kacem's response will be. He's going to tell me that he loves me as much as I love him."

Dave was doubtful about this, although he was aware that the two teachers had recently become friendly. Kevin had invited Kacem over for lunch a few times and was constantly visiting him at his parents' house. Still, when Dave had seen them together, he hadn't sensed any vibrations coming from the Moroccan, and he certainly was more of an expert at these things than Kevin was.

"Take it slow, Kev," advised Dave. "Believe me, it's the best thing you can do."

"That's bullshit!" exclaimed Kevin. "I'm telling you Dave, I know what I'm doing. You can talk all you want about being careful and not moving too fast, but this time I know what's best for me. Tomorrow night, I swear to you, Kacem and I are going to make love, and it's going to be the most wonderful night of my life."

"Oh?" asked Dave. "And just exactly how do you plan to let Kacem know the way you feel? Are you going to blurt it out over lunch, the way you nearly did just a few minutes ago, right in front of Lateef? Or maybe while you're watching the sheep being slaughtered? And then what? What's going to happen once the two of you fuck? Didn't Kacem say that his best friend was coming for a visit from France? Are all three of you going to spend the holiday together?"

"Of course not!" said Kevin. "Given the choice, I'm sure Kacem will want to be with me! He just has to!" Dave thought Kevin was about to cry. "Anyway, I haven't thought that far ahead. But when the time comes, it'll all work out. I … I know it will! And I wish you'd just … Oh, go to hell!"

Kevin got up and stormed out of Dave's bedroom. A few seconds later, Dave heard Kevin's own bedroom door slam shut.

Good luck, thought Dave sadly. You'll need it.

Returning to the living room, he sat down next to Lateef. There was no longer any steam rising from the *tajine*, and the fried potatoes looked like they'd gone soggy.

"What was that about?" asked Lateef.

"Just another of Kevin's tantrums," replied Dave. Normally, he hid nothing from Lateef, but he was uncomfortable discussing Kevin's sex life as long as sex remained a bone of contention between him and Lateef.

"*Rhadi f'hali*, Mr. Dave." Halima had just entered, announcing her intention of returning home. She was wearing her *haïk* and veil. Wishing her employer a happy vacation, she promised that she would drop by faithfully every day to see that the house was in good order and that no burglars had broken in.

Dave wished her a happy holiday. "Marcie told me that you and she are going to buy a sheep together at the *souk*."

"Yes, Mr. Dave. That's where I'm off to now. I have to hurry, or there won't be any sheep left."

"*B'slama*, Halima," said Dave, and Lateef echoed his good-bye.

"*B'slama*, Mr. Dave. *B'slama Si* Lateef," said Halima, and then muttered under her breath, "*Rhali bezaff. L'haouli rhali bezaff.*"

She was saying how expensive sheep were this year. Poor Halima, thought Dave. Even though he and Kevin had given the maid a bonus this holiday, as had Janna and Marcie, the Moroccan woman would doubtless have to go into debt in order to pay for the sheep, which custom dictated must be bought. Going without a sheep for the *Aïd El Kébir* would have brought *heshuma*, or shame, on her family. Such a thing was unheard of, she said.

Will I ever understand Moroccans? thought Dave as the maid left. Halima would spend the rest of the year repaying the relatives and friends who had loaned her the money.

Dave and Lateef were finally able to finish their meal in peace. As usual, Lateef offered to wash the dishes. Rising from the *banquette*, he collected the dirty lunch things and exited the room. Just then, Kevin stuck his head in the living room door. "I'm going out for a walk," he announced, and a second later he was gone.

Dave shrugged his shoulders. Things had not been going well so far today, and they were unlikely to get any better once Lateef knew about the results of the *conseil* and Dave's interview with the governor.

The next several minutes dragged on as if each were an hour, but finally Lateef had returned to the living room and was seated on the *banquette* next to Dave. "Now tell me," said the young Moroccan. "How bad is it?"

As sensitively as possible, Dave informed Lateef of the *proviseur*'s refusal to award him *tableau d'honneur* and of the governor's near certainty that he would not be granted a passport. He watched as the hope faded from Lateef's eyes.

"I knew it," said the young man. "I knew it was all too good to be true." His face was grim, his eyes filled with tears. He had never looked so helpless, so vulnerable, so in need of comfort.

Gently, Dave placed his hands on Lateef's shoulders, then squeezed firm. "It's not over yet," he insisted. "We won't let it be over." Pulling the Moroccan towards him, he held him tightly in his arms.

After what had happened six months ago, Dave was expecting to feel Lateef pull away, but instead Dave found the Moroccan returning his embrace, holding on to his friend as if for dear life, as if Dave were the only thing solid enough to keep him from falling into the depths of despair.

Dave felt Lateef's cheek against his own, felt the warmth of his skin's touch. Dave's lips were next to Lateef's ear. The urge to speak the truth was irresistible. "I love you," he whispered.

Lateef did not say a word, but the tightness of his arms around Dave seemed to speak volumes.

Suddenly it all felt so right to Dave. Lateef's being here in his embrace, his face so close to Dave's lips, so ready to be kissed.

Dave touched his lips to Lateef's cheek, and then, emboldened by Lateef's lack of protest, by what seemed to be an unspoken consent to what was about to happen, moved them to press against Lateef's mouth.

Their lips touched.

Unlike the last time, Dave did not attempt to penetrate Lateef's mouth with his tongue. He simply let their lips remain gently pressed together and savored the contact of skin to skin.

The feeling was exquisite, and even more exquisite was Lateef's surprising acquiescence. Dave felt Lateef's hands begin ever so slightly to massage his back. The Moroccan's lips seemed, ever so slightly, to be responding to Dave's kiss. He could have sworn that he felt the tip of Lateef's tongue touch his own, ever so slightly.

And then the doorbell rang. A loud harsh stinging ring, as if its volume had been raised to many decibels its normal level.

"I'll get it!" said Lateef, and shot to his feet, nearly tearing himself from Dave's arms. In a second he was gone from the room, leaving Dave suddenly alone and wondering if he had only dreamed what had just taken place.

A minute later, Lateef returned to the living room looking as if nothing had happened between them.

"That was Halima," he said. "She'd left her money pouch in the kitchen. She was so relieved to find it there. She thought she might have lost it, and today's the day she's buying her sheep for the *Aïd*."

"Oh," said Dave, still unsettled by the memory of Lateef's lips responding to the touch of his own, or had he just imagined that?

"About what we were discussing," the Moroccan was saying, "my passport and all that. Don't worry about it. I'll be all right. The honor roll's not going to help me to pass the *baccalauréat*. And maybe something will work out with my passport. If not, it's not the end of my life, is it?"

"No," agreed Dave numbly.

"Anyway, we'll think of something else. Maybe between the two of us, we can come up with some new strategy." Lateef's enthusiasm seemed intended to convince himself as much as to convince Dave. "And in the meantime, let's really enjoy our trip to the South. I've hardly ever been outside Aïn El Qamar. We'll have a great time!"

Now Dave was really beginning to think he had imagined the aborted love scene with Lateef.

"I've got a few things to take care of before we leave," said the Moroccan. "But I'll be by early tomorrow morning, all packed and ready for departure, okay?"

"Sure," said Dave. "I'll be expecting you."

"Okay, so …" Lateef seemed antsy to be on his way. "I'll see you tomorrow morning, all right."

"See you tomorrow morning," replied Dave.

Lateef smiled his usual radiant smile, leaned over to kiss Dave on both cheeks in his usual friendly, non-sexual way, and then he was gone.

Dave got up and walked over to the window, looking out at Lateef's departing figure, watching him until he was out of sight.

What had it all meant?

If the response of Lateef's lips to his own had indeed not been a figment of his imagination, what had it all meant?

Could it be that Lateef was coming to a new awareness of his feelings for Dave? Had the Moroccan's insistence on his heterosexuality been merely a vain attempt to convince himself that he was not interested in Dave in a romantic and physical way? Was he now ready to admit that his feelings for his American friend ran much deeper?

Lateef had once been turned on enough to have intercourse with Dave. And today, he had started to kiss him back in a decidedly non-platonic way.

Was it possible that Lateef had wanted sex with Dave last June, not because he considered Dave a temporary substitute for a woman, but because it was Dave himself that he desired? Was Lateef's problem not that girls like his childhood sweetheart Naïma were unavailable, but that he did not desire them in the first place?

Perhaps the next two weeks would reveal the answers to these questions.

In any case, for the first time in months, Dave began to feel hopeful about his relationship with Lateef.

Despite the results of the *conseil de classe* today …

Despite the uncertainty of Lateef's ever being granted a passport …

Despite Lateef's insistence that he was not gay …

Despite all of this, Dave could not help feeling a new and unexpected optimism about the future.

CHAPTER 11

▼

The dream still haunted him, even now, months later. He could no longer remember the Greek girl's face, but the image of her naked body entwined with Marcie's remained. He told himself that he had only imagined it, that it had been the result of intense fatigue and a confused brain. Why then was he unable to erase it from his mind?

The image obsessed Jean-Richard. He could not see Marcie at school without remembering that he had imagined her having sex with the Greek girl. He wondered if she could sense that there was something amiss between them, something holding him away from her. At times, when she looked at him, there seemed to be an expression close to pity in her eyes.

Jean-Richard often recalled that evening when she had told him of her arrival in Morocco. She had been so vibrant, so full of passion for her new life that he had wanted to share in her excitement, to accept from her some of the joy that had gone out of him. But she had questioned him about France, and he had shut himself off from her warmth.

Later that same evening at her house, when he had tried to rekindle the spark that had momentarily brought them so close, Marcie had again broken the spell by mentioning her fiancé. Jean-Richard still could not think of that moment without anger and jealousy. And this too troubled him. He had not once been jealous of a woman in his ten years in Aïn El Qamar. Why should it matter that she was engaged? It wasn't as if ...

Whatever the reason for his feelings, Jean-Richard had kept his distance from Marcie during the past two months, not wanting to give her the chance to penetrate the armor that shielded him from hurt and betrayal. He had tried his best to think about her dispassionately, and at times he felt he had succeeded in putting her out of his mind.

But had he really been successful? If so, then why did her presence beside him now in this late afternoon *conseil de classe* excite and trouble him so greatly that he was unable to concentrate on the reading of his students' names and grades, that he had to be called upon to give an opinion, and that even when this happened, he responded as if he had been awakened from a deep sleep, as was the case at this moment.

"Monsieur Moreau!" the voice of the *proviseur* was saying. Jean-Richard brought himself back to the present, back to the office of Monsieur Rhazwani where the final *conseil* of the trimester was being held, where Jean-Richard as the *professeur de sciences naturelles* and Marcie as the class's English teacher had found themselves sitting side by side.

"Monsieur Moreau, *faites attention!*"

"*Pardon, monsieur,*" apologized Jean-Richard. "You were saying?"

"What about Chafik?" Monsieur Rhazwani asked again.

"*Tableau d'honneur en sciences naturelles,*" said Jean-Richard. "An excellent student."

Marcie was looking at Jean-Richard. She seemed concerned about his distant, distracted manner. "Are you all right?" she whispered.

"*Bien sûr!*" answered Jean-Richard a bit too sharply. He wanted out of the *conseil* and away from this girl who seemed to radiate light and joy.

"The next student is Abderrahim Drissi ..." The *proviseur* continued down the list of names until he reached number thirty-eight, the last student on the list, and the *conseil* was over. Finally, thought Jean-Richard, finally I can get out of here! He nearly bolted from the *proviseur*'s office into the now darkened courtyard.

But Marcie would not let him go. Catching up with him, she took his arm. "What's wrong, Jean-Richard?" she asked. "Are you ill?"

He jerked his arm away from her grasp. "I told you before that it was nothing," he insisted. "So just leave me in peace!"

Jean-Richard left a bewildered Marcie standing open-mouthed as he hurtled across the courtyard towards his waiting car. He could hear her calling something behind him, but he refused to listen. All he could think of was the touch of her hand on his arm. And of the way it had nearly burned him.

I must escape from this place, this town, this country, Jean-Richard told himself as he turned on his headlights and drove from the parking lot. If I don't have a complete change of scene, I'll lose my mind.

It wasn't only Marcie. This past trimester had been a living hell. Constantly having to cope with the incompetent and often stoned lab assistant who had never bothered to learn his duties properly had worn Jean-Richard out. One day, when things were going particularly badly, the *proviseur* had chosen to inspect him. He had not been impressed, he said afterwards, and Jean-Richard had had the overwhelming desire to strangle the man then and there. But he had done nothing. Maintaining his job meant not making waves, even at the price of his dignity and self-respect.

At least now he was going to have a couple of weeks of temporary escape. The morning after tomorrow night's party at his house he would be on a plane heading towards the Canary Islands, which lay off the Moroccan coast but were a Spanish possession. For ten days he would be able to feel himself worlds removed from Aïn El Qamar and school, and from the troubling presence of Marcie Nelson.

If only he didn't have to go to the party tomorrow night! But Claudette had insisted on his being there. "It's going to be held at your own house, for God's sake!" she had exclaimed, and Jean-Richard had not been able to refuse his closest friend. Still, how could he stand having to look at Marcie all evening, so fresh, so beautiful, so unaware of life …

Jean-Richard had been driving through Aïn El Qamar for nearly five minutes, seeing nothing of his surroundings, and he was startled now to find himself heading out of town. He felt a moment of near panic. Had he let his brain become so clouded by his recent problems that he didn't even know where he was going? Then, suddenly, he remembered his destination and the fear passed. Jean-Richard's plane ticket for the Canary Islands was ready and waiting for him at the Hotel El Qamar according to the phone call the school had received today, and he was requested to pick it up without delay.

As Jean-Richard approached the hotel now, a car sped past him returning in the direction of Aïn El Qamar. It was a Renault 12, and in the light from his headlamps Jean-Richard caught a glimpse of Claudette at the wheel with Fareed, the tennis pro, riding next to her.

As usual! thought Jean-Richard in disgust as he pulled into the parking lot of the modern tourist hotel. Claudette's behavior had, in the two months since she began her liaison with Fareed, become a public scandal. She was seen with him constantly, at the hotel restaurant, at the post office, at the Epicérie Mondiale, her arms around him, sometimes kissing him on the cheek, sometimes even on the lips. Claudette was throwing away years spent protecting her good name. And for what? It was true that she was already several years past forty, but with her style and personality and gift for life, there would always be men attracted to her. Was Claudette willing to risk everything that she had achieved just for the companionship of a man like Fareed?

Claudette claimed that Fareed loved her, but did she really believe this? If so, why did she feel the need to shower him with gifts—rings, and clothes, and even an expensive new stereo system? And why was it she who paid for everything when they went away on their weekend trips to Marrakesh or Casa? It was obvious to Jean-Richard that she felt it necessary to buy the man's affections, and he worried about what would happen when the tennis pro tired of her—long before she tired of him, Jean-Richard was sure.

A cold silence hung in the air between the two formerly close friends these days. Jean-Richard avoided conversations with Claudette, knowing that they would lead to arguments. He spent most of his time upstairs in his room rather than be with the two lovers, who were either in the downstairs living room or next door to it having audible sex in Claudette's bedroom. He occasionally would come down during the hour of aperitifs, but only because Fareed left when there were French visitors. Apparently he felt uncomfortable under their hostile gaze, although he seemed to delight in parading his conquest in front of other Moroccans when he and Claudette were out in public together.

As today …

Jean-Richard recalled the speeding Renault 12 he had just seen leaving the Hotel El Qamar, where he now sat parked, and he wondered how long this impossible situation would last. Oh God, let it be over soon! he thought as he turned off the headlights and got out of his Fiat.

As Jean-Richard walked towards the hotel entrance, he could hear Christmas music coming from within. There was even a tall, brightly-decorated tree in the spacious lobby. But it didn't feel like Christmas to the Frenchman. With both Claudette and Marcie causing him such misery, it had never felt less like Christmas in his life.

The desk clerk was apparently new to Aïn El Qamar, for he did not recognize Jean-Richard. "*Un billet d'avion pour les Canaries?*" he asked. "Yes, I did notice a ticket for the Canary Islands. *Une minute, s'il vous plaît.*" The man returned a moment later with Jean-Richard's ticket. "*Votre carte d'étranger, s'il vous plaît,*" he asked, and Jean-Richard handed him the pocket-sized green identification booklet that all foreigners were required to carry. Satisfied that this was indeed Monsieur Jean-Richard Moreau, citizen of France and resident of Aïn El Qamar, Morocco, the clerk presented him his ticket. Departure would be from the Marrakesh airport in two days' time, at 10:35 a.m. Jean-Richard wrote the man a check on his Moroccan bank account, and accepted the ticket. Just looking at it made him feel more cheerful. It was his passport away from the unpleasantness of the past two months.

As he was leaving the lobby, in strode Dominique Moulin, who walked past him without a glance, the inevitable cigarette between her lips. Jean-Richard knew that she had never forgiven him for his lack of interest after their one-night stand. That liaison had been so brief and painless to end. Why couldn't he feel about Marcie as he did about her? Things would be so much simpler.

As Jean-Richard went out into the early darkness, he heard Dominique ask for her plane ticket to France. So she too needed to escape, thought Jean-Richard, as he got back into his car for the return drive to Aïn El Qamar.

Claudette's Renault was parked out front of their house when he arrived. He wondered if Fareed was inside. He didn't see the man's new motorcycle—was that also a gift from Claudette?—so he supposed that he had left, thank God.

Inside, Saadia, their longtime maid, was working in the kitchen. At first, Jean-Richard wondered what she was doing here so late in the day, then realized that she was probably helping to prepare for the big fête tomorrow evening.

Saadia beckoned to him from the kitchen and he joined her. The maid was not her usual cheerful self this evening, Jean-Richard thought. She looked worried about something. My God, he realized, she's been crying!

"Has anything happened?" he asked the woman. In years, she was doubtless closer to his own age than Claudette's, but she looked at least fifty. Life had not been easy for her, scrounging to make enough money to feed and clothe her children—her husband had divorced her years ago and she was their sole support. Despite her troubles she remained a cheerful optimistic woman, and Jean-Richard wondered what had upset her so.

"*C'est mademoiselle!*" she said. "Oh, Monsieur Jean-Richard. *Quelle honte!* Miss Claudette's become such a disgraceful woman! She's throwing her life away. She's … she …" The maid was in tears and unable to continue. Jean-Richard reached for his handkerchief and handed it to her.

"*Assieds-toi,* Saadia," he said sympathetically. "Sit down and talk to me about it."

"I'm just worried sick about Miss Claudette," said the maid through her sobs. "I know she's done foolish things in the past, but this time … She's never done anything like this before! Everybody in town is talking about her, Monsieur Jean-Richard, and saying the most terrible things. They're calling her *la putain française*, the French whore! No one respects her anymore. They think she's trash! And do you know how that makes me feel? Mademoiselle Claudette's like a sister to me, and I cry all the time now thinking about what she's doing to herself. But when I beg her to stop, to think about what other people will say, she just laughs. Now I'm trying to get ready for this big party, and I can't think about what I'm supposed to be doing. I can't think about anything except Mademoiselle Claudette!"

Jean-Richard had never before heard Saadia make such a long speech. Never before had she uttered more than a few sentences at a time, and he was surprised and touched by the depth of her feelings towards Claudette, towards both of them, he supposed.

"I'll try and talk to her too, Saadia," he said reassuringly, though he didn't know if it would do any good.

"*Merci*, Monsieur Jean-Richard," she said. "I'll be getting back to my work now. If you'll excuse me."

Jean-Richard nodded and, leaving the kitchen, went into the living room to wait for Claudette. He had been there for at least twenty minutes when she finally came into the room wearing a low-cut clingy green dress, her thick auburn hair hanging wildly to her shoulders

"*Alors*, we meet for a change," she said. "I am surprised not to find you upstairs hiding." Claudette made no move to sit down, but remained standing by the door. "To what do I owe the honor?"

"*Arrête*, Claudette!" exclaimed Jean-Richard. "The innocent act doesn't work on me. I know you too well."

"I have no idea what you're talking about," said Claudette.

"Don't play games with me. If I'm downstairs for a change, it's because it's time for us to talk about the way you've chosen to destroy yourself in front of the people who care about you, and everyone else in this town for that matter. God, don't you realize that when this absurd affair is over, you'll be left with nothing!"

"Who says it's going to end?" said Claudette defensively. "Fareed loves me. You have no idea how many times he's told me so."

"Yes, I'm sure … like the time you bought him that fourteen carat gold ring, and the time you paid for the brand new stereo system, and all the times he's had all-expenses-paid vacations in Marrakesh and Casa and wherever the hell else you've taken him, I'm sure he told you he loved you and proved it too—in bed. But God, do you have to humiliate yourself again and again just for a fuck? How low can you sink?"

Claudette looked at him in fury. "I've known you for ten years, Jean-Richard, but I've never realized what a despicable, vulgar man you can be. I've known you to be cold … and unfeeling … and I've seen how many women you've hurt, but

I had no idea you could be so cruel and vicious. How does it feel to be a man with a block of ice in place of a heart!"

"That's unfair and you know it!" shouted Jean-Richard. "Damn it, Claudette, I can't help who I am, and you of all people ought to understand that."

"Yes, I know all about your dirty laundry, Jean-Richard," spat out Claudette. "I know all about what happened to you in Paris ten years ago, and I know how much it still tortures you."

"Then why dredge it up tonight?" asked Jean-Richard.

"Because after the filthy insinuations you've made about Fareed, you deserve to suffer, you bastard! You only want to destroy my happiness because you're incapable of it yourself. Well, let me tell you, Jean-Richard, if you say another word to me against Fareed, I'll make you hurt like you've never hurt before!"

Jean-Richard wanted to answer her, wanted to scream back that she was being inhuman and unjust and even sadistic, but the words would not come. He could only sit there in silence, looking at her, knowing the horrible truth of her words, and unable to respond.

Fortunately for both of them, the silence was broken by the ringing of the doorbell.

"That's Fareed now," said Claudette. "If you don't want to see him, I suggest that you go up to your room."

Jean-Richard got up and stalked past Claudette into the entry hall, but when he reached the foot of the stairs leading to his bedroom, he could not find the power to take even the first step up. The house was surrounding him, enclosing him, the walls pressing nearer and nearer. It was ten years ago in Paris, and the stairs led to an apartment door behind which … Oh God, he had to get out!

Pulling the front door open, he came face to face with Fareed, dressed in an expensive and obviously new sport jacket. "Your meal ticket is waiting for you," he sneered, and pushed past the Moroccan into the chill night air. His hands were trembling, but not from the cold, and he wondered if he had the strength to stand. Staggering over to his car, he stumbled in and jerked it into motion. He had to get away, he had to go somewhere, anywhere!

Jean-Richard drove and drove, unaware of his direction, unaware of the pedestrians that he nearly ran over, knowing only that he had to get as far as he could from the memories Claudette had stirred up within him.

He had been a fool to try and reason with her. She was beyond common sense. All she could do was lash back at him with her own accusations. Jean-Richard wondered if he could ever forgive her.

Certainly, now, all he wanted to do was rid himself of the image of her accusatory green eyes and the mouth which had spat out such venom. He had to find peace, somewhere, away from the pain of his own past and the scandal of Claudette's present. He had to find …

Jean-Richard discovered that he had instinctively driven in the direction of Marcie's house, that without realizing it, he was almost there.

Marcie. Marcie.

Her name echoed inside his tortured brain. She alone would be able to illuminate his darkened spirit. She alone could erase the torments of his past.

Jean-Richard stopped his car in front of her door, summoned his courage, and got out.

CHAPTER 12

▼

The wine and the candlelight and the music had gone to her head, and now, as Claudette sat gazing across the dinner table at Fareed, she thought: At last I have found the man I have been searching for since I first became aware of love's existence. Fareed was so strong, so virile; he made her feel beautiful and desired. He never failed to be near her when she needed him. He satisfied her sexual hunger as no man ever had before.

He was gazing at her now, with that deeply erotic look in his eyes that said, "You excite me and you please me and I want you."

"What are you thinking, *mon amour?*" she asked softly.

"You'll find out."

"You don't mind that I sent Saadia home early and cooked for you myself?" asked Claudette.

"The meal was delicious," replied Fareed, and she could almost hear him add, "as delicious as you."

Oh God, she loved him so, and needed him. She would do anything for him. Anything to keep him with her always.

"I have prepared a special dessert for you, *chéri,*" she announced. "Wait here and I'll bring it to you."

Claudette cleared the table of the dinner things—she had made her scrumptious mushroom omelet—and returned from the kitchen with two crystal bowls of chocolate mousse and a large one of fresh whipped cream.

"*Mousse au chocolat!*" she announced. "*Ma spécialité.* I prepared it just for you."

She sat down and gave him one of the crystal bowls, taking the other for herself. She was about to spoon out some whipped cream onto his mousse when she suddenly changed her mind. "We'll save that for later," she said, "for the *pièce de résistance.*"

"And what might that be?" asked Fareed, but Claudette merely smiled. Sticking her finger into her mousse, she held it up to Fareed's mouth. He licked it off.

"*C'est délicieux,*" he said.

"Not half as delicious as what comes next," hinted Claudette provocatively.

Fareed ate his mousse with obvious pleasure, and when he had finished, Claudette put the two empty bowls on the sideboard behind her.

At the other end of the room, a new record fell down onto the turntable and the sensuous voice of Véronique Sanson filled the room singing "*Amoureuse.*"

"She sings my feelings," said Claudette. "I can never never regret the moments we have shared. I pray only that they will last forever."

Claudette leaned over the table and began unbuttoning Fareed's shirt. "Take off all your clothes," she said. "I want to see you naked in the candlelight."

As Fareed obeyed her, Claudette unfastened her green dress and let it slide to the floor. She was wearing nothing underneath.

They stood looking at each other's nude bodies across the table in the dimly lit room. Then Claudette lay down supine on the tablecloth, her face looking up invitingly at Fareed's.

"Now you can have the whipped cream," she whispered. "Spoon some on me. I am your dessert."

Fareed eagerly took her suggestion and began to drop the whipped cream onto Claudette's full round breasts. He spread it around with his fingers, and she moaned at the feel of the smooth silky cream and Fareed's tender but demanding hands.

"*Je suis ton dessert,*" she reminded him. "So don't just touch me. I'm tasty too."

Claudette felt herself shiver with pleasure as Fareed's mouth descended on her breasts, sucking, licking, massaging, as his tongue spooned up the thick sugary cream.

"I've never tasted anything like this before," he said.

"Put some topping on my pussy, and see how that tastes," suggested Claudette.

Fareed covered the triangle with mounds of the white whipped cream and buried his face in it. Claudette could feel his hungry mouth suck in the tantalizing mixture of the cream and her own sex juices. His tongue plunged deep within her, making tiny circles around her tenderest tissues.

"Oh God! Oh God!" she moaned. Fareed was once again bringing her to the peaks of ecstasy. She felt herself coming in orgasm after orgasm. "Now!" she screamed. "Fuck me now!"

Fareed climbed on the table atop her. He thrust his waiting cock into her wet whipped-creamy pussy, filling her with his love.

"Fareed! Fareed!" she cried. "Never leave me! Never!"

Claudette was alone now in her bathroom, showering after the rapturous interlude with Fareed. The water cascaded down over her breasts, soothing them after the bruising passion of Fareed's mouth. Fareed, she thought. *Je t'aime tellement*! Oh how much I love you!

He was waiting for her in the living room now with something important to tell her, he said. Well, it had to be something wonderful, thought Claudette. All of Fareed's gifts to her were wonderful. And the greatest of them all was making her feel young again.

How terrible it had been to look in the mirror and see breasts that were no longer as firm and proud as they once had been, to see hips that were getting broader and legs that were no longer so smooth and sleek. How terrible to see those tiny lines around the eyes and mouth, to feel the looseness of the skin under the chin. How terrible to feel herself growing older and yet incapable of doing anything about it.

Well, if Claudette couldn't help herself, at least Fareed had been able to, with his attention and his kindness and his love.

Yes, love, damn it, in spite of what Jean-Richard had said. Fareed did love Claudette, and if she chose to return his love by giving him things which she knew would please him, then that was her affair and no one else's. It was her way of repaying Fareed for the precious gift he had given her. Because of him she was a girl again, and more sure of herself than any beauty treatment or cosmetic surgeon's knife could ever have made her.

So what if she kissed him in public! What was so wrong about kissing the man you loved more than life itself?

So what if she paid for their trips together! She earned more than he did, and it was absurd to pretend otherwise simply in order to please a town full of narrow-minded bigots. She was still the queen of Aïn El Qamar society; her house was still its palace. Tomorrow it would be filled with people who could have left on holiday, but had chosen to remain an extra day in order to be able to say that they had attended Miss Claudette Verlaine's exclusive *soirée de Noël*.

Her reputation was intact, would remain intact! All that was new in her life was what she had denied herself so foolishly for ten long years, a man who was wholly and completely her own, yesterday, today, and forever!

Fareed was sitting in the living room smoking when she came back in feeling fresh and clean from her shower, wearing a black silk dressing gown. She knelt in front of him and encircled his waist with her arms, laying her head against his chest, feeling the strength of his body and the beating of his heart.

"I'll never tire of you, *mon amour*," she whispered.

Fareed pushed her away from him with both hands.

"Is something wrong, *chéri*?" she asked in concern.

Only now did Claudette notice that the lights had been turned on and that the music had stopped. What had happened to the romantic atmosphere of only minutes before? And why was Fareed suddenly so distant?

"I said I had something to tell you," he was saying, his voice glacial.

Claudette looked into Fareed's eyes, the same eyes that minutes ago had drunk in her beauty and held such warmth and adoration, or so she had thought. They were indifferent now, and cold. Oh God! she cried within. This can't be happening!

But he seemed unaware of her distress. Rising from the *banquette* to stand above her, he calmly and dispassionately announced his decision to leave Aïn El Qamar.

"No!" she screamed, a cry of shock and despair that tore through the room. Oh God, she couldn't believe what he was saying. It couldn't be true that he was moving to distant Tangier for a new job in a resort hotel, and that he was leaving this very evening! It couldn't be true that he was discarding her like a piece of old rubbish!

Claudette threw her arms around his knees and held on for dear life, imploring him not to leave.

"I'll do anything! Anything!" she cried. "Whatever you want, it's yours. Just tell me what I can give you."

"My freedom," he said simply.

"Your what?" murmured Claudette numbly.

"Let me make this crystal clear. Until now, I've been up for sale to the highest bidder, which happened in this case to be you. But I'm tired of Aïn El Qamar and I need to get out. And to tell the truth, Claudette, I'm even more tired of you!"

"But you told me you loved me!" protested Claudette. "You said that you needed me and that you'd never get enough of me."

"Those were your words, '*mon amour*,' not mine," said Fareed. "You were hearing your own echo."

"*Oh Dieu!*" screamed Claudette. "Don't let this happen! Fareed! My love! My life! I can't go on without you! Stay with me! Stay with me forever!"

"Forever?" Fareed was incredulous. "In your dreams, lady! I'm saying good-bye right now, and *that's* forever! So good-bye, Claudette. And good riddance!"

"You son of a bitch!" shrieked Claudette.

Fareed was already on his way out. Lurching to her feet, Claudette reached him as he was nearly at the door.

"Are you deaf?" asked Fareed, turning to face her one last time. "Well, let me spell it out in words that you can understand. You, '*chérie*', are an aging faded joke! And I stopped laughing a long time ago."

"Bastard!" screeched Claudette, reaching for his face and drawing her sharp fingernails down his cheek. Blood oozed from where she had scratched him.

"Cunt!"

Suddenly, she felt the back of Fareed's hand strike her jaw and the next minute she was lying on her back, staring up at his sneering face.

"I hope you die!" Claudette shouted, hatred in her voice.

"Go to hell, bitch," replied Fareed, and strode out of the room.

She spat after his retreating figure, then collapsed in sobs that wracked her body and blocked out the slamming of the door.

Oh God, they had all been right! Fareed had been taking advantage of her and lying to her and making a fool out of her. Why hadn't she listened to her friends' warnings? How had she let herself get into such a situation? Now she was left with nothing. The love she had thought she felt for Fareed had died the moment she had realized the brutal truth. And all that remained in its place was bitterness and hatred, towards Fareed and towards herself.

Yes, she hated herself now, hated what she had become. A woman past her youth who had paid with her money and her self-respect for the illusion of love.

Slowly, painfully, Claudette rose to her feet, her head still swimming from Fareed's blow. She staggered over to the sideboard where a bottle of whiskey stood. Unscrewing the cap, she raised the bottle to her lips and took one long deep swallow, feeling the liquor burn her throat.

Fareed had been telling her the truth when he had called her old. She was nearly forty-five, for God's sake, the bloom of her twenties and thirties and even half of her forties a thing of the past. No longer was she young enough to be desirable to men, or at least to the kind of men she wished to be desirable to. Fareed was right to insinuate that the only love she could expect from now on was the kind that had to be bought.

And so now what do you do, Claudette? she asked herself. What in the name of God do you do?

Perhaps she should just give up, just give up and go into hiding. Accept the fact that from now on, her life would be nothing but an empty desolate shell of what it once was. That just might be the easiest solution.

"And the most cowardly!" Claudette cried aloud. "No, damn it! I will *not* give up! And I won't live a sexless sterile life either! If I have to pay for sex and the illusion of love, then so be it!

"I'm damned if I'm going to spend the rest of the evening here, a solitary self-pitying drunk. I'll show you Fareed! I'll show you that you can't destroy me! I'm resilient, do you hear me! I will not crawl into a hole and die!"

Claudette had seen the virile young men who congregated around the bar and *discothèque* at the Hotel El Qamar each night. Surely, a generous gift would be persuasion enough for at least some of them. Well, if they were for sale, as Fareed had been, then she was willing to buy. But no more commitments. No more fidelity to one man alone. Emotional involvement was a thing of the past. She was available. And ready … for all the men she could have.

"I will not sleep alone tonight!" she cried. Nor would she be alone at her party tomorrow night. She would be making love to some muscular young stud every night of the coming vacation, and the more different men the better. She was no poverty case. She could afford them.

"I'll show the world I'm not defeated," she swore.

No, God damn it! Miss Claudette Verlaine was never defeated!

CHAPTER 13

▼

Marcie had so much news to tell that she had decided to write one letter now and another after tomorrow's *Aïd El Kébir* celebration and the party at Claudette's.

She was sitting at the desk which she had bought just a few weeks earlier after searching for ages it seemed. It was no fine piece of furniture, but she liked its sturdy construction and after she herself had varnished it, the grain of the wood shone through and made it an attractive addition to her house.

Last week she had finally surrendered and bought a *butagaz* heater after feeling the rooms grow colder and colder as autumn progressed. It had taken a large chunk of her savings, but since she would be staying with a friend and not in hotels during vacation, it was worth the expense just to be warm for a change.

So now, after a quick after-school snack, she sat in comfort at her new desk and tried to compose a letter to the man to whom she was still officially engaged, but who had become more a name at the top of a page than someone she truly loved.

"Dear Eddy," she wrote. "These past few days have been the most exciting so far in what has been the most incredible experience of my life, exploring the many worlds of Morocco and of Aïn El Qamar.

"Classes have ended and today my final *conseil de classe* took place. I felt so proud to be sitting among my colleagues, knowing that I was a professional member of the school faculty myself. While it is true that many of the French teachers have negative attitudes or insufficient training to teach successfully, there are a good number of exceptions who make me feel that I truly am a teacher, and not just a crazy American off in some strange country.

"Unfortunately Monsieur Rhazwani, was as mean and harsh as usual. I don't think he likes anyone, students, teachers, or his fellow administrators. So far I've been one of the few faculty members to escape his scrutiny. I just try to be nice to him and hope that some of my friendliness will rub off, although I'm afraid this will be a losing battle.

"Anyway, to change the subject, tomorrow is the *Aïd El Kébir*, which by the way means 'big holiday.' This holiday celebrates the day that Abraham, who was willing to show his love for God by sacrificing his own son, was told by God that he had proven his devotion and could sacrifice a sheep instead. It surprised me at first that this same story should be both in our Bible and in their Koran, but I've since learned that parts of the Koran are similar to or the same as the Bible.

"In any case, each Moroccan family buys a sheep, and performs a ritual sacrifice by cutting the animal's throat. This of course gives them enough meat for the rest of the week, and each day is in itself a celebration.

"Tomorrow I'm going to Halima's house to observe the sacrifice and today we picked up the sheep at the *souk*, by far the biggest *souk* ever. I've never seen so many stands and displays and tents—and people of course. As always there were the fruit and vegetable merchants who make the rounds of the weekly *souks* in this area, and those that sell kitchen supplies, or spices, or shoes, or fabric, or jewelry. The displays of produce were as colorful today as always, with all the different fruits and vegetables arranged in neat piles before the merchants.

"It was terribly muddy there today after a lot of rain last night, but the sky was clear and it was almost warm, so no one was complaining. The *souk* grounds are located below the level of the town itself, so that looking up you could first see Aïn El Qamar, and then the famous *qsar* on a hill behind it, and in the distance, the snow-capped Atlas. Forgetful Marcie had left her camera at home, so that picture will remain preserved only in my memory. It's such a beautiful one, though, that I don't think it'll fade away.

"I still can't get over the number of sheep at the *souk*. There were literally thousands of them, wherever you looked, and of course you could smell them too! Poor Halima (and she is poor in both senses of the word) could only afford to buy the scrawniest of animals, and still it must have set her back a great deal. She bargained and bargained, but the demand is so high that the sheep owners are able to stick to what they are asking. The maid is unaware of the economics of the situation and could only complain that things were just getting more and more expensive and couldn't the King do something about it?

"You should have seen the two of us parading through town leading that sheep by a length of rope. Just imagine what the American tourists on their rest stop at the bus station must have thought. A veiled Moroccan woman and a blonde foreigner walking a sheep down the boulevard? We must have made a strange sight!

"Anyway, tomorrow is the big day. The *Aïd* at Halima's and then the long-awaited party at Claudette's and Jean-Richard's house, but I'll write you about that once the excitement is over, maybe from Fez where I'll be spending a week with Judy Murata, my friend from training who lives there.

"Take care of yourself and (I almost forgot) Merry Christmas! (Christmas seems worlds away here.)

"As always,

"Marcie"

Marcie folded the pages she had filled with her careful handwriting and placed them in an airmail envelope. She would drop it in the mailbox tomorrow.

Suddenly feeling an urge for coffee, Marcie went into the kitchen to put a kettle of water on the stove to boil. Then, as her new *butagaz* heater only could heat a single room and the kitchen was chilly on this December evening, she hurried back into the living room.

Pulling over a leather *pouf*, she sat in front of the heater, staring at the burning orange plaques which radiated welcome heat.

She had signed the letter to Eddy "as always," which seemed appropriate since her feelings for him remained as they always had been. Unfortunately, she was beginning to realize that such feelings were not enough to base a marriage on. Naturally, she did not tell Eddy this, preferring to dwell on safer topics, such as her day-to-day life in Aïn El Qamar.

Another subject she did not mention was Jean-Richard and the troubling whirlpool of emotions she felt surrounding the man. She certainly could not speak of the way she had been unable to concentrate on the goings-on at today's *conseil* because of Jean-Richard's disquieting presence beside her. She had both relished his nearness and feared the dangerous depth of this relish, dangerous because of what she knew about the Frenchman.

Jean-Richard's reputation was clear and widespread, and it didn't matter that she sensed that he was a deeper and more complex individual that most would admit, she still was afraid of what might happen if she gave in to her feelings. She had not come to Morocco to become some lothario's bed partner for one night, and the facts were indisputable. In his ten years in Aïn El Qamar, Jean-Richard's affairs had never lasted longer than the briefest of periods. Who was she, Marcie Nelson, to think that she might be the exception? No, it was better to keep her distance.

Not that Jean-Richard had appeared particularly attentive to her lately. He seemed to be avoiding encounters with her as much as she was with him. Perhaps that meant that he had lost interest in her, though at times she caught him staring at her and wondered if he was all that indifferent. What was the mystery of his character? He was so complex, she didn't know if she would ever be able to unravel him, but then again, did she really want to take the chance and try?

Today, he had seemed almost ill in the *conseil*, but when she had tried to find out the reason, he had quite literally run away from her. What was troubling him so, and worse than that, why was she still thinking of him almost constantly?

Perhaps this vacation, and some good heart-to-heart talks with Judy, would help her to straighten out her thoughts. Maybe ...

Suddenly, two things were happening at once. The doorbell was ringing and the kettle of water was whistling to be removed from the flame.

Marcie ran to the door and there of all people stood Jean-Richard. Hardly giving herself time to feel shock at his unexpected arrival, Marcie told him to come in, come in, then ran back to the kitchen to turn off the burner.

Returning to the living room, she found the Frenchman sitting on a *banquette* and staring into space with an expression of near desolation on his face.

She hurried over and sat opposite him. "What's happened, Jean-Richard?" she asked in concern.

Jean-Richard seemed not to have heard her question. He said in an almost expressionless voice, "You've made some changes here. You only used to have one *banquette*."

All right, thought Marcie. If you don't want to talk about what's on your mind, we'll have it your way.

"That was months ago," she answered. "I bought this one soon after your visit, when I'd gotten paid for the month. And the desk and heater are new too. Slowly but surely things are coming together."

"You have good taste, Marcie."

"I have some coffee almost ready," offered Marcie. "Let me get you some."

"Don't bother," said Jean-Richard.

"It's no trouble," said Marcie. "I was making some for myself anyway."

She left the room and went to the kitchen. As she prepared two cups of Nescafé, she thought: I've seen Jean-Richard withdrawn and distant before, but never like this. The man is suffering but he refuses to admit it. Well, if he just wants someone to talk to, I guess I can be as good a listener as anyone else.

Jean-Richard looked up as she reentered the living room carrying a tray with the coffee things.

"You didn't need to do that," he said.

"Don't you listen, Jean-Richard?" replied Marcie, setting down the tray. "I told you I was having some. Didn't you hear the kettle whistling when you arrived?"

"I didn't notice."

"Well, have some coffee. I made it strong. You look like you could use some."

Jean-Richard accepted a cup from Marcie and took a gulp of the strong hot coffee.

He grimaced. "*Il n'y a pas de sucre!*" he exclaimed.

"*Oh pardon!*" laughed Marcie. "You have to add sugar yourself, American style. I take mine without." She was pleased that the missing sugar had unexpectedly lightened the atmosphere.

"*Vous, les Américains, vous êtes bizarres,*" said Jean-Richard, and Marcie could perceive the first trace of a smile.

"Not any stranger than you French are," she countered.

As Jean-Richard sipped from his cup, Marcie kept telling herself: Don't pry. Don't let your natural curiosity get the best of you. Don't start asking him questions.

Strangely enough, though, it was Jean-Richard who began to speak unbidden.

"I had to get out. Things are pretty bad between Claudette and me. We've been avoiding each other, but tonight I made the mistake of trying to talk with her."

"I see," said Marcie understandingly. "I was just thinking about Claudette earlier this evening. I don't know her well, but I admire her, or at least I did at first. Her behavior lately has seemed pretty self-destructive though."

"That's exactly it," said Jean-Richard. "She thinks that what she's doing is the solution to her troubles, but it's just the opposite. She's creating more problems than she's solving, and the new ones are worse than any she had before."

"And you told her this?" asked Marcie.

"I tried to, but she refused to listen. She simply refused. We started fighting almost like animals, tearing at each other with our words. We've had arguments in the past, but tonight … Tonight it was different. I was only trying to help, but she attacked me with something close to hatred."

"Perhaps she's afraid of the truth," suggested Marcie. "People can do such stupid things in order to avoid reality."

"You may be right," said Jean-Richard pensively, and she wondered if he was thinking only of Claudette. "But the truth is precisely what she needs in the long run. She's created a fantasy world and the day she finally realizes that it's nothing more than a fantasy, it may just be too late for her to accept the facts."

"Well, you can't blame yourself for trying to help, Jean-Richard. You were being a good friend, and if she chose not to listen, then that was her prerogative, and her mistake."

"I realize that," said Jean-Richard, and took another sip of his coffee. "But did she have to …?"

"Yes?" asked Marcie, wondering why Jean-Richard had stopped.

"*Ce n'est rien,*" he replied, and his face once again closed up. "It's really nothing. *Sans importance.*"

Marcie sensed that Jean-Richard had come close to confiding in her some of what was troubling him and had been troubling him for so long. But he had apparently thought twice, and the moment of near-revelation had passed.

Jean-Richard finished his coffee and stood up.

"You don't have to go," said Marcie impulsively. "It's nice having a guest for a change."

"But I'm imposing …"

"It's no imposition," insisted Marcie. "Please stay and keep me company."

"Thank you, I will" said Jean-Richard. "You're not the only one who's enjoying this visit."

Marcie walked over to her cassette player and put on a tape of Chopin's Nocturnes, which she often listened to while reading or correcting papers in the evenings. Then she returned to her seat. She was pleased that Jean-Richard had sought out her presence, and though she sensed the danger in his being so near, she did not want to see him leave. Besides, she was only having a simple conversation with the man.

Marcie spoke of her visit to the *souk* today and of returning to town with the maid's sheep in tow. She spoke of growing up in River Falls, Wisconsin, though she scrupulously avoided referring to Eddy. She spoke of her vacation plans, and of amusing classroom incidents, of her students' unintentional puns which she attempted to translate to Jean-Richard in French. She spoke of her invitation to spend the *Aïd* with Halima's family, and of her mixed feelings towards the sacrifice of the very sheep she had accompanied back to the maid's house today. She spoke …

As usual, Marcie told herself, you're talking too much, but when she mentioned this to Jean-Richard, he merely smiled and told her that she was being foolish and that she should go on.

When, finally, she looked at her watch, she saw in surprise that it was nearly ten o'clock. He had been here for hours. And yet the time had passed so quickly. She had not even thought about dinner.

"Would you like something to eat, Jean-Richard?" she asked. "No, don't say you're not hungry, because I'm sure you're as famished as I am. There's some left-over *tajine* in the kitchen, and I'm sure there's enough for two. You wait here and I'll go heat it up."

"*Oui, mademoiselle*," said Jean-Richard obediently. "It will be my pleasure to be your dinner guest."

An hour later, Marcie was standing at the living room door with Jean-Richard. It had been a lovely evening, she thought, really it had, and she had perhaps been wrong to think that the Frenchman was a threat to her. He was a kind, thoughtful man who merely needed a sympathetic friend and she felt flattered that he had chosen her to fill that role.

"*Merci*, Marcie," said Jean-Richard, and then chuckled at the rhyme in French.

"Not the ideal combination," agreed Marcie. "But then again, my parents had no idea when they named me that I'd be living in Morocco one day. You're not the first French person who's found it amusing."

"*Non*, Marcie," said Jean-Richard and laughed again. It sounded so much like "No, thank you" in French.

"Really," he continued. "When I offer you my thanks, I ought not to laugh. I'm grateful to you for making me feel so much better. This evening has been a refreshing change for me."

"If I've helped, I'm glad."

"You have," Jean-Richard assured her. "And now, perhaps I can return home a bit more cheerful than when I left. With luck, Claudette won't be in."

"Thank you for coming, Jean-Richard," said Marcie. "*Bonne nuit*."

Jean-Richard looked into her eyes and smiled. "*Bonne nuit*, Marcie," he said, and kissed her lightly on the lips. Then, as he was about to leave, he turned back to her and kissed her again, but this time his kiss was passionate and demanding. Marcie found herself kissing him back, feeling his lips at once tender and firm, experiencing sensations she had never before felt. Jean-Richard's arms were around her and she felt warm and needed and loved.

"Oh *chérie*," he said between kisses. "I want you."

He reached for the buttons of her blouse. Marcie knew she ought to protest, knew she ought to say, "But I'm not willing to be just another of your endless liaisons," but she was silent, accepting his kisses and caresses without opposition, returning them with equal fervor.

And then it happened.

He called her Nicole.

Oh God, thought Marcie. He wants to make love to me and he can't even keep me straight from the others.

She withdrew her arms from around his back, turned her face to one side, and pushed him away.

"I'm Marcie!" she cried. "*Je m'appelle Marcie!*"

Jean-Richard seemed uncomprehending. "I know who you are. You're the woman I want to make love to."

"Then why did you call me Nicole?"

The color suddenly drained from Jean-Richard's face. "I … I'm sorry Marcie. I'm so sorry."

"Being sorry doesn't help! I care about you Jean-Richard, but to you, I'm nothing but another name on an endless list of your conquests. And that's not good enough for me. Not good enough at all. So go ahead and enjoy your shallow life. Enjoy your meaningless one-night stands. Enjoy your party tomorrow night. Enjoy it without me. I won't be there."

"But Marcie, let me try to explain," pleaded Jean-Richard.

"No. Just get out of here and leave me alone!"

She could barely see Jean-Richard's shocked expression as he turned to leave. Her eyes were glazed with tears. She felt worn out from her angry words.

Marcie stumbled over to the *banquette* and collapsed upon it, her mind swimming with questions. Why had she reacted to Jean-Richard with such fury? What was the man's power over her that he could make her lose all control? What dear God was happening in her life?

Then, all at once, Marcie knew the answers to these questions. The truth was so simple that she was surprised never to have seen it before. She had fallen in love with the man. In spite of the things she had heard about Jean-Richard—and she knew that they were true—she had fallen in love with him, painfully, desperately in love.

I've got to get away from here, Marcie realized suddenly. I've got to get far away from Aïn El Qamar and from Jean-Richard. I need time to think, and I need to put distance between us in order to be able to do that.

Calmly, Marcie made up her mind. She would go to Halima's house tomorrow as planned, then be on the next bus leaving for Fez. This would mean missing the party she had been looking forward to for weeks now, but how could she possibly enjoy it with Jean-Richard's presence a constant reminder of her hopeless situation?

Yes, she would leave Aïn El Qamar tomorrow. She would go far away and attempt to sort out her thoughts. At the moment they were so confusing and conflicting that she didn't know where to begin her soul-searching. One thing was undeniable, however. Marcie knew with absolute certainty that despite the distance she was putting between herself and Jean-Richard, it would be impossible to forget the feel of his arms around her and the caress of his lips kissing hers. That was something she would carry with her for the rest of her life.

CHAPTER 14

▼

It had come as no surprise to Kevin, his inability to sleep last night. After all, today was going to be the most important day of his life. And the most fulfilling, he added to himself as he lay in his bed on this chilly December morning, countless thoughts racing through his head, memories of the distant and not so distant past, images of what he was sure was about to be.

He could see Jamey Morales's face, and it was as if he could hear Jamey's voice saying to him, "It's time for you to start loving again, Kev. You've mourned me long enough. Now, get on with your life."

Jamey, thought Kevin. I still love you and I always will, but I've found someone new, someone as wonderful as you were, and he and I are going to share the happiness I would have known with you if only things had been different.

Kevin now turned his thoughts to Kacem, the man who had given him new hope and a new reason for living. He owed everything to Kacem Hajiri. Because of him, he had come out of a black tunnel into the sunlight and had felt his life begin to fill with promise.

Damn Dave and his idiotic warnings! Who did he think he was to suggest that Kevin was only imagining Kacem's feelings for him! Hadn't Dave noticed the way Kacem smiled at Kevin whenever they met in the *salle des profs*? Hadn't Dave seen the warmth of the Moroccan's greeting whenever he stopped by at Dave and Kevin's at the latter's invitation? Those were not just friendly smiles! Such warmth could not be merely platonic! How could a love as strong as Kevin's be one-sided?

Dave had the audacity to suggest to Kevin that it was he who had invited himself to Kacem's farm for the *Aïd El Kébir* celebration. But he couldn't be more wrong! Kevin had only casually mentioned that he had missed the *Aïd* festivities the previous year (which was a lie, but what did that matter?). It was Kacem who had suggested that Kevin join his family for the holiday. Dave had no idea what he was talking about!

But he'd see. Just wait until Kevin came back from two glorious weeks spent traveling with Kacem. Then Dave would realize how wrong he'd been. Then he would eat his words.

Kevin had no doubt that Kacem would change his holiday plans in order to spend his vacation with Kevin. He could wire his friend in France that he was ill and ask him to come another time. No promise made to a mere friend could come before a commitment to a lover!

Kevin could already imagine the nights he and Kacem would be spending together, and the first of them would be this very evening. He would tell Kacem how he felt, just as he should have told Jamey if only he had not been so foolish, and Kacem would do as Jamey surely would have, declaring his own love for Kevin. Then the two of them would fall into each other's embrace, kissing passionately, eagerly ripping off the other's clothes. Naked in each other's arms, their two bodies would meet, and that would be the start of a lifetime of love and commitment that they would share with one another.

Suddenly, Kevin felt himself too excited and restless to stay in bed even a moment longer. Throwing off the blankets, he quickly made his bed, then tried to decide what he should pack. In theory, he was only staying overnight and returning tomorrow. Should he take enough for two weeks and seem obvious? No, he'd better just pack what would look normal. The farm was only half an hour from Aïn El Qamar, Kacem said. He could easily come back tomorrow and get the rest of the things he needed.

Kevin packed his overnight case, then went to the bathroom to wash and shave. Returning to his bedroom, he pulled on a pair of snug-fitting charcoal slacks and a black turtleneck sweater. Pretty sexy, he thought as he looked at the outfit in the mirror, and he knew that Kacem would think so too.

The light of a new day was beginning to enter the room through the cracks in the bedroom shutters. Kevin walked over to them, opened the windows, and threw back the shutters. The sky was once again cloudless, and Kevin supposed that today would be even warmer than yesterday had been. It would be a perfect sunny day and a beautiful romantic night.

A few children were already playing in the street in front of Kevin and Dave's house. They had obviously put on their best clothes which, although they were not of high quality, were clean and colorful. Even the little girls who usually looked rather unkempt were well-groomed. An older woman walked past the children wearing her *haïk* and veil. The children cried out joyously *"Aïd Mbrok! Mbarek l'Aïd!"* Happy Holiday! Happy *Aïd!* Two little boys began pretending that one was the sheep and the other the butcher. The first one got down on all fours and went "Baaaaaa Baaaaaa" while the other played at slitting his throat with an imaginary knife. Evidently these boys were not turned off by the gore of the slaughter. It was a part of their lives, as much as Christmas and Thanksgiving were a part of the lives of American children.

Kevin decided he couldn't wait inside even a second longer. There was a cafe by the bus station where he could sit until Kacem came. He put on a windbreaker against the morning chill and grabbed his overnight case. Quietly, so as not to awaken Dave, he closed the windows, turned off the heater and light, and hurried out to begin his walk to the station.

People were beginning to fill the streets. Children were standing outside the small *hanoots* buying little whistles or balloons with the few *ryals* that had been their holiday gift. Kevin passed one of his students who wished him a "Happy Holiday" in English and Kevin returned the greeting in Arabic. A young boy was dragging an unwilling sheep behind him—apparently a last minute purchase. It looked as though the animal knew what was coming and was uneager to accept its fate.

The bus station was much less crowded than usual. Most people had already returned home the day before, and few buses were in service today. As always, though, there was the smell of gasoline and oil and exhaust fumes, in spite of the fact that the buses waited in the open air. Kevin could hardly control his impatience to be on the old bus that ran the line from Aïn El Qamar to Douar El Ayash, the village where Kacem's family had their farm.

Kevin took a seat outside the station cafe and ordered a coke. Most of the men sitting there were drinking mint tea, but Kevin knew that he would be served glass after glass at Kacem's.

Time seemed to be passing at a snail's pace, despite the colorful spectacle of people strolling along the street and stopping to greet each other, despite the catchy music of the Moroccan group Jil Jilala coming from a radio inside the cafe, despite the excitement that was everywhere in the air.

Kevin kept looking at his watch, but whenever he thought that perhaps fifteen minutes had passed, he would discover that the minute hand had advanced no more than three or four. Would Kacem ever arrive? Kevin asked himself again and again.

And then, finally, he was there.

God, he just gets more beautiful, thought Kevin as he looked up at the man standing before him with his warm dark eyes and thick black hair.

Kacem kissed him on both cheeks and wished him a "Happy Holiday." Kevin felt his heart pounding like a sledge hammer, and just the sight of Kacem was making him hard. Be patient, he told himself. Tonight will come soon enough.

Kacem sat down beside him and asked him how he was enjoying the day so far.

"It's so different from the States to see everyone outside celebrating," answered Kevin. "At home, everyone stays indoors at family gatherings."

"That's the case here, too," explained Kacem, "but later on once the actual preparations for the sacrifice have begun. Now is the time for people to meet their friends and wish them *Aïd Mbrok.*"

Kacem asked Kevin about his *conseils* yesterday, and they discussed the problems which they and the other teachers were having with Monsieur Rhazwani. When Kacem inquired as to Kevin's plans for the rest of vacation, the American muttered something about not really being sure yet. "Ask me again tomorrow," he added cryptically, thinking: By tomorrow, there'll be no need to ask.

Finally, the bus arrived. It looked like something out of the forties, thought Kevin, old and rickety, its red paint chipping, one of those buses in which there was never enough room for your legs, and where you froze in the winter and sizzled in the summer. Kevin could never understand why Moroccans insisted on keeping the bus windows shut during the most sweltering of trips. Some kind of fresh-airphobia, he supposed.

"It's fortunate that Douar El Ayash is such a short distance from Aïn El Qamar," said Kacem.

"You aren't kidding," agreed Kevin, as they got up and headed for the ticket window. "At the speed this thing must go, it'd probably take six hours to get to Casablanca." Casa was only a little more than two hours away by car.

Kevin and Kacem joined the other people who were crowding around the window. There were a good number of them, doubtless taking advantage of the fact that this was to be the only bus of the day going to Douar El Ayash. Eventually, their tickets purchased, they boarded the ancient vehicle. Kevin put his overnight case and Kacem's satchel in the overhead rack, then took the window seat, Kacem sitting down beside him. To be so close and yet not be able to do anything about it was almost too much for Kevin to bear.

Even after the bus was nearly full, the driver's seat remained empty—buses never left on time in Morocco. An old woman dressed in rags entered the bus, one of the dozen or so beggars who congregated around the station at all times.

She slowly progressed down the aisle, chanting verses from the Koran, blessing those passengers who gave her a *ryal* or two. Kevin had long ago become immune to the poverty of the beggars. It was not that he was heartless, but simply that there were so many of them that it was impossible to feel generous towards them all. Kacem gave the old woman a four *ryal* piece, though, and not wanting to seem stingy, Kevin followed suit.

"Here comes the driver now," said Kacem. "I recognize him. He's from Douar El Ayash so he probably volunteered to drive today and then just remain in the village until tomorrow. It's hard to find bus and taxi drivers when there's a holiday."

The driver, a dark-complexioned man with a paunch, caught sight of Kacem and smiled. Kacem wished the man a happy holiday, and the driver returned his greeting.

"Now maybe we'll be off?" said Kevin hopefully. But no, they waited another fifteen minutes until the engine was fully warmed up. Also, according to Kacem, there were still a few empty seats and the driver didn't want to leave without a full bus.

Finally, though, he pulled out of the station, honking the strident horn at the children playing in the driveway. As the bus lumbered out onto the main street, Kevin could see the Moroccan flag with its green star on a red background everywhere, and there were strings of lights suspended over the streets, which would be turned on this evening as the people once again left their homes for a walk through town.

The sky was an intense blue, and the fields outside Aïn El Qamar were beginning to show tiny green wheat sprouts after the recent rains. Kevin tried to concentrate on the beauty of the surroundings, but it was nearly impossible to with Kacem's body touching his. Kacem was telling about his family farm, and about his mother and sisters who were busy preparing the day's festivities. He said that his father was probably praying at the mosque at this moment.

"Will he be the one to slaughter the sheep?" asked Kevin.

"No, there's a local butcher who makes the rounds of the houses each *Aïd*. He must be over seventy now, but his hand is still steady and no one would think of denying him his traditional role."

The bus ride was taking even longer than the expected thirty minutes. The driver insisted on stopping whenever someone flagged him down or a passenger wished to get off along the way. Kevin was beginning to wonder if they would ever reach Douar El Ayash.

But at last they arrived. The town was hardly more than a village with a very small downtown area which consisted of a few shops, most of which were closed at this time. Kacem's family farm was about a ten minute walk, he said, so he and Kevin got off the bus and began the journey on foot. It was getting warmer now, and Kevin stopped to take off his windbreaker. Then they proceeded on towards the small brown box-shaped farmhouse which Kacem pointed out in the distance. The land was flat, and one could see for miles in all directions. As always the Atlas Mountains formed a spectacular white and green backdrop.

As they reached the farmhouse, Kevin could hear sounds of movement from within. A woman's voice was shouting, "Behave yourselves and let me work!" and from the front door came running two young children, visibly overjoyed at the day's festivities. Kevin recognized Kacem's youngest brother Abdenbi, who had served them when he had eaten at Kacem's house last October, but he didn't know the little girl.

"This is Souad, my sister Fatiha's daughter," explained Kacem.

Abdenbi ran over to Kevin and kissed his hand. Touched at the gesture, Kevin leaned over and kissed the boy on both cheeks. Then the little girl held up her face and Kevin did the same to her.

"*Sbah-el-khir*," said Kevin. "Good morning. *Aïd Mbrok*!"

"*Marhababek*!" answered the two children in unison. "Welcome!"

Kevin's long awaited "Happy Holiday" had begun.

Now, nearly an hour later, the sheep was about to be slaughtered. The men in the family, the same whom Kevin had met in October, had gathered in the central courtyard, which was open to the sun. Kacem's father, who had returned from his morning of prayer at the local mosque, was wearing his finest white *jellaba*. The others were dressed in what in the United States would be referred to as their Sunday best, though Kevin supposed that since this was Morocco, it should be called their Friday best.

The bleating sheep had been brought out and was lying on its side, one of Kacem's younger brothers holding it still as Kacem bound the front legs and then the rear. The others all watched in curiosity and expectation.

Then the elderly butcher Kacem had told Kevin about stepped up with a sharp freshly-wiped knife. He was wearing a loose-fitting white shirt which showed traces of his morning's work at the homes of other families, and he had tucked his traditional *serwal*, baggy white Moroccan trousers, into a pair of knee-high rubber boots.

He murmured a brief prayer from the Koran, the only word which Kevin could recognize being *Llah,* or God. Then, leaning over, he slit the sheep's throat almost before Kevin was aware of it. The two young men holding the sheep jumped back as the animal began to writhe in the agony of death, a pool of blood forming at its throat. Kevin was intrigued by the sheep's jerky movements that seemed to deny the inevitability of its demise.

The rest of the actions took place rapidly as if they had been choreographed and rehearsed in advance. Kevin supposed this was true, as Moroccans had been sacrificing sheep for centuries on end.

The butcher now proceeded to sever the dead animal's head completely. Kevin assumed that one of the family members would take it away, but they did nothing, just left it to stare eerily into space.

Next, with his now bloodied knife, the old man removed the cords which bound the animal's limbs. He cut a slit in one of the sheep's rear legs and then, to Kevin's amazement, began to blow into it. The man had incredible lung power, for the animal's skin soon started ballooning around its body.

Kacem looked at Kevin and said, "That's to make the skin easier to remove," and Kevin nodded.

Then the headless wool-covered body which only moments before had been a living breathing sheep was hooked by its rear leg to a rope hanging from the branch of a tree which stood in the courtyard. The butcher used his knife to begin pulling the animal's skin down over its body.

Eventually the skin had been completely removed and lay inside out on the ground beneath the carcass it had once surrounded. When the butcher began cutting into the carcass in order to pull out the animal's entrails, Kevin felt his stomach begin to turn, and said to Kacem, "Would it be all right if we went inside?" Kacem smiled as if to say, "I understand," and escorted the American back into the house, his arm around his shoulder. It was just a friendly gesture, but it made Kevin want to fall into Kacem's arms right then and there. Just keep your shirt on, Kev, he told himself. You'll be taking it off soon enough, along with all the rest of your clothes, and Kacem's as well.

It won't be long now, Kevin told himself as he sat with Kacem and two of his brothers playing Moroccan rummy. It was quite unlike the card game he had played in the States, so it had taken him some time to learn. Also, different players seemed to have different rules, so that Kevin was never quite sure which variety he was supposed to be playing.

The rest of the day had gone surprisingly quickly after the sacrifice of the sheep. He and Kacem had been served *brochettes*, bite-sized pieces of meat on skewers. Only afterwards had he learned that they were liver and lung *brochettes*, and if he had not found them so tasty, he probably would have been ill. Then there had been an enormous *tajine*, and the rest of the men in the family had joined them. Kevin and Kacem had spent most of the afternoon exploring around the farm and the village. Kacem had taken him to the imposing new bridge which had been built over the nearby Oum Rbia River, the longest in Morocco. Kevin had been surprised to see such a modern construction in a small, traditional Moroccan village. They had walked down by the edge of the water, throwing stones across the surface and talking—about Kacem's studies in France, about the problems of Moroccan students confronting a severely crowded job market, about their experiences in teaching and their attitudes towards education. At times they were silent, and Kevin felt that their silences were more meaningful than their words.

The only upsetting note had come when Kacem had asked Kevin to tell him about Michèle Perrault. Why on earth was he interested in knowing about Michèle? wondered Kevin, who told him what he knew about the Frenchwoman as succinctly as possible, and hoped that Kacem would drop the subject, which thankfully he did.

Now, it was hours later. They had had dinner—another *tajine*—and mint tea. The sun had set at five o'clock, and with no television in this rural farmhouse which had only kerosene lamps for lighting, the four young men found themselves playing cards around the table and talking. Kevin could not follow much of what they were discussing in Arabic, but he managed to say enough for them to comment on how well he spoke—for a foreigner.

Kevin was praying for the game to end, for he knew that once it did, the two younger brothers would leave and he and Kacem would remain alone in this room to spend the night together. It was a typical Moroccan living room, with a half dozen *banquettes* against the walls, which doubled as beds in the evening.

Finally, the older of the two brothers put down his hand. "Rummy," he called out, and the game was over at last. The two younger brothers kissed their older brother good-night and shook hands with Kevin.

"It's been quite a day, hasn't it," said Kacem. "I for one am exhausted. Let me make up a *banquette* for you while you use the bathroom. *D'accord?*"

Kevin took his toothpaste, brush, soap, and towel into the small room which contained a sink and toilet and nothing else. He washed his face and hands and brushed his teeth, the better to kiss Kacem with, he thought. He hoped Kacem wouldn't be bothered by the roughness of his face, and wished he hadn't had to shave so early in the morning.

Kevin returned to the living room and Kacem took his turn using the bathroom. When he had changed into his pajamas, Kevin sat down on the *banquette* to wait for Kacem to return. A few minutes later, the Moroccan was back, also wearing pajamas. "Well, it's been a long day," he said, "and you must be as tired as I am. So I'll let you get a good night's sleep, and we'll see each other again in the morning. *Bonne nuit*, Kevin."

Kacem pulled back the bedcovers on his *banquette* and got between the sheets. He turned off the light switch on the wall next to the *banquette*.

The room was now lit only by the rays of the moon entering through the ceiling skylight. The perfect atmosphere, thought Kevin as he tiptoed to the side of Kacem's *banquette* and knelt down next to the Moroccan.

He had often wondered how he would reveal his feelings to Kacem, had thought of many possible ways to begin, but it seemed to Kevin now that the best way would be the boldest, and yet also the simplest.

Leaning over until his face was only a breath away, he pressed his lips to Kacem's, his mouth so hungry for Kacem's that, almost despite himself, he found his tongue beginning to make its way inside.

The feeling was electric, and Kevin waited for the Moroccan to become aware of what was happening and to respond to his kiss with equal fervor, as Kevin was sure he would.

Then, without warning, Kacem sat bolt upright in bed, his abrupt movement sending Kevin reeling back onto the floor. Kacem's eyes registered shock, and Kevin realized with dismay that this was not at all the reaction he had been expecting.

"What the fuck were you doing?" asked Kacem, dumbfounded. "You can't possibly think that ..."

"But we love each other!" protested Kevin, his brain in turmoil. "You love me as much as I love you. I know you do."

"You're ... you're queer?" stammered Kacem. "And you thought I was too?"

Kevin reached out his hand to touch Kacem's arm, but the Moroccan thrust it away. "Don't do that!" he exclaimed. "Don't touch me!"

Suddenly Kevin was on his feet. His brain was still spinning, and reality of Kacem's reaction had only just barely begun to sink in, but he knew that he couldn't stay in this room, in this house, in this village even a moment longer. He stumbled over to the armoire when he had hung up his clothes and pulled them off the hangers. Now where had Kacem put his suitcase, God damn it! Kevin's eyes scanned the room, but it was nowhere in sight.

"What are you doing?" asked Kacem. He was standing now, his face a mixture of shock and confusion.

"Isn't it obvious? I'm going to take the next bus back to Aïn El Qamar. I can't stay here, can I? You obviously don't want me to. I know what you must be thinking."

"I don't know what to think," replied Kacem. "I must still be in shock. I never in a million years imagined that you were … And that you were interested in me? What would make you think …"

"I have to get out of here!" cried Kevin. "I have to get back to Aïn El Qamar!"

"But you can't."

"What do you mean?"

"I mean there are no buses and taxis until morning," said Kacem. "I told you that before, because of the *Aïd*."

"Then what can I do!" Tears were streaming down Kevin's cheeks.

"Just go back to bed and try to get some sleep," Kacem told him. "I'll go spend the rest of the night with my brothers. We'll talk about this in the morning."

"There's nothing to talk about, Kacem," said Kevin dully. "I can see how much you hate me. Good night."

"I don't hate you, Kevin," said Kacem. "I don't know what I feel. I … I just never expected this from you. I'll … We'll talk in the morning." And then he was gone, leaving Kevin standing alone in the room. He had never felt more alone in his life. Spotting a pack of Marlboros and a box of matches on a table, he reached down and took a cigarette. He lit it and inhaled. The smoke made him cough, as he had smoked only occasionally in high school and then quit. But it felt good. It filled the emptiness he felt in his chest and in his heart, at least for the moment.

Well, he had learned his lesson now, and in the hardest way possible. There was no happiness to be gained from love. Love only brought so much pain that you wished you were dead.

"I loved you Kacem," he said to the empty room. "I was so in love with you I thought I'd die if I lost you. But I never really had you to lose."

And then he cried out in an agonized wail:

"Jamey!!!"

CHAPTER 15

▼

It feels so good to be feeling better for a change! thought Janna as she slipped on the strapless black dress she had chosen to wear to Claudette's party. The dress was one of her favorites. It made her shoulders look pale and creamy, and brought out the red in her hair. It raised her spirits which were already higher this evening than they had been in many weeks.

Janna went into her living room to wait for Dave, who was due to come by for her in about twenty minutes. She sat down on one of the *banquettes*, lit a cigarette, and tried to put together her feelings about her life, and about this evening which so many people had been eagerly anticipating for such a long time.

Looking around the living room, Janna thought with pride of the wonders she had accomplished in furnishing and decorating it. She had converted a cold white box into a warm and attractive room, or at least it was attractive now after the morning she had spent putting everything back in order after having let things go for so long. Luckily, Halima had been taking good care of her plants. They looked none the worse for the wear. What was different now was that the room, with its colorful posters and sunny yellow curtains, seemed cared for and cared about.

Thank God for Michèle and even for the fact that Janna herself had been too stoned to remember yesterday's *conseil de classe*. Michèle's compassionate and caring advice, as well as Janna's shocking realization of how unforgivably she had let down her students, had been enough to make her decide to snap out of the depression that had overcome her recently.

Not that she had been depressed without reason. Janna had given so completely of herself to Lahcen, taught him so much about love and commitment, that for him not to have written in weeks, to have apparently forgotten about her completely after having been so close to her, was a betrayal of everything they had shared.

But Janna had not fought the depression. She had surrendered to it, even abetting it with the *keef* that had only increased her feeling of abandonment. Her letters to Lahcen had become nearly hysterical in their pleas for an explanation of his silence. And as his had become less and less frequent, hers had begun to be mailed nearly every day.

Michèle had made Janna face the reality of what she had been doing, both to Lahcen and to herself. Her repeated trips to the post office had only served to push Lahcen even further away, to destroy whatever affection he might still feel for her. And her increasing reliance on drugs had sent her into a world where she was unable to communicate with the people around her, or they with her. Thank God classes had already ended when she went on her latest binge. What would have happened if she had tried to teach a lesson stoned? Janna prayed that her spaced-out manner had not been too obvious during the last weeks of classes.

In any case, when she got up this morning, Janna made a vow to attempt some changes in her life. They began with a thorough floor to ceiling housecleaning. The kitchen disgusted her with its filth, and she was glad that she could clean up the mess before Halima saw it.

Then she wrote to Lahcen, one final letter, apologizing for her recent barrage of mail—harassment would have been a more apt choice of words. She told him she had not been well, and asked him to forgive her, adding that she hoped he was enjoying life in the United States. "I understand that you are very busy and that you have little time to write," were her words. "Please know that my thoughts are with you and that I wish you much happiness in your new life."

The part about understanding was a lie, of course. She didn't understand in her heart how a relationship that had seemed so real and solid could crumble so quickly into nothingness. No, she didn't understand, and she wanted an answer to her letters. She wanted him to beg for forgiveness and swear to her that he still loved her. But she knew now that this was unlikely to happen and that until she accepted this bitter reality, she would be unable to get on with her life.

Janna's new calm and her efforts to once again become her usual self remained shaky, though. She felt as if she had to keep moving, keep busy, in order not to fall once again into the depths of depression where *keef* was her only escape.

For this reason, she decided at the last minute to accept Halima's request to celebrate the *Aïd El Kébir* with the maid's family. It would get her out of the house and into the atmosphere of merriment and joy that this day brought to every Moroccan home. Maybe some of this excitement would rub off on her.

Marcie was going. Usually, Janna found Marcie too sweet and perfect for her own taste. She was skeptical of people who never seemed to see the bad in anyone, and she didn't recall ever hearing Marcie say a mean word about Morocco or Moroccans, or anyone else for that matter. And God, who could live here for any length of time without having at least something to complain about?

How strange it was then to find Marcie so quiet and withdrawn today at the maid's house. Janna, who thought that Marcie's innocent schoolgirl enthusiasm might lift her spirits, was surprised to find the young woman hardly listening to anything anyone said. She scarcely smiled, and when she did it was a joyless half-smile, and her eyes remained bleak.

Marcie volunteered nothing about what was bothering her, and when Janna asked if anything was wrong, she replied "Of course not," a bit too insistently to be credible, Janna thought. Later, when Janna asked her if she was looking forward to Claudette and Jean-Richard's party, Marcie looked away suddenly and muttered something about having decided not to go. Janna was incredulous. No one was more enchanted by the French than Marcie, the eternal romantic. What could have possessed her to leave Aïn El Qamar the very night of this year's biggest social event?

Strangely enough, Marcie's gloomy, distracted demeanor actually served to buoy Janna's own mood, as she now felt it her responsibility to try to brighten the other woman's spirits, or at least to keep the conversation going. So she found herself telling Marcie about her childhood in Boston, her adventures in Berkley and Europe, and her experiences working in the political jungle of Washington D.C. Marcie seemed not to be paying much attention, though, and when Janna asked her about her own upbringing, Marcie appeared at first not to have heard. Janna repeated her question, and Marcie said, "Nothing in my life in River Falls prepared me for Morocco," with such bitterness and finality that Janna understood that the subject was closed.

Well, thought Janna now as she sat dressed for Claudette's party, glancing occasionally at her watch to see if it was time yet for Dave to arrive, I only hope that getting away from Aïn El Qamar will help you Marcie—and help me as well. It looks like both of us are in need of strength.

Janna looked at her watch once again. Damn! Dave still wouldn't be here for another fifteen minutes. Suddenly, the thought of idly waiting here for a quarter hour more was unbearable. She couldn't sit doing nothing even a moment longer, and besides, Dave's house was only a five minute walk from hers. The sooner the two of them were on their way, the sooner they would be at the party.

Janna ran into her bedroom to get her forest green *burnoose*, which resembled an elegant opera cape. She recalled the day she had bought it in Fez during her travels with Lahcen last summer. Don't think of that, she told herself. The only way you're going to get through the days and nights is by pushing memories of him out of your mind. Or at least by trying to.

The night was cool but not cold as Janna went out. Today had been so beautiful with its warm sun and clear sky. At the moment, it felt more like mid-autumn than December. Perhaps the change in the weather had helped her mood. If so, Janna could only hope that during the next two weeks she and Michèle would have dawn to dusk sunshine in Agadir.

Think about the coming days on the beach, she told herself as she began the walk to Dave's house along the quiet side street. Don't think about the thrill you got every time you saw Lahcen at your door, even before you were lovers. Don't remember the way he smiled and laughed. Don't recall how he used to hold you in his arms throughout the night.

Janna could feel the terrible despondency descending on her once again. Don't give in to it, she ordered herself. Fight it! Fight it for the sake of your life!

Thank God she had nearly arrived at Dave's house. It must be the darkness of the night that was depressing her so. Hadn't she been fine this morning, while she was cleaning, and this afternoon at Halima's? She needed to keep busy, to be with people. The party would help. It had to help!

Janna was just a few blocks from Dave's door when she suddenly realized that she was being followed. She could hear footsteps behind her and they were neither fading away nor making any attempt to pass her. Janna felt her heart pounding so loudly she was sure that her follower could hear it. She wanted to look around, to tell whoever it was to leave her in peace, but she was too frightened. There was something strange and terribly threatening about the steady pace of whoever was behind her.

She became aware that he was getting closer and closer. He was almost at her back now. She nearly screamed when she felt the touch of his hand on her shoulder.

Janna turned around to see his face.

"You very byootifool tonight," said a voice in accented English, and Janna recoiled from the burst of fetid breath. It was a student-aged young man with an unshaven face and uncombed hair. There was something vaguely familiar about him. "You alone," he continued. "Is very dangerous at night. I walk with you."

"You get away from me or … or I'll scream!" Janna's voice was unsteady.

"I bet you not scream with Cherqaoui," said the young man. "Or maybe you scream a lot, in bed." He reached out and touched her face.

Half terrified, half enraged, Janna grabbed his wrist and tore it away from her cheek. "Leave me alone!" she exclaimed, then turned on her heels and literally ran the remaining block to Dave's door. She pounded on it with all her strength. Fortunately, he opened it almost immediately.

"Janna, what are you doing here? Has anything happened?" he asked in concern, then added, "You're shivering." Janna became aware that she was indeed trembling, and it was not from the cold.

"A young man … he was following me … he touched my face … I … I was so scared!" she stammered, and fell into Dave's comforting arms.

"It's all right now," Dave reassured her, patting her gently. "Nothing happened. You're fine, and he's gone. Don't think about it anymore. It was probably somebody out drinking in the olive groves, and now he's on his way home to sleep it off."

"You're right," said Janna. "This isn't New York City after all. And it isn't as if my life was in danger, is it? In any case, it's partly my own stupidity for having been out walking alone at night. I should have waited for you to come for me at my place. I was just so eager to be on my way, I couldn't sit still another second. Anyway, it's over now."

She removed herself from Dave's arms, resolved to put the disturbing incident behind her. Tonight was a night of celebration after all.

Dave was giving her an admiring once-over. "You look fantastic tonight, by the way" he said.

"So do you," responded Janna. Dave was wearing a white linen sports jacket with a flowered body shirt underneath, and tight black denim slacks. She found the combination of flora and brawn quite appealing.

"Well, since you're here, let's be on our way," said Dave, turning off the house lights and locking the door behind them. Janna replied with an eager "*Yallaho*," which was the Moroccan equivalent of "Let's go."

"I wouldn't be taking any more strolls after dark if I were you," advised Dave as they began walking towards the main street leading to Claudette's house.

"I won't be," Janna reassured him. "There was something really scary about that guy. Something almost crazy about his eyes. And I have the strangest feeling that I've seen him before, though with my brain in the shape that it's been for the past weeks, my memory's pretty foggy, and it may just be some inexplicable case of déjà vu, for all I know."

"I wouldn't worry about it if I were you," said Dave. "He probably just freaked out seeing an attractive woman walking by herself at night."

"Well, you're here now to protect me," smiled Janna, "so I can relax and start getting back into my party mood."

"It looks like a party everywhere tonight," commented Dave as they approached the main street. There were crowds of promenaders, both old and young, who had obviously enjoyed a splendid day of feasting and wanted to share their joy with each other. As Janna and Dave joined the happy throng, Janna once again felt that the depression which had so nearly overtaken her only minutes ago was becoming a thing of the past. She would begin a new life tonight, and enjoy the evening to its fullest.

Dave seemed aware of the change in her. He mentioned that he'd been a bit concerned about her recently, but that she seemed to be doing fine tonight. "You know you can count on me anytime you need a friend," he told her, and she squeezed his hand gratefully.

The two Americans were stopped frequently on the way to Claudette's house by groups of their students and by Moroccan colleagues who wished them *Aïd Mbrok.*" Once a student made Janna laugh when he asked her if she had eaten a sheep that day. "You mean, 'Did you eat mutton?'" she corrected. "I can't eat the entire animal." "I can," said the student, and he was such a little thing that both she and Dave burst out in laughter.

"I'm glad to see you so happy," said Dave.

"Happy?" said Janna wistfully. "Not quite. At least not yet. But I'm trying."

They had almost reached Claudette's neighborhood when Michèle drove up beside them.

"Hi there," she called from the car window. "I stopped by your house, Janna, to see if the two of you wanted a lift, but you'd already gone. Hop in, and I'll drive you the rest of the way." The two Americans got in and Michèle commented, "You both look smashing! Like some Hollywood *couple du jour.*"

"I feel like I'm on the way to a Hollywood party," agreed Janna, thinking how wonderful it felt to be smiling again.

"Well, here we are," announced Michèle as they pulled up about a block from Claudette's house. "Or at least as near as we'll get. Look at all those cars! Half of Aïn El Qamar must be here!"

The three of them left the Renault and headed for the front door. An excited merry hodgepodge of voices and music and noise was coming from Claudette's house. Apparently the party was already in full swing.

Saadia, the maid, opened the door. This was *her* night too, and she was dressed in her finest yellow and green caftan with a matching scarf on her head and big gold earrings, necklaces, and bracelets adorning her ample body. "*Marhababikum*! Welcome!" she greeted them enthusiastically. "*Aïd Mbrok*! *Bonne fête*!" they replied. Saadia took Janna's *burnoose* and Michèle's fur-collared coat. "You look sensational, Janna!" exclaimed Michèle. "Black does wonders with your hair and skin. And I'm so glad to see you feeling better!"

Michèle was her usual neo-hippie self, with a peasant dress embellished with a half dozen or so long multi-colored scarves making her look like a psychedelic gypsy. "You approve?" she asked, modeling the outfit.

"It's you, Michèle!" said Dave with a wide grin, and added, "It'll be my pleasure to escort both of you ladies into where the action is."

"So, what are we waiting for?" said Janna and Michèle, almost in unison. The three teachers moved from the entry hall into Claudette's living room, which was already crowded with guests. Most of the furniture had been removed—*banquettes*, poufs, and the big dining table—so there was more room than Janna had expected there to be. Labelle's "Lady Marmalade" was playing on the stereo, and several couples were dancing to it in one corner. "*Voulez-vous coucher avec moi*?" they sang along with the refrain, and this was one crowd which understood the meaning of the suggestive lyrics. Other people mingled, smoking cigarettes, drinking wine or cocktails, discussing various vacation plans. Some were traveling inside Morocco, others returning to France. A few intended to visit Spain, and one adventurous couple announced that they were going to drive all the way to Algeria.

A Frenchman whom Janna recognized as Pierre Arrier, a history teacher at Lycée Mohamed Cinq, came up with a tray of drinks. "*Champagne*?" he offered, and began speaking with Michèle and Dave in French. Janna accepted a glass of champagne and drifted away. Saadia came up and asked her if she was enjoying herself so far. "Yes," she replied in Arabic, "but I would be even more if I spoke French well." "But you speak our language beautifully," said Saadia. "You don't need French. Besides, you're a *Mirikania*!" Janna smiled. She doubted if Saadia had any idea where America even was. "Did you see the tree?" asked Saadia proudly. No, she hadn't! At the opposite end of the room there was an eight-foot Christmas tree brightly decorated with lights and foil ornaments. "My oldest son cut it down," explained Saadia, "and I made the decorations. So that all you Christians would feel at home." How sweet, thought Janna, and kissed Saadia. She had nearly forgotten that Christmas was only a week away.

Saadia went off to answer the door again and Dave came up behind Janna. "Sorry about shutting you out of our conversation," he said, "but Pierre's English is limited to 'How do you do?' and virtually nothing else."

The record had changed and now the couples were boogieing to the Bee Gees' "You Should Be Dancing."

"Shall we?" asked Dave.

"You know what? I actually do feel like dancing," replied Janna brightly. "And I haven't wanted to dance for months and months."

The two Americans moved over to the corner where the dancing was going on. Dave broke into a series of hip and torso movements that took Janna by surprise. "Wow!" she exclaimed admiringly. The other dancers, much more sedate, kept moving, but most of them had their eyes glued to the American couple. Janna could feel the music lead her body in its spell, and she was happier than she'd been in longer than she could remember. Just make life a *discothèque*, she thought, and everything will be all right.

She and Dave had been dancing for perhaps twenty minutes when they became aware that everyone had turned to watch a new arrival. Miguel Berthaud was entering, dressed as of all things a pirate, with a bandana around his head, a patch over one eye, a penciled-on mustache, and a voluminous white shirt open to the waist. He was carrying an umbrella in place of a sword, and was pretending to fight away an invisible enemy with wide, slashing movements. The entire room was in hysterics at Miguel's latest stunt. Then, he seemed slowly to become aware of the laughter around him. He looked at each of the guests, all dressed in his or her most special clothes for this most special of evenings. His mouth fell open and there was an expression of exaggerated dismay on his lean angular face. His bulging round eyes seemed larger than ever as they feigned shock and confusion. "But … but …," he stammered, and the guests just laughed louder. "I thought … I thought this was to be a masquerade!"

The laughter swelled, mixed with applause, and then died down as the dancing started again and Miguel began to mingle with his friends. Janna noticed that Saadia had brought in a tray of elegant canapés. As the Moroccan woman served them, Janna realized with a start that one of the women who accepted an hors d'oeuvre was Dominique Moulin, but a Dominique she scarcely recognized, despite her customary cigarette and scowl. Poor plain Domino, as Michèle referred to her, was neither poor nor plain tonight. She was wearing a pair of gold lamé lounging pajamas, her face strikingly made up for evening, her ordinarily mousy brown hair pulled tightly back in an elegant chignon at her neck. Janna could hardly believe her eyes.

When the song she and Dave were dancing to ended, Janna excused herself and went to find Michèle. The Frenchwoman was standing talking to Miguel, the pirate.

"Ah Janna," said Michèle. "Have you greeted Captain Long John Berthaud?"

Miguel said something in French, and Michèle translated. "He says that if all American women are as beautiful as you, he will set sail for the United States tomorrow."

"Tell the Captain that if all Frenchmen are as dashing as he is, I'll take the next airplane to Paris."

"No Paree," said Miguel in comic English. "Paree very beeg and dirty. *Capitain* Berthaud is from zee South. Marseille!"

"*Pardon, monsieur,*" said Janna with mock seriousness. "Marseille. Of course."

Miguel excused himself in order to greet the other guests and Janna was left with Michèle. "He's a riot!" exclaimed Janna. "Marcie's told me some of the things he does here, but I didn't know what a character he really is."

"There's only one Miguel Berthaud," agreed Michèle. "And speaking of characters, did you get a load of Domino?"

"I know," said Janna. "I was just noticing myself. What's happened to her?"

"I haven't the foggiest. Maybe it's her departure for France tomorrow, or the idea of a party to perk up the boredom of Aïn El Qamar. She was still dressing when I left, so I'm as astounded as you are to see her now. I only hope the change will last."

Just then, the subject of this brief discussion appeared beside the two women. She said hello, but made no attempt to speak English with Janna. Even after her make-over, she remained the same sour individual at heart, thought Janna, who got a hint of why Dominique had dressed so elegantly when she heard her inquire about the whereabouts of Jean-Richard, who had not yet made an appearance at the party. Janna couldn't follow Michèle's answer, but Dominique was obviously disappointed and walked away sullenly.

"She saw him at the Hotel El Qamar last night and decided to give one last stab at getting back into bed with him," explained Michèle.

"If she keeps looking like that, she might just get him back," said Janna.

"Oh, look at *that* glamorous couple!" said Michèle sarcastically, and Janna turned to see Laurent and Christiane Koenigsmarck enter. The short, plump Frenchman was wearing a loud yellow and black striped sports jacket and a pair of bright yellow pants too tight for his chubby legs, the ensemble making him look like an oversized honeybee. Christiane was heavily made up as always, and had chosen of all things a white frock with red polka dots which gave her the appearance of a sleazy farmer's daughter. Her blond-streaked hair was teased high atop her head and a cigarette hung from her fire-engine red lips.

"Oh God, if I'm not careful, I'll be in stitches," said Janna, and bit her lip to maintain control.

"Pretty hideous, aren't they?" said Michèle.

"I wonder if she has any idea how cheap and vulgar she looks," commented Janna.

"She probably thinks she's the belle of the ball."

"Who are you talking about?" asked Dave, who had come up behind them. "Christiane, the local tramp?"

"Dave, don't talk so loud," cautioned Janna. "She'll hear you."

"Are you kidding? She can barely speak French, let alone English."

Michèle excused herself to talk to some of the other guests. Dave turned to Janna, then exclaimed, "Look over there. Jean-Richard's finally shown up."

"He looks different," commented Janna as she took in the handsome blond Frenchman who wore a simple white dress shirt and dark slacks. "I mean, not the way he's dressed. He's got that same understated elegance, as always. But he's almost too animated tonight. Look at the way he's smiling and gesturing. It's like he's putting on a show."

"I think you're imagining things," said Dave.

"Maybe," replied Janna, "but I still think it's curious."

As the evening wore on, there was still no sign of Claudette, and Janna asked Saadia if anything was wrong. For a moment, the Moroccan woman looked near the point of tears, then she said, "Miss Claudette is still in her room. She's … she's getting dressed."

Janna noticed that Claudette's bedroom door was shut tight. She wondered what Claudette had chosen to wear to impress her friends on this most important and memorable of evenings.

Michèle came up to Janna. "Jean-Richard isn't himself tonight," she said.

"So you've noticed too," commented Janna.

"He was talking to me, flirting is more the word, but his heart didn't seem to be in it, and he kept looking around as if he was trying to find someone. Anyway, I gave him the cold shoulder as usual. I simply have no time for the man, despite his widely proclaimed charm. But there's something troubling him tonight."

"What could it be?" wondered Janna.

"Your guess is as good as mine," replied Michèle. And then, with a gasp, she added, "Oh my God!"

Janna turned to see what was so shocking.

There, standing at the door was Claudette. Her auburn hair hung thickly to her shoulders and there were bits of glitter in it which sparkled in the dimly lit room. Her face was dramatic and spectacular as always. But it was not that which had attracted the attention of all the guests. The music played on, but the room was otherwise silent as everyone stared in open-mouthed astonishment at their hostess who was wearing only the sheerest of negligees and absolutely nothing else! It was possible to see her nipples beneath the bodice, and below her waist, her crotch was scarcely hidden by the diaphanous gown. She turned as if to model the negligee, and Janna saw in horror that a lipstick heart had been sketched on her left buttock.

"Oh God, she's gone insane!" exclaimed Janna. "How in heaven's name can she show up at her own party dressed like some porno queen?"

"*Bienvenu, tout le monde!*" cried Claudette. "Welcome *chez moi*! Tonight marks the dawn of a new era in Aïn El Qamar. I am the new Claudette Verlaine! Welcome to my new world!" Janna noticed that Jean-Richard had turned away in disgust and was walking across the room in an obvious attempt to distance himself from Claudette. Some very strange things are happening in this household, thought Janna. She recalled the look of sadness which had crossed Saadia's face earlier, and she wondered what had been going on behind closed doors to cause it.

"Oh lord," said Michèle. "She's coming this way."

"'ello, ladies of *l'Amérique!*" she exclaimed. "Veree wonderful evening, *n'est-ce pas?*"

Janna stammered out a greeting, but after that she found herself at a total loss for words.

"You wonder at zee new Miss Claudette, *oui?*" said the Frenchwoman, and Janna could scarcely restrain herself from staring at her blatantly exposed body. "I 'ave seen that I was wrong to think of others and what zey say. From now on, I live onlee for myself and for *mon plaisir sexuel.*"

And then she was gone, mingling with the other guests, and Janna could see that most of them were as tongue-tied as she was. "I thought I was a pretty cool lady," she said to Michèle, "but even I have never seen anything like that."

"After the way she's been acting in public with her Moroccan lover these past weeks, I'd believe just about anything about Claudette Verlaine. At least you were ..."

Michèle stopped, embarrassed.

"At least I was more discreet with Lahcen," said Janna. "You may be right. But in the end, where did it get me?"

"I'm sorry, love," apologized Michèle. "I shouldn't have said anything."

Janna suddenly found herself very near the point of tears. She had been hiding her feelings so well, both from others and from herself. She had almost begun to enjoy the party. But once again, Lahcen was with her, even though an ocean and half a continent away.

"Please forget what I said," begged Michèle.

"It's all right," answered Janna. "I guess I'm just realizing that coping with loneliness isn't going to be as easy as I'd hoped."

Michèle kissed her affectionately on the cheek. "It'll get better love," she said.

But after that, the party was no longer the same as it had been. Claudette's entrance had soured the festive atmosphere, and already some of the guests were leaving.

In one corner, Dominique stood smoking a cigarette and sulking. Jean-Richard had apparently been as uninterested in her as ever, despite her newly glamorized self.

In another corner, Janna was astonished to see the French playboy flirting with, of all people, Christiane. It was shockingly clear that he was putting the make on her while her husband was discussing the latest soccer scores with several colleagues in another part of the room. Janna couldn't believe the attention Jean-Richard was paying to the tall cheap-looking Frenchwoman. She was so completely the opposite of the women who usually seemed to attract him. What was going on?

"That's one pairing up I thought I'd never see," said Dave, who had come up beside Janna to offer her another glass of champagne.

She accepted the drink and said, "People certainly do the strangest things. First Claudette and now Jean-Richard."

"I think I know what's brought about the change in Claudette," said Dave. "Fareed's left town for a new job in Tangier."

"Just like that? No wonder she's upset. But still, what does she expect to gain from the way she's acting tonight?"

"I think your answer is standing at the door. And also the reason why it took Claudette so long to come out of her bedroom tonight."

"Oh dear God!" exclaimed Janna as she looked at the young man who was about to enter the living room.

"What is it?" asked Dave.

"N … nothing," she stammered. "I'm … I'm just going to freshen up. Excuse me."

Janna bolted out of the room, past the cause of her distress, and into the bathroom off the entry hall. Falling to her knees, she vomited into the toilet. He had been … he had been …

Get hold of yourself, Janna, she said silently. Just because you see a Moroccan who bears a resemblance to Lahcen … That's no reason to …

But they were so alike! The same curly brown hair. The same eyes shaped like two almonds. The same tall strong young body.

Stop it! she told herself. Don't let this get to you! Go back to the party and face what's upsetting you. Don't run away from it!

Slowly, she pulled herself together. Reaching up to flush the toilet, she rose, washed her face and mouth at the sink, then returned to the living room. The young man was no longer there.

Was it only my imagination? Janna asked herself. Perhaps in the dim light I only thought he resembled Lahcen.

Dave came up to her and asked, "Are you all right now?"

"Fine," she answered. "I don't know what came over me." No, neither the young man nor Claudette, for that matter, were anywhere to be seen.

"You had me worried," said Dave. "It seemed like you'd seen a ghost."

"I suppose in a way I had," she answered, and when she saw the blank expression on Dave's face, she added, "Never mind."

"Let me get you another drink," offered Dave. "You look like you could use one."

Janna nodded her head and took a cigarette from a nearby table. She lit it as Dave returned with more champagne.

"Hardly seems appropriate tonight," commented Janna, looking at the bubbly liquid. "No one seems to be celebrating much of anything." She was beginning to feel calmer and almost to wonder if the young Moroccan had indeed been a figment of her imagination.

"Look who's leaving," said Dave.

"I don't believe it," exclaimed Janna.

Jean-Richard had his arm around Christiane and they were quietly heading out of the living room, oblivious of the people around them.

"Impossible," said Janna. "He's really sunk low this time. And what about Laurent?"

"Take a look," said Dave, and pointed to the short, bald Frenchman who was standing next to Dominique and whispering something in her ear.

Michèle came up and said, "So you've seen the new couplings too. Jean-Richard connects with Laurent's wife and Domino is about to be seduced by Laurent because Jean-Richard found her ever so resistible."

"What on earth can she possibly see in him?" wondered Janna.

"I've progressed beyond the point of trying to analyze Domino," said Michèle. "She hates Aïn El Qamar so much, I think she'd do anything for a change."

"But Laurent?" gasped Janna.

"He *is* quite a few steps down from Jean-Richard," agreed Michèle.

Janna noticed that there were other guests who had decided to make their exits. The music continued, but only two or three couples remained on the dance floor. This evening was certainly not turning out the way everyone had anticipated. Perhaps Marcie had been right to decide not to come.

"They're leaving together!" exclaimed Dave.

"Who?" asked Janna. "Oh, I don't believe it! Dominique and Laurent!"

"They better not decide to use our place for their love tryst," said Michèle between her teeth. "I'd throw them out, and Domino for good!"

"It looks like there are going to be quite a few scandals tonight," said Dave. "Here comes Claudette again with her new boy toy. I heard she picked him up last night at the Hotel El Qamar *discothèque*. Rumor has it that he bragged to the bartender that she was going to pay him a hundred *dirhams* to spend the night with her."

Janna stood mute, scarcely hearing Dave's words. Claudette was indeed back, her body still almost totally exposed by the nearly transparent negligee. But now she had her arms enfolded around the young Moroccan and he was fondling her breasts. She wrapped her legs around him and rubbed against him with her sex.

However, scandalous as this spectacle was, it was not the sight of Claudette's wanton sexual hunger that had Janna in a state of utter shock and panic, but the young man's face. No, she had not been wrong before. The resemblance to Lahcen was uncanny. And it was as if instead of being with Claudette, he was with some seventeen-year-old high school cheerleader and it was her breasts he was caressing and her crotch rubbing against his leg.

He lied to me when he said he loved me! she thought. He took advantage of the fact that I was older and more experienced in order to have an easy bed partner and sex tutor. Moroccan virgins weren't available and whores were too expensive. He used me, and now he's fucking someone else, telling her he loves her. Maybe he's even laughing about his English teacher, making fun of my stupid naive belief that he cared about me.

"I've got to get away from here!" she cried out, pain and desperation in her voice.

"What?" exclaimed Michèle.

"I'm leaving!" repeated Janna, stumbling towards the entry hall.

"Wait Janna!" called Michèle. "Let me drive you!"

"Do whatever you want," said Janna as she accepted her *burnoose* from Saadia. "I just want to get home. I never should have come in the first place!"

Saadia gave Michèle her coat and the two women left the party, the music and the noise continuing behind them.

As they walked the block to Michèle's car, the Frenchwoman pleaded with Janna to tell her what was wrong.

"Nothing," lied Janna. "I didn't feel like staying, that's all."

All the way back to Janna's house, Michèle tried repeatedly to get her friend to reveal what was upsetting her so, but Janna refused, insisting that she merely felt tired.

When they arrived, Michèle asked Janna if she should come in and stay with her until she felt better.

"No, Michèle," replied Janna. "I'll be fine. I just need to be alone after being around all those people."

"All right, love," said Michèle. "I'll be by to pick you up in the morning. Don't forget to pack some summer clothes. It'll be warmer in Agadir than in Aïn El Qamar."

"Agadir?"

"Of course, Agadir. We're leaving tomorrow!"

"Oh, that's right," said Janna tonelessly. "I'd forgotten. I'll … I'll be ready." She managed a half smile. "Thanks for being my friend."

"Nonsense," said Michèle, and kissed Janna good-night. "You'll feel better once you're on the beach at Agadir."

Janna left the car and went into her darkened house. She had no desire to turn on the bright lights. Feeling her way into the living room, she lit a candle with her cigarette lighter. Then, holding on to the candle, she went in search of her *keef* pipe.

She had hidden it away that morning when she had felt strong enough to face the world. But she had been wrong. She knew now that only the sweet smoke of the *keef* could help her forget Lahcen's horrible betrayal.

Tonight I'm going to get stoned like I've never gotten stoned before! Janna told herself in agony.

Sinking to her knees, she buried her head in her hands. "Oh, Lahcen," she wept. "I loved you so much!"

CHAPTER 16

─────────── ▼ ───────────

His short pudgy fingers were fooling with her pussy as his fat slobbering lips descended on her tits.

Merde! thought Dominique. What did I ever do to deserve this? Laurent Koenigsmarck was nearly drooling as he bit one of her nipples.

He moaned, "*Oh, mon bébé, quelle poitrine!*" and tried to swallow her right breast with his wet gluttonous mouth.

Dominique nearly screamed, but she resisted the temptation. After all, it had been her own choice to leave the party with Laurent in order to spite Jean-Richard for having chosen Christiane over her.

"Gotta get me a taste of some cunt," panted Laurent, and lowered his head to lick between her legs. "Spread wider, sweetie," he begged.

Oh God, I'd love to squeeze your shiny bald head between my legs until it bursts, thought Dominique.

"How does that feel, *mon bébé*?" asked Laurent.

"*Fabuleux*," said Dominique sarcastically.

How could she tell him that she felt nothing? And never did.

There must be something wrong with me, she thought. I must be frigid.

Sex never was for her what it was cracked up to be. Even Jean-Richard had not been able to make her feel anything, though she'd been so angry at his indifference that she'd wanted to go to bed with him again just to put an end to the feeling of rejection.

"You taste like sweet honey," enthused Laurent. "I'm going to suck your twat dry!"

And I'd like to throw up on your fat ugly head, thought Dominique. I'd like to …

"Oh my God!" she exclaimed.

"*C'est bon, n'est-ce pas?*" asked Laurent.

"No … no …" stammered Dominique.

"What's the matter, baby?"

"It's … it's your wife!"

"Forget about Christiane. Just think about my tongue inside your pussy!"

"She's … she's standing at the door!"

Laurent jerked his head up from Dominique's sex as his wife cried out, "At least you can get yours up!" She began to laugh wildly.

Laurent and Dominique stared at her, speechless. Dominique tried to cover herself, but Christiane said, "You've got nothing to hide, *chérie*. At least you're getting laid. That Jean-Richard Moreau and his great reputation? *Quelle merde*! After he took me upstairs with him, he just hung there like a wet noodle."

Christiane had been undressing as she spoke, Dominique looking on in shocked disbelief. "At least *you* are a man!" she exclaimed now, leaning over and taking Laurent's engorged cock in her full red mouth.

Dominique knew she should feel horror and disgust at the sight of Christiane fellating Laurent as he lay in bed with another woman. But instead she felt stirrings in her loins that were unknown to her. She could not resist imagining Christiane's lips and tongue on her own sex, licking it, exploring it.

And then, as if Christiane had been reading her mind, Dominique's fantasy became reality as Christiane's mouth met her pussy. And it was the fulfillment of a long repressed dream.

So, this was what she had wanted all along, thought Dominique. How could a man give her what another woman could? The kisses and caresses which from men had felt slimy and obscene now became the source of a deep erotic gratification when administered by Christiane. The scent of the other woman was like no other she had ever inhaled. She ran her fingers through the blond woman's hair and caressed the nape of her neck. As Christiane's kisses moved from Dominique's groin up her belly and towards her chest, Dominique reached down to grasp and fondle her partner's large pliant breasts.

Out of the corner of her eye, she could see Laurent. He was kneeling at the end of the bed, his eyes wide as saucers, his hand at his erect cock.

Christiane was kissing Dominique now, full on the lips, her tongue eagerly probing her mouth as Dominique's did the same to Christiane's. She felt a finger insert itself deep between her legs until it found a spot that Dominique did not know even existed.

She was overtaken by an infinity of orgasms, she who had never before felt any pleasure in the act of sexual intercourse. God damn Laurent, who was masturbating at the sight of the two women making love. God damn all men who considered themselves gods! Dominique Moulin knew at this moment that all she had ever wanted from life was the love and fulfillment that could be found only in the arms and in the bed of another woman.

Tonight the dream was worse than ever. Marcie and the Greek girl were once again lying together naked, but now they were laughing at him. "You're not a man!" they cried. "You tried to make love to Christiane and you failed! You fail at everything! Failure! Failure!"

And damn it, they were right, thought Jean-Richard as he woke in a cold sweat, nearly screaming.

His whole life was a failure. He could never make a commitment to a woman because that meant a belief in the future. He could only relive past memories and push aside any woman's attempt to get inside him, to understand him, to love him.

Tonight, though, he had failed as never before. For the first time, he had found himself impotent. And the thought of his inability to prove himself a man had tormented him long into the night.

Christiane had done everything possible to excite him. She had used her mouth in ways that even he had found inventive. And yet he had hung limp and unresponsive.

Was it that she was cheap and common? He had slept with cheap common women before, and Christiane's body was not without its curvaceous charms.

Was it because he felt guilty at having sex with a married woman? No, that was ridiculous. A wedding ring had meant nothing to him in the past.

Or was it that as he lay with Christiane, he had heard Marcie's voice crying out, "You're destroying yourself! You're destroying yourself!" and had known the horrible truth of her words?

Thank God the pain had finally numbed. With each toke of the sweet fragrant smoke, Janna felt Lahcen's betrayal a little less, until finally she felt nothing.

Sitting in the dark, she smiled a joyless smile. The images of Lahcen making love to a faceless American girl remained before her eyes, but at least they no longer hurt. She could still hear Lahcen saying, "That woman meant nothing to me." She could still hear him laughing at her for her naive stupidity. But his words did not wound her. She could almost laugh at them. Almost.

Screw Michèle and Dave and everyone else who had tried to bring her back to life. Screw them for their well-meaning but futile efforts. Didn't they realize that it was too soon? It would take time, weeks, months, perhaps even longer, for her to recover from the pain of Lahcen's rejection. And for the time being, there was only one way to go on living, day to day, and that was to drug herself, to drug herself senseless, until she once again had the strength and the courage to confront the ugly face of reality.

Dave knew it was only a dream, but still he surrendered to it willingly. Lateef was kissing him, on the eyes, on the cheeks, on the lips. He had wrapped his body around the American's and Dave could feel the electricity of his touch. And then Dave was inside Lateef, and Lateef inside Dave, and the intensity of their double climaxes was like none that either of them had ever known.

Dave awoke, his bedclothes sticky with semen. Despite himself, he chuckled. He hadn't had a wet dream like this since high school. Getting out of bed to find clean sheets, Dave thought to himself: Until today I believed that Lateef was untouchable, unreachable. But he kissed me, and even if it was for the briefest of moments, that kiss was real, it meant something, and I'm going to find out what!

Dave suddenly found himself eagerly awaiting the new year, and what it might bring.

Miguel Berthaud had never before felt so miserable as he did tonight. He had gone to Claudette's party expecting to see his friend as radiant as she always was whenever she opened her house to all of Aïn El Qamar for one of her eagerly anticipated fêtes. He had gone there expecting to laugh, and to make others laugh. He had gone there if not expecting at least hoping that the company of her friends would snap Claudette out of the insane self-destructive behavior that she had adopted recently whenever she was with Mohamed Fareed.

What he had not expected was to see the catastrophic change in Claudette. Whereas before she had had a carefree openness about sex, now she was blatantly and offensively vulgar.

Miguel knew that her descent into what could only be called depravity was due to Fareed's sudden and vindictive exit from Aïn El Qamar.

But why had Claudette chosen to react in a way that could only bring her more pain and misery?

Miguel could imagine a different ending to tonight's events. He saw it so clearly that the illusion almost became reality.

Claudette had come to him in tears. "My life is in ruins," she cried. "Fareed has left me and I am empty inside. I am old and faded and desired by no one."

Miguel laughed. "Old? Faded?" he exclaimed. "Can't you see how beautiful you are? The changes you think you see in your mirror are only in your mind. You possess a beauty that can only come with having lived a full life. When you enter a room, every eye is on you in envy and desire. And you are equally beautiful from within. Your spirit of adventure and your *joie de vivre* are as exquisite as your face and body."

Claudette remained silent, drinking in Miguel's words, scarcely able to believe them. Then, finally she said, "How foolish I have been! Why didn't I see that all my searching must eventually lead to you, Miguel? I have said that other people do not go below the surface when they look at me. But I myself have been a blind fool. Only tonight have I beheld your own inner beauty, Miguel, an inner beauty I have never found in any other man."

And then she was in his arms telling him how much she had always loved him if only she had not been so blind.

"It's all right," he consoled her as he tasted her kisses. "We have the rest of our lives to make up for our foolishness."

That was how it had been in his imagination. That was how it should have been. That was how it never would be.

Claudette lay awake and stared at the young man beside her. The light which filtered in from the street caressed his hard naked body. He slept silently, and in sleep his face was that of a child.

It had been good having him make love to her, worth the hundred *dirham* note she had slipped into the pocket of his skin tight pants last night at the Hotel El Qamar *discothèque*. He was strong and virile and he made her feel young and free. He was a stranger, but as they had merged in the ecstasy of passion, she had loved him and she had felt that, momentarily, he had loved her.

Now only emptiness remained. There was no love, no youth, not even the illusion. There was nothing. Nothing at all.

And tomorrow her useless, endless search for … something … would begin again.

It's not working, thought Marcie as she lay sleepless on one of the *banquettes* in her friend Judy's house in Fez. It seemed that no matter how much distance she put between herself and Aïn El Qamar, the clearer she saw Jean-Richard's handsome face and troubled eyes.

That face. Those eyes. They had stayed with her all last night and had been before her at Halima's house today. They haunted her still, as she stared at the darkened ceiling of Judy's living room.

Why had she fallen in love with a man who could not keep her straight from all the other women he had made love to? What was it that had made her feel that she might be different, that she might be the one who could change him, make him love one woman and one woman alone? Who was she to think herself so unlike the rest?

Stop asking these absurd questions! Marcie ordered herself. Forget about Jean-Richard. The man is only going to complicate your life and bring you unneeded pain and heartache.

But I am already in pain, she responded. And I'm beginning to realize that there's only one way to end it.

The way is escape, one half of her argued. You were right not to have gone to the party. You're right to be putting last night out of your mind.

But I can't, the other half answered. There's only one solution to my problems and that is to give Jean-Richard a second chance. There must be some reason why he is so afraid of loving a woman and of being loved in return. I think that if I don't try to help him, he may never get another chance. And if he has no second chance at happiness, then neither perhaps may I.

When she returned to Aïn El Qamar in January, Marcie swore to herself, she would find a way to reach Jean-Richard, and in so doing, to discover the man that she knew somehow to be hiding deep inside his seemingly hollow shell.

Kevin found no peace this night as he lay sleepless in the room where he and Kacem Hajiri were to have consummated their love. He was alone now, Kacem too disturbed by his presence to remain in the same room with him.

This was to have been his night of passion, and now he was left with nothing, not even hope, which at least had been in his heart up until today.

Was there some curse on him, a curse that would forever deny him the joy of being loved? Jamey had been murdered. Kacem's feelings had proven to be platonic at best. What would be the next manifestation of this curse? How would he next be forced to suffer?

No, God damn it! He was through with love and the pain it brought him. Love could not be depended on. Love created nothing; all it could do was destroy.

Only work brought Kevin happiness. Only work brought him peace. His students were his rock. They would always be on his side. They would never let him down.

Kevin knew he was already an excellent teacher. He vowed now to become the finest in his school. No! The finest in all of Morocco, and his students unsurpassed as well. Instead of spending his time dreaming of Kacem, he would plan lessons that would dazzle with their brilliance. His explanations would be so clear that even the slowest learner could not fail to understand. Together, he and his students would achieve results that no one had ever dreamed possible.

This, and not love, would be his salvation!

I think I may be the only sane person in Aïn El Qamar, thought Michèle as she awakened to hear Dominique returning to their house. Her bedside clock showed five in the morning. I hope you had a good night, thought Michèle. Although with Laurent, I'd be surprised.

Yes, only Michèle seemed to be sane. Claudette flaunted her wanton sexuality. Janna wallowed in her despair. Jean-Richard was obviously seeking something in his endless seductions.

And here am I, thought Michèle, untouched by the misery and self-destruction around me.

I've just finished a wonderful trimester of work. The *proviseur* hasn't harassed me. I awaken every day to find something new and exciting in my life in Aïn El Qamar.

And perhaps I've found a man as well.

Kacem.

She repeated the name.

Kacem.

It was gentle, sweet, but it had an inner strength, just as did the man himself.

Kacem …

Yesterday at the *conseil* had only been the beginning.

Michèle sensed that there was much more to come.

Dawn had not yet arrived, but the student was wide awake. All night long sleep had eluded him. Ms. Gallagher's face remained before him hours after he had closed his eyes.

Now he rose from his bed, lit a candle at his desk, and opened his diary. He reread what he had written earlier that evening in his erratic script.

"I put my hand on her cheek tonight. Her skin was soft and white. I know now how Cherqaoui felt when he touched her. But he's gone, and I am here.

"I know that Ms. Gallagher won't refuse me when the time comes. I just need to find a way to get her alone with me. It may take time, but I can be patient."

He reached down and felt his erection. He was more of a man than Cherqaoui ever was, and this was the proof. When the time came, it would be his means of making Ms. Gallagher his own.

MARCH 1977

CHAPTER 17

▼

The pretty redhead who stood at the front of the classroom seemed hardly awake at all. Her few movements were lethargic. Her eyes stared blankly ahead. She seemed almost unaware of the sea of faces before her.

Some of her students attempted to follow the lesson, but others stared out the windows or worked on assignments for other classes, and some even used the time to share gossip with their neighbors.

Janna had drawn no amusing pictures for this lesson. She asked her questions in a slow toneless voice.

"Where are you going to … travel next summer …"

Several hands rose hesitantly, but she did not seem to notice them, so the answers came simultaneously.

"I'm going to I'm travel to travel to Casablanca I going in Tetuan to Marrakesh next summer in next summer the next summer …"

Several students laughed at the cacophony of mistakes, but their laughter held no pleasure or enjoyment of the lesson. Other faces showed confusion. What could be considered correct when their teacher accepted all answers indiscriminately? Once again Ms. Gallagher paid no attention to the errors, and she made no attempt to quiet the giggling students. She obviously had no control over these young Moroccans, and it was clear that they were either bored or annoyed or perhaps even a little sad to be in this class rather than studying physics or geography.

"Where are you going to travel … next summer …"

More laughter followed the teacher's unintentional repetition of the previous question.

One of the students, whose name was Abdellah, answered:

"Next summer I'm going to travel to Casa and Rabat."

He waited in vain for Ms. Gallagher to show approval. She said nothing. Once, she had done so much to help this intelligent but painfully shy student to gain confidence in himself. Now he wondered if she even knew him from the others.

This Ms. Gallagher was so unlike the young woman who had taught him his first words of English only five months ago that he sometimes imagined that the real Ms. Gallagher had left Aïn El Qamar and some extraterrestrial twin had taken her place, someone with uncombed hair, vacant eyes, and a face that never smiled.

Abdellah still loved Ms. Gallagher, though it was no longer easy to. If there were a way to bring her back to what she had once been, he would do anything to find it. But there seemed to be no solution.

Of course, she was not always so distant and removed from reality. Some days he could still see traces of the teacher he had known last fall. But today was one of the bad days. One of the really bad ones. And seeing her like this tore at Abdellah's heart.

An increasing number of students swore that Ms. Gallagher smoked *keef*, not occasionally as did some of them when they were nervous about a test, but every day, and even in the mornings. One student had gone so far as to suggest that they try and steal her purse to see how much she had stashed inside, but Abdellah had summoned his courage and told the other student he would kill him if he even attempted to search her handbag. Ironically, few students ever mentioned her relationship with Lahcen Cherqaoui anymore. They had her current behavior to gossip about now.

Abdellah had once felt confident that he would actually be speaking English by the end of the school year, less than three months away. Now he had grave doubts. Ms. Gallagher's explanations were often so confusing that he didn't really understand what she was having him repeat, and because his mistakes were no longer being corrected, he did not know if his English was improving. Before, he had trusted Ms. Gallagher to teach him everything he needed to know. Now he had to rely on a second-hand book he had bought at the *souk*, but the book had been written and published in France, and he wondered if the English in it was accurate.

"Where ... When are you going to travel to ... Casa?" asked Ms. Gallagher now.

A few students blurted out different answers. Abdellah doubted that any of them were correct. The faces of most of his classmates showed only boredom and a wish to be elsewhere. Abdellah recalled how there had once been cheerful laughter at Ms. Gallagher's clever, funny questions, and how she had once pretended to be afraid of a little toy mouse she had brought to class. Then, Abdellah's heart had been filled with love and admiration. The love remained, but the admiration was replaced by pity and an intense painful sadness.

Shit! thought Janna. Is the fucking bell ever going to ring! Would this hour never end? Janna knew that the lesson was going badly. At times she would almost forget what she was teaching. At times she was almost unaware of where she was. She knew that the students only partially understood what they were saying, and she even heard many of their mistakes. But while a part of her said, You shouldn't be letting this happen, a greater part of her was saying, So what. Does it really matter if they learn or not? Does anything really matter?

Janna had never intended to let herself get into this state, she was occasionally sober enough to realize. She had only wanted to dull the pain of Lahcen's rejection. She had never expected to become reliant on a drug to help her do so.

It was funny now. She was almost sure that if she stopped smoking *keef*, she would find that even without its numbing effects she could think of Lahcen without hurting, which was surprising, since at one time she had thought that she could not go on without him.

He had not once written her again after his last letter in—when was that? Early November? Four months ago.

It seemed almost beyond comprehension that winter should already have passed and that it should now be nearly spring, her second spring in Aïn El Qamar.

Last year at this time, she and Lahcen had been merely teacher and student. If only things could have stayed that way, Janna would not be in this impossible situation. Her initial motivation for smoking *keef* hardly existed any longer. Time had indeed made Lahcen's silence easier to accept and she could almost think of him dispassionately, as someone she had once cared deeply for, but for whom she now felt virtually nothing except regret that their doomed relationship had ever even started.

Well, perhaps she did not really regret the time they had spent together. Those had been beautiful months, and whether or not they had been based on falsehoods, the memory of them was still, if not sweet, then at least bittersweet.

Janna could still recall back in October when smoking *keef* had been a lark, an easy way to get high for the evening. If only she had let it remain so. But in December and January, when she had needed it emotionally, she had started smoking as soon as she got up in the morning in order to dull the pain that always struck the moment she returned from sleep to reality. During Christmas vacation she had spent entire days on the beach at Agadir under the influence of *keef*. Michèle had been powerless to stop her from returning to their room every few hours to revive the drug's effects on her body and on her mind.

Back in Aïn El Qamar, Janna had made no attempt to stop using. She relied on the lesson plans she had prepared during her first year in Morocco and was somehow able to get by, scarcely aware of what she was teaching. Many students no longer paid attention in class, but Janna had reached the point where she simply did not care what her students did or thought.

Now, if only the bell would ring, she could get out of this classroom and into the nearest bathroom to sneak a few more tokes. Janna hated the feeling of coming down, and she could already feel her high fading rapidly.

Glancing at her watch, Janna saw that it was already five to eleven. The bell should have rung minutes ago, but that old fool whose only duty was to ring it was probably napping as usual. Janna wanted to give the students permission to leave, but Kevin had recently dismissed his students before the bell had rung, and the *proviseur* had herded them back to class and reprimanded Kevin in front of them. So Janna continued asking questions in her dull monotone, and if she was repeating herself, that was the bell ringer's fault and not her own.

Finally, she heard the sound of the bell, and the students got up to leave the classroom. No one came to her desk today to ask questions. It had been a long time since they had last done so. Janna was aware that she was not teaching as she used to, but she found she didn't really give a damn. All that was important was staying high and floating through the rest of the year. Aïn El Qamar was a place filled with painful memories, and all she wanted now was for the year to end, and to be on a plane going anywhere as long as it was out of the country.

The class *responsable*, whose duties included keeping the class attendance book, had given her today's list to sign. He had written the names of seven students who had not come to class. It crossed Janna's mind that she had once had perfect attendance, but the thought was brief and did not faze her.

Leaving the classroom, Janna headed for the faculty-staff lavatory, which was located in the administrative wing of the school. On one of her good days, she might have waited until she was home before using her *keef* pipe, but today she was in such a hurry to feel the effects of the drug that she disregarded the fact that any of her colleagues, male or female, might use the restroom after her. She took out the long *keef* pipe which she always kept hidden in her purse under all her teaching things, and after filling the tiny bowl, she lit it and inhaled the strong thick smoke. Life was so much easier when you had something to cushion the blows.

As Janna left the lavatory for the *salle des profs*, she noticed Kevin Kensington walking towards her, but he passed her with only the slightest nod, and she herself ignored him. Janna had never particularly liked Kevin, and now she found him almost obnoxious in his obsessive dedication to teaching. In her few recent conversations with him, he had so bored her with his self-centered ramblings about what he was doing in class, new techniques he was trying, the "amazing" progress of his "brilliant" students, blah, blah, blah … that Janna had simply stopped talking to him at all. It wasn't just that she found him boring; there seemed to be an implied put-down of the rest of the faculty in his egocentric bragging.

The *salle des profs* was nearly full when Janna entered. Almost mechanically, she walked over to the large table where the mail was left each day. She had long ago stopped waiting for letters from Lahcen, but after weeks of rushing to the *salle des profs* only to have her hopes dashed, the habit of checking her mail remained. There was nothing on the table with her name on it, but this did not bother Janna in the slightest. There was no one she was particularly interested in hearing from.

Janna was about to leave the *salle des profs* when Kevin stalked in, heading purposefully in her direction. What on earth has got him so pissed? she wondered. As if I care, she added silently.

"Where the fuck do you get off smoking dope in school?" exclaimed Kevin without preamble, and although he was speaking in hardly more than a whisper, Janna could hear the indignation in his voice.

"What are you talking about?" she said, feigning innocence.

"You know damn well. I saw you coming out of the bathroom just as I was about to go in. God, that room still stank of your filthy smoke."

"What makes you think I was the one who was smoking? It could have been anyone else. You know, Kevin, you've really got your nerve!"

"You're a fine one to be talking about nerve! You must be out of your mind to smoke your disgusting weed right here in school. You might as well have been doing it in front of the students."

Janna reached into her purse for a cigarette. She lit it and said, "Listen, little mister perfect teacher of the year, you can just take your goddamn unsolicited advice and shove it!"

"Good Lord, Janna, don't you have any respect for the work you're doing? Don't you ever think of what you're putting your students through, of the way you're letting them down? And if you don't care about your students, at least think about Dave and Marcie and me. What you do rubs off on all of us!"

"You know something, Kevin," exclaimed Janna, "I don't give a shit!"

"Well, you'd better start, or you're going to have everyone in this school against you. We don't need your kind here. You're going to pull us all down with you!"

"Well fuck you all!" shouted Janna. By now, both she and Kevin had abandoned all pretense of keeping their voices down. "And especially you, Kevin Kensington, you son of a bitch faggot!"

Suddenly Kevin's hand had struck her face, and in the hush that ensued, the eyes of the entire faculty room were glued to the pair of Americans. Then the silence was broken by the ringing of the eleven o'clock bell—ten minutes late as usual—and the other teachers filed out, carefully avoiding the two Americans.

"You're a real cunt, Janna," spat out Kevin, "and I hope you rot!"

He stormed out of the *salle des profs* without another glance in her direction.

Oh God, thought Janna, I didn't mean for that to happen. Why won't people just leave me alone?

Michèle had come up to her and put her arm around Janna's waist. "Do you have another class, love?" she asked.

Janna shook her head.

"Neither do I," said Michèle. "Come on, I'll drive you home."

"I can walk," insisted Janna. "It's only a few blocks."

"You're in no condition to walk even that far," replied Michèle. "Come on."

Janna allowed herself to be led out of the *salle des profs* and towards the parking lot.

"You're lucky that there wasn't anyone in the faculty room who could understand what you said to Kevin," said Michèle as she unlocked her car. She and Janna got in. "Kevin's sexuality has nothing to do with his ability as a teacher or his worth as a human being," she continued as they left the parking lot in the direction of Janna's house. "And you know that as well as I do."

"All Kevin thinks about is school," said Janna. "It drives me crazy. Why can't he just mind his own business?"

"He probably thinks it is his business," said Michèle. "He's so concerned about his own students that he must be doubly worried about what's happening to yours."

"I'm still teaching them," insisted Janna. "They haven't complained … have they?"

"Not yet that I know of," Michèle reassured her. "And that's where you're lucky." She was pulling up in front of Janna's house. "Your poor students still remember you the way you used to be, and they're still fond of that memory. I think they're afraid of hurting the teacher they once loved so much."

Janna said nothing, nor did she attempt to leave the car, so Michèle continued:

"You're also very lucky that Monsieur Rhazwani inspected you early in the school year. If he'd waited until now, you'd be in even bigger trouble. Just keep your fingers crossed that he continues to stay clear of your class."

"Michèle," said Janna. "You know, I really don't care. I probably should give a shit, but I don't."

"This is not you talking, Janna," said Michèle. "This is a drug that has screwed with your mind. Come on, now. Get out. You've got some pretty heavy thinking to do."

Janna got out of the car and Michèle followed her to the door. "You can come in if you want," said Janna. "Halima was here yesterday, so it's not in too much of a mess."

"I think I will," replied Michèle. "You and I haven't finished our talk yet."

"I really don't know what there is to talk about," said Janna as the two women went into her living room. It was in darkness, as the shutters had not yet been opened.

"If you'd let in some air and light," said Michèle, "you might see that it's nearly springtime." She threw open the windows and the shutters. "Come here," she said to Janna. "Just look outside. Winter's almost over. Feel how warm the air is. Let some of it inside this house, and inside you."

Janna had come up to the window to stand beside Michèle, but she now withdrew and took a seat on one of the *banquettes*. Lighting a cigarette, she said, "Why can't you understand, Michèle, that I'm content to let things stay the way they are? Don't you see that I enjoy getting high? It's not that I can't stop. I just don't want to."

"You're lying to yourself," said Michèle, turning to face Janna. "You're hooked, and you know it. You've got a habit that you're incapable of breaking."

"Don't you listen?" said Janna. "There's no question of being capable or incapable. I simply don't want to quit."

"Have it your way, then," said Michèle. "Go on throwing your life away. I've seen you at your best and I've seen you at your worst. And if you want to stay down where you are now, which is pretty low and hopeless let me tell you, then just stay there. I've talked and talked and I've seen you ignore my advice again and again. Well, this time, I've had enough. I wash my hands of you, Janna. I'm your only real friend in Aïn El Qamar, and if even I can't help you, no one can. In any case, I'm fed up with trying."

"Well, then just get out of here and see how much I care," said Janna. "Friends like you I don't need. Meddle in someone else's life for a change, Michèle."

"I never thought you'd come to this, Janna," commented the Frenchwoman sadly, "and I'm damned sorry for you."

"Take your pity and leave!" cried Janna. "Go on. Get out of here! And never come back!"

Sadly, resignedly, Michèle rose and, without a look back in Janna's direction, walked out of the room.

And out of my hair, thought Janna. Out of my life.

She found that last phrase curiously intriguing. Out of my life. Out of my life. Lahcen was out of her life. Happiness was out of her life. So was hope. And now Michèle was out of her life as well.

My life. My life.

Stop it, Janna, she thought. Don't start thinking that your life is worth something, or you'll begin to wonder if Michèle is right and that you are throwing it away. She reached for the *keef* pipe in her purse.

But something held her back from lighting it. She sat staring at it for she had no idea how long. She was alone, completely and utterly alone, and suddenly the thought of going on without even Michèle in her life and on her side was unbearable. Michèle's friendship was the last thing she had going for her and if she lost that …

Jumping up from the *banquette*, Janna raced to the door. If only she was in time to catch Michèle before she had driven away. If only she could reach her before she had indeed driven out of Janna's life.

"Michèle!" shouted Janna as she threw open her front door. And miracle of miracles, the Frenchwoman was still sitting in her car. Hearing Janna's cry, she looked up, startled.

"Michèle!" said Janna again, and ran to the car. Michèle reached over to open the passenger door.

"Help me!" begged Janna as she got in beside Michèle. "Please help me!"

CHAPTER 18

▼

The air was becoming warmer and drier as the bus moved farther from Rabat on its way to Aïn El Qamar. The traffic and skyscrapers and crowds and noise of the big city seemed hardly more than a vague memory. Now, as far as the eye could see, there were fields of wheat grown green and high after the winter rains. Gloriously colored patches of wildflowers were everywhere. The same land which had been brown and dry during the summer months was now radiant with new life and growth.

Dave and Lateef were returning from Rabat this morning, their spirits as high as the ripening wheat which gave promise of a memorable harvest. It hardly seemed possible that only two months ago, Dave had sat at the *qsar* staring down at Aïn El Qamar feeling the future to be bleak and desolate. Now, incredibly, it seemed that Lateef would indeed be accompanying the American back to the United States in July.

And this amazing reversal of fortune was due to, of all people, Claudette Verlaine. At the depths of his desperation, Dave had come to the sudden realization that there was only one person who had been in Aïn El Qamar long enough and who knew enough people to possibly be of help, and he had gone to visit her.

"*Je t'en prie*, Claudette," he had implored. "Is there anything, anything at all, that you can do?"

"And why should I?" she had asked coolly. "Moroccan men are all the same. Fareed was a bastard, and so is every last one of them!"

"If Lateef is, at least let me find that out for myself. I'm begging you, Claudette. You're my last hope. Is there anyone you know who might help us? I'm just asking for a name, someone I could contact, someone who …"

"Very well, you silly boy," interrupted Claudette. "I can see you're as besotted as I was. I'm actually quite touched. I'll speak to the governor directly."

"You know him?" Dave was astonished. He knew Claudette had a large circle of friends and acquaintances, but the governor himself!

"We were lovers many years ago," Claudette explained, "long before he reached his current exalted position. Let me have a little chat with him. He's actually quite a decent man, and if his decency doesn't suffice, I have several of his love letters in my memory chest, which I'm sure he would not wish his wife to read. They were newlyweds at the time he and I became involved. Theirs was not a love match, obviously. And as for the rest, you silly naive fool, don't come crying on my shoulder when your little Moroccan love breaks your heart too. I've had enough of heartaches to last a lifetime."

And hardly two weeks later, Dave had received word of Lateef's passport being approved.

Now, if only Claudette's prediction did not come true, Dave thought, his life would be perfect. Or nearly perfect, he corrected himself.

In the two months since he had felt Lateef respond to his kiss, Dave had tried repeatedly to recreate the magic of that moment which had brought Lateef into his arms. But the young Moroccan seemed deliberately to be keeping his distance. Oh, he was still as warm and caring and attentive as always, but invariably he managed to stay just far enough from Dave to prevent the American from further probing his feelings. Even when Dave had told him the good news about his passport, Lateef had seemed to be holding back, as if wanting to avoid another reason for finding himself in Dave's embrace.

Now, as the two of them sat in the Rabat-Aïn El Qamar bus, Dave both relished and resented Lateef's closeness to him on the narrow seat. Everything was so different from what he had expected back in December when his despair had turned suddenly to hope, a hope which had soon turned, if not back into despair, then at least into a kind of resignation that his relationship with Lateef had gone as far as it was to go. Well, if the relationship *was* going nowhere, at least he and Lateef were going there together.

"Do you think there'll be any problem with my visa?" the Moroccan was asking now.

"It doesn't look that way," reassured Dave. "You know how optimistic the consul was yesterday."

"But, things don't always turn out the way we expect," said Lateef, and Dave couldn't help thinking about his own situation with the young Moroccan.

The bus was pulling into Khoribga now, which marked the halfway point between Rabat and Aïn El Qamar. Dave looked at his watch. It was half past ten. They ought to be back in Aïn El Qamar by one, in time for him to put together a lesson for his three o'clock class.

"We should be here for about fifteen minutes," said Lateef. "Are you hungry?"

"Not particularly, but if you are, I'll buy you a *brochette* sandwich," offered Dave, as the two young men squeezed past a ragged beggar who was making his way down the aisle. Feeling generous, Dave gave the old man ten *ryals*, hardly more than a dime, but perhaps four times what he usually received.

Khoribga's bus station was built around a large square where there were almost a dozen buses now parked, each a different color and representing a different line. The town had grown rapidly in recent years, as there were abundant phosphate deposits nearby, but here it hardly looked different from the other towns where the bus had already stopped and would continue to stop on its way to Aïn El Qamar. One thing all of them had in common were the stands where *brochette* sandwiches were sold. Skewered cubes of beef or liver were quickly cooked over charcoal, then served between half loaves of round Moroccan bread. They were Morocco's closest equivalent to hamburger stands.

Dave approached one of the tiny booths and listened as a Moroccan asked the price of six *brochettes* and half a loaf of bread. Foreigners were often overcharged, and Dave had acquired the habit of finding out the going price before ordering anything. Today, as usual, it pleased him to ask for a *brochette* sandwich in Arabic—he was finally making some progress with Lateef's encouragement—and when the vendor quoted him a tourist price, and Dave replied by saying that the would only pay thirty-three *ryals* and not a *centîme* more, the man's shocked expression was a sight to behold. When the sandwich was ready, Dave took it over to Lateef who was drinking a Pepsi at a nearby soda stand.

"Did he try to overcharge you?" asked Lateef, and when Dave nodded, he added with a twinkle, "Welcome to Morocco!"

And now they were back in Aïn El Qamar. As Dave walked with Lateef towards his house, he realized how much his own feelings towards the town were influenced by his mood. When it had seemed that Lateef's passport would never be granted, he had noticed only the filth and the poverty and the ugliness. He had been disgusted by the litter in the streets, and by the rags that some children were forced to wear. He had seen the people as narrow-minded and unenlightened. The town had appeared carelessly thrown together and poorly constructed.

Today, everything was different. The men who sat leisurely sipping their mint tea in cafés reminded him that people in Aïn El Qamar did not share the Western obsession with time and money. The sight of wagons loaded with fresh fruit and vegetables was evidence that this was not yet a culture whose food was polluted with chemical preservatives and additives. Nor was the air impossible to breathe. Besides all this, there was also the special feeling a foreigner got whenever he observed the color and exoticness of Aïn El Qamar, evident in its architecture, in the dress of its inhabitants, and in the language they spoke. Although Dave still eagerly looked forward to his return to the United States, on days like this he knew that it would not be easy to tear himself away from Aïn El Qamar.

Lateef seemed to sense his mood. "You look like a tourist who's seeing Morocco for the first time," commented the young man as they walked with their overnight cases in the direction of Dave's neighborhood. "Sometimes I think this town disgusts you but not today."

"No, not today," agreed Dave. "Today I feel as if nothing can go wrong."

"I'm happy too," seconded Lateef, "so I've decided to make lunch for you today. Kevin probably doesn't know what time we're getting back, and after all the trouble you've gone to for me, I'd like to return the favor, even though I can't do that much."

"I would be delighted to have you cook for me," replied Dave.

"All right, then," said Lateef. "If you'll take my case for me, I'll leave you now and pick up what we need for … a lamb *tajine*?"

"That would be delicious!" exclaimed Dave, reaching into his pocket for his wallet.

"No, you don't," protested Lateef. "I've got enough money to buy food for us. I'm tired of taking from you. I want to give something back for a change."

"You owe me nothing," insisted Dave, but he accepted Lateef's overnight case without further attempting to pay for the meat.

"I'll see you in about fifteen minutes," called Lateef as he walked in the direction of some nearby shops.

Dave watched as the handsome young Moroccan moved away, then continued on to his own house.

It really did feel good to be back in Aïn El Qamar after twenty-four hours in Casablanca. Being in the big city always invigorated Dave at first, and he enjoyed the busy cafes and the window shopping he could do, but after a short time it became a bit too hectic, and he longed for the calm of Aïn El Qamar.

Arriving now at his house, Dave was greeted by the smell of cigarette smoke and a cry of "I hope the trip was worth your missing a day and a half of school!" Oh God, thought Dave, and I was just thinking what a quiet and welcoming place this was.

Kevin was obviously in one of his moods today. The foul odor was the result of Kevin's having become not just a smoker after his return from Kacem Hajiri's farm, but a heavy one at that. And the angry greeting was typical of Kevin's recent attitude towards anyone who did not share his obsession with teaching.

"Forgot something, Kev," shouted Dave. "Talk to you in a few minutes." He had in fact forgotten nothing, but a confrontation with Mr. "Teaching-Is-My-Life" would only spoil his good mood. After leaving the two overnight cases in the entry hall, Dave sat down on the front step, closing the door behind him. Several little neighborhood children came up and greeted him in Arabic. When he had returned their hellos, they mercifully went away to play.

It was sad now to recall the excitement Kevin had felt before Christmas vacation, and his naive optimism. Throughout the two weeks Dave had spent with Lateef in the South of Morocco, he had found himself nearly praying that everything had worked out as Kevin had insisted it would. Dave had almost convinced himself that when he returned to Aïn El Qamar he would find his friend brimming with happiness and fulfillment.

But of course, his initial fears had been well founded. At first Kevin had refused to talk about the events of the *Aïd El Kébir* celebration at Kacem Hajiri's house. But it was obvious that he needed to speak with someone, and in the evening, after the two Americans were well into their second bottle of wine, Kevin had finally revealed what had happened that night.

"He wasn't mean or vicious or anything like that," Kevin said, "but it seemed pretty clear that he doesn't think gay people are normal, and though he didn't say so in so many words, I'm sure that given a choice, he'd rather not have anything to do with a *pédé* like me."

"You don't believe him, do you?" asked Dave. "That there's something wrong with being gay?"

"There are people who change, aren't there? Who get married? Who have children?"

"That kind of 'change' is only superficial," said Dave. "What really happens is that they end up living a lie and ruining their lives and the lives of the people they deceive. Listen, Kev. Some people are just gay, just like some people are left-handed. We're not worse than straight people, we're not better, we're just different. You know as well as I do that we can love just as deeply and with just as much commitment as heterosexuals do."

"But wouldn't you change if you could?" wondered Kevin. "If you could be reborn, wouldn't you rather be born straight?"

"That's a pointless question, Kevin," said Dave. "And an unfair one. How would you feel if you heard a black person say that he wished he'd been born white, or a Jew that he'd been born Christian. You'd call them racist, or anti-Semitic, or just plain ashamed of themselves. Isn't that what liberation is about, accepting yourself and loving who you are? I like being gay. I didn't choose it, Kev, and neither did you. It's just who I am. And I like the feelings I have for other men. Those feelings feel right to me. They feel good. And I see no reason to try to change them."

"I thought that how I felt about Kacem was right and good myself," said Kevin, "but now … I just don't know, Dave. I just don't know."

That had been Kevin's reaction to Kacem's rejection, and Dave had wondered then how his friend would fill the void left in his life. He shouldn't have bothered wondering. It was as he had feared, only worse. Kevin plunged back into his work with a fury that made his "obsession" with it after Jamey's death seem only a passing interest. He never stopped planning, preparing, revising, and rehearsing his lessons. He would spend hours correcting student assignments with meticulousness that Dave found absurd considering how little time the students had doubtless spent doing their work. When a composition or exercise was good, not outstanding but merely good, Kevin would read it aloud as if it were a masterpiece. At times Dave would hear Kevin shouting "Idiot!" or "Moron!" and he would know that one of his brighter students had disappointed him. Dave had weeks ago decided to converse as little as possible with his friend, because their talks always ended up being so one-sided.

The situation wouldn't be so bad if Kevin didn't also insist upon other teachers' devoting as much time and energy to their own work as he did. Recently, though, he had gone up to teachers he hardly knew and criticized them merely because of what he had heard his students say. Kevin's natural tendency was to be a loner, but he was carrying this to extremes by alienating his fellow faculty members, by making them his enemies.

Something is going to give some day, thought Dave. Once again Kevin was putting all his energy into a single interest. The end result of his consuming passion for Kacem was to submerge himself in his work when that relationship failed. What would happen if Kevin's students did not conform to his expectations? Dave shuddered to think what the consequences of that might be.

Judging from Kevin's greeting when Dave had opened the door a few minutes ago, an argument was about to take place unless Dave could do something to avoid it, though he didn't know what.

Noticing Lateef approaching in the distance, his arms full of groceries, he decided to wait for the young man to arrive. Perhaps Kevin would be less inclined to criticize his friend if someone else was present.

When Lateef had reached the door, Dave told him about Kevin's reaction upon his arrival, and Lateef agreed to do his best to help. "When Kevin gets in his moods," said the Moroccan, "he seems a little crazy."

"He's hardly a model of stability," agreed Dave as they entered the house together.

"I'll help you with lunch in the kitchen, Lateef!" shouted Dave so that Kevin would hear him and know both that he was not alone and also that he had no intention of joining him for a discussion that would no doubt turn into a quarrel.

Lateef smiled at Dave and winked. "I'll be glad to have your help!" he shouted back.

As Lateef was browning the lamb he had bought, and Dave was peeling potatoes, Kevin came into the kitchen, smoking as usual.

"I'm sorry I yelled at you when you first came in," he said. "I was looking over Akazou's test paper and it had me so disgusted that I took it out on you."

Dave was glad to hear Kevin's apology, but he wasn't about to let him get away completely with his thoughtless remarks. "I hope it won't happen again," he said. "If you keep going on at me about what you obviously think is my sloppy work, we're never going to make it through the next few months. And if you don't put out that cigarette right away, I'm going to scream. You know you promised not to smoke in the kitchen or while we're eating. It's bad enough to live in the smokers' capital of the world without having your own home start smelling like an ashtray." Kevin sheepishly put out his cigarette in the sink. "And as far as my trip to Casa, you know that I went there on important business. I don't miss school for nothing, and you know that better than anyone else."

"You've made your point," said Kevin. "Forgive me? Please?"

"All right," said Dave. "But only this time."

"So how was your meeting with the consul?"

Lateef smiled at Kevin and said, "I think I'm going to be studying in the States next year."

"That's really wonderful," said Kevin, but he seemed preoccupied. "I'm happy for you both. And now, I'd better get back to my work."

Kevin was about to return to his room when he suddenly exclaimed, "Oh, I nearly forgot! A letter came for you yesterday afternoon. I'll go get it." Reentering the kitchen a few seconds later, he continued "It's from some female in the States. I don't think I've ever heard you mention her name."

"What name is that?" Dave asked.

"Miranda Cox," said Kevin, handing Dave the letter.

"Mandee Cocksucker! Well, I'll be damned."

"Mandee who?"

"A girl I knew in college," explained Dave. "She was known as the hottest fuck on campus. Gorgeous black hair, enormous tits, and a pussy that needed a daily dose of dick, if you'll *pardonner* my *français*. There was hardly a guy she hadn't screwed, myself included. She was so wild with her tongue, she almost had me convinced that I was as straight as she was. Believe it or not, we actually dated for a few months, till I met Ethan that is, and knew without a doubt that they don't get any gayer than yours truly. God, I wonder what's prompted her to write?"

"Well, open the letter," urged Kevin, "and find out."

As Dave skimmed the note, his mouth fell open in shock.

"What is it?" exclaimed Kevin.

"She says she wants to come stay with us for a week or two."

"She what?"

"Listen," said Dave, and read from the letter. "'I was talking to Peggie and Jake the other day and when I mentioned that I was traveling to Europe this coming May, they suggested that I take advantage of the proximity and go visit you. Well, I checked and it'll be so cheap for me to fly down to Casablanca that it would be silly for me not to make the trip. From what I hear, Moroccan men are prize studs, although that can't possibly be news to you, wink, wink. Anyway, if there are any who'd rather fuck a girl than your own ever-charming self, could you let them know that Mandee's on her way? See you soon. Love, Miranda.'"

"You don't look very happy about her visit, Dave," commented Kevin. "What's the problem? You've had other friends from the States come stay with us, and none of them have ever gotten this kind of reaction from you. She obviously knows you're gay. So what's the problem?"

Dave glanced meaningfully towards Lateef, who was slicing tomatoes for a salad. "That's the problem," he whispered to Kevin.

Miranda Cox, once she had laid her eyes on Lateef, would want to lay more than just her eyes on him, and with Lateef such a frequent visitor, there was no way he could keep the two of them apart. What then? How could Dave prevent her from trying to sleep with Lateef, knowing that she would surely make the attempt? Would he be able to stop her before she had made good on her nickname? Just the thought of Mandee Cocksucker in bed with Lateef was enough to make Dave physically ill. No, that was something he could never let happen. He had to find a way to prevent it. He had to!

CHAPTER 19

I forgot to add salt, realized Michèle as she tasted the sauce in which her *navarin de mouton*, or lamb stew, was simmering. Now if she could only discover where Kacem had put the shaker. Cooking in someone else's kitchen was quite different from doing it in your own, and when the kitchen was that of a bachelor, it was even worse. He must have put the salt shaker somewhere, but where?

"Damn it Kacem," she said aloud, even though the object of her annoyance had not yet arrived back from school. "Don't you have any sense of organization?" Finally, she found the salt under the sink of all places. Now whatever had possessed the man to leave it there? Michèle had no idea, but after adding a teaspoonful of it to the *navarin*, she returned the salt to its peculiar hiding place. She was not here to reorganize Kacem's kitchen, only to cook for him.

She had in fact needed to do a good deal more than cook, though, the first time she had come here. Kacem's decision to rent a house of his own had pleased them both, but a large part of his salary still had to go towards supporting his family, and now that he was paying rent as well, he had no money left to hire a maid. On Michèle's first visit, the place had been a disaster area. So I became the cleaning lady, she thought ruefully, though she had to admit that since her first visit and her exclamations of horror at the disorder she had found everywhere in the house, Kacem had done his best to keep things tidy.

Now, as Michèle stood watching the *navarin de mouton* to make sure that it did not boil, she thought to herself how much both Kacem's life and her own had changed since their first long conversation in the *salle des profs* last December.

She hadn't seen him again until school started. During vacation, she had often caught herself thinking about him, recalling his warmth and his concern for the welfare of his students during the *conseil de classe* and his courage in standing up for what he believed in. She had wondered if he would appear the same to her once she was back in Aïn El Qamar or whether she would find that her first impression had been merely an illusion.

He hadn't changed. That first day back at school, they had begun a conversation in the *salle des profs* which had so interested them that Michèle had invited him over for lunch to continue it. Dominique was going to be out, so Michèle knew that her French friend's sour disapproval of things Moroccan would not spoil their meal.

It had been a delightful lunch. Kacem not only talked intelligently about his own background and education and hopes for the future but he listened attentively as well, fascinated by Michèle's accounts of her experiences in France, the United States, and Morocco. Michèle had deliberately omitted several stories of the sexual escapades she had observed and even been a part of in Southern California, and she had made no mention of her unfortunate affair with the married man. She sensed that in spite of Kacem's impeccable French and his European veneer, he remained Moroccan at heart. Michèle had therefore made a deliberate effort not to come on too strong, feeling that this might only scare the man away.

The first day, she had driven Kacem back to his family's house, and after their second lunch together as well. Dominique was rarely in these days, so it had been easy to invite Kacem a third time, and a fourth, and …

After several meals, Kacem himself had suggested that he not be seen in Michèle's car with her. "It's not for me," he had explained. "If people start to gossip, they'll only tell me how lucky I am to have found a European girlfriend. They'll probably congratulate me on it. You're the one who'll be hurt. They'll start calling you a loose woman, or making jokes about how Frenchmen aren't good enough for you. Do you see what I mean? You know and I know that there's nothing for them to gossip about, but even if they were aware that we were only friends, that wouldn't stop their tongues from wagging."

Michèle had been touched by Kacem's concern. It was true that they had never slept together, but Michèle foresaw that it was only a matter of time until they did, and she realized that Kacem was right. The sooner they started being discreet, the better. Both of them had seen how quickly gossip could spread during Claudette's liaison with Mohamed Fareed.

Was it after their fifth or their sixth lunch together that Kacem and she had finally made love? Michèle couldn't recall exactly. She could only remember the pleasure he had given her, and the feeling of having found someone truly special to fill a void in her life. Now that she and Kacem were together, her daily experiences in Morocco gained new meaning, as she saw them not only through her own eyes but through Kacem's as well, and through the eyes of love.

Now that the *navarin* was simmering gently, Michèle took plates and silverware for two into the living room and set them on the low table which stood between the two *banquettes*. Then Michèle sat down on one of the *banquettes* to wait for Kacem to arrive from school. As she waited, she recalled the day when Kacem had announced his decision to rent a place of his own.

"I'm tired of always having to visit you and wonder if Dominique will be out or not," he had said. "I know she doesn't approve of me, and whenever she's around, I can feel her hostility."

"You know it's nothing personal," Michèle said. "She's like that with everyone."

"Whatever the reason for her dislike, I don't want to worry about whether or not she'll be around. I've found a small house in the Bab-Jdid quarter. It's a decent neighborhood and the house is almost hidden from the others, so that it's nearly impossible for anyone to see who's coming and going."

"But won't they recognize my car?" asked Michèle.

"It's possible, of course," answered Kacem. "But there are hundreds of white Renault 4's in Aïn El Qamar. Also, since yours was bought in Morocco, it has standard Moroccan license plates, and not the yellow ones that foreign-bought cars have."

"Still, I wouldn't put it past some people to recognize my license plate number," said Michèle.

"Listen, love," replied Kacem. "We can't stop rumors entirely, but if we stay away from public places and keep our conversations at school casual, like they've always been, we can at least prevent the kind of gossip that was being spread while Claudette and Fareed were … you know …"

"Your discretion is charming," said Michèle. "And I can see your point. All right, if you've found a place, move in, and I promise to do my best not to give your neighbors any more food for gossip than humanly possible."

And so Kacem had taken the house last month, and Michèle had become a frequent visitor. They had worked out a plan whereby if Kacem had Moroccan friends over, he would leave one particular shutter closed. Seeing this, Michèle could drive quickly past and return later. If Moroccan friends came by when they were together, Kacem simply didn't open the door, and let them suppose that he was out, or if they became too insistent, he would shout out that he was busy preparing a difficult physics lesson, and they would leave him alone.

It had not taken Michèle long to realize that she had fallen in love with Kacem. And because of her love for him, she was happier than she had been in years. The one thing which had been missing from her previous enjoyment of life in Aïn El Qamar was now present. And how wonderful it was to be involved with someone who was totally, completely free, and what a change it was from her previous self-destructive relationship. How wonderful that Kacem did not have to share his time with anyone else.

If only ...

In recent days there had been disquieting complications in the guise of Claudette Verlaine. The Frenchwoman had never recovered from the breakup of her relationship with Fareed, and for the past few months she had been seen with dozens of young Moroccans. Her promiscuity was becoming a public scandal, but it was not Claudette's countless one-night stands that troubled Michèle. It was the sudden attention she had begun paying Kacem Hajiri.

This overnight interest had started about two weeks ago when Claudette had unexpectedly invited Kacem over for dinner one evening. When he had politely refused, she had not let the invitation drop. A few days later, she had presented him with an expensive physics handbook, saying that she had noticed it that weekend while perusing the shelves of a Marrakesh bookstore and had thought immediately that it might be of use to Kacem. He had had no choice but to accept the gift, and Claudette had promised to be on the lookout for anything else that he might find beneficial in teaching his classes.

This was almost a week ago, and Michèle wondered if Claudette had showed up with anything new today. As far as she knew, the Frenchwoman remained completely in the dark about Michèle and Kacem's affair. Would it be better to let Claudette know that Kacem was already taken and risk having the news spread around Aïn El Qamar? No, unsolicited as Claudette's attentions were, they were still preferable to having all of Aïn El Qamar gossiping about Michèle and Kacem.

Michèle looked at her watch. It was nearly quarter past, and Kacem should be arriving shortly. In fact, there he was now. She heard his key in the front door lock as he opened the door. Then Kacem was entering, smiling his dazzling smile. Michèle hurried over to him, her arms outstretched. He took her in his embrace and their lips met. As Kacem kissed her long and tenderly, Michèle let her worries about Claudette fade away.

"Let's not have lunch right away," suggested Michèle. "I got started a bit later than I expected, and at the moment there's something I want more than food."

"*Moi aussi*," agreed Kacem, and led her into the bedroom where they undressed each other unhurriedly, savoring the leisurely revelation of their bodies. They lay on the bed together, naked, entwined in each other's arms, kissing deeply and searchingly. Michèle loved the way Kacem's strong but sensitive hands went from experience to the places where their touch excited her the most. She could not stop from moaning when they danced across her belly or when they lightly stroked the skin of her inner thighs. She herself delighted in returning this pleasure to Kacem as she sucked playfully on his nipples, or more deeply on his pulsating manhood. She relished the way his own mouth returned the favor, especially when his tongue found her own sex and explored its every secret place. They had each learned that lovemaking between them was best when they built up their sexual lust until both were panting for those final moments of ecstatic release. Today, as always, when Kacem entered her, she felt a rapture that she could never have found words to describe.

And then it was on to more commonplace pleasures. "What's that delicious smell coming from the kitchen?" Kacem asked, and Michèle replied, "You're in for a treat. You've had lamb *tajines* before, but today I've made you a French *navarin de mouton*. I hope you'll like it. Just remember that the spices are more delicate than in Moroccan cooking, so don't expect them to jolt you. Let them caress your taste buds."

"Like this?" asked Kacem, as he kissed Michèle, circling her tongue sensually with his own.

"Nothing tastes quite as good as you," she whispered between kisses.

They could have stayed there for hours, but the aromas wafting in from the kitchen were now too powerful to resist.

They dressed. Then, while Kacem waited in the living room, Michèle took the *navarin* off the stove and filled two plates with the mixture of meat, peas, and tiny onions, and an exquisitely seasoned sauce. She brought them in, hot and tempting with steam rising from the plates.

"Would you like wine today?" asked Michèle, as she set the plates on the table.

Kacem smiled and nodded his head. Michèle returned with a bottle of Cabernet du Président which she had bought yesterday at the Mondiale.

"Sometimes I wonder how I ever lived without you," said Kacem. "My life has changed so much in these past months, and it isn't just that I now have wine with my meals," he added, taking a sip of the Cabernet.

"*C'est bon?*" asked Michèle.

"*Délicieux*," replied Kacem. "And so is this *navarin*," he added as he took a bite. "I ought to get the recipe for my mother."

"And who would you say it was from? Kacem, you know as well as I do that our relationship would be difficult at best for her to accept. She's a traditional Moroccan woman, you're her eldest son, and I'm a foreigner who's five years older than you are."

"*Ne t'inquiètes pas*," reassured Kacem. "To start with, you don't look a day over twenty-three. And secondly, my mother and my father will accept whatever woman I choose to be with. They know I spent years away from home living in France. So just stop worrying about things that aren't really important."

"*Oui, monsieur!*" said Michèle with a mock salute. "And would you please be so kind as to eat this scrumptious food I've slaved over a hot stove to prepare!"

Now it was Kacem who was pretending to salute Michèle, and then protesting, "You don't expect me to eat this with a knife and fork, do you? Mother never taught me how!"

"Just shut up and eat!" commanded Michèle as she forced herself to stop from laughing. "With your knife and fork!"

After lunch, Kacem's jocular mood seemed to change. As they sat in the living room drinking coffee—he had helped her wash the dishes, which showed how far Michèle had come in her efforts to liberate him—Kacem suddenly became silent, his eyes staring into space, a worried furrow on his forehead.

"What is it love?" asked Michèle. "Is it Claudette again?"

"I almost wish it were," said Kacem. "She at least I can handle."

"Don't be so sure about that," cautioned Michèle. "Claudette is a determined woman, and right now she seems to have set her sights on you. She won't give up that easily. But if it's not Claudette, then what is it?"

"You left school too early to see the builders arrive and begin work on Monsieur Rhazwani's latest brainstorm."

"What's he up to now?" asked Michèle, wondering what more the man could do.

"I mentioned to you that a lot of the boarding students have been secretly leaving the school grounds now that it's virtually impossible for them to get official permission to go out," said Kacem. "*N'est-ce pas?*"

Michèle nodded. "They really have no other choice but to scale the wall if they want to see their friends and families."

"Well," said Kacem gravely, "it looks as if those days have ended. There's a construction crew at the school now with orders from the *proviseur* to add another three feet to the school wall and to top it with barbed wire and fragments of broken glass."

"*Oh mon Dieu!*" exclaimed Michèle. "That man is sick!"

"You're damned right he is," agreed Kacem. "Sick with a lust for power, for total domination of the school. He won't be happy until everyone kowtows to his authority."

"Can't anyone do anything to stop him?" asked Michèle.

"I wish we could, but Rhazwani claims he's only enforcing school regulations restricting student passes."

"But adding on to the school wall can't be cheap," said Michèle. "Does Lycée Mohamed Cinq have so much money budgeted for school renovation?"

"Probably not," agreed Kacem. "But apparently the quality and quantity of the food in the dining hall has fallen drastically in the past few weeks, though there's no way to prove this. You can be sure that if an inspector came, the students would be eating like kings for that day. The money for building onto the wall may represent what's being saved on food. It's also possible that he may be misallocating funds set aside for books or equipment."

"*Mais c'est affreux!*" exclaimed Michèle. "That man is an insult to humanity! He's …"

Michèle's expressions of outrage were interrupted by the ringing of the doorbell. Neither she nor Kacem had any desire to answer it, but the ringing would not stop. Getting up to look through the window, Kacem called out, "I'll be right there." Then, turning to Michèle, he explained, "It's a message from the secretary of the Cinéclub."

As Kacem went to open the door, Michèle recalled how it was he, with the help of several other teachers, who had organized Aïn El Qamar's first Cinéclub just after Christmas vacation. Kacem felt that the students deserved to be exposed to the finest of European, American, and Arab films, so now students, faculty, and interested members of the community were able to attend weekly showings of motion picture classics and the best of recent cinema. Discussions were held afterwards, which Kacem moderated. Michèle wondered what message from the Cinéclub secretary could possibly be so important.

Kacem was returning now, and his face made it clear that the news he held in his hand was not good.

"*Merde! Merde! Merde!*" he exclaimed.

"*Qu'est-ce que c'est?*" asked Michèle, rising from the *banquette*.

"Two things, actually," he replied. "First of all, Monsieur Rhazwani wants to meet with the Cinéclub committee late this afternoon to discuss boarding students who attend film showings '*illegalement.*'"

"What does that mean?" asked Michèle.

"It's the same thing I was telling you about earlier. *Internes* jumping the school wall because they feel they have as much right to be Cinéclub members as students who live at home. Rhazwani's probably going to boast to us that he's solved the problem by making the damned wall higher."

"Well, at least that's nothing new," said Michèle. "*C'est à dire* ... you already knew about that, didn't you? So what's the other thing, the one that's really bothering you?"

"See for yourself," answered Kacem, and handed Michèle the letter he had just been delivered. "Look who signed it."

"Oh shit!" said Michèle as she read the name "Claudette Verlaine" followed by the title "Acting Secretary." "You don't think ..."

"What else is there to think? Claudette couldn't care less about the Aïn El Qamar Cinéclub."

"Then it's just ..."

"*C'est ça*, Michèle," agreed Kacem. "Unless I'm mistaken, this is Claudette's latest scheme to get her hands on me."

"Then there's only one thing for you to do and that's resign," said Michèle.

"And let Rhazwani destroy the Cinéclub I worked so hard to set up? I can't do that Michèle!"

"But now Claudette will have an excuse to see you whenever she wants!"

"I know," groaned Kacem. "I know."

CHAPTER 20

▼

There must have been fifty men riding horseback, each wearing his finest *jellaba*, each holding an antique-looking rifle high in the air, stampeding in a single line across the field. Faster and faster they rode, closer and closer to the crowd of spectators gathered at the opposite end. Marcie stood among the onlookers, her hand firmly in Jean-Richard's grasp, her heart pounding as the horsemen sped towards them. There was no way the horses would be able to stop in time! Oh God, they were going to be trampled!

Then, as if they were a single rider, the horsemen pulled in unison on their reins, and as the dozens of speeding animals slowed almost instantly to a stop only inches from the spectators, a chorus of fifty rifles fired simultaneously. The crowd roared its approval and Marcie impulsively hugged Jean-Richard in her enthusiasm.

The horsemen were returning now to the other end of the field, obviously pleased that their performance had been so successful, preparing, Marcie supposed, to surpass that success with their next attempt.

"*Alors* ... did you enjoy the spectacle?" asked the young Moroccan who was standing with Marcie and Jean-Richard.

"Now that my heart has finally stopped beating like a drum," replied Marcie, "*oui, c'était extraordinaire.*"

"Sometimes the *fantasia* is a miserable failure," continued the Moroccan.

"*Fantasia?*" asked Marcie.

"That's the name given to the horse show you've just seen," answered their guide. "Sometimes, the riders stop too soon, and the crowd is disappointed.

Other times, they don't stop soon enough and unless the spectators move back quickly, people are hurt."

"Then I was right to be worried a few minutes ago," exclaimed Marcie. "We might have been killed."

"That's rather unlikely," said the Moroccan. "Today the riders are outstanding, the true champions of this area. Did you hear how they all fired their rifles at one time? It sounded like a single shot. Occasionally there's one who's a second late, and then of course the crowd breaks out in laughter instead of applause."

"Shall we stay here and watch them perform again?" asked Jean-Richard.

"Not from this close," answered Marcie. "I don't think my heart's up to it. Next time, the riders may not have such good timing, and I can just see my parents' expressions when they receive a telegram informing them that I've been hospitalized, the victim of a stampede. I've had a hard enough time convincing them that Morocco isn't a primitive backward desert. After news like that, they'd never believe another word I said."

Seeing that the riders were now lined up again at the opposite end of the field, the three spectators pushed their way back through the crowd and away from the precarious front line where they had been standing.

"There's a tent over there where we can have some mint tea," suggested the Moroccan. "The owner is a real expert at making it."

Marcie looked up at Jean-Richard who nodded. "We'd love to," she exclaimed. As they walked towards the open canvas tent, Marcie thought how lucky they had been to find their young guide, or rather to have been found by him. The Moroccan had been one of Jean-Richard's students several years back, and his delight at meeting his former science teacher had been evident. Now, thanks to the young man, whose name was Abdelhaq El Hassani, they were seeing this *moussem*, or festival, through the knowing eyes of a native and not simply as foreign tourists.

Abdelhaq introduced them to the middle-aged man whose tent they had come to, and when Marcie addressed him in Arabic, his already welcoming smile broadened and he insisted that they sample his tea *bla floos*, free of charge. The three visitors sat down under the canvas shelter which was completely open on one side allowing them a panoramic view of the surrounding action. Their host called out to a young boy—Marcie thought he referred to him as "nephew"—and asked him to bring them a half-dozen *sfinj*.

"He shouldn't be going to all this trouble," whispered Marcie to Jean-Richard, but secretly she was thrilled. *Sfinj* were airy Moroccan donuts, quickly fried in boiling oil until they were crisp and golden on the outside and light and fluffy on the inside. A few minutes later, the boy returned with the pastries, and Marcie was fascinated by the way they had been threaded through a long thick blade of grass which the boy wore around his neck like some kind of pagan necklace.

"They look delectable," exclaimed Jean-Richard, as the boy cut the grass with a knife and gave a *sfinj* each to the two foreigners and one to Abdelhaq. Meanwhile, their host had finished boiling water for their tea on a *mijmar*, a round, smoke-darkened and worn portable barbecue. This was the stove and heater of Moroccan families who could not afford gas burners, and of course it was essential outdoors where one could not easily carry the heavy *butagaz* bottles. The Moroccan man now prepared the mint tea as Kevin had described to Marcie back in October. She had been fortunate enough to observe and participate in the tea ceremony several times since then, at various Moroccan homes to which she had been invited, but the precise manner in which the tea was brewed to perfection never ceased to fascinate her. Thank goodness she had not let her pre-Christmas depression continue into the new year. Think of all the wonders and excitement she would have missed if she had let her love for Jean-Richard torment her instead of admitting it with joy. She would not be here now, and he would not be at her side.

"Do you realize," Jean-Richard was saying, "that in my ten years in Aïn El Qamar, I have never before been to a *moussem*?"

"You were spending all your time with other French people at parties and in fancy hotels," Marcie reminded him. "The only Morocco you knew was the one you'd created for yourself."

"*C'est vrai*," agreed Jean-Richard. "I'd constructed my own private world within the real world of Morocco, and I never saw outside its limits. Until now …"

Jean-Richard looked out towards the colorful spectacle of the *moussem*, and Marcie followed his gaze. The hills of the village of Aït Attab, high in the mountains an hour and a half from Aïn El Qamar, were studded with what looked from here like black diamonds. Actually they were the countless tents of wealthy Moroccan sheiks who had congregated in this mountain village to celebrate, as they did every year, the birthday of Saint Moulay Brahim, and to worship at the white-domed *marabout*, or shrine, where he was buried. Their celebration included the *fantasia* horse show, music, dancing girls, and much socializing. The crowds of people were multitudinous, some dressed in traditional *jellabas*, others in modern clothing, apparently big city residents returning to seek their roots, or perhaps only wanting to see how the other half of Morocco lived. Many of those who wore *jellabas* had come on foot or on horseback from neighboring villages,

while the dozens of cars parked nearby testified to the presence of the more affluent observers. There were even a handful of foreign tourists with their inevitable
cameras. Several of them were walking past Marcie and Jean-Richard now and
Marcie could sense how envious they were of the lucky foreigners who had been
invited to drink tea *à la marocaine*.

"*Barakallahoufik*, Abdelhaq," said Marcie. "Thank you for showing us what
most tourists can never see."

"It's my pleasure," said the Moroccan as he handed Marcie and Jean-Richard
each a glass of piping hot mint tea. "Monsieur Moreau was such a fine teacher
when I studied in his class at Lycée Mohamed Cinq that I'm glad to be able to
return some of his kindness. I wish I'd been a better student, but my family here
in Aït Attab is so poor that I had to work in my spare time to earn extra money,
so I wasn't able to concentrate on my studies as I should have."

"I'm glad you've told me," said Jean-Richard. "I always wondered why your
work wasn't as good as I knew it could have been. I suppose that back then I just
wasn't aware that my students had private lives, that they were real people with
real problems. Maybe now I'll start looking a little deeper under the surface. I'm
sorry I didn't with you."

Marcie couldn't help noticing how much Jean-Richard's attitude had changed
in the past few months, and the change pleased her. Not only was he discovering
his students as people; he also seemed to be rediscovering his own worth as a
human being.

"How did you find the time to come here today?" Abdelhaq was asking.

"We both taught from eight to ten," explained Jean-Richard, "but our day was
free after then. It was Mademoiselle Nelson who'd heard that there'd be a *moussem* here today, and I'm delighted now that she convinced me to come. This is a
remarkably beautiful place."

All around were lush green hills, and beyond them the higher peaks of the
Atlas Mountains. In the distance, the village itself was visible, but it was merely a
small conglomeration of modest houses and tiny shops. Most people lived on
small farms in the surrounding hills.

"We are Berbers, you know," said Abdelhaq. "Not Arabs. More than a third of
Moroccans are Berbers. The country was ours long before the Arabs invaded,
pushing us back into the mountains. They still dominate us, holding better positions, imposing their language on us in the schools, although here in Aït Attab
you hear mostly Berber spoken. Perhaps eventually things will change, but for
now we remain second-class citizens."

"I may be a romantic," commented Marcie, "but I think you're lucky in a way to be living in the mountains. Everything is so much more beautiful here than in the plains around Aïn El Qamar. Where you live, it's green the whole year, and cooler in the summer, and there must always be interesting places to explore. Except for the spring months, the flat plains are so dull and brown."

Abdelhaq looked pensive for a moment. Then he said, "I'd never thought of it that way. I guess I'm too close to the poverty to appreciate just how much beauty there is here. When people don't have jobs, and freeze in the winter because they lack the money to buy wood, it's pretty hard for them to value the things they do have."

"I see what you mean," said Marcie. "I suppose that my own relative affluence has blinded me to much of the reality of Moroccan life."

"Well," said Jean-Richard. "You're discovering it now. We both are."

The man who was serving them tea said something to Abdelhaq. "What was that?" asked Jean-Richard. "Don't ask me," replied Marcie. "I don't speak Berber."

"Our host wonders if you would like some more tea," Abdelhaq translated into French.

Marcie looked at Jean-Richard who shook his head. "Thank you, but …" Marcie hesitated to refuse the offer, so she suggested, "Could you perhaps take us around and show us some of the other things there are to see?"

"*Bien sûr*," replied Abdelhaq. "I'd be delighted." He apparently explained to their host in Berber that he would be guiding the foreigners around the *moussem*. The middle-aged man shook hands with them, thanking them in Arabic. Marcie told him how much she had enjoyed the tea, and Jean-Richard, who understood nothing, simply smiled and nodded his head in agreement with whatever she was saying.

The three of them got up and started to explore their surroundings. There were a number of stands which looked very much like the ones usually seen at *souks*, and Abdelhaq explained that many people took advantage of an excursion to the *moussem* to do their weekly shopping. One vendor was selling balloons for a *ryal* apiece to excited children who had the day off from school. Another group of youngsters had gathered around a magician, and Marcie noticed over their heads that the man was removing egg after egg from the mouth of one little boy to the delight of the onlookers. An old veiled woman sat cross-legged before small piles of powdered herbs and other plants. "Are those spices?" asked Marcie. "Some are," replied Abdelhaq, "but others are medicines or love potions or beauty preparations." There was another old woman who was reading someone's palm, and Jean-Richard asked Marcie if she'd like to have her fortune told. "No," she replied, and added, "Remember what we said about taking things one day at a time."

Now the two foreign visitors and their Moroccan guide were approaching the big black tents they had seen in the distance. Music was coming from within, and crowds of people had gathered around them attempting to peer in.

"There are dancing girls from the mountains inside the tents," explained Abdelhaq, "and only those who are invited in may observe them. The people outside have not been asked to enter."

"Oh, I do wish we knew the owner of one of those tents!" exclaimed Marcie, and then wished she hadn't spoken. Perhaps Abdelhaq was one of those unimportant folk without connections.

"Then wish no more," Abdelhaq was saying with a smile. "I know the man who owns that tent, the one way over there." He pointed to a medium-sized tent almost at the top of one of the hills. "He's a distant cousin, and if you don't mind the climb, I'm sure he'd be delighted to welcome you."

"Of course we don't mind," replied Marcie. "But is it … I mean is it all right for me …?"

"Foreign women are allowed to sit in the tent among the men," said Abdelhaq reassuringly.

"Then there's no problem," said Jean-Richard. "Let's go. It's not that far. And it's sure to be worth the walk."

The climb up the hill ended up being a good deal more difficult than it had looked from down below, and by the time Marcie and Jean-Richard were standing outside the tent, they were both out of breath.

"My feet ache from the stones," said Marcie between gasps. "But you," she added, looking at Abdelhaq, "you look like you've hardly climbed an inch."

"This is nothing for me," insisted Abdelhaq. "I've been scaling the cliffs around Aït Attab all my life."

As Marcie and Jean-Richard caught their breath, the young Moroccan slipped through the crowd gathered around the tent and entered. A few seconds later, a large smiling man with a dark beard and a white turban came out to greet them.

"This is my cousin Kaddour," introduced Abdelhaq, and the bearded man invited them into his tent in eager but somewhat broken French. Abdelhaq explained that his cousin had fought with the Allies during the Second World War and had learned French in the army.

Marcie and Jean-Richard were asked to remove their shoes once inside the tent so as not to soil the beautiful multicolored wool rugs covering the ground.

Marcie was amazed at how spacious the interior of the tent was. There must have been at least fifteen or twenty *banquettes* forming a circle around the rugs, and already a large number of young and old men were seated there, smoking cigarettes and drinking mint tea from small silver tables laid out about the tent. Marcie felt a moment of embarrassment as she entered, but the men were polite and did not seem to notice her. Perhaps they expected foreign visitors at such celebrations. There was a group of musicians performing at one end of the tent. One played a fiddle, another a wooden flute, and a third beat on a long cylindrical drum called a *tarija*. As Jean-Richard and Marcie took seats at one end of the tent, Abdelhaq explained that this was Berber music, and Marcie had to admit that it was unlike what she usually heard in Aïn El Qamar, more lively and infectious. Their host came over to offer them mint tea, which they gladly accepted.

Marcie wondered if they would have to wait long for the dancing girls to arrive, though strangely enough she was in no great hurry for the performance to begin. The unusual, somewhat discordant music was surprisingly soothing, and she found herself content just to sit back with Jean-Richard at her side and think back over what had happened after Christmas vacation.

Upon her return to Aïn El Qamar, Marcie had offered her friendship to Jean-Richard on the condition that it remain just that—friendship. Marcie knew in her heart that what she really longed for was more than that, much more. But if she surrendered to Jean-Richard as things stood between them now, it would mean the end of whatever relationship they did have.

Surprisingly, Jean-Richard had accepted her offer. She thought he had seemed almost relieved that there was no longer sexual promise, or danger, in their relationship. "*L'amitié*," he had agreed, and they had been with each other as friends ever since, seeing films together at the Cinéclub, dining out or at one of their houses, playing tennis, or merely enjoying a cup of coffee, heedless of what Aïn El Qamar might think, because they knew in their hearts that they were doing nothing worth gossiping about.

But as time passed, Marcie found herself beginning to vacillate in her determination to keep their relationship platonic. Always before, she had been convinced that to sleep with a man before marriage was wrong, immoral, a rejection of her upbringing and religious principles. Now, she wondered how much longer she could stand not having Jean-Richard's arms around her and the feel of his body pressed against her own.

Today, she … It wasn't that she suddenly wanted to jump into bed with Jean-Richard and forget everything which had come before. It was simply that she was no longer sure that she really believed what she had been telling herself about her feelings. Perhaps it was being here in this Berber tent, hearing music unlike any she had known in the United States, feeling herself worlds removed from her past and even her present in Aïn El Qamar. It was as if all that counted was this precise moment and the closeness of the man she loved. If he asked her now, at this very second, to give herself to him, would she have even the slightest hesitation to do so?

Marcie saw with relief that the dancing girls had arrived. Her thoughts had become too dangerous for her own good.

What a surprise to see that the girls looked hardly like the half-naked belly dancers she had been expecting. The four young women—two of them did not look a day over fifteen—were completely covered in snowy white caftans, and their long black hair was pulled back demurely and hidden under spangled black scarves. The fine blue lines tattooed on their foreheads and chins showed that they were Berbers. The only evidence of their being less than respectable was the red lipstick they wore and the cigarettes they were smoking. Marcie had only seen Moroccan women smoke in big cities, and even there that was rare, at least in public. But here were these young dancing girls, puffing away and chatting gaily among themselves despite the sea of male faces that stared at them in obvious interest and even lust.

"The two younger girls are from a village high in the mountains," explained Abdelhaq. "The older ones have been dancing for several years, and it was while traveling that they discovered the two young members of the troupe."

"But didn't their families object to the girls' leaving?" asked Marcie in shock, fearing that these young girls did more than dance, considering the way they were behaving in public.

"As I told you earlier, *mademoiselle*," continued the Moroccan, "we are a poor people. You must understand. For their families, it meant one less mouth to feed, and the girls can now live a comfortable life."

The four young women were now moving to the center of the tent in order to begin their dance. At times swaying to the music as a group, at times individually, the dancers captivated the audience with their rhythmic movements. Their bodies undulated with sensuous grace as they jingled the tiny finger-cymbals they held. Now and then they sang along with the musicians; at other times one heard only the sounds of the instruments. At this moment the four girls were dancing together in a circle around a low table, their hands joined. Then, one by one, each girl performed a solo dance on the table above the others. A man in the audience threw up a long scarf which the girl who was now dancing tied around her hips. The other girls moved back so that the dancer on the table could have the full attention of the spectators. The scarf emphasized her swaying hip movements, or perhaps they were belly movements—Marcie was not sure. The music increased in speed and intensity as the audience began to clap rhythmically, faster and faster. Finally, in one tumultuous burst of applause, the dance was over.

"*Magnifique*!" exclaimed Marcie. "Thank you so much for letting us see this!" she added to Abdelhaq. As the young man's cousin approached, she told him how much she had enjoyed the performance.

Then, looking at Jean-Richard, Marcie was surprised to see a strangely distant look in his eyes, and she wondered where his mind had wandered. But then he smiled at her and said, "I was only thinking, as I seem to be doing quite a lot lately, just how much I owe you." He took her hand in his, and despite what the men around them might think, Marcie did not object. She owed him as much as he owed her—for showing her what it was like to truly be in love. It was at moments such as this that she knew she dared not hesitate any longer before writing Eddy to tell him that their engagement was off. She ought, in fact, to have done so long ago.

"Would you like to stay on for lunch?" asked Abdelhaq. "Our host insists that you remain for the *meshoui*."

Marcie looked at Jean-Richard. "Oh, I know you probably feel as out of place here as I do, but please, can we stay? Opportunities like this don't happen every day."

"You're not the only one who's enjoying herself," said Jean-Richard. "Of course I'd love to stay."

"Wonderful!" exclaimed Abdelhaq. "Come with me. I must show you how the *meshoui* is prepared."

The young Moroccan escorted Marcie and Jean-Richard outside to the rear of the tent where several sheep carcasses were being roasted over open fires on thick long poles which women kept turning in order to make sure that the meat was evenly cooked. "The *meshoui* is our most special way of preparing lamb," explained Abdelhaq, "and it is only done on the most important of holidays."

"It smells so tempting, I can hardly wait!" exclaimed Marcie. "We often barbecue meat in the United States, but I've never seen anything done on such a grand scale."

"We can go back to the tent," declared Abdelhaq, "or you can walk around a bit more if you'd prefer."

Marcie looked at Jean-Richard. "Let's go up to the top of the hill," she said. "To the very top. The view must be spectacular."

"Very well, young lady," smiled the Frenchman. "Today I can refuse you nothing. Only remember when you hear me complaining of sore feet all day tomorrow who the culprit is."

"I take only partial credit, or blame," laughed Marcie. "Will you excuse us, Abdelhaq? We'll meet you back at the tent in say ... twenty minutes?"

"That will be fine," said the Moroccan. "Enjoy yourselves. Even I, who've lived here all my life, find the view spectacular."

And he was right. From the top of the peak, Marcie and Jean-Richard, standing hand in hand, could appreciate the *moussem* in all its splendor, and incredibly, the horsemen were still riding, never seeming to tire of their sport. Some people were leaving, but still others were arriving, either by car on the narrow winding road which led through the mountains, or on foot, or riding horses or donkeys along precarious mountain paths.

"I'm almost afraid to say it," declared Jean-Richard, "but at this moment I'm happier than I can ever recall being in this country. And it's all because ..."

"Don't," cautioned Marcie, and held her fingers up to Jean-Richard's lips. "Just be glad for the way you feel, and stay happy. You owe it—not to me, not to anyone else—you owe it to yourself."

In the quiet, high above the village of Aït Attab, Marcie felt closer to Jean-Richard than ever before, and when the twenty minutes had passed, she could hardly bear to tear herself away from this place where she felt such contentment and peace in order to return to the tent to partake of the *meshoui*.

But return they did, and as Marcie was pulling hot chunks of tender lamb from the roast, following the example of the other guests, she thought that this just might be the most delicious meal she had ever been served in Morocco. The mixture of the barbecue smoke with the juices of the meat was superb and she felt honored to be participating in this feast.

Naturally, there was *couscous* following the *meshoui*, and fruit to follow that. Finally, there was more of the inevitable mint tea, and when Abdelhaq noticed Marcie's deliberately small sips, he insisted, "You must drink at least two glasses of tea after such a big meal. It's excellent for the digestion." Well, thought Marcie, I've eaten so much already, a few glasses of tea won't kill me. And surprisingly, she found that the liquid did indeed help to settle her stomach.

"Are you stuffed?" she asked Jean-Richard.

"At this moment, not even one of Saadia's most tempting plates could appeal to me," he answered. "I may not eat for the rest of the week. But I have no regrets about today's meal. Believe me, I'll never forget it."

After they had finished eating, and had washed their hands in the traditional ceremony which Kevin had once described to Marcie, cigarettes were passed around to the satisfied diners. Jean-Richard, who had not smoked since he had begun seeing Marcie, refused, but Marcie accepted one. The harsh smoke made her cough, but it was gratifyingly calming.

No, she wanted to tell Jean-Richard, I'm not going to become a smoker just when you've quit, for she knew he must be wondering about her reasons for accepting a cigarette, she who had never smoked except occasionally during her student days before final exams. She wondered if he had any idea that it was because she had just come to the most momentous decision of her life, the thought of which so frightened and exhilarated her that she had felt the sudden need for a cigarette. Dear God, she prayed, let this decision be the right one, both for me and for the man I love!

Today, when everything between Jean-Richard and her was so perfect, Marcie had the absolute certainty that she should no longer resist the physical side of her love for him. Far from Aïn El Qamar, her reservations seemed foolish and puritanical and infantile. She was a grown woman who loved a man, and refused to offer him her love. Today, though, this would change. She could not let this moment pass by as had all the others before. If so, she might regret it for the rest of her life. Today, today finally, she would reveal to the man she loved the depth of her emotions, withholding nothing, giving all.

Today would be the day!

CHAPTER 21

▼

What he saw in the *salle des profs* filled him with disgust. How dare they call themselves teachers, thought Kevin as he scanned the faces of the men and women who waited in the faculty room between classes this afternoon. These people weren't professionals. They were dedicated to nothing but the pursuit of their own selfish pleasures.

Look at Claudette, for example. The woman spent more time deciding what to wear than in preparing her lessons. Or perhaps, to put it more accurately, in deciding what not to wear. What depravity had provoked her to leave her blouse unbuttoned so low that her full breasts were nearly hanging out? God, you could even see the outlines of her nipples through the flimsy fabric! To think that Kevin had once considered her his friend. Well, those days were past. No longer could he admire her style and verve or sympathize with her romantic problems. These days she looked and acted like a whore, with the exception that it was she who paid. And what must her students think of her? Thank God most of them were too young—only twelve or thirteen—to realize what a tramp Miss Claudette had become.

And then there was Laurent Koenigsmarck, the short pudgy stupid little man whose main interest these days seemed to be in discussing soccer scores with his cronies while pretending not to notice his wife's "friendship" with Dominique Moulin. The man taught French, yet he knew less about French grammar than Kevin, and it was his own language. Kevin thought of the hours he himself spent reviewing English sentence structure despite being a native speaker, and Laurent's indifference and incompetence revolted him even further.

Laurent's wife Christiane and Dominique Moulin had obviously become lovers. The signs were unmistakable to Kevin. The caresses Dominique gave Christiane, even in plain view of their colleagues, left no doubt in his mind that she was having sex with the vulgar Frenchwoman. Clearly, she was going to great pains to please Christiane, for she was now taking particular care of her appearance, and it was almost possible to consider her attractive these days. However in devoting all her time to her affair with Christiane, Dominique had lost the right to call herself a teacher.

Christiane had never been a teacher to begin with. She was perhaps even more crude and unschooled than her husband, if such a thing were possible. Her presence in this room was a farce, an insult to pedagogy, to the students, and to the school.

Kevin noticed Michèle now entering the *salle des profs*. She still chose to dress like a hippie, thought Kevin, the embroidered Moroccan tunic she had on today being the kind of garb favored by drugged-out American outcasts congregating around the *souk* in Marrakesh, and entirely inappropriate for an institute of learning.

I wonder what she can possibly have to say to me, Kevin asked himself now, as Michèle came walking in his direction.

"We need to talk, Kevin," said Michèle, "after what happened this morning between you and Janna."

"I don't know what there is to say," replied Kevin coolly.

"I'm sorry, but I disagree," declared Michèle, surprising Kevin with her bluntness. "Now don't get defensive. I haven't come here to argue with you, only to ask you to be more understanding with Janna in the next few weeks."

"After the way she insulted me in front of everyone this morning?"

"I grant you her choice of words wasn't the kindest," admitted Michèle. "But they were hardly slanderous, just a bit coarse and most definitely lacking in tact. You've got to realize, Kevin, that it wasn't Janna talking but the *keef* she'd been smoking. You two may not be the closest of friends, but Janna really respects you as a teacher and as a person, and what you told her about her condition today is nothing that she wasn't already aware of deep down. The point is, she's asked for my help in breaking the habit, and I've agreed. But my help isn't going to be enough. Please, Kevin, Janna's truly sorry about what she said this morning. Can't you give her a break just this once? She needs all our help and support."

"All right, Michèle," agreed Kevin. "I'll do what you ask, but only because Janna's students need their old teacher back. They're the ones who've been suffering, and they're the ones who need a break. But if she slips up again, I'll be on the phone to Peace Corps in Rabat before Janna even comes down from her high."

"Thank you," said Michèle with a grateful smile. "Oh look, you didn't tell me that Dave was back from Casa."

You hardly gave me the chance, thought Kevin, as Dave walked towards them.

"Well, how was the big city?" asked Michèle.

Dave told her excitedly about Lateef's visa being virtually a sure thing, and as Michèle offered him her congratulations, Kevin noticed Kacem approaching them. He was walking at a strange angle so that his back was turned to one side of the *salle des profs*, as if he were trying to avoid someone.

The conversation switched to French upon his arrival. "I don't want Claudette to notice me," he explained to the group.

"*C'est quoi le problème*, Kacem?" asked Dave. "You're not saying that Miss Claudette has set her sights on *you* now?"

"Unfortunately, it seems so," replied the Moroccan. Then, turning to Kevin, he asked, "How have you been?" Since Christmas vacation, Kacem had mostly kept his distance from the American, though at moments like this, it appeared that Kacem was trying to make up for their misunderstanding.

"Fine, thank you," answered Kevin, attempting to return his cordiality.

"That's good," said Kacem, but his thoughts seemed to be elsewhere. "Can any of you see Claudette?"

"I'm afraid you're in for a visit," said Dave sympathetically, as the Frenchwoman began walking in their direction.

"Kacem, *chéri!*" exclaimed Miss Claudette. "Did you get my note?" She had positioned herself next to the young Moroccan in such a way that her partially exposed left breast was literally touching his arm. Leaning her head up to his, she whispered something into his ear. Kacem was obviously embarrassed by this overtly sexual display, and Kevin thought disgustedly: At least I knew how to be discreet. Claudette was no better than a common slut, and if Kacem weren't such a gentlemen he would tell her so. Instead, he was saying, "*Bien sûr*, I'll be at the meeting. At six o'clock, *n'est-ce pas?*"

Claudette nodded her head, her body still pressed close to Kacem's.

"*Pardonnez-moi*," said the Moroccan, "but I have a physics experiment to set up, so I've got to get to class early. If you'll excuse me?" His last remark was clearly directed towards Claudette.

"Very well," pouted the statuesque Frenchwoman. "But I'll be expecting to see you later," she added, and the kiss she planted on Kacem's cheek landed precariously close to his mouth.

"*Quel homme!*" exclaimed Claudette, after Kacem had left the *salle des profs.* "He's one hundred percent man! How could I not have noticed him before? No woman could remain unsatisfied with a man like that in her bed."

Claudette would doubtless have continued singing Kacem's praises ad infinitum, but the bell sounded at that moment, summoning the teachers back to their classrooms.

Kevin excused himself from the group with whom he had been standing. He was doubly eager to get to class today. First, because hearing Claudette speak of Kacem with such brazen sexual lust had sickened him. If Claudette succeeded where Kevin had failed … No! That was too painful and humiliating a possibility to even consider! His other reason for hurrying to class was that he had prepared a pop quiz for his students, and he needed to arrive early in order to write the questions on the blackboard.

The inspiration for the quiz had come to him just after lunch. Now he wanted to give the test while the idea was still fresh in his mind. He had explained and drilled yesterday's lesson so clearly that he was certain his students would all ace the quiz. Their near perfect scores would be unmistakable proof both of the excellence of his teaching and of their own brilliance. He could hardly wait to see their faces when they saw their exceptional results.

Kevin's students were already seated expectantly when he entered the classroom. They were an eager, lively group in their second year of English class. Most of them were eighteen or nineteen years old, and though they were a bit boisterous, Kevin knew that this was due to their excitement about learning and not to rudeness or lack of interest. They had been his students since his arrival in Aïn El Qamar eighteen months ago, and he had specifically requested to continue teaching them this year.

After setting out his things on his desk, Kevin turned to the blackboard and wrote the words "Surprise Quiz" in bold letters. As he began copying the first question from his notebook, he heard murmurs running throughout the class. "*Mtihan?*" the students were saying. "Test?"

Kevin turned around and said, "This is an English class. You know the rule about not using Arabic in class."

A student named Hashimi, one of the few in the class Kevin didn't particularly like, raised his hand, and when Kevin called on him, said:

"Why you give us test, Mr. Kensington? You not say anything yesterday about test!"

"The question is 'Why *are* you *giving* us *a* test?' and I *didn't* say anything about it because it's a surprise quiz. We call them pop quizzes in the United States, where they're very common."

"We don't like surprise, Mr. Kensington," exclaimed Hashimi, a number of his fellow students nodding agreement.

"But we've been studying this material for the past three days. I know none of you will have any trouble answering the questions. So take out a piece of paper and a pencil."

Kevin waited for them to obey, as they always did. Today, though, a disturbing babble of Arabic-speaking voices followed his instructions, and Kevin wondered what had come over these students who had always been so eager to learn from him. Today they seemed almost hostile.

"What's happening here?" demanded Kevin. "I asked you to take out paper and a pencil."

"No, Mr. Kensington," said Hashimi.

"I don't understand."

"We do not take the test," continued Hashimi, and several other students joined in saying, "No test. We take no test."

Kevin was in a state of sheer disbelief. He had been teaching these students for nearly two years now. They couldn't possibly be turning against him.

"When I tell you that you're going to have a test, I mean it."

"We're sorry, Mr. Kensington," repeated Hashimi. "But we are not going to take the test."

Kevin's shock turned to self-righteous anger. "When I tell you that we're having a test, that means that we're having a test!" he declared. "No ifs, ands, or buts!"

"No test, Mr. Kensington!" insisted Hashimi, and several other students repeated, "No test! No test!"

Kevin could not believe his ears. "I'm the teacher in this classroom, not you!" he shouted. "What I tell you to do is what you do! And damn it, today you are going to take this test!"

The faces of most of Kevin's students indicated that they were as astounded by this sudden tirade as he was by their refusal to take the test, but one of them giggled nervously, and this infuriated Kevin even more.

"You *will* take the test!" he ordered them. "If not, you will fail this class! I don't just mean that you'll fail this test. Your grade for the entire trimester will be zero!"

"No!" cried Hashimi, and the other students joined in his protest. "You can't do that!" Then, unable to fully express himself in English, he continued in French, "*Vous avez changé, monsieur.* You used to be fair with us. But lately your assignments have been unjust. You try to accomplish so much in an hour that when we get home in the evening, we can barely remember half of what you've taught us. And your homework often takes longer to finish than all our other classes put together! We work for hours and still you give us more compositions to write and more exercises to finish. We have other subjects to study, Monsieur Kensington, and just before this class we had a history exam. Monsieur Alaoui asked such difficult questions that most of us can hardly think straight. There's no way we can take another test, especially one that we're not prepared for."

"But you are prepared for this quiz!" protested Kevin in English. "Anyone who's been paying attention for the past week should have no problem in answering the questions."

"*Vous avez notre décision, monsieur,*" announced Hashimi. "Our minds are made up. There can be no test today. There will be no test."

"All right then," seethed Kevin. "We'll just sit here for the rest of the hour or until you change your minds. If you leave this room without taking this test, your grade will be zero, and yesterday's lesson will have been your last!"

Kevin sat down behind his desk to wait. He still could not believe what had happened. His students were betraying him, after all he had given them. Well, he was not going to give in. He was the teacher, not they, and damn it, before the end of the hour they would recognize that fact. Didn't they realize how much he loved them and needed them? Didn't they see that it was because of this love that he demanded so much of them, that he wouldn't let them get away with this childish, pointless behavior? It hurt to punish them, but punish them he would unless they did as they were told.

The minutes dragged on, and still Kevin sat and waited in front of a group of close-mouthed, sullen faces. If one of them tried to voice a dissenting opinion, he was quickly shamed into silence. This was clearly to be a war of wills between Kevin and his students. They had number on their side, but Kevin was still the teacher, and as such held the power to make final decisions regarding grades. If they knew what was good for them, they would realize that in the end, there could be only one victor, and that would be Kevin.

A glance at his watch showed him that already fifteen minutes had passed. Then five more. Finally, unless he was mistaken, there were signs that many of the students were starting to have second thoughts about their actions. It was becoming clear that they were beginning to realize the rashness of their decision.

It would certainly be better for them to take the test, whatever grade they received on it, than to fail the course.

Kevin attempted to keep his face expressionless, but inside he was smiling. He had known that they would come around eventually. Their challenge to his authority had been foolish and impulsive, but forgivable. Already several students were making weak attempts to raise their hands. Soon they would have the courage to admit their error and the situation would be resolved, Kevin would forgive them for their adolescent protest, and all would be well between them once again. It was only a matter of time before …

Suddenly the classroom door was flung open and in strode Monsieur Rhazwani, the *proviseur*, grown fatter in recent months, and more arrogant and overbearing than ever.

"Monsieur Kensington," he said. "A classroom monitor has informed me that there seems to be some kind of disturbance here. *Quel est le problème?*"

"*Il n'y a pas de problème, monsieur*," said Kevin, "at least nothing I can't handle myself."

"I asked you the cause of the commotion, Monsieur Kensington," insisted Monsieur Rhazwani, "and not whether you felt capable of dealing with it. That is beside the point."

Kevin could hardly control his anger. How dare Monsieur Rhazwani offer help when none had been requested or was needed!

"Didn't you understand my question, Monsieur Kensington?" continued the *proviseur*. "Or are you deaf?"

"I heard you, *monsieur*," said Kevin. Reluctantly, he explained, "There's been a disagreement about a test. But I'm sure that …"

"Do you mean to say that there has been an attempt to subvert the discipline and order of my school?" cried Monsieur Rhazwani, in mounting indignation.

"Not exactly, *monsieur*," replied Kevin. "It's true that the students were unwilling at first to take the test, but I'm confident that they …"

"What!" screeched the *proviseur*. "They dare to question the authority of my *lycée*! Such behavior is unpardonable!"

"But I'm certain that they were about to change …"

"Discipline must be maintained!" continued Monsieur Rhazwani, ignoring Kevin's protest. "You!" cried the *proviseur* and pointed at Ahmed Shakiri, one of the brightest and best-behaved of the students. "Come up here at once."

The student cowered under the towering form of Monsieur Rhazwani. He seemed at the point of tears.

"I told you to come forward!" repeated the *proviseur*.

"But he has nothing to do with …" Kevin was saying.

"Do you hear me, boy!" The *proviseur* appeared oblivious to Kevin's presence in the classroom.

There were silent tears streaming down Shakiri's boyish face as he rose and began to walk apprehensively towards Monsieur Rhazwani. Oh God, thought Kevin, what's going to happen to him? Shakiri was one of Kevin's favorite students, hard-working, cheerful, uncomplaining. Even today he had been among the first to show displeasure with Hashimi's protest and the class's refusal to take the test.

The frightened Shakiri was standing in front of the *proviseur* now, scarcely able to control the trembling of his lower lip. Kevin wished he could do something to stop whatever was about to happen, but his body was paralyzed. Why couldn't he speak, damn it! Was Monsieur Rhazwani scaring him too? The man's malevolence was overpowering.

Monsieur Rhazwani started to scream at the boy in Arabic, and though Kevin attempted to follow the words, it was impossible to in his current state of distress. The *proviseur*'s tirade seemed endless, and Kevin realized that he was using the one terrified student who stood before him as an example to all the others.

Finally, the *proviseur* became silent and a terrible expectant hush descended over the class.

Then, Monsieur Rhazwani grabbed the boy's hands from his sides and pulled them out so that his arms were extended, the palms of his hands facing down. From within the depths of his *jellaba*, the *proviseur* withdrew a long polished rod. Then, turning so that the entire class could observe his actions, he began to administer slow, steady, savage blows to the back of Shakiri's hands, to his fingers, his knuckles, his wrists. The boy was scarcely able to hold back his cries. His face was bathed with tears, contorted in agony. Each time his brutalized hands began to drop from the pain, the *proviseur* forced them up again. Dear God, thought Kevin, was the man never going to stop?

And then, finally, he did. Monsieur Rhazwani returned the rod to the hidden recesses of his *jellaba* as the savagely beaten boy let his battered hands fall lifelessly to his sides. Monsieur Rhazwani had gone to throw the classroom door open, and now he returned to Shakiri and literally kicked him out of the room. Through the window, Kevin could see the boy start to run in stark terror from the place where he had been so cruelly and unjustly punished for a crime of which he was innocent.

"I have solved your problem for you, Monsieur Kensington," announced the *proviseur.* "*Continuez.* There will be no more protests." And then, as abruptly as he had entered the classroom, the man was gone.

Kevin walked silently to the blackboard, his movements those of an automaton. He was scarcely aware of what he was doing. When he had finished writing the exam questions, he turned to the students and said in what was hardly more than a whisper, "With only a pen and a sheet of paper on your desks, please answer the questions."

And then, returning to his desk, Kevin added, almost inaudibly, "I'm sorry," but no one seemed to have heard. Kevin sank into his chair, watching as the defeated students began answering the questions he had so eagerly prepared for them only hours before.

Oh God but he hated Monsieur Rhazwani, as he had never hated anyone in his life. He hated him for having usurped his authority as a teacher. He hated him for his sadistic violence, and for the terror he had instilled in the students Kevin loved so dearly. It was true that half an hour ago Kevin had claimed to be willing to fail them all, but he had known instinctively that they would eventually agree to take the test. He loved his students. He could never intentionally hurt them.

As it was, though, they would hate him for the rest of their lives. They would never realize how horrified Kevin had been by Monsieur Rhazwani's vicious display of violence. They would assume that because he had said nothing, he supported the wicked, power-hungry sadist. They would never believe that nothing could be further from the truth.

How could he ever face Shakiri again, that gentle studious boy? Whenever he looked at him, he would recall the youth's terrorized face and the sight of his bloodied hands. In his eyes, he would see nothing but hatred towards the teacher who had been too cowardly to defend him against Monsieur Rhazwani's barbarous punishment.

As Kevin looked at his broken students barely able to concentrate on the test they had been forced into taking, he felt an almost unbearable sense of pain and remorse. He had survived the loss of Jamey, and then Kacem's rejection. How much longer could he continue to bounce back from such heartbreak?

It seemed that the bell would never ring, and all Kevin wanted now was for his students to leave the classroom, to leave him alone as he deserved to be left. If only he never had to face them again.

But at last, thank God, the hour was over. As the students filed out of the room one by one, Kevin could not bear to look at their faces. He kept his head bowed, his eyes shut tight, until he heard the last student leave.

There was silence in the classroom now. They had all gone. Kevin was alone, abandoned by his students because he had abandoned them when they had needed his support most.

Suddenly, Kevin was no longer able to subdue his emotions. His eyes flooded with tears as his body shook with sobs he could not control. Never had he cried like this, not after Kacem's rejection, not even after Jamey's murder. It was as if all the tension and nervous energy that had been building up in him these past months now exploded within him. Kevin tried to stop from sobbing, but he found himself unable to. "Forgive me! Forgive me!" he moaned to the emptiness around him, but there was no one to hear his repentant cries.

And then, incredibly, he was not alone. He felt arms around him and heard voices saying, "Don't cry, Mr. Kensington. Please don't cry." Kevin looked up uncomprehendingly. He thought they had all left, but here were three of his dearest students kneeling at his desk beside him, telling him that they loved him and begging him for forgiveness.

"Me, forgive you?" wailed Kevin. "Oh God, don't you see that I'm to blame for what happened, for not stopping the *proviseur* from beating poor Shakiri. I could have stopped him, but I didn't!"

"We understand how you felt," said Salah Guirrou who was Shakiri's best friend. Speaking in French, he continued, "We never expected you to go against Monsieur Rhazwani. If you'd spoken up, he might have fired you, and then you'd never teach us again."

"Yes," said one of the others. "We want you to stay our teacher. We aren't angry with you. We know that you're our friend and that you didn't want to see Shakiri punished."

"We should be asking you to forgive us," said the third student. "Just because we were tired was no reason to turn against you. It's true that you make us work hard, but Hashimi was exaggerating when he said you overworked us. We know that what you require of us is no more that what you yourself do. What happened in class today was because Hashimi and a few others pushed us into it. They're just a bunch of lazy bums!"

"That's right," agreed Guirrou, "so please stop crying." He was rubbing Kevin's back as one might comfort an injured dog. "Who's got a handkerchief?" he asked, and one of the other two handed him one. "Wipe your eyes, Mr. Kensington," he ordered, as if he were the teacher and not Kevin. "Take a few minutes to calm down and then we'll walk you home."

"I'm all right now," protested Kevin, his tears finally coming to an end. "Please, hurry to class or you'll be late. Please. I don't want to cause you any more trouble."

"It's no trouble, Mr. Kensington."

"Please," insisted Kevin. "I'm going to be fine."

"But isn't there anything we can do to help?" asked Guirrou.

"Just explain to Shakiri how sorry I am that I let him down."

"Mr. Kensington," replied Guirrou, "our teachers have been striking us with rods since we were only four and five years old and attending Koranic school, and they haven't always been fair. Today wasn't the first time for Shakiri, nor would it have been for any of us if someone else had been singled out. Shakiri knows that you're our friend. He loves you, just as we all do, and once his hands have stopped hurting, he'll forget this ever happened."

"I can hardly believe that," said Kevin, "but thank you for saying so. Now, hurry to your next class. Go on. Run."

Kevin watched as the three students turned and began reluctantly to move away. So … it was not as bad as he had thought. They really did love him in spite of everything. What had just happened between these three students and himself was something that he would never forget. For the first time, he had been shown love when he needed it most, and for this he would be forever grateful.

But never, never would he forgive Monsieur Rhazwani for what he had done. Never again would he submit to that man's insane wishes. Never again would he allow the man to dominate him as he had today.

The test papers were still on Kevin's desk, a tangible reminder of this afternoon's terrible events. He could not bear to look at them. Trying to correct them would be torture. Slowly, deliberately, Kevin took the papers and ripped them in half, then into smaller and smaller pieces. Finally, in a sudden fit of violence, he hurled them across the classroom where they floated to the floor, one by one.

Thank God this classroom was vacant at this hour. If anyone other than his students had seen him in tears …

Well, "what ifs" were of no use now. He could torment himself for the rest of the year wondering what would have happened if he had had the courage to stand up to the *proviseur*.

But it was the future that counted. Kevin now must think only of the final months of the school year, of the little time that remained. He prayed that his students would indeed forgive him. But regardless of whether they did or not, one thing was certain. From now on, and regardless of the consequences, Kevin vowed that he would never again fail to oppose the *proviseur* openly and publicly if it meant preventing the man from continuing in his evil sadistic unjust ways!

CHAPTER 22

▼

As Claudette sucked on the puny, flaccid penis, feeling it slowly begin to pulsate and grow hard in her mouth, and as she inhaled the unwashed stink of the man's bulging body, she was filled with revulsion. She could barely prevent herself from vomiting on his exposed crotch, but she knew that she had no choice but to continue her ministrations. The road she had chosen in December had inevitably led to this, and if she was now forced to perform fellatio on Monsieur Rhazwani, the *proviseur*, the fact was that she had no other option.

The man's body was so enormous that his cock seemed even tinier by comparison, although regardless of its owner's proportions, Claudette would have found it laughably small. At times she asked herself whether the *proviseur*'s insistence on flaunting his power stemmed from a need to prove that he was more of a man than his pitiful tool would testify to.

Now, though, Claudette had no time to wonder about the man's motivations. Her job was to bring him to climax, and the sooner the better. So she bathed his cock with her saliva, and the lubrication seemed to make him more sensitive to the suction of her tongue and lips. Oh God, why wouldn't he just come and get it over with? But no, the detestable man was holding back today, wanting to savor as long as possible the sensation of having Miss Claudette Verlaine kneeling before him submissively, as she filled her mouth with his virility.

Filled it? Virility? Claudette nearly bit into the man's "virility" as she attempted to refrain from laughing at the thought. Maybe his dick would fill one of Jean-Richard's test tubes, but it would be a loose fit.

Merde! she screamed inwardly. Climax, will you? She felt like shouting, "You've got ten more seconds before I have you declared clinically dead!" but she knew that would do no good. Patience was the only solution.

And finally, when she had almost stopped expecting it, her persistence paid off. As she felt his cock begin to spurt forth its white cream—though his was more like skim milk—Claudette jerked her head back and pushed away from the man. Monsieur Rhazwani's semen made a pathetic attempt to shoot out, but managed only a centimeter or two trajectory before falling back onto his naked groin.

The *proviseur* wiped himself dry with a handkerchief, a smug satisfied smile on his face. Once again he had prevailed over Miss Claudette Verlaine, the most passionate and sexually insatiable woman in Aïn El Qamar. She was his whenever he wanted her.

Today, when Monsieur Rhazwani had summoned her to his office twenty minutes before the scheduled meeting of the Cinéclub committee, she had known what to expect, just as had been the case last month when he had originally asked to see her.

He had made it clear that first time that Claudette's recent promiscuity was becoming a public scandal. Since the night of Fareed's precipitous departure, Claudette had slept with more different men than she cared to remember, and sometimes even two at a time. She met them by the pool at the Hotel El Qamar on sunny days, or in the hotel bar on rainy afternoons, or late at night in the discotheque. Most were tall, strong and muscular, but she was not choosy. Each had confirmed to her that she remained desirable, at least until the next morning when she would once again find herself alone and in need of further proof.

People were beginning to talk, the *proviseur* had said that first time as he stood in front of his desk before her. He himself was becoming quite concerned about the school's reputation. He admired Mademoiselle Verlaine very much, he insisted, and knew from his earlier inspection that she was *un professeur superbe*, but what other choice did he have but to report her to the *délégué*? After all, there were children involved.

Claudette had seen at once the game Monsieur Rhazwani was playing. She knew that he had the power to have her dismissed in disgrace from her post at Lycée Mohamed Cinq, and then where would she go? How could she support herself and her way of life and her sexual needs and desires? Monsieur Rhazwani could take all this away from her unless she agreed to give him the satisfaction he was so obviously soliciting.

So she had pretended to quail under the *proviseur*'s veiled threats, declaring her admiration and esteem for the man and promising to do anything … anything … in order to please him.

She was already on her knees in feigned subservience, so it had been easy enough to gently raise the man's *jellaba* from the floor as he stood before her. Going down on a man was nothing new to her, and always it had pleased her as much as having a man's head descend between her own legs. But that first time with Monsieur Rhazwani had been as revolting as it was today, and when it was over, the *proviseur* had told her that of course, he would do nothing to jeopardize her future in Aïn El Qamar, that is if she didn't mind seeing him in his office from time to time.

What could Claudette do but accept his conditions? And so, at least once every week she would receive a summons to his office, he would lock the door, and she would fulfill his needs … until the next time.

The *proviseur* was lowering his *jellaba* now, and smiling at Claudette. His manner was friendly, but once again that of an administrator dealing with a teacher. For him, pleasure was over and it was business as usual.

"The members of the Cinéclub committee should be arriving soon," he said as he crossed to the door and unlocked it. "I'm sure that they will all be delighted that you have agreed to replace Madame Rousset as secretary while she is in France on maternity leave."

"It will be my pleasure to fill in for her," commented Claudette, thinking gleefully of the opportunities she would now have to be near Kacem Hajiri, one of the founding members of the Aïn El Qamar Cinéclub.

Kacem … Kacem, *mon amour!* How is it possible that I never noticed you until so recently? I must have been blind not to have fallen in love with you from the moment I arrived at Lycée Mohamed Cinq.

When was it that he had first caught her eye? Two weeks ago? Three? Whatever the exact date, from then on he had begun to fill her thoughts day and night. Continuing to meet and sleep with other young men had not prevented her from desiring Kacem, and even as she held another in her arms, even as she lay naked beneath him, even as he thrust himself deep within her, Claudette would think to herself: If only he were Kacem.

How incredible it had been to discover, after endless weeks of futile searching, that her emotions had not died after Fareed's departure. Precisely when she had thought that she was no longer capable of feeling anything, Kacem Hajiri had entered her life. She was in love, deliriously, passionately in love, as she had never been before. Kacem was all she had ever wanted in a man, all she would ever want. And he was going to be hers.

True, he had been slow so far to respond to her charms, but he would in time, of that Claudette had no doubt. It was only a matter of time until he too realized that they were destined for each other. It was only a matter of time …

Claudette's thoughts were interrupted by a knock at the *proviseur*'s door. "*Entrez*," he said, and two Moroccan teachers wearing their inevitable dark suits and ties came into the room, followed by Paul Durand and Janine André, two French members of the committee, and Dave Casalini, the lone American. Miguel Berthaud was next, and he kissed Claudette on both cheeks when he saw her. *Mon cher* Miguel, she thought warmly. Always my champion. Unlike Claudette's more casual friends who no longer came to her house for aperitifs, no doubt disapproving of her conduct, Miguel remained faithful to her, and always would.

"*Nous sommes tous présents?*" the *proviseur* asked, as the seven teachers took seats in the half-circle of chairs facing his desk.

"All present except for Monsieur Hajiri," said Paul Durand, who like Kacem taught physics. But he has to come! thought Claudette in dismay. If he chose not to attend, she would have gotten herself on this damn committee for nothing!

"I have neither the time nor the patience to wait for those who do not have the courtesy to be punctual," proclaimed the *proviseur* as he too was seated. "We shall begin this meeting at once. And," he added, looking sternly at the two Moroccan teachers, "the meeting will be conducted exclusively in French."

Monsieur Durand asked the *proviseur* why they had been called together. After all, the committee had met only three days ago.

"There are several reasons," explained Monsieur Rhazwani. "First of all, I wished Mademoiselle Verlaine to become acquainted with our activities. She has generously agreed to substitute for Madame Rousset during her absence."

Claudette smiled beatifically at the others. Inside she was thinking: Where the devil is my man! Kacem must realize how much this meeting meant to her. He couldn't let her down. He just couldn't!

"I also intend to speak to you about a certain film you have chosen to present."

"And which film exactly is that, if I may be so bold as to ask," said Kacem Hajiri, who had just entered the room. He's here! thought Claudette, her previous concern replaced by a joyous sense of relief. Claudette lifted her purse from the chair she had saved by her side. "*Assieds-toi, chéri*," she sighed, and Kacem took a seat only inches from her body. What delicious proximity, she thought.

"The film to which I am referring is *Mourir d'Aimer*," said the *proviseur*. "*To Die of Love*. I am shocked that such trash was shown to our students. Not only did it present the story of a young student having a love affair with his teacher, a much older woman, something which violates all standards of decency and professional conduct, but it also glorified student rebellion against authority. I will not allow this kind of subversive garbage to be shown to students of Lycée Mohamed Cinq."

"*Pardonnez-moi, monsieur*," said Kacem emphatically, "but I must object. *Mourir d'Aimer* is the true story of a historical event. The romance between the two leading characters is told in impeccable taste. Nothing lewd or even suggestive was shown. Student-teacher romances may be seen by some as unprofessional or even immoral, but no one seeing this film can deny that in this case their love was sincere and selfless. And as far as the strikes which took place in France in 1968, they are a part of modern history, and a valuable lesson to our students."

As Claudette listened to Kacem, she felt overwhelmed with love and admiration for the man. He was so forceful and dynamic. No wonder she adored him!

"There is no value in smut," declared the *proviseur*, who had clearly blocked his recent sexual encounter with Claudette from his mind. "And this film is nothing but smut, case closed."

"But *monsieur*," protested Kacem.

"Now, you all may feel entitled to your own opinions, however mistaken they may be, but I as *proviseur* of Lycée Mohamed Cinq am responsible for defending the moral character of the students at my school."

Claudette could hardly hold back from bursting out in sarcastic laughter. How could the man who had only minutes earlier shoved his cock into her mouth claim to be a protector of morals any more than she herself could? At least she was no hypocrite.

"And as *proviseur*," Monsieur Rhazwani continued pretentiously, "I alone have the right to determine which films the students at my school may view. There will be no more showings of filth that does not meet my standards. And as for the boarding students, they will remain on school grounds at all times. Their days of attending Cinéclub illegally are over!"

"But why?" asked an incredulous Dave. "Shouldn't Cinéclub be for all students at Lycée Mohamed Cinq? Why allow the *externes* to attend and not the *internes*?"

"Because I say so!"

"Is that why you've decided to build on to the wall surrounding the school?" asked Kacem, and there were several exclamations of surprise among the other teachers. "You didn't know that, did you? Yes … soon there will be another three feet of stone around Lycée Mohamed Cinq, making the unfortunate *internes* who live here virtual prisoners."

"*Mais c'est incroyable*," muttered Miguel Berthaud under his breath, and Dave added, "*Ce n'est pas juste.*" One of the Moroccan teachers said something in Arabic, but grew silent under the *proviseur*'s glare. Paul Durand and Janine André were mute.

Claudette too said nothing though she longed to tell the *proviseur* that *Mourir d'Aimer* was the story of Gabrielle Russier, a woman who had dared to defy convention just as Claudette did. She wished she could cry out that he was a maniac for power who must be stopped. But she knew that he could make a sound case for her dismissal from the school faculty, so she did not open her mouth. Still, how proud she was of Kacem's bravery and integrity! Once he and she were together, her need for adventure, which others labeled promiscuity, would cease and the *proviseur* would have no more ammunition to use against her. Kacem would not stand for it.

Kacem was truly wonderful! And she was so near to him. If only she could …

It would be so easy to take her right hand and slowly move it so that it was behind Kacem's back. *Voilà*. She had actually done so and no one was aware of a thing. And now, it was child's play to slide her fingers gently into Kacem's pants, to fondle the skin of his buttocks. Surely he must be as excited by her touch as she was.

"What gives you the right to disagree with me!" the *proviseur* was exclaiming. "You have no say whatsoever in the matter. The wall will be built and students will not be shown trash like *Mourir d'Aimer* anymore!" Claudette could feel Kacem's skin tingle as she touched it. "I did not summon you here to ask for your advice, only to announce my decision."

Suddenly Kacem had shot to his feet leaving Claudette's hand dangling limp at her side.

"Do as you like, Monsieur Rhazwani," declared Kacem. "I for one am resigning from the Cinéclub committee. I can be no party to an organization that enforces censorship and repression."

"Don't leave us," pleaded Miguel Berthaud. "This committee needs your decency and integrity."

"*Merci*, Monsieur Berthaud," said Kacem. "Thank you for the compliment. I do appreciate it. But it makes no difference whether I stay or go as long as we members have no power. You know as well as I do that from now on, we won't be the ones to decide which films will be shown and who has the right to see them. I see no point in remaining a puppet to someone else's whims. *Mesdames, messieurs*, good luck in your endeavor. I'm afraid it will be a futile one."

And with that remark, Kacem strode forcefully from the room, leaving Claudette in a state of total dismay. She wanted desperately to follow him, to show him that she was on his side. But what could she do? He was young and a fighter, and if anyone could triumph against Monsieur Rhazwani, Kacem could. She, on the other hand, had in recent months felt defeated by life, a victim of the cruel and inexorable process of growing older and less desirable. She did not dare let the *proviseur* use his weapons against her. She must remain with the others for the time being.

It seemed, though, that Kacem was not to be alone in his departure. Dave, too, had risen to his feet and was saying, "I agree with Monsieur Hajiri. He's absolutely right to have resigned from this committee, and that's why I too have decided to quit. I'll be leaving Aïn El Qamar in just a few months, so whatever happens to me between now and July is of absolutely no concern to me. Someday all of you,"—Dave's glance included the *proviseur*—"will realize that the eventual result of repression is rebellion. I myself refuse to be a part of this sort of repression, and so if you'll excuse me ..."

The room was silent as Dave exited. The other teachers knew that Monsieur Rhazwani could determine their own futures, and they had neither Kacem's idealistic zeal nor the safety of Dave's position as a volunteer to fall back on.

"Are there any other comments, suggestions, or ... criticisms to be made?" asked Monsieur Rhazwani, his voice glacial.

No one answered the question.

"*Très bien*. You are to submit a list all selections for future Cinéclub showings to this office without delay. Understood?"

The defeated committee members nodded in unison.

"And now," continued the *proviseur*, "since I have finished wasting my time with you, this meeting is adjourned."

Realizing that there was nothing more they could say or do, the intimidated faculty members began walking out of Monsieur Rhazwani's office.

"Mademoiselle Verlaine," said the *proviseur* as Claudette was leaving. "Do not forget our appointment for next week."

She turned to glare at him, but felt compelled to lower her eyes under his dictatorial regard. "*Très bien, monsieur*," she replied in resignation, and turning once more, walked defeatedly from his office.

The other teachers were talking in furious whispers outside the *proviseur*'s office when Claudette emerged. Miguel then suggested that it would be wiser for them to cross to the *salle des profs* where they were less likely to be overheard, and the others nodded agreement.

Once they were all gathered there, along with Dave, who had been waiting for their arrival, Miguel began once again to speak, and Claudette suddenly realized that since the beginning of their meeting with the *proviseur*, her dear friend's usual buffoonery had been nowhere in sight. "*Ecoutez*," he said soberly. "It's too late for complaints. We had our chance during the meeting, and none of us were brave enough to act, except of course for Monsieur Hajiri and Monsieur Casalini here. Perhaps this issue does not touch us deeply enough. After all, it's the students who are most concerned, and not ourselves as teachers."

"But it could be us next time!" exclaimed Madame André.

"*Exactement*," said Miguel. "But will we be in any stronger a position then to protest?"

"I for one dare say nothing to provoke Monsieur Rhazwani," declared Monsieur Durand. "I have my wife and children to consider. I have no tenure in France yet. I must not lose this job."

"We're in basically the same situation," said one of the two Moroccan teachers.

"Then that means we say nothing," stated Miguel, "and pray for the sakes of the students and teachers at this school that Monsieur Rhazwani will somehow find a way to hang himself. He's not a reckless man, but it could happen."

There were dubious mutters from among the other teachers, but they seemed to realize that this was their only hope. It was in a state of dejected submission that Paul Durand, Janine André, and the two Moroccans left the *salle des profs*.

Claudette found herself standing with Dave and Miguel, who had remained. "You beautiful men," she said. "How would you like to join me for an early aperitif? There will doubtless be others dropping by in a short while. I personally would rather not wait until then for a drink."

"*Moi aussi*," agreed Dave. "I still can't believe that I had the guts to tell off the *proviseur* the way I did. Hopefully, he'll realize that I'm leaving in a couple months and not try to take revenge on me. Although you know what, I'm actually ready for a fight, if that's what he wants."

"Come now," insisted Claudette. "Let us forget the horrendous things that have just been said by that filthy man and get out of this school which he so passionately and self-righteously defends."

"Claudette is right," said Miguel. "This school is …" Suddenly he had taken on the arrogant overbearing mannerisms of Monsieur Rhazwani as he had at Claudette's house in October. "This school is mine to protect and defend. Without me, it will fall into chaos and anarchy. I am the savior of Lycée Mohamed Cinq. I am the savior of you all. Worship me, peasants!"

Claudette's body shook with laughter and tears streamed down her face. "Stop it, Miguel! You'll have me in convulsions."

"And me too," said Dave. "Come on. Let's get out of here."

Miguel handed Claudette a handkerchief to wipe her eyes. Thanking him, she followed the two men out of the *salle des profs* and towards the parking lot. "I'll give you a lift, Dave," she offered. "Miguel, *on se revoit chez moi?*"

"I'm on my way," said Miguel as Dave and Claudette got into her Renault 12. She pulled out of the parking lot and turned in the direction of the French *quartier*.

A few minutes later they had arrived at her house, Miguel just ahead of them in his car. Claudette and Dave joined him outside her front door. Unlocking it, she led the two men into the living room. As usual, everything was spotless after Saadia's cleaning, though as soon as the mistress of the house had been home for even a few minutes, the room would begin to look as if Hurricane Claudette had struck.

"What will you drink, Dave?" asked Claudette. "Miguel, I know, wants a Ricard."

"Do you have any whiskey?" asked the American. "After my encounter with Monsieur Rhazwani, I need something with a kick." He sat down opposite Miguel, who offered him a cigarette which he refused.

Claudette arrived carrying their drinks and her own Martini Rouge. Then she ran into the kitchen, returning with a bowl of black Aïn El Qamar olives and another of mixed nuts.

"Let us drink a toast to better days," she suggested "To better days and … happy endings."

The three teachers raised their glasses.

"I can't believe the situation at the school could get much worse," said Dave after he had taken a long sip of his whiskey.

"Do you know," said Claudette, "in spite of everything, I am feeling more optimistic now than I have in months. I sense that my life is about to change in the most marvelous of ways. Can … can I trust you two men with a secret?"

"You know us, Claudette," said Miguel. He shut his mouth tight and mumbled something unintelligible through his nose.

"What was that?" Claudette asked Dave.

"I think that's Miguel's quaint way of telling us that his lips are sealed."

Miguel lifted his glass to his mouth, which remained tightly closed. When he tilted the glass as if to drink from it, the liquid dribbled to the floor.

"*Arrête*, Miguel!" laughed Claudette. "You'll stain my rug. Please! You've convinced me you won't say a word to anyone."

"*Exactement,*" said Miguel. "You know, the Ricard loses some of its punch when you try to drink it that way."

"*Assez!*" cried Claudette. "Now listen to me both of you. My days of searching are over. At last I am truly in love!"

"Again?" gasped Miguel. "I thought you were through with love."

"Not 'again,'" corrected Claudette. "For the first time in my life! And this love will last forever! The man I have found will give me everything I have been seeking since the day of my birth. He will love me and protect me and adore me until I die!"

"Do … do we know the man?" asked Miguel.

"*Mais bien sûr*! *C'est* Kacem!"

Miguel's mouth fell open.

Dave began to choke on his whiskey.

"Dear men," exclaimed Claudette. "Whatever is the matter? Aren't you happy for me?"

"Of … of course," stammered Miguel.

"It's … wonderful news," added Dave when he had stopped coughing.

"The most wonderful news of my life!" agreed Claudette.

"If you say so," commented Miguel halfheartedly.

"*Ecoutez,*" said Dave. "I'm really sorry, but I've just realized that I promised Kevin to run an errand for him. I know I've only just arrived, but will you two please excuse me?"

"Can't you stay a little longer?" protested Claudette. "Besides, you have no car. Wait a bit and one of my guests will drive you downtown."

"I can take him now," offered Miguel. "I'm terribly sorry, Claudette, but I too must be on my way. I truly am sorry."

"Very well," agreed Claudette reluctantly. "If you must go, I suppose I can't stop you."

And then, before she was hardly aware of it, the two men had risen and were leaving. "*Au revoir,*" she said lamely, closing the door behind them.

What had happened? Why hadn't they been elated by her news? Didn't they realize that a new day was about to dawn in her life? Damn it! Now she would have to celebrate her joy alone. Claudette lifted her glass to her lips and drank a silent solitary toast to love, and to the life she and Kacem would soon be sharing.

CHAPTER 23

━━━━━━━━━━━━━━ ▼ ━━━━━━━━━━━━━━

Sometimes he felt as if he had become another person. Sometimes it seemed that he could look at the old Jean-Richard as if from a distance and hardly recognize him as the man he now faced every morning in his bathroom mirror. What had happened to the pain in his eyes, to the even greater pain in his soul? Now when he smiled, his face lit up with joy, and he smiled often. If friends had told him a few months ago that his life would change so radically, he would have laughed in their faces. But radical changes had indeed taken place, and as Jean-Richard walked with his hand in Marcie's on this perfect March day, he knew that if he had become a new person, he owed the change to her.

"It's so peaceful and quiet here," said Marcie dreamily. "I don't think there's a living soul within miles."

They were walking through a shady grove of olive trees they had noticed not long after leaving the *moussem* in Aït Attab. It was Marcie who had asked if they might stop there and walk for a while.

"I can't face Aïn El Qamar quite yet," she had said. "Couldn't we please spend a little more time away from the noise and the people? The *moussem* was so crowded, and Aïn El Qamar will only remind me that I have lessons to plan and papers to correct. Please, let's stay here and just be by ourselves for a little bit."

Jean-Richard had not protested. He himself felt a release at being far from Aïn El Qamar. The town was too closely related to the person he had been and to the meaningless life he had led. Though the past had not changed, Jean-Richard thought of it less and less, and recently he had begun to hope that because of Marcie, he might be able to once again love and trust another person.

As they walked now, their fingers entwined, tall leafy trees above them and soft mossy ground at their feet, Jean-Richard felt a joy he had scarcely imagined in recent years. What if he had never met Marcie? What if …? But no, that was foolish. He had met her. It must have been meant to be. What other explanation could there be for such a fundamental change in his life. It must be destiny.

"What must be destiny?" asked Marcie.

"*Quoi?*" Jean-Richard hadn't realized that he had been thinking aloud.

"You said that something must be destiny. What did you mean?"

"I … I was just thinking that I can't imagine not having met you, Marcie," replied Jean-Richard. "It seems as if I've always known you, as if nothing or no one that came before you held the slightest importance."

"But all I've done is offer you my friendship," she protested.

"Is that all it is, Marcie? Just friendship?"

Marcie was silent for some time, and Jean-Richard wondered if his question had violated their agreement not to invade each other's privacy. Then, as she spoke, he realized that she had merely been pondering his question.

"I've known since … since December that it was more than friendship. I've loved you …"

At the first mention of the word "love," Jean-Richard stopped short. He had sensed that she would speak it, and yet it had come as a shock to hear it for the first time. He took her other hand in his, and she looked deeply into his eyes. Her own were warm and intent and profoundly caring. He wanted so much to believe and trust her.

"I first knew I loved you," she continued, "that night I threw you out of my house just before vacation. I thought I was throwing you out of my life as well, but I was wrong, and it took me only days … or maybe it was only hours … to realize that your presence in my life was something I neither could nor wanted to eliminate. Living without you would only be possible if I could erase from my mind every moment we'd been together. But those few moments had become such a part of me that to try to pretend they'd never happened would have been foolish and futile. Like it or not, you were in my life, and nothing I could do was going to change that."

Was it possible that Jean-Richard was hearing her speak these words, and not retreating in fear? Always before, the slightest possibility that a woman might have fallen in love with him had made him want to run away and hide. And yet here was Marcie telling him that life without him was unimaginable, and here he was listening to her words, not fleeing from them, but believing them, drinking them in as something precious for which he had long thirsted.

He kissed her, and nothing mattered but the present moment. The past was blotted out under the tenderness of her lips. The cares of his day to day existence faded away under the fragrance of her hair and skin. She did not protest as he began to undress her. When he kissed her bare breasts and heard her whispering again and again that she loved him, it was as if she was the first woman he had ever been with. She was the virgin, and yet he felt that he too was making love for the first time. He was gentle with her, and surprisingly hesitant. He did not want to rush things, either for himself or for her. They lay down on the cool earth of this lush verdant forest, two lovers alone in the unspoiled natural beauty of their surroundings, rejoicing in each other's adoration. He could not remember taking off his own clothes. All he knew was that their two naked bodies were together as they had always been meant to be. Finally, when the moment came, he was almost afraid to enter her, knowing that it was her first experience at lovemaking. But she told him not to worry. Any pain she might feel would be exquisite proof of her love for him. When their two bodies had at last united, Jean-Richard knew that the wasted years were over and that a new beginning had taken place.

They lay naked in each other's arms for he did not know how long, the breeze which blew through the trees caressing their bodies and the song of birds delighting their ears.

"I wish we never had to go back," said Marcie. "I wish it could just be you and me alone together here for the rest of our lives. Today has been like a dream, a beautiful precious dream, and I can't bear to see it end."

"Then forget about going back," whispered Jean-Richard. "We can stay here forever if you like."

But Marcie's reminder of the outside world had returned them both to reality. Reluctantly, they realized that their idyll must come to an end. As Marcie dressed, she said to Jean-Richard, "I never thought I could stand unclothed in front of someone, and feel no shame, but it's as if I ... I exult in being naked with you. I want nothing to separate us anymore, not clothes, not misunderstandings, not secrets."

For a moment Jean-Richard felt a stab of panic. But it passed. He had been so afraid that she would press him to talk about the past. And that, even now, was something she must never do. The past must remain buried within him, as it had always been.

"Today has been the most perfect day of my life," Marcie was saying.

"I still can hardly believe ..." began Jean-Richard.

"That I finally … gave myself to you?" completed Marcie. They had finished dressing and now began walking towards Jean-Richard's car, which he had parked some distance away by the road.

"I thought it was against your … moral code," said Jean-Richard.

"It was, as long as I wasn't really in love. It's easy to say no to a man when you're not in love with him, and I never felt anything but friendship for Eddy. That's why I was able to preserve my own myth. I wanted to make love with you that first night back in October when you brought me home from aperitifs at your house. I realize that now. Let's just say I'm about four months late."

"We have so much time to make up for," agreed Jean-Richard.

"And we'll have that time, *mon amour*. Now that we're together, nothing will keep us apart."

They were at Jean-Richard's car now, and he was opening the door for her.

"If only we didn't have to get in and begin the drive back to Aïn El Qamar," sighed Marcie. "Back to the real world."

"Do you think this isn't real, this moment here and now?" asked Jean-Richard, though he understood her meaning.

"Of course it is. It's more real to me than my day to day life in Aïn El Qamar. It's just that going back means having to consider things other than our own happiness. You have your problems with Monsieur Rhazwani, and it can't be easy living with Claudette these days. Also, there's having to consider what others will say about our relationship. People in a small town can be such gossips."

"Forget them all," insisted Jean-Richard. "Think only of yourself, and of me, and of our amazing good fortune."

"You're right, and I'm just being silly," agreed Marcie. "Why put up obstacles to happiness? I'm ready to go back now."

Jean-Richard got into the Fiat beside Marcie and together they continued the return ride to Aïn El Qamar. Spring had truly arrived, not only in the trees and wildflowers and lush greenery which surrounded them, but in Jean-Richard's wondrous feeling of rebirth. Oh God, he prayed, don't let this end. The painful memories were still so near the surface. They must not interfere with his new-found peace and contentment.

The road seemed all too short on this return trip, and Jean-Richard found himself driving more slowly than usual to prolong the journey. As they approached the Hotel El Qamar, several kilometers outside of town, Jean-Richard suddenly suggested, "Why don't we stop here for a while? The day is so beautiful, and it's still light. We can sit by the pool, and have something to drink, look at the mountains, and forget just for a few minutes longer the crowds and the noise and the sight of students."

"Jean-Richard, there's no need to convince me. I have no more desire to go home right now than you do. Of course let's stop."

Jean-Richard pulled into the parking lot outside the tourist hotel, then walked with Marcie towards the entrance.

They sat down by the pool. There were a few Spanish tourists swimming, though in Jean-Richard's opinion it was still too cool for that. He recognized several other teachers who waved to him and Marcie with friendly smiles.

"Let's hope we're lucky and that we don't have to wait forever for service," smiled Jean-Richard. "The waiter here is infamous for his laziness."

"I don't mind how long we wait," insisted Marcie. "He can come tomorrow, for all I care. I'm content just to sit here and be with you."

But today, the waiter was atypically attentive to his customers' needs. There were, after all, few other people, this being a school afternoon.

Jean-Richard ordered a gin and tonic and Marcie a glass of white wine, and the waiter was remarkably prompt in bringing them their drinks. The gin and tonic tasted good, refreshing. With soft music coming in from the lobby, and the light breeze that played across his face, and Marcie's presence beside him, Jean-Richard closed his eyes and the past seemed worlds away.

He must have dozed off, for when he reopened his eyes, there were two women swimming in the pool who hadn't been there before.

"I didn't notice anyone else arrive," he commented to Marcie.

"You were napping," she replied.

At first, Jean-Richard did not recognize the playful swimmers. Then, in spite of their wet hair, he realized that they were Dominique Moulin and Christiane Koenigsmarck.

"Those two certainly have become good friends lately," remarked Marcie, "though I don't see what they have in common."

Jean-Richard scarcely heard Marcie's words. His eyes were glued to the two women, who were alternately splashing and lightheartedly wrestling with each other in the pool. He watched in growing horror as Christiane's and Dominique's hands explored one another's bodies in the guise of innocent horseplay. Marcie might assume that these were merely two friends enjoying a dip in the pool, but Jean-Richard knew only too well that when two women touched each other as these two were doing at this moment, their relationship was not platonic. There was hunger in their eyes and desire in their every move, lust for the moment when their naked female bodies would entwine.

"Jean-Richard, you seem a million miles away," commented Marcie.

Paris was indeed miles and years away, yet at this moment it was closer than it had been in months. If he didn't get away from this place soon, he'd …

Jean-Richard bolted from his seat and began fleeing towards the hotel lobby, a bewildered but concerned Marcie only steps behind him. As he was about to enter the lobby, a man bumped into him heading in the opposite direction towards the pool. It was Laurent Koenigsmarck, and he was obviously very drunk.

"*Salut les amants*," he said sarcastically, and Jean-Richard recoiled from the stench of alcohol on his breath. He tried to push past the short pudgy man, but Laurent grabbed his arm.

"Where's my Christiane?" he growled.

"You're drunk," spat Jean-Richard. "Get out of our way!"

"Not until you tell me where my Christiane and her little plaything are."

"What's he talking about?" asked Marcie. "What's happening here?"

"I'll tell you what's happening, little Miss Goody Twoshoes," exclaimed Laurent, holding the couple back. "I came here looking for my wife and her lovergirl, that's what's happening. I saw Dominique's car outside, so I know she's around someplace. And wherever she goes, my sweet Christiane is sure to be following. Or hadn't you noticed, little Miss Innocence? My wife doesn't want my cock anymore. She prefers the taste of pussy, of Dominique's honey-filled pussy. So stay clear of the *salope*, or she might just try to stick her tongue up yours!"

"Make him stop!" pleaded Marcie.

But Jean-Richard was hearing another voice saying, "No man can excite me the way she can. No man ever could!"

"Jean-Richard! Jean-Richard!"

"Oh God, Nicole, that's enough!" he cried.

And then suddenly, he returned to reality, back to the present where he was standing with Marcie, who was begging him to take her away from Laurent and his vulgar ravings. God damn the man for his filthy drunken words! God damn him!

Jean-Richard could no longer control his fury. The man must be silenced and now! In sheer rage, Jean-Richard swung at Laurent, hitting him in the jaw, knocking him to the ground.

Marcie stared on in horror, then broke into a run, through the open sliding glass doors and out into the lobby. Jean-Richard wanted to chase after her, but his body would not move. He stood paralyzed, staring at Laurent's inert form, aghast at what he had done. Not just at knocking out the disgusting Frenchman, but at calling Marcie by that other name again. And yet all this had made him come to his senses. Lies. Deception. Betrayal. That was all women were capable of. And nothing more!

If only he could believe that Marcie was the exception, but the past few hideous minutes had brought Jean-Richard back to reality. Today had been an illusion created by being far away from Aïn El Qamar in an almost fairy-tale world. But magic and illusions were not reality, and reality was all that mattered.

Jean-Richard did not know how long he stood over Laurent's unconscious form, thinking of the misery of his past and the bleakness of his future. He hadn't even noticed the waiter who had come over and was sprinkling water on Laurent's forehead, the check for Jean-Richard and Marcie's drinks in his hand. Laurent was beginning to come to now, and Jean-Richard could not face hearing what he might have to say. He stepped over the man's pudgy, revolting body and, ignoring the waiter's calls, bolted through the lobby towards his car. Marcie was standing beside the Fiat, crying softly. She looked up when she heard him approach, silent tears streaming down her face. "Where have you been?" she wept.

Jean-Richard did not answer her. Walking around to Marcie's side of the car, he unlocked the door, then opened his own and got in.

"What's happened?" cried Marcie. "What's happened to our beautiful day? Everything was so perfect, and now it's all ugliness and filthy words and horrible insinuations. And you ... you called me by that name again. Why, Jean-Richard? Who is Nicole?"

"I was a fool to think that we could return to reality and still be as happy as we'd been in the mountains," said Jean-Richard numbly, as if he had not heard her question. "It's over between us, Marcie. Don't ask me any questions. Just accept what I'm saying. We have no future together. *C'est terminé.*"

"But Jean-Richard, I love you!" protested Marcie.

"Don't you see," exclaimed Jean-Richard, "that we can never be happy together? There's no hope for us, Marcie. There's no hope for me with any woman!"

Jean-Richard could bear this conversation no longer. He turned the key in the ignition, backed out of his parking place, and pressed hard on the gas pedal. The sooner Marcie was back at her house and out of his life the better.

"But Jean-Richard," she continued as the car raced towards Aïn El Qamar. "If you love me ..."

"That's beside the point!" he insisted. "Just don't ask me any more questions."

"You can't be doing this, Jean-Richard! I know I can make you happy. I swear to God I can make you forget the past."

"Not even you can. Not even you," replied Jean-Richard tonelessly, oblivious of the pedestrians and animals in the street as he sped along. "No Marcie, you've got to let go."

"But today …"

"Today was a dream, a fantasy. It won't happen again. It can never happen again."

"Jean-Richard, don't do this to me, to us! Before I knew you, I could live without love. Now … never! Tell me what's eating at you, tearing you apart. Tell me and let me help you!"

"Just forget it!" cried Jean-Richard. "Forget me! Forget today ever happened. When you see me at school, look the other way. Get a transfer next year. Let me get a transfer. I don't care either way. Just live your life without me!"

They were at Marcie's house now, though Jean-Richard had no recollection of having driven there.

"I think it's time we ended this conversation," he said. "There's nothing further to be gained from it."

"Very well, if that's what you want," replied Marcie, suddenly calm after her emotional outburst. "But let me say just one more thing, Jean-Richard. And I want you to listen carefully, because I'll only say it once. It's taken me my entire lifetime to fall in love. Obviously I'm not easily infatuated. And now that I am in love, my feelings are not just going to disappear overnight. I don't care how many times you tell me to get out of your life, to forget about you, it simply won't happen. If you want, Jean-Richard, I'll keep my distance. But I won't stop loving you or wanting you. And I'll be patient. It doesn't matter how long it takes. Someday, when you finally come to your senses and realize that a life alone is worthless, I'll still be waiting for you and loving you. You can count on me, Jean-Richard. You can count on my love."

Marcie leaned over and kissed Jean-Richard gently on the cheek, much as he had first kissed her months ago, and then got out of the car.

Jean-Richard watched Marcie go into her house and close the door behind her. Why couldn't she have told him to get out of her life as she had once before? Why did she have to leave open the possibility of a reconciliation? They could never have a future together. Why couldn't she realize that and just tell him good-bye?

Pulling away from the curb, Jean-Richard began the lonely drive back to his own house. He wished he did not have to return home, to face Claudette, but there was nowhere else to go. If only he were in a big city like Casablanca or Rabat, he could find a place to hide. But this was Aïn El Qamar, and there was no escape from reality.

When Jean-Richard had arrived at his house, he saw Claudette's Renault parked outside. Don't let her hear me come in, he prayed. Let her be too busy with her aperitif guests to know that I'm back.

He entered quietly, hardly daring to breathe. Fortunately, there were voices coming from the living room that blotted out his footsteps, and no one heard him begin to climb the stairs.

Alone, he thought as he entered his room. Alone at last. Alone. Not just for the moment but forever.

Jean-Richard sat down on his bed, the bed in which he had made love so many times without feeling love, and buried his head in his lap. He wanted to hide, not only from others but from himself as well.

He could not risk being hurt again! He would not risk it! Even feeling nothing was better than once again facing the possibility of being subjected to unbearable, unending pain.

Marcie would get over him. She would find someone else, someone without secrets, someone completely trusting, someone who could share her innocent belief that all was perfect in this world, or at least that it could be.

And *he* …

For the first time that he could remember, Jean-Richard was surprised to find his cheeks wet and to realize that he was crying, shedding tears because he had come so close to happiness—it had been almost within his reach—and now was gone forever.

His tears were soundless, but they would not stop, and later, much later, they still fell, testimony to his profound sorrow and emptiness.

CHAPTER 24

$$\blacktriangledown$$

"Kevin!" called Dave from their kitchen. "Will you come in here and help me for a minute?"

Kevin left the living room where he had been sitting with Miguel Berthaud and joined his friend.

"Put on some music in there for God's sake!" exclaimed Dave. "The gloom in that room is so thick you could cut it with a knife. I asked Miguel over for dinner, not for a wake."

"Couldn't you have let me know he was coming?" protested Kevin.

"I would have if I'd known in advance," answered Dave as he tasted the sour cream sauce he was preparing for their Beef Stroganoff.

"I wish you'd just let me pretend to be sick or something. I don't know how to make lighthearted chitchat after what happened to me in class today."

"You should be glad that your students stood by you. Listen, Kev. Miguel's been a good friend to us since we arrived in Aïn El Qamar, and I could see that he wasn't too thrilled when Claudette told us about her latest infatuation."

"So what do you want me to do?" asked Kevin grudgingly.

"Just put on some music, anything that'll lighten the atmosphere, and I'll try to get in as soon as I can. Keep filling his glass with wine, and your own too, and try to think of something positive to say."

"Damn it, Dave. There's nothing positive in my life to talk about!"

Dave started to answer Kevin back, then decided that what he really wanted to say would only make his friend angrier. He was fed up with Kevin's constant moodiness, and if he told him how disgusted he was, there was sure to be an explosion.

"Oh all right," answered Kevin, smiling sarcastically. "I'll just think about how wonderful life is and how happy I am that all my dreams have come true."

He left the room in a huff just as Miguel was calling out to ask if they needed any help. "Everything is fine!" called back Dave. "I should be out pretty soon." Thank goodness there had been several filets in the refrigerator. Dave had known that he could invite Miguel for a dinner which would be both tasty and quick to prepare. He hadn't even had to stop at a neighborhood *hanoot* on the way home because there was already a can of mushrooms in the kitchen. It was fortunate that he had anticipated not feeling like shopping on the evening of his return from Rabat. Knowing that everything was there for a fancy dinner, he had been unable to resist inviting Miguel once he saw the Frenchman's expression upon leaving Claudette's house.

Dave heated a skillet, then melted butter in it and began browning the meat. The sour cream sauce was ready, the mushroom can open. Water was about to boil, almost ready for him to add the rice, and in the living room the table was already set. With luck, fifteen minutes from now, they'd be seated and enjoying the meal.

With luck. The expression stuck in Dave's head. Was he the only lucky one in Aïn El Qamar? In the past two months things had been getting steadily worse for his friends and colleagues with Kevin and Claudette and Janna sinking deeper and deeper into their depression. Were their woes contagious? Did this mean that he too was heading for emotional disaster? Aïn El Qamar seemed to be wrecking so many lives. Was his to be next?

Claudette wondered what was keeping Jean-Richard. The last of her aperitif guests had long since gone, dinner was on the table, and still he had not descended from his room. She had called up to him several times, finally getting an answer, but there was still no sign of him.

"Jean-Richard!" she called out once more from the foot of the stairs. "I'll start dinner without you if you don't get down here at once, and you know you can't stand cold soup." They were having *potage de légumes* which Saadia had prepared at noon and Claudette had reheated.

She waited for the sound of Jean-Richard's footsteps, but when they did not come, she made good her word and returned to the living room to sit down without him.

The soup was hot and full of delicious vegetables and Claudette could only wish that Kacem were sitting across from her sharing it with her. The next time

Jean-Richard and Marcie were dining out, she would invite Kacem. It would be their first dinner together, and it would be unforgettable.

Merde! If only she had been able to truly share her joy with someone today, but first Miguel and Dave had left so precipitously, and later her company for aperitifs had been people she knew less intimately, people she didn't feel she could confide in. Now, Jean-Richard was hiding in his room for some strange reason. Was there no one to whom she could reveal the overwhelming passion Kacem inspired in her?

Claudette had nearly finished the potage when Jean-Richard walked slowly into the room, a blank expression on his face, his hair mussed. What on earth can be wrong? thought Claudette. Just this morning he had been full of excitement telling her of the excursion he was going on with that innocent young sweetheart of his. Now he looked as if he had just learned of someone's death. It wasn't like Jean-Richard to neglect his appearance, and at the moment he looked simply dreadful.

"Do you think there's still time for me to request a transfer to another city, or preferably to another country?" he asked dully as he seated himself opposite her, not even tasting the soup.

Claudette could not believe her ears. Jean-Richard had always been perfectly content in Aïn El Qamar. In fact, he had seemed almost afraid to even contemplate leaving.

"You want to go somewhere else?" asked Claudette in shock.

He seemed oblivious to her question. "Do you think it's too late? If I can't get a transfer, then I'll just leave, go anywhere, find a job somehow …"

"But Jean-Richard, that's foolish," protested Claudette. "You have another year left on your contract. Besides, it's much too late in the year to ask for a transfer back to France."

"I said nothing about France," continued Jean-Richard in the same monotone. "I didn't even say I wanted to continue teaching. I just want to get away, and if that means sweeping streets, then I'll do it."

Was it possible that this was the same man she had seen only this morning? How could she tell him her good news in the state he was in now?

"*Qu'y-a-t'il*, Jean-Richard?" asked Claudette, and there was concern in her voice. "Has something happened between you and Marcie? Did she tell you she wanted to end your relationship? Is that it?"

The Frenchman laughed humorlessly. "Nothing could be further from the truth. She says she loves me. She says she wants to spend the rest of her life with me."

"And you complain about that?" asked Claudette in astonishment.

"I will not be hurt again, not ever again!"

"So you're leaving Aïn El Qamar. You're running away from the possibility that maybe you'll be hurt rather than staying to face the possibility that this girl might make you happy. Truly, you are the most self-pitying man I've ever met!"

"You don't understand!" cried Jean-Richard. "You've never really loved anybody but yourself, so you can't possibly comprehend the way I feel. I should never have come down."

Rising from his seat at the table, leaving his soup cold and untouched, Jean-Richard hurried out of the room and back upstairs.

Claudette walked over to the *banquettes* at the other end of the living room. She lit a cigarette and sat down to think. It was clear that she could do nothing to help Jean-Richard, who insisted on behaving like a fool. Infinitely better for her to concentrate on her own happiness, which at least was within reach. So far, Kacem had not demonstrated his feelings in any overt way, yet Claudette knew that he was attracted to her. It was only matter of remaining patient just a short time longer.

In no time at all, he would be as head over heels in love with her as she was with him.

In no time at all, he would make his feelings known to her.

In no time at all, he would be hers forever!

"You don't mean she actually stuck her hand down your pants in front of all the other teachers?" asked a dumfounded Michèle, who had come over to Kacem's house after Dominique's arrival with Christiane had made her feel like an intruder in her own. She could tell when she got to Kacem's that something was bothering him, and recalling his worry about the surprise Cinéclub meeting, she had wondered if Claudette had anything to do with his mood. Apparently she was right.

"I don't think the other teachers were aware of what she was doing," commented Kacem. "After all, what was happening was going on behind their backs … and mine. Still, I could hardly keep from blushing. And I must admit it took some effort to try to listen to what that bastard Rhazwani was saying."

Kacem was reclining on a *banquette* with his head in Michèle's lap, and she was stroking his forehead soothingly. Moving her fingers to gently caress his lips, she said:

"I'm really proud of the courage you showed today. I know I never would have had the strength to stand up to Monsieur Rhazwani like that."

"The Cinéclub isn't the problem," declared Kacem. "It's only one example of the *proviseur*'s maniacal desire to control us all, to strip away our authority as teachers, to be the final boss in all cases. He won't be happy until he achieves total domination of every one of us."

"But you used to say that one day he'd go too far, that all we had to do was wait and he'd hang himself."

"I think that I was just being naive," said Kacem thoughtfully, "and I realized that at the meeting today. That's why I did what I did. The *proviseur* has got to see that there's opposition to his quest for power. We may not change much, but at least maybe he'll think twice before making another decision like the one about the school wall."

"But what will he do to you?" asked Michèle apprehensively.

"Let's not worry about that for now," said Kacem. "I'll put on some music and the two of us will lie back and think only about us. All right?"

Kacem crossed over to his cassette recorder and inserted a Georges Moustaki tape which Michèle had brought from France. Returning to Michèle, he sat beside her and put his arm around her shoulders. "Not another word about Claudette or the *proviseur* tonight," he declared.

Together, they listened to the soft guitar of the Greek who sang in French, and to his poetic words.

"We will take the time to live, to be free and to love. Come. I am here. I wait only for you. Everything is possible. All is permitted …"

Kacem kissed Michèle, and as their lips met, she forgot everything but the present moment and the rapture she and her man would soon be sharing.

Oh God, how had she ever let Michèle remove all the *keef* from her house? Janna knew it was no use looking for any. She had shown Michèle all her hiding places. Already, though, she was beginning to wish that she had set aside just enough for one pipe-full, for just one toke. But no, it looked like she was going to have to spend the night stone sober.

Not that deep inside she didn't want to. What Michèle had told her today was nothing that Janna hadn't been aware of, at least subconsciously, for some time now. Still, how much easier it had been to float along on the cushion that *keef* provided than to attempt certain fundamental changes in her life. Had she simply been too scared and unsure of herself to see if it would indeed be possible to get along without the drug?

If only Michèle were with her! Now that everything was so clear, the lines around the objects in her living room so sharp, nothing dulled or blurred by *keef*, being alone was almost too much to bear. Please ignore what I told you about giving me time to be by myself tonight, pleaded Janna silently. Please come by, if only to check up on me. Don't make me spend the evening all by myself. I don't know if I can make it without help!

The ringing of the doorbell brought Janna out of her reflections. Oh thank God! she thought. That must be Michèle now.

Janna ran to the door and flung it open, then gasped in shock. A young Moroccan was standing outside, a disrespectful smirk on his face, and the way he was looking at her made Janna shiver.

"I come to see you, Ms. Gallagher," said the young man in thickly accented English. "I want you not be alone."

Janna tried to slam the door in the stranger's face, but he had already half-stepped into her hallway.

"Who are you?" she asked angrily. "What do you want?" There was something familiar about the young man, but she couldn't put her finger on it. "What do you want?" she repeated, feeling more and more uneasy by the moment.

"I ... say to you before. I not want you be alone. You have a good friend last year. A very good friend. Maybe lover? He's name Cherqaoui. I think, maybe, you feel lonely and ... Maybe you and I ... Maybe you wanna fuck?"

"You get the hell out of my house!" shouted Janna, furiously shoving her knee into the young man's groin. She recognized him now. Twice before he had spoken to her, and always in the same sly, vulgar, insinuating manner.

The Moroccan staggered back, obviously stunned and in pain. If she could just shut the door before he recovered enough to ...

Incredibly, in the darkness outside, Janna could almost swear she spotted Marcie walking by herself. It hardly seemed possible that the other American woman would be alone in the street at night, but it looked so much like her.

"Marcie! Marcie!" Janna called.

"Janna?" answered the young woman. It *was* her, thank God! "Come over here quick, please!" cried Janna.

The young Moroccan turned around quickly, saw the other woman approaching, and broke into a limping run. Janna was trembling when Marcie reached the door.

"What was Faress doing at your house?" asked the blonde.

"You ... you know him?" gasped Janna."

"Yes ... he's ..."

"Please … please come inside," begged Janna. "I've got to get this door shut and locked. Thank God I saw you walking past, Marcie. He wanted to come in and … I don't know what else."

Janna closed the door behind them and fastened it securely. When she had gone with Marcie into the living room, she asked:

"Did I hear you right? You said you knew that young man?"

"Yes, I do," replied Marcie. "His name's Larbi Faress. He's my student."

"Wait. That seems to ring a bell," said Janna as she sank into one of the *banquettes*, Marcie beside her. "Yes!" she exclaimed, snapping her fingers. "The first time he spoke to me on the street—months ago that was—he told me you were his teacher. I remember thinking I ought to point him out to you, find out what was going on in his head. I saw him again the night of Claudette's party, although it's only now that I've realized that it was the same person. He followed me to Dave's house. It was pretty spooky. But after that … I haven't seen him since then."

"He was in an accident," explained Marcie. "He spent weeks in the hospital, and then even after he came back he looked awful for the longest time. It's only recently that he's been regaining his strength."

"That explains why he hasn't bothered me since December," said Janna thoughtfully. "Thank God you know who he is. Now that he realizes that you've seen him, he'll probably leave me alone." What would have happened if Marcie hadn't recognized him? What if she hadn't been where she was precisely at that moment? What if …?

"Marcie, what in God's name are you doing out alone after dark?" Janna suddenly asked. "You must be crazy!"

"I … just felt so cooped up inside, and Dave and Kevin were having a guest over, so I thought I'd go out for a walk. I needed to think, to try to figure some things out. I suppose that instinctively I started walking in this direction. I needed to be with another woman. But then, when I got near your house, I wasn't sure if …"

"If maybe you'd find me stoned … as usual?"

"Well … not so much that as … just not wanting to impose myself on you. I know that you and I … well we're two such different people and you know as well as I do that we've never really been that close."

"Your visit tonight is hardly an imposition," smiled Janna. "Not only am I not stoned, for a change, but I was just wishing I had someone to keep me company. Let me fix us some coffee and then you can tell me your troubles. Maybe that'll help me put my own in perspective."

"Thank you Janna. Thank you for being willing to listen."

It was probably an hour later that Marcie finally finished talking. She had told Janna everything about herself and her relationship with Jean-Richard, and Janna had listened with a growing awareness that Marcie was a much deeper and more complex person than she had imagined. For the first time she thought that they might become friends.

"Oh God Marcie," exclaimed Janna. "I don't know what to say. I'd like to help you. I'll do anything I can. But considering the way I've screwed up my own life, I don't know if my advice would do any good."

"You've already helped, Janna, just by listening, just by not making me feel so alone. The rest is up to me. You're finding the strength to cope with your own problems. Now I've got to do the same with mine."

Once again the student sat in his candle-lit room, filling his diary with the same erratic nearly illegible handwriting he had used in his other entries:

"I lost my chance to be alone with Ms. Gallagher tonight, and I may never have another. I would have gone to see her sooner, but the time I spent in the hospital prevented me from acting. And now my teacher knows that I attempted to enter Ms. Gallagher's house and she must have told her who I am. If I try anything more, they'll stop me."

The student removed from his desk a picture he had taken of Ms. Gallagher earlier in the week. She hadn't seen him with his camera that day, but he had gotten a good likeness. Now, with a pair of scissors, he cut around the head, and then pasted it into his diary. With a black ink pen, he carefully drew on a neck, and then bare shoulders. He added two full breasts, sketching the nipples with care. Then a slender waist and rounded hips, and legs spread wide open to expose her genitals. He drew from the memory of a similar picture he had masturbated over in a magazine a friend had once lent him. Under the picture he wrote:

"I wanted to see Ms. Gallagher like this tonight. I would have, too, if my teacher hadn't come. Do I dare to hope that she will forget my visit in time? Maybe if I stay away from school for the next month or so, people will think I've left Aïn El Qamar. I can spend my days in the olive groves, making plans ..."

The student paused in his writing, his eyes shut in thought. Then he resumed the latest entry to his diary:

"My mind is made up. I will 'disappear' for the next month, perhaps two. That should be enough time for Ms. Gallagher to forget that I even exist. Then ..."

Staring at the naked drawing, Larbi Faress unzipped his pants, pulled out his cock, and smiled.

MAY 1977

CHAPTER 25

▼

They hadn't intended to return so late, but wanting their weekend in Marrakesh to last as long as possible, they had remained in the discotheque until three that morning.

It had been a wonderful, unforgettable weekend, thought Dominique as she sped along the unlit two-lane highway which led from Marrakesh to Aïn El Qamar and then eventually on to Fez. Christiane was sitting beside her, dozing, looking beautiful and even innocent in sleep. With her lover at her side, as they had been all weekend, Dominique thought that she had never been this happy.

The road was dark, and she could see ahead only as far as her high beams would illuminate, but it was straight and virtually deserted this early in the morning. Rarely would another car pass them going in the direction of Marrakesh, and Dominique had only counted three cars that they themselves had overtaken in the hour and a half since leaving Marrakesh.

Dominique put one arm around Christiane's shoulder, feeling her soft flesh through the fabric of the summer dress she wore. The weather was pleasant now, even at four-thirty in the morning, though by noon it would be quite warm. At the moment, though, with the fresh night air and the stillness all around her, it was more than comfortable. It was soothing and relaxing. The calm of the night allowed Dominique to think.

This affair had been going on for over four months already, and still Dominique had not begun to tire of Christiane. She wondered sometimes at the rapidity with which she had responded sexually to the other woman that night in December when Christiane had joined Dominique and Laurent in bed. But then she thought to herself that she would never have been so quick to fall under the spell of the blonde Frenchwoman if she hadn't already felt lesbian urges. People who saw her nowadays often marveled at the ways she had changed. Gone was the sour complainer of earlier months, and in her place was a lovely young woman who seemed to have bloomed under the Moroccan sun. Dominique knew that much of her former unhappiness had been caused by a self-enforced repression of her true sexuality. She had almost convinced herself that she was the frigid, unresponsive woman men found her to be. Then, after her affair with Christiane had begun, she had known that she was neither frigid nor unresponsive. It was simply that no man had ever brought out the sensual side of her nature. No man ever could.

Yes, Christiane was vulgar at times. She said what she thought, and didn't bother to pretty up her language. Other people looked down on her, called her common. But Dominique found this side of Christiane one of her most endearing. She was fed up with the boring, pseudo-intellectual friends of her university days in Paris. Christiane was everything they weren't, and especially when she would utter those crude, erotic suggestions during their lovemaking, Dominique knew that she would not change Christiane for the world.

How blissful it was now to be alone with her lover, speeding along this nearly deserted highway, just herself and Christiane and the night. If only this precious moment would never end. If only …

Christiane would leave her one day, Dominique knew. She would go back to Laurent who waited patiently for her return.

"It's not the first time I've cheated, and it won't be the last," Christiane had told Dominique early in their relationship. "Neither one of us can be satisfied with just one person forever."

Christiane, unlike Dominique, considered herself bisexual. She declared herself equally turned on by both men and women, and among her past lovers had been members of both sexes. "I dig it when a man stuffs his dick inside me, but I like to go down on a woman too, just as much," Christiane had told her. "So when I get my fill of cock, I switch to pussy, and then back again. You know what they say about variety."

As for Laurent, "He's got his girlfriends in Aïn El Qamar," explained Christiane. "There's been about a dozen whores over the years, and it seems there's always one of his girl students who's willing to screw him in the olive groves if he gives her a passing grade. Some of them aren't a day over fourteen. If it weren't for you, I wouldn't mind a taste of that teenage snatch myself."

If it weren't for you …

She can't say she loves me, thought Dominique, but I know she does in her heart, at least for now. And that's enough for me. Leaning over, she kissed Christiane's hair affectionately. The car swerved slightly, but as there was no one else on the road, no harm was done. Dominique could not see the donkey-drawn wagon a few miles up the highway. It was still some distance ahead, and although red reflectors were required by law, this wagon had none. You would have to be almost on top of it before it would become visible in the darkness of the night.

Dominique was blissfully unaware of the wagon as she caressed Christiane's shoulder. No doubt the sexually adventurous woman would tire of Dominique some day, and go back to Laurent for a while, and then on to another woman or to a man perhaps. For now, however, she remained attached to Dominique, and Dominique did everything she could to keep it that way, from her loving compliments, to her occasional inexpensive but thoughtful gifts, to the care she took with her own appearance in order to please Christiane.

Dominique's caresses seemed to be awakening the other Frenchwoman now, and she sighed in pleasure. Instinctively, Christiane moved one hand towards Dominique's chest, the other to touch the side of her neck. Not in the car, thought Dominique, but she was too excited to protest aloud. She felt Christiane's hand open and enter her blouse, slowly, sensually. It was almost impossible to keep her foot steady on the gas pedal as Christiane's fingers knowingly caressed the tender skin of her breasts. Then she was lowering her head in order to taste Dominique's nipples, her tongue and lips sucking them, lubricating them, nibbling on them playfully.

The next thing Dominique knew, Christiane's hand had reached under her skirt and her fingers had begun expertly probing the area between her legs. She inserted one, then two fingers into Dominique's already drenched pussy. Don't stop, prayed Dominique. Don't ever stop!

Dominique could not resist closing her eyes as she luxuriated in the ecstasy of Christiane's adept lovemaking. But although she closed them for hardly more than a few seconds, it was a few seconds too long.

When she reopened them she saw the wagon. The stupid idiot who drove it hadn't bothered to put on reflectors! She was coming up to it so rapidly, could she swerve to the other lane in time? Dominique jerked the steering wheel to the left, hardly aware that Christiane was still making love to her. She was in the left hand lane now, the wagon beside her when ... Oh dear God, it couldn't be! She hadn't known that there was a bend in the road just ahead. She hadn't known that another car was speeding along in the opposite direction heading towards Marrakesh. Only now did she see the headlights, almost on her own. She couldn't swerve back to the right where the wagon plodded along. There was only time to try to get over to the left shoulder. But, oh sweet Jesus, that was just what the other car was doing!

Just before the two speeding vehicles met head-on, Dominique noticed in the glare of her own headlamps that the driver of the other car was a middle-aged Moroccan seated next to a veiled woman, and there seemed to be several children in the back, perhaps in their early teens.

Then, in a burst of crashing steel, the two cars collided, sending flying debris in all directions.

Christiane was killed immediately, her head smashed against the steering wheel. Amazingly, Dominique survived the initial impact, trapped in the car by her lover's dead body, wishing only for the end to come soon, for she realized more than ever how much she loved Christiane and that life without her would be meaningless. Seconds later, as she had prayed, flames burst out and enveloped her.

One of the children in the other car had been thrown to the side of the road where he watched helplessly as the two wrecks burned, their flames illuminating the night. Before he lost consciousness, he caught a glimpse of his parents' charred faces.

The driver of the wagon stared on in horror at the violence of the shooting flames that swallowed the two demolished vehicles. He thought to himself how dangerous it was to drive these days, and thanked Allah that he could only afford his donkey-pulled wagon.

CHAPTER 26

▼

Dave and Kevin were having coffee and croissants for breakfast. As they sat in their sunny kitchen—the days were getting long once more—it hardly seemed possible to Dave that the end of the school year was less than two months away. Classes would last another week, perhaps two, and afterwards all that would remain would be a series of three national exams to proctor and correct, one for passage from elementary school into *lycée*, another for the *Certificat d'Etudes Secondaires*, given to what in the United States would be ninth graders, and finally the all important *baccalauréat* examination. Dave and Kevin might be summoned to administer the oral part of the *baccalauréat* English test in another city, and there was always the possibility that they would have written copies to correct, perhaps as many as a hundred. These would be numbered and unsigned, and the teacher would then have to travel to Rabat, where the results of all subjects would be totaled by a group of correctors and decisions made as to who would pass and who would fail. This might seem a heavy schedule to the uninitiated, however in fact it was child's play compared to the work involved in day to day teaching. Once classes ended in just a week or two, Dave would finally have the free time he longed for in order to plan his and Lateef's departure from Morocco. He had already started counting the days.

Kevin, on the other hand, seemed to be taking the finality of these last days of classes rather hard. He had become so devoted to his work in recent months that the mere mention that his students would soon be departing was enough to send him into a fit of rage.

This morning, Dave was tempted to comment on how excited he was that he would soon be able to sleep in on Mondays, but he thought better of it. As usual,

Kevin, sitting opposite him, was only picking at his food, less interested in break-fast than in the lesson plan he was examining.

"Have some breakfast or you'll get sick," ordered Dave, but he knew it was useless to make a fuss. Kevin hardly listened to anyone these days. He smoked constantly, and it was only because Dave had insisted that the kitchen was off limits that Kevin was not doing so now.

Poor Kevin, thought Dave. He was a bundle of nerves since the day the *proviseur* had chastised one of his students before his very eyes. And although things seemed to be going rather smoothly between teacher and class, Dave knew that Kevin had never forgotten their refusal to take his test, which he termed their "betrayal," and he lived in fear that they would turn against him again. In addition, he was convinced that the *proviseur* was hounding him, and perhaps this was true. Monsieur Rhazwani had summoned Kevin to his office several times to inquire about the behavior of the American's students, and although Kevin insisted that there were no problems and even once had gone so far as to tell the *proviseur* that he must have more important things to worry about, the *proviseur* did not seem to be letting up on him. He apparently felt that Kevin's roll-taking was inaccurate, for several times he had sent messengers to verify it. Also, Kevin suspected that there was a student spy in his classroom, reporting to Monsieur Rhazwani on his actions. Both he and Dave had heard stories before of such things occurring in Moroccan schools, but until now they had paid little atten-tion to them, and Dave still felt that there was no need to worry about unsub-stantiated rumors. Kevin, though, was overly conscious of his every word in the classroom, obsessed with the idea that the *proviseur* was out to "get" him.

"Have you written to Barry Pennington yet?" Dave asked Kevin now as he buttered another croissant. Barry was the coordinator of Peace Corps teachers throughout Morocco.

"Damn it, Dave," exclaimed Kevin. "When I write him I'll tell you. Until then, just drop the subject. I haven't made my decision yet, but when I do, you'll be the first to know."

Kevin was talking about his decision whether or not to remain a third year in Aïn El Qamar. Barry had asked that all volunteers decide before the first of May whether or not they were extending their two year stays. There was no question of Dave's continuing on, and until recently he had been sure that Kevin would be leaving too. Then, one day not long ago, Kevin had spoken of what he could accomplish if he remained with his students next year, and since then he had been vacillating between wanting to stay, and wanting to get away from Aïn El

Qamar, from the *proviseur*, and from the unhappy memories that this town held for him.

Dave knew it would be foolish to respond to Kevin's last remarks, but he could not hold back. "You probably think this is none of my business," he said, "but if you don't decide soon, you may find the decision made for you. And what if you discover that your position has been filled by someone else because you were too slow to make up your mind?"

"All right damn it!" shouted Kevin. "I'll come to a decision before the end of the week. I've got other things to think about now. So if you don't drop the subject, I'll go somewhere else to work."

"You can't go into the living room or you'll wake Mandee," reminded Dave, referring to his college friend Miranda Cox, who had made good the letter she'd sent him by arriving in Aïn El Qamar at the end of last week. "And if Mandee finds your adorable sandy-haired boyish self hovering over her *banquette*, she might just unzip your fly and perform oral sex on you. They don't call her Mandee Cocksucker for nothing."

"Oh go to hell!" cried Kevin and stalked out of the kitchen. Dave knew he should have kept his mouth shut, but if he was careful about everything he said, he would have to be mute.

"What's all the commotion, Davey?" asked a husky female voice, and Dave looked up to see Miranda Cox enter the room, wearing only one of Dave's pajama tops and, he supposed, panties underneath, though with Mandee one could never be sure. This morning, as always, she looked like she was ready to jump into bed with anyone at the slightest provocation. Her pale skin contrasted with her jet black hair which hung thick and wavy to below her shoulders. Even without make-up this morning, her eyebrows and lashes were dark enough to hardly need accentuating. There was a bit of Claudette in her, thought Dave, despite the fact that the curvaceous Mandee was only five foot two or so. It was not surprising that she had been able to appeal to Dave in his early college days before he had realized definitely that his sexual interests did not lie with women.

"I thought I'd try sleeping a little later this morning," continued Miranda, "but no luck. There were children playing outside as usual and you and Kevin were having some kind of argument in here. Needless to say I'm up with the birds as I seem always to be these days."

"Let me pour you some coffee," offered Dave.

"Thanks, I could use some," said Miranda as Dave handed her a cupful. "Where is Kevin, by the way?"

"Busy preparing for today's lessons as usual," answered Dave. "I'd just leave him alone if I were you. He's likely to blow up at any minute."

"Maybe an hour with me would be just what he needs," suggested Miranda, but Dave just smiled and shook his head.

"Sorry, Mandee. Wrong gender. Although you may be right. Kevin's probably as much in need of a good fuck as anyone I know. But his biggest problem is just being here in Aïn El Qamar. He needs to get out of this town worse than anyone else I know, and still he's thinking of staying."

"I thought you said you two guys had it made here," remarked Miranda as she sipped her coffee and accepted a croissant from Dave. "Jobs that you enjoy, a beautiful foreign country, gorgeous men ... Especially that student of yours who's always dropping by. Lateef?"

"Hands off, Mandee," cautioned Dave for the umpteenth time. "You know I've got dibs on him."

"Dibs, schimbs! You told me yourself that this is an unrequited love affair ..."

"It is," conceded Dave. "But hopefully not for much longer," he added a bit over-optimistically. If anything, Lateef had seemed even more stand-offish in recent weeks, and since Mandee's arrival, Dave had caught him staring at her in a way which made Dave wonder if he found her sexually attractive. He had informed the young man in no uncertain terms that he was to stay away from the house when the two American men were out. "In order to avoid gossip," Dave had lied, and Lateef had not seemed pleased by his friend's request.

Fortunately for Dave's sanity, he had recently begun a casual affair with an Egyptian university student whom he had met in Rabat on one of his many visits regarding Lateef's visa—which had been granted as expected—and other documents required for their return to the United States. Like Fareed, the Egyptian, whose name was Galeel, was wild, unashamed, and totally uninterested in any kind of emotional commitment, which suited Dave perfectly. But he would give up Galeel in an instant if Lateef would once again kiss him as he had back in December. That, however, seemed even more improbable in recent weeks, and especially in the days since Miranda had arrived. What if Lateef decided to test his sexuality with the ever available Mandee Cock-sucker? No! The mere thought of the two of them together was nauseating beyond belief.

"So, Davey ..." Miranda was saying now. "Where are the hunks you promised to line up for me? My patience is wearing thin."

"Keep your shirt on, Mandee. At least until Thursday when we're having a party in your honor."

"But that's still three days away," pouted Miranda.

"I promise you the pick of the best looking straight Frenchmen and Moroccans in Aïn El Qamar."

"I still don't know why you won't lend me Lateef, at least until I meet someone else. I promise I'll return him to you, if not in mint condition, then at least with the widest and most satisfied grin you've ever seen, or my name isn't …"

"Don't even think it," interrupted Dave with such ice in his glare that Miranda was forced to look away. "And now, I'd better get dressed for school. I'd invite you to observe my classes, but we've got a *proviseur* … excuse me, a principal …, who objects to just about everything we do, so you'd better not pay a surprise visit. But there's a girl, one of my former students, who lives just down the street, who told me she'd like to have you over for tea. Her English is pretty good. She passed the *baccalauréat* last year but her parents wouldn't let her go off to the university, poor thing. I know she's dying to meet you."

"I suppose it's a way to pass time," said Mandee, "until the party …"

"You'll have fun," Dave assured her. "I almost wish I could turn invisible and join you. As a man, I have no idea what you'll see today. It's a part of Aïn El Qamar that's completely off limits to Kevin and me. And now, if you'll excuse me, I've got to go change. I'll be home a little after twelve and you can tell me about your morning then. See you," he added as he left the kitchen and headed for his bedroom.

Twenty minutes later, Dave called a quick good-bye to Miranda, then joined Kevin at the door to begin the ten minute walk to Lycée Mohamed Cinq. Kevin hardly spoke the whole way, doubtless preoccupied with the lessons he was about to teach, and Dave couldn't help thinking of how different his prospects were from his friend's. While Kevin faced an uncertain future, not knowing if he was staying in Aïn El Qamar or going elsewhere and unable to reach a decision, Dave's future was already decided, and it looked pretty bright. In just a few months he would be starting a new life as a graduate student, and Lateef would be studying English at the same school. That the young Moroccan would remain a part of Dave's life even after his return to the United States was a dream come true. If only …

Dave felt a sudden chill as he recalled Mandee's obvious interest in Lateef this morning. But no, there had to be straight sailing ahead! Lateef would never sleep with Mandee!

Would he?

CHAPTER 27

▼

The young Moroccan sat in his room, rereading an entry in his diary dated Monday, April 25. This would be his last chance to examine the words before putting his carefully laid plan into action.

"Today I went to Ms. Gallagher's house pretending to work for the Department of Water and Power. I knew before going that Ms. Gallagher would be at school. She teaches on Mondays from ten to noon. Monday is also a day when her maid comes to clean. The woman is illiterate, probably not even able to write her name. When I showed her my student I.D. card, it never occurred to her that I wasn't a worker sent by the D.W.P. It was easy for me to pretend to have come to check the water pressure inside Ms. Gallagher's house. The foolish old hag never even questioned my story.

"The visit was a success. I now know the layout of Ms. Gallagher's house. I know where the living room, bedroom, and kitchen are situated. I also discovered a small unlocked storage closet off the entry hall, hidden from the rest of the rooms, empty, and large enough for a man to fit into if he sits.

"When Ms. Gallagher is at home, the front door is always locked, but the maid leaves it open when she works in case a neighbor wants to come in and gossip. All I have to do is get through the door without being noticed. Then I can crawl into the storage closet and hide. After that, I only have to wait until Ms. Gallagher arrives back from work and the maid leaves for home. I'll be alone in the house with Ms. Gallagher and I'll finally have what I've been wanting for months and months."

The Moroccan now turned to the next entry in his diary. It was dated Monday, May 2, a week ago today. He read:

"Today my plan failed miserably. I waited all morning in a small park down the street from Ms. Gallagher's house, hoping that the neighbors who were sitting out front would leave so that I could sneak in. The door was half-open the whole time, urging me to enter, but I would have been seen. School ends in just a few weeks, and once Ms. Gallagher has stopped teaching, she will be home on Monday mornings and the door will remain locked. If I don't have better luck next Monday or the one after, I will lose my chance forever."

Last night he had written the most recent entry. It said:

"Tomorrow I will try again. I'm sure that by now Ms. Gallagher will have forgotten my visit two months ago when Miss Nelson saw me there. Like everyone else at Lycée Mohammed Cinq, she too must believe that I have dropped out of school and left town. She will be expecting nothing. Not she, not anyone else, has the slightest idea of what I intend to do.

"I must have better luck this time than the last. I will pray that some distraction takes the neighbors' attention away from Ms. Gallagher's door. Anything is possible: a street quarrel, an accident, a fire … If it is Allah's will, no one will notice my entry. Allah must will it so."

The student closed the diary and hid it under some old magazines in his desk. Crossing to his small chest of drawers, he removed a rolled-up pair of socks and a two foot length of rope which he had left there expressly for this day. These he put into his satchel along with the textbooks with which he filled it daily in order to convince his aunt and uncle that he was still attending school and not hiding out in the olive groves behind Aïn El Qamar. He called good-bye to his aunt who was busy in the kitchen.

His heart was pounding as he left his house and headed towards Ms. Gallagher's. The walk, which took only a matter of minutes, seemed longer today, longer than it had the previous times he had gone to Ms. Gallagher's house. Somehow he was sure that today he would be successful, and in his impatience to finally achieve his aim, the road to her house seemed endless.

But at last he was there, seated in the small park in which he could remain unnoticed and observe the comings and goings in Ms. Gallagher's neighborhood.

The student lit a cigarette, and glancing at his watch, saw that it was nearly ten past ten. Ms. Gallagher would be in class now, teaching her lesson, unaware of what would take place in just hours.

The minutes dragged on, and still the Moroccan sat waiting in the park. He wanted desperately to move into action, but like the previous week the front door of Ms. Gallagher's house was never for a moment left unguarded. Once, the maid came out to dispose of a pail of garbage, but she locked the door behind her so that even if the coast had been clear, he would not have been able to enter.

The student kept looking at his watch, amazed that the minutes were passing so slowly. And then suddenly he was aware that on the contrary time was rushing past all too quickly. It was already half past eleven, and still he had been unable to make his entry. In a bit more than half an hour it would be too late and he would have lost yet another chance at attaining what he sought.

And then he heard it. The innocent sound of a flute accompanied by the rhythmic beating of a clay drum. The music was getting nearer and nearer, and unless he was mistaken …

The young Moroccan turned around and there in the distance he could see … Yes … Yes! A wedding procession was heading this way! Allah was answering his prayers. This would be the distraction he had been waiting for!

A man was leading a donkey-drawn wagon piled high with wedding gifts. There were bottles of cooking oil and several large sacks of flour, baskets of oranges and a huge pyramid of watermelons, and even a sheep which would soon be slaughtered. Behind the wagon walked the musicians whom the student had heard playing before he was aware of what their music signified. And following them were dozens of men and women. The women came first, women of all ages, some wearing *haïks* or *jellabas*, others of school age wearing smocks over short skirts and carrying satchels. Then came the men, from the old and bearded to the young and long-haired. All were clapping in time to the music and singing in unison. The wagon moved slowly along the street towards the park where the young Moroccan sat, heading steadily in the direction of Ms. Gallagher's house. Occasionally the caravan stopped, and new celebrants joined the others, delighted to find something to relieve the boredom of their day.

And now they were at the park. Along with several other people who were sitting there, the young Moroccan joined the crowd which followed the wagon. He pretended to add his voice to those of the others, but his mind was elsewhere. His eyes were fixed on the front door of Ms. Gallagher's house. He could see that the people standing near it had all turned in the direction of the approaching wedding caravan. If they continued to pay attention to it and not to the door …

He was nearly there now. Please, he prayed, let the wagon stop here. Let it …

Now was his chance. The festive group had paused almost directly in front of Ms. Gallagher's door. There was no doubt that it was Allah's will that he go through with his plan. Everything was working out to perfection this time. Last week had only been a test of his resolve. Now was the reward for his patience.

The student slipped away from the crowd among whom he had been standing. As Ms. Gallagher's neighbors moved to approach the wedding parade, as her maid stood with them admiring the numerous gifts atop the wagon, the young man crept around behind them, slowly, casually, until he was standing with this back against the wall of Ms. Gallagher's house, only inches away from the door, the neighbors crowded around the caravan, blindly unaware of where he stood. And then, in a matter of seconds at most, he had slipped through the half-open door and was standing inside the house.

His heart was pounding so fast and hard that he was sure its beat was echoing though the entry hall, but no … That was only the sound of the drum coming from outside.

The small closet was there as he had remembered it from his previous visit. Unfastening the latch, the young man crawled in, pulling the door shut behind him, and sat to wait for the inevitable moment when there would be only he and Ms. Gallagher in this house.

CHAPTER 28

▼

The bell had rung, and rather than continue straight through into the second of the two hours he spent with this class every Monday morning, Jean-Richard decided to give them a break. It was not that he thought they were becoming tired or restless, nor even that he himself needed a short recess from his work. If he could finish the remaining hours of this school year without pausing for an instant, working ceaselessly for two or three days just to have them over with that much sooner, he would do it. No, today he had offered them this break in order that he might rush to the *salle des profs* to see if the all-important letter he was expecting from France had arrived. Usually the morning mail delivery was at ten o'clock, but today it had not come on time, so Jean-Richard had spent the last hour wondering if the letter he was anxiously awaiting had been delivered while he taught. Now was his chance to see.

"Monsieur Moreau," asked one of his students who had come up to Jean-Richard's desk, evidently with a question. "Could you explain …?"

"Not now," interrupted Jean-Richard. "I'll talk to you at the end of the second hour. Please excuse me."

The student looked hurt at Jean-Richard's brusqueness. It was not like this teacher to ignore the questions of his class, though in recent days Monsieur Moreau had changed a great deal.

Jean-Richard hurried out of the science laboratory past groups of milling students. It was true that he was less dynamic, less involved in his lectures, than had been the case previously, and he knew that this loss of interest and dedication was due wholly to the pretty blonde teacher he could see walking out of the *salle des profs* at this minute. Thank God Marcie was on her way home now after her morning at school. Their few meetings these past two months had been painful and strained. At least this morning she would be gone by the time he reached the faculty room.

Jean-Richard had tried desperately to put Marcie out of his mind since the afternoon of the *moussem*. He had traveled frequently, visiting friends on weekends, being introduced to attractive single women, making love to them. But there was something missing in his affairs, something he had felt that wonderful spring day when everything had seemed to open up for him. Rarely in the past had he noticed any emptiness in his sexual adventures. Since he had experienced love with Marcie, though, it was the emptiness and meaninglessness that struck him the most. And each new experience only confirmed what he had known from the start, that without Marcie in his life, he hardly felt alive at all.

Why had he met her? Why did she have to complicate a day to day existence that had been so much simpler before her arrival? Why did he have to keep on loving her when all he wanted was to forget that he had ever known an American girl named Marcie Nelson?

Well, at least for the moment she was gone from his sight, out of the *salle des profs*, out of the school … but never, God help him, far from his thoughts.

The mail had arrived, Jean-Richard could see as he entered the *salle des profs*. If only the letter he was waiting for was there …

Jean-Richard had not changed his mind about leaving the country at the end of the school year, though unfortunately his request for a transfer had been dismissed without explanation. Now his hope lay in the answer to a letter he had written a little more than a week ago to a friend he knew in France. If the answer was not encouraging, Jean-Richard still planned to leave Morocco, but it would mean without the certainty of a teaching position, and it might mean accepting anything he could get in order to put food in his mouth.

Ordinarily Jean-Richard would have gone over to talk with some of the other teachers in the *salle des profs*. Michèle and Kevin were conversing in one corner while in another area Jean-Richard could see Dave with Janna. It seemed incredible that these teachers could be present and not know that Jean-Richard's whole life depended on whether or not there was a response to his letter. If René had answered his request right away, the reply could be on the table in the middle of the *salle des profs* at this very moment. Today was the first mail delivery of the week. If it had arrived over the weekend …

Jean-Richard hurried across to the table, ignoring the several greetings he only vaguely heard. As he sorted through the mail, he prayed silently, "Let it be here! Please!"

And then he found it. A plain white envelope with the return address reading "Académie Fernaud, Lyon, France." Inside might lie the key to his future or the end of all hope. Tearing open the envelope, Jean-Richard read:

"*Cher* Jean-Richard,

"*Je viens de recevoir ta lettre*! What a wonderful surprise to hear from you after so many years! Yes, much time has passed since we last saw each other, but you have never been far from my thoughts. I have often pictured you in your far away corner of the world.

"You write that only recently did you recall that since our days at the university I have become director of this small private school in Lyon. Let me say that your forgetfulness has been most fortuitous.

"If you had written me several months ago at the time when job requests are normally submitted, I would have told you how sorry I was that I had nothing to offer you. We have so many more applications than we have positions to fill.

"May I compliment you on your timing? It so happens that your letter arrived only days after one of our best teachers, Marlène Michelet, announced to me that she will be going on maternity leave during our summer session, and plans to take the following year off to spend with her child during its infancy. I could I suppose offer the job to one of those who applied months ago, but as you are an old friend and apparently quite eager to work at the Académie Fernaud, the position is yours if you want it. I cannot offer you more than a year's contract, but the possibilities of its being extended are very good, especially in your case.

"Please let me know your decision as soon as possible. I do hope it is a positive one.

"*Amitiés sincères*,

"René"

Jean-Richard could hardly read to the end of the letter. His eyes were blurring and he could feel the blood rushing through his head. Never had he dared to hope for such luck, but the unbelievable had happened. He had a job, or would have as soon as he answered René. What a wonderful, true friend the man was!

Of course it was only a one year contract. Of course the job would mean a return to France, the country from which he had fled years before. But Lyon was not Paris, and at the moment even France with its unhappy memories seemed preferable to Aïn El Qamar where every day he was forced to avoid Marcie, forced to pretend that they had never found each other only for him to run from the promise of her love.

Jean-Richard had been so intent on reading his letter that he had not noticed the two policemen who had entered the *salle des profs*. Only now, when the blood-curdling scream tore through the air, instantly plunging the room into silence, only now did Jean-Richard look up to see Laurent Koenigsmarck crumple into the arms of one of the policemen. What in the name of God had the man been told?

The second policeman was speaking to Michèle, offering her a handkerchief which she refused. Kevin, who had been conversing with Michèle before the policemen's arrival, wandered over to Dave and Janna, his eyes wide with shock. The news must have been awful, thought Jean-Richard, for as Kevin spoke to the other Americans, Dave turned white as a sheet and Janna could hardly light the cigarette she was holding.

Suddenly Jean-Richard could restrain his curiosity no longer. Hurrying over to where the three teachers had gathered, he blurted out:

"*Que ... que'est-ce qui c'est passé?*"

"*Il y a eu un accident,*" replied Kevin grimly. "Christiane and Dominique were killed early this morning in an automobile crash."

"Oh dear God!" gasped Jean-Richard.

"They ... they were coming back from Marrakesh, it seems," continued Kevin, "and crashed head-on into another car. Three people were killed in the other vehicle. It appears that one child survived, but Christiane and Dominique were killed almost instantly."

Jean-Richard thought for a moment that he, like Laurent, was going to faint. Kevin, in fact, reached out to support him in case he fell, but the Frenchman found the strength to pull himself together, forcing himself to erase the image he saw in his mind of the two women's horribly battered bodies.

Michèle was approaching them now, visibly shaken by the news she had just heard. Dave held out his arms as if to take her in them, but she shook her head. "It's all right," she said. "It's just that I can hardly believe that it's happened. I can hardly believe that Domino's gone."

"I understand, Michèle," said Dave soothingly. "After all the time you spent with Dominique, you have every right to mourn her loss."

"But Dave ... When they told me she'd been killed, I had the strangest and most awful first reaction. I thought to myself how lucky she was, how damned lucky."

"What do you mean?" asked Dave.

"Don't you see? How many people are fortunate enough to find the kind of happiness that Domino found with Christiane? How many people end their lives never having known what it's like to really be in love? Oh, I know that some narrow-minded people might say that their relationship was wrong, but Dominique loved her. She loved her. That's why, when they told me the news, I couldn't help thinking how lucky Dominique was. When she died, it was with Christiane, it was with the woman she loved."

Jean-Richard heard Michèle's words, and it was as if in the briefest of seconds the past had returned once more to torment him. "She died with the woman she loved," Michèle had said. "She died with the woman she loved."

The words kept repeating themselves in Jean-Richard's ears, torturing him, tearing at him, for it was not just Michèle who was speaking them, it was another voice as well, telling him, "I want to be with the woman I love, and when I die, I want it to be with the woman I love, not with you Jean-Richard, with the woman I love!"

Jean-Richard threw his hands up to his ears to blot out the angry, hateful words, but still they continued. She was with him once again. She would never let him alone!

"*Arrête*, Nicole! Stop it!" he screamed. "God damn it, stop!"

Turning sharply, Jean-Richard broke into a run. He ran from the startled teachers with whom he had been standing. He ran past the students who crowded around the faculty room wondering what the commotion was about. He ran across the courtyard, past the gatekeeper, towards his car, fumbling in his pocket for the keys. His whole body was shaking as he got in, and he was sure he would be sick. The words still raced through his head as if Nicole were a part of this present moment, and he could see her, not as she had been in life, but lying bruised and bloody by the side of a deserted highway as flames enveloped the car she had been driving. In her arms was another woman, and even in death it was clear that theirs was a lovers' embrace.

He could visualize the scene so clearly. It was as if he were there at the site of the accident, a witness to its terror and devastation. And then he *was* there, slowly approaching the lifeless victims, afraid to see their faces but morbidly wanting to confirm the identities of Nicole and the woman she had loved. "The woman I love," re-echoed the words. "I want to die with the woman I love!"

He was near them now, leaning over their bodies, his hand trembling as he reached down to turn the face of one of them towards his own and to see ... Oh dear God! Nicole's lover was Marcie!

Jean-Richard threw open the door of his car, leaned out, and vomited on the pavement beneath. His forehead was covered with cold sweat. He felt that he had no strength in his body.

And then suddenly someone was beside him, holding on to him, pulling him up, asking him what was wrong. Jean-Richard opened his eyes to see Dave, who must have rushed out after him from the *salle des profs*. The mental image of Nicole lying dead with Marcie in her arms had apparently lasted no more than seconds, though it had seemed to stay with him an eternity.

"*Qu'est-ce qu'il y a?*" Dave was repeating. "Jean-Richard, are you all right?"

"I … I'm fine now," said Jean-Richard weakly. "It must have been the shock. I'm sorry I frightened you. I just …"

"I understand," said Dave, kneeling beside the car despite the stench of Jean-Richard's vomit, handing the Frenchman a handkerchief to wipe his mouth. "It's been a shock for us all. Is there … is there anything I can do?"

"No, nothing," replied Jean-Richard, and then changed his mind. "Yes. Will … will you go to the science lab and tell my students not to expect me for the second hour? I've got to get away from here."

"Of course," said Dave. "Are you sure you're all right?"

"Yes, I'm fine," insisted Jean-Richard. "Please … please don't let me keep you from your work."

"Don't worry about your students," reassured Dave. "I'll think of a good excuse to tell them. Just go on home now and try to relax and forget what's happened."

"*Merci*, Dave," said Jean-Richard as he watched the tall American walk away. "I'll go home and try to forg …"

Forget? Who was he fooling? There was no way to forget the dreadful image of Marcie and Nicole lying dead in each others arms. It remained horribly vivid in his mind, and much too real. There was no way to forget. There was n …

Or was there? Perhaps … perhaps if he were to see Marcie alive and vital as always, if he were to see her as she truly was, innocent, full of hope, untouched by hatred and spite, perhaps then he could replace the nightmare with reality, with the reality that was now his only hope for salvation.

"I've got to see her!" Jean-Richard cried. "I've got to see her now! I'll lose my mind if I don't."

In a single movement, Jean-Richard pulled the car door shut and turned the key in the ignition. Without even a glance to see if anyone was behind him, he backed out of his parking space and raced past the gatekeeper, through the open gate, and out into the street. Marcie would be on her way home now. Let her not have taken a different route to go shopping or visit someone! Let her …

Jean-Richard was squinting to see in the distance when he spotted her walking towards her house, unaware as yet of the drama which had exploded after her departure from the *salle des profs*. He increased his speed until he was just past her, then jerked to a stop. Leaning over to open the right hand door, he called out:

"Marcie, *s'il te plaît*! I have to talk to you!" She was at the car door in an instant, a look of concern in her eyes. Thank God. He had been so afraid that she would turn away from him after the pain he had caused her.

"Please get in," begged Jean-Richard, his voice shaky, his face still pale from shock.

And a second later she was by his side, Jean-Richard asking her, "Would you … would you mind if I came over to your place … just for a while? There … there are things I've got to tell you, things you have every right to finally know."

"Jean-Richard, there's no need to even ask," said Marcie. "I told you I'd be around if ever you needed me. I don't break my promises."

The Frenchman gave her a faint half-smile of thanks, too drained from the scene in the school parking lot to fully express his feelings. She could have told him to go to hell, but she had reaffirmed her emotional commitment to him. He needed her now, and she had not abandoned him. Jean-Richard drove on the few remaining blocks to Marcie's house. Parking the car outside her door, he stumbled out and joined her, still trembling, as she unlocked the door and invited him in.

The living room was as he had remembered it from his previous visits, though she had accumulated even more furnishings—vases and a brass candleholder and a small rug—since the last time he had been here, months ago.

"Can I get you something?" asked Marcie after Jean-Richard had sat down. "I have some Scotch a girlfriend brought me. Let me get you some."

Not waiting for an answer, Marcie ran into the kitchen, leaving the Frenchman momentarily alone.

Jean-Richard sat with his head cupped in his hands, forcing himself to replace his nightmare vision with the real one he had just seen, of a beautiful vibrant girl, alive and full of warmth and tenderness.

And then she was there once again, sitting beside him, handing him a glass of whiskey which he gulped down in one swallow, its fire jerking him back to the reality of the present moment. Marcie was next to him, her body touching his, her hand on his shoulder, understanding, begging to help.

"You said you wanted to talk, Jean-Richard. You said there were things you thought I had the right to know. Does that mean that you're finally ready to let out whatever it is you've kept bottled up inside for so long?"

Jean-Richard wondered if Marcie had any idea of the truth of her words. He had indeed kept things inside for longer than he could remember, resisting every urge to set them free until the pressure had built to the point where, at this moment, if he didn't let her know everything, he felt that he would explode with his secrets.

"There ... there was an accident this morning ..." Jean-Richard began, and told her of the deaths of Dominique and Christiane. "And when Michèle said those words, 'She died with the woman she loved,' it wasn't Michèle's voice I heard. It was Nicole's, and she was telling me she wanted to die with the woman she loved."

Marcie did not interrupt Jean-Richard's painful revelations, perhaps understanding that today, at last, the full story must finally come to light.

"When I called you Nicole, those other times, it wasn't what you imagined. I know you thought that it was because I couldn't keep you straight in my mind from the other women in my life. But it was much more than that. The feelings you were awakening in me were feelings I thought had died, with her, with Nicole, and it was as if she was back with me once again, not as I had finally discovered her to be, but as she had been when we first met, when we were first married."

"M ... married?" stammered Marcie, her eyes wide with incredulity.

"Yes. Nicole was my wife."

Marcie did not speak. It was clear to Jean-Richard that she was too dumbfounded to utter a word.

"We were married for nearly three years."

Jean-Richard waited for some kind of response from Marcie, for her to ask him how it was possible that in his ten years in Aïn El Qamar, no one had ever even intimated that he had once been married, how it was possible to keep such a secret buried so deep within him. But when she said nothing, he continued, forcing himself to answer these unasked questions whether bidden to or not.

"I met Nicole when we were both hardly out of our teens," he told Marcie. "I was completing my science studies at the university and Nicole was finishing hers in economics. She was the most beautiful thing I'd ever seen, tall, slender like a fashion model, and with a face like one you'd see on the cover of *Elle* or *Vogue*.

"I myself was ... Well, I was very different from the person I am now. I was so young, and so romantic. In fact, when I now think back on that much younger version of myself, I realize that I had many of the same ideals and values that you now have. I'd spent most of my life in a small provincial town, and Paris was a revelation to me. My first years at the university, I didn't socialize much, though I had a few friends I enjoyed spending time with. I suppose that the size and scope of Paris and all it had to offer was just too great for me to totally accept at first. There were … no romantic involvements for me at that time. I was actually quite inexperienced.

"Then, one evening after I'd been in Paris for several years, I let a couple of my friends convince me to go to a party they'd been invited to. They more or less had to drag me there, as I found being surrounded by strangers both intimidating and at the same time rather boring.

"Unfortunately, being at that particular party was as dull and unpleasant an experience as I had imagined, until I saw Nicole. She was sitting by herself at the other end of the room, and … I don't know what my first impression was. Did I first notice her beauty, or was it the fact that it seemed so incredible to me that someone with her obvious allure should be alone? She seemed to feel as out of place at the party as I did.

"I'm not sure to this day how I ever found the courage to go over to her, but it was as if there was some force outside myself pulling me in her direction. I asked if I might sit down beside her and she looked up at me to answer. I could tell that she was about to say that she didn't want company, that she preferred to be left alone. Then, she seemed to change her mind. She smiled at me, a demure bewitching smile, and invited me to join her.

"You'd hardly know it from the reputation I've acquired in Aïn El Qamar, but I was shy in those days. I especially found it difficult to talk to attractive women. And a woman as beautiful as Nicole would normally have intimidated me to the point of absolute speechlessness. How then can I explain why I felt totally at ease with Nicole, right from the beginning? I told her how I felt about having been dragged to the party, and she replied that she too had let herself be convinced to come. I found myself describing my studies, and she seemed sincerely interested in what I was doing. We talked for hours, though it seemed like only minutes. Or perhaps I should say that I talked. Nicole spoke briefly about her school work, but she scarcely mentioned her private life. I attributed this to shyness, and since she was such a good listener, I didn't think anything about it.

"We were the last guests to leave the party, at … it must have been past three in the morning. She lived just down the street, so I walked with her to her flat in the silence of that new day. Most people who know me now would find it hard to believe that I made no move to invite myself in. But I was a different person then. I was in no hurry to go to bed with her, and I was very young and thought that we'd have all the time in the world, especially when she told me that she'd enjoy seeing me again.

"I knew when I left her that morning that I'd ask her to marry me. There was no doubt in my mind that in the short time I'd known her, I'd fallen as deeply in love as I ever would in my life. I knew that it was more than infatuation. No man could love a woman as much as I loved Nicole at that moment.

"I should have realized back then that she was hiding things from me. There were parts of her life that she would never talk about. She gave me only the barest skeleton of her growing up, saying that the past was too painful to discuss, and in any case, things that happened before we met meant nothing to her anymore. The present was all that counted.

"I should have pressed her to tell me everything, but I believed her. I was so naive then that I couldn't even conceive of her being capable of duplicity.

"When finally I found the courage to ask her to become my wife, I nearly fainted at her response. She said yes. She told me that she too had known from our first meeting that we would someday be husband and wife.

"So we were married, just a week after we'd both graduated from the university. And I felt as if a whole new life was beginning for me. I'd fallen in love, so totally and completely in love that nothing I'd known before had any meaning for me, and the woman I was in love with had agreed to share my life. The first weeks, months, of our marriage were the kind of storybook perfection that you read about but never hope to find.

"Why ... why couldn't I have seen from the beginning that Nicole was keeping a side of herself from me that I was never allowed to glimpse? While I was at my job as a fledgling *prof de sciences* in the *banlieu* of Paris, did I have any idea of how she filled her days? I'd asked her if it bored her, staying at home when she could be working at her own chosen profession, but she told me that she preferred to devote herself to making a home for me. So I simply assumed that she shopped and cleaned and exchanged gossip with the other housewives who lived in our building. I never had the slightest idea of what really went on in our flat while I was away.

"Life was bliss for me for the first two years of our marriage. But it was a blind bliss, deliberately ignorant of the signs that Nicole was holding things back from me, hiding so much of her life, of her past, and of the present I thought we were sharing.

"One day, about a week before we were to celebrate our second wedding anniversary, I was scheduled to attend a conference in Marseille. I'd canceled classes, so when, at the last minute, I learned at school that the conference had been called off, I was left with a free day on my hands.

"I wanted to telephone Nicole right away to let her know of our luck, but I remembered that our phone was out of order, and wouldn't be repaired until the next day. Besides, I thought it might be nice to surprise her. Why not celebrate our anniversary a bit in advance when we could be together without my job coming between us?

"So I picked up the most special bottle of champagne I could find at a price I could afford, and left for our flat, as happy and optimistic as I can ever remember being. This would be a day to drink toast after toast to the happiness we'd found together and then to fall into bed gloriously drunk and make love for the rest of the afternoon."

Suddenly, Jean-Richard broke off his narrative for the first time and buried his head in his hands. "Oh God!" he moaned. "If only I'd known what I'd find when I reached our flat … If only I'd had some way of anticipating the horror of what I saw, it might have eased the devastation I felt."

Jean-Richard threw his head up, looking Marcie in the eyes, his own wide with near frenzy.

"Who am I trying to fool!" he cried. "No amount of preparation could have helped me to accept what I found! I … I walked into that flat expecting to see Nicole dusting or having a snack or reading. But instead … instead I saw her there … naked, on the bed we'd shared for nearly two years … lying there naked in the arms of another woman!"

"Oh, Jean-Richard!" gasped Marcie.

"Nicole looked up at me and … I don't think I'll ever forget the expression in her eyes at that moment. Shock, fear, embarrassment, and yes, even relief, they were all there in those brief seconds before she bolted from that bed and into the adjoining bathroom, locking the door behind her, the sound of her muffled sobs echoing in the ensuing silence.

"I looked then at the woman with whom Nicole had been sharing her bed, thinking she'd cover herself, if not in shame then at least in embarrassment, but she just sat up in bed and screamed, 'What the hell are you doing here? What the hell right do you have to interrupt our privacy! Get the fuck out of here!'

"I stared at her in shock and disbelief, unable to say a word. The woman—I learned later that her name was Suzanne—could have been mistaken for Nicole's sister. She was equally beautiful, with the same long hair and feminine body, but her face at that moment was twisted with more hatred than I'd ever seen in anyone in my life. 'You fool!' she shouted. 'You idiot! Did you really think she loved you? Couldn't you see that she just closed her eyes and gritted her teeth when you had sex? Couldn't you tell that she married you for camouflage, so that no one would ever suspect that she and I had been lovers since long before the two of you met?'

"I prayed that she'd stop, but she was like a river of venom and the flow of her words went on and on. 'You could cope with another man, couldn't you? But not with this! I can see it in your eyes. You and all other men who think that we women must get down on our knees and worship your revolting cocks. You're all alike, vain, egocentric monsters. Well, let me tell you, Jean-Richard, you don't mind if I call you that do you, no man could ever satisfy Nicole like I do. Not you, not any man!'"

Jean-Richard was unable to control himself any longer. The tears he had been holding back throughout his agonized revelations now spilled from his eyes, and as Marcie took him in her arms, he found himself sobbing like a baby.

Finally, when he had calmed down slightly, he said, "I walked out of that flat and never went back. What Suzanne had told me had shattered me, and I knew that I'd never be the same again. I felt totally bereft. I wanted desperately to hate the two of them, but I couldn't even do that. I could only feel that my life had, in an instant, become devoid of meaning. My one great love had been destroyed. Nicole had used me and made a fool of me and left me with nothing in the end, I who had had so much, or at least so I thought.

"That was when I vowed never to love again. If you loved, you were hurt. The more you loved, the greater the wound. So for me the only solution was escape, from promises which had turned out to be a mockery, from a city and a country which held only pain and disillusionment for me.

"Nicole and I were never divorced, you know. I never even got the chance to confront her, to find out from her own lips if she had truly despised me as much as Suzanne had claimed. The very next day she was dead, killed in a terrible automobile accident just south of Paris.

"But do you know what the final irony was? Not only had I lost Nicole forever, the accident was undeniable proof that our marriage had been a sham. You see, Nicole didn't die alone. Suzanne was with her in the car when it happened. Even death could not separate Nicole from the true love of her life. Not even death."

Jean-Richard said nothing more. The whole painfully traumatic story lay exposed in front of Marcie's compassionate eyes. After months of evasions and half-truths, he had finally told her everything.

"Oh dear God, Jean-Richard!" Marcie moaned. "What anguish you've been through. What torture! I understand now what I'd only guessed before. You're in no way the callous, uncaring man that people have thought you to be. That was only an act, a way of protecting yourself from being hurt again.

"But there's no more need to pretend, Jean-Richard. Now that I know what you've feared all these months, all these years, now that I know how terrified you've been to commit yourself and your love to another woman because you couldn't bear the thought that she might hurt you and betray you the way Nicole did, now that I know what my enemy is, I can fight back. I can devote all my strength and my love towards proving to you that you no longer have anything to be frightened of. I've told you that I love you, and I've told you that you're the first man I've ever loved. I swear now before you and before God that I'll never, never do you hear me, do anything to hurt you or disappoint you or make you lose your trust in me. So please, Jean-Richard, give me the chance to be for you in fact what Nicole only pretended to be. Give yourself the chance to forget the past and rediscover the promise of the present. Give us both a chance for a future together. Please, Jean-Richard. Please!"

It had been so long since he had trusted anyone, so long since he had believed in the possibility of happiness, that he hardly understood anymore what the words trust or happiness even meant. But as Jean-Richard looked into Marcie's eyes, as he saw the way they pleaded with him to give her the opportunity to erase his past sorrows, he knew that he must take the chance this one last time. Dear God, he prayed. Let her words be the truth. Let her be the woman who can give me back what I've lost.

And as Jean-Richard fell into Marcie's waiting arms, he knew at that moment that his prayers were being answered.

CHAPTER 29

▼

As Janna returned the test papers her students had given her the previous Friday, she could not help but think of the hurdles both she and her classes had overcome during the course of this school year. This first year class especially had had its problems, and Janna was painfully aware that she had caused many of them. Her second year students had been better able to cope with that two or three month period when she had been so distant, first from a combination of the pain caused by Lahcen's forgetting her and the *keef* she smoked to dull the ache, and then simply from the effects of the drug, long after she had ceased to suffer from her lover's rejection. Her second year students had already learned enough English to piece together her disjointed explanations and to verify or correct the misunderstood sentences they had heard in class. They had continued learning despite her. But this class of beginners had truly suffered. After those first few months of quick progress and high hopes, they had suddenly lost the teacher they had so quickly grown to love and admire. Though her shell remained, her teaching skills appeared to have vanished, leaving these students confused and disillusioned. But then, even more suddenly than the first change had taken place, the former Ms. Gallagher had made her reappearance two months ago, and in that time she had done all in her power to make up for the time they had wasted. Now as she handed back the test papers whose results were so gratifying, Janna knew that she had finally overcome the loss of Lahcen's love. Working together, she and her students had rebounded brilliantly, they in their academic work and she in her emotional comeback.

Janna was about to hand back the test paper of Abdellah Fadeel when she stopped to reread the short paragraph he had added at the end. Abdellah had once been painfully shy, and she had gone to great lengths to bring him out of his shell. Even during the period of her mental absence, she had dimly perceived the way he was struggling to understand in spite of her vagueness and confusion. Now, those days were over, and as Janna reread Abdellah's comments, written in French, she felt tears begin to fill her eyes.

He had written:

"*Cher professeur,*

"It's almost the end of our year together as students and teacher. Before we part, I would like to tell you what I have learned from you. I have discovered for the first time that being in class can be fun, even when you're studying. We laugh together, but that doesn't mean that we are not serious. Other teachers seem to think that it is wrong for students to enjoy school. They don't care that their lessons are dull. If someday I become a teacher, as I hope to, I want to teach my students the best I can, and as much as I can, but I will always want them to have fun learning, the way we have this year. *Merci*, Ms. Gallagher.

"From your student,

"Abdellah"

Janna knew that it would embarrass Abdellah if she said anything, so she returned his A+ paper without any comment other than the grade which spoke for itself. As she continued handing back the tests, she thought of how much both she and her students would have lost if she had resisted Michèle's efforts to straighten her out. It was sadly true that Lahcen had probably gone on to other loves and interests in the United States, but the scores on this exam—and she had intentionally made it difficult in order to see just how much she had gotten across—these outstanding scores were proof of her accomplishments despite her personal problems, and nothing could ever change them.

Michèle had indeed been her true friend in time of crisis. She had come to visit Janna frequently during the past two months, not just to check up on her, but to encourage her in her recovery and to congratulate her on her progress.

It hadn't been easy at first. Those initial drug free days had been excruciating, her vision razor-sharp, her hearing brutally clear. But as the weeks had passed, Janna had come to appreciate and even relish sharpness and clarity, because they were confirmation that she was still a living, breathing, feeling human being.

Now, handing back the last of the test papers, she was filled with optimism that when she left Aïn El Qamar in July, after her two year stay, not only would her memories of the town be **happy** ones, but her students, friends, and neighbors would carry positive, fond memories of her.

The bell rang, signaling the end of another morning of class, and as the students rose to go, several came up to Janna holding out their high scores and telling her how hard they had prepared. "We did it to make you happy," said one of them, and once again Janna could barely control her emotions. They had wanted to make her happy, after her dreadful unhappiness had spoiled so many of their hours together. How truly beautiful these young people were!

Leaving the classroom, Janna headed towards the *salle des profs*, recalling as she walked how great the suspense had been back in October and November each time she had gone to the faculty room knowing that there might be a letter from Lahcen. Those days were ancient history now, and today Janna felt happy just to be alive and drug free and supported by caring friends.

Several of those friends were gathered in the *salle des profs* when she arrived, and suddenly Janna recalled what had happened there just one hour ago. Oh God, how could she have let herself forget about Christiane and Dominique? And yet in her pleasure at being with her students and at seeing their marvelous progress, the tragic deaths of the two Frenchwomen had faded to the back of her mind.

Michèle was standing with Dave and Kevin, still looking stunned from the morning's events. Janna went over to them as Michèle was saying:

"It's not that we were ever close. You know that quite the opposite was true. But recently she'd been so much happier and easier to live with that it was almost pleasant having her around. I don't know how I'll be able to face seeing her clothes and her other things … now that she's gone."

"Don't worry about that, Michèle," said Janna as she joined her three colleagues. "You can stay with me for the next few days, for as long as it takes you to deal with what's happened."

"I wouldn't be putting you out?"

"Nonsense!" exclaimed Janna. "You were there for me when I needed someone to lean on. Let me help you for a change."

"Thank you, love," replied an obviously grateful Michèle. "It's not going to be easy for me without you in Aïn El Qamar next year."

"Why don't you come over for lunch now? I'm sure Halima's made enough for two."

"I'd love to, but … I've already made plans with someone else to have lunch with … with her."

Janna guessed that Michèle's lunchtime companion would be Kacem Hajiri, and not an anonymous "her." However, not knowing if Dave and Kevin had gotten wind of their affair, Michèle was clearly doing everything in her power to maintain discretion.

"We've got to get home too," said Dave. "Kevin and I have a house guest to feed and entertain, and she's probably wondering what's keeping us. Take care, both of you. Everything'll work out."

Janna smiled after the departing Americans, then turned back to Michèle and said, "You can stay with me as long as you want, and when you do finally decide to go back to your place and arrange Dominique's things, I'll be with you to help, and to lend my moral support. God knows you've done enough for me."

"Thanks Janna. It means so much to me to have a friend like you in my life. I really do love you. And now, I promised Kacem I'd join him for lunch. He didn't have classes this morning, so I guess I'll have to break the awful news to him. At least his shoulder will be there for me to cry on. Can I give you a ride back home on my way?"

"Thanks, Michèle, but I think I'll walk the few blocks. I have a couple things to pick up at the local *hanoot*."

"All right," replied Michèle. "I'll see you this evening, or … don't you have a class at three this afternoon? We can get together here in the *salle des profs* and discuss what time to expect me tonight. *D'accord? Ciao!*"

"Bye, Michèle," said Janna as her friend left, thinking again how glad she was to be able to repay her debt to the Frenchwoman. If there was anyone to whom she owed her present mental well-being, it was to Michèle.

Janna left the *salle des profs*, returning the waves of several students who were standing outside the school cafeteria waiting for lunch to be served. On a day as sunny and beautiful as this, it hardly seemed possible that tragedy had struck Aïn El Qamar only hours before, to think of Laurent who, unpleasant and crude as he was, must be suffering greatly at this moment.

Janna stopped at a *hanoot* a block from her house to buy milk and a pack of cigarettes. Tobacco was all she smoked these days, and even that was something that she had cut down on. Smoking an occasional cigarette had become no more than a social device. Janna was done with relying on anything other than her own strength to see her through the days.

When she had arrived home, she could hear Halima in the kitchen finishing the lunch preparations. Janna left her school things in the living room, then joined the maid, whose visits she enjoyed as a chance to practice her Arabic and to gain a deeper knowledge of people and things Moroccan. Halima always had stories to tell of her family adventures and troubles. Today, though, her first words were about the accident. Apparently, the news had spread through Aïn El

Qamar by word of mouth almost as quickly as if it had been announced on the radio.

"Wasn't it awful?" exclaimed Halima. "Many, many people killed, and two foreign teachers. Were they friends of yours?"

Janna explained that although she had known Dominique and Christiane, she had not been close to them, but that of course she felt terrible about what had happened.

"It is dangerous to drive in this country," declared Halima unnecessarily. "There are accidents almost every day, right in the streets of Aïn El Qamar. Once there was a crash just two blocks up from this house. Four people were killed, and three others were injured. The drivers here are like maniacs. I prefer to walk."

"I agree with you," said Janna. "You're much safer on your feet than behind the wheel."

Halima nodded her head in agreement, then returned to the chicken *tajine* she was preparing. Janna knew that it had kept her busy, since to make it the maid had had to buy a live chicken, have a neighborhood man kill it—this was not considered an appropriate task for a woman—then pluck and clean it herself, and finally cook it in much the same way she prepared a lamb or beef *tajine*, first browning the meat in oil, then letting it slow cook for several hours. Janna had been astounded the first time Halima had served her a chicken *tajine* once she learned how much time and effort the maid had gone to, but Halima insisted that it was no trouble and that Janna needed to eat more than she did. It was her duty to look after her employer's welfare.

"There was a wedding parade outside this morning," commented Halima as she checked the meat's tenderness. "The bride's family must be very rich. There were many, many presents, and lots of people following the wagon. Of course, I was too busy to spend much time watching the singing and dancing, but I did step outside for a minute or two, just to be able to tell you about it."

The maid was now apparently satisfied with the results of her cooking. Protecting her hands with a towel, she lifted the clay *tajine* and carried it into the living room, where she set it on the dining table. Janna followed her in, anticipating with pleasure the savory taste of the chicken which the maid had seasoned with lemon and saffron.

"Sit down and eat, now," ordered Halima. "You're a busy girl and you need your strength. Removing the cone-shaped lid from the *tajine*, she left the room to return to the kitchen. Janna broke off a piece of bread from the loaf Halima had left on the table, and dipped it into the sauce. It was as delicious as she had expected. What a shame Michèle hadn't been able to come over for lunch. Janna had been right to say that there would be more than enough for two. Well, they could have the rest for dinner that evening.

Halima stuck her head in the door as Janna was finishing. "Is there anything else I can do, Miss Janna?" she asked, though from the fact that she was veiled and ready to leave, it was clear that she already knew the response.

"No, thank you Halima," said Janna. "Everything's fine. Hurry home to your family. I'm sure they're starving and looking at their watches, waiting for their own lunch."

"I'll see you on Thursday then, Miss Janna," said the maid. "Those poor teachers … dead … both of them …" she muttered as she walked away.

Despite herself, Janna could not help but smile bemusedly at the maid's gory appreciation of the accident. Without money to buy a television or even to attend the movies, the drama of real life was her only entertainment. One could not blame her if she felt a certain relish at thinking about the troubles of others.

When Janna had finished the *tajine*, or at least as much as she intended to eat of it this meal, she took it into the kitchen and recovered it. It would stay fresh until the evening. Though the days were warm, the house remained cool, the shutters being kept closed during the day to guard against the midday heat, so Janna was sure that the food would not spoil. She washed and dried her silverware, then returned to the living room to wipe off the table. Finally, she gathered her teaching materials to plan the afternoon's lessons. Since her recovery, Janna spent more time than ever working on her lesson plans, not of course to the extent that Kevin did, but enough to make up for the time she had lost in the previous months.

Opening her notebook, she sank down on a *banquette*, leaning against several pillows, and began to jot down ideas for the presentation of this afternoon's key structures. A rather inventive lesson had just begun to shape up—if she could allow herself this lack of modesty—when Janna's attention was caught by a noise corning from the entry hall. That's strange, she thought. Had Halima come back? Janna hadn't heard the front door open, only some muffled sound, but there was no denying that she had heard something. Were there mice in that small storage closet off the hall? It was possible. Janna had once heard of a woman volunteer who had lived for months in a house which a rat invaded on a nightly basis, and who had barricaded herself in her bedroom until sunrise each morning.

I'd better go see what it is, thought Janna. If it should be mice, Halima will know what to do to get rid of them.

Rising from the *banquette*, Janna set down her notebook and headed towards the living room door. Then she stopped. What if it wasn't mice, but someone who had broken in? The idea seemed inconceivable. There were always people outside her door to prevent anyone from sneaking past, and the windows were barred. Still, anything was possible. It certainly wouldn't hurt to carry some kind of arm.

Janna spotted a brass candlestick on her desk. It would be heavy enough to serve as protection. Holding it firmly in her right hand, she tiptoed towards the open door. When she was about to go through, she raised the candlestick above her shoulder in case there should be any danger.

Then it happened.

Before she had even the slightest chance to use the weapon, a karate-like chop struck her right forearm, making her wince in pain and causing her to loosen her grip on the candlestick, which fell to the floor. She felt a cold hand press against her face, clamping her mouth shut, preventing her from screaming, while a strong arm reached tightly around her waist.

Janna swung wildly with her arms and hands, but they hit only air. She tried to struggle with her assailant but he was too powerful for her. He held her pinioned against him, stifling her screams so that only the slightest peep escaped from her mouth.

Oh dear God, she thought. What's happening? She wanted to shout at the man, Take anything you want! Just don't do anything to hurt me! But his hand was too firmly pressed against her mouth to allow her to speak.

Then, suddenly, he had removed his arm from around her waist. She thought this would give her the chance to escape, but his grip on her head was too strong. Then, even that eased for a second, but only long enough for her to feel a hunk of rolled-up cloth being stuffed savagely into her mouth. She tried with all her will-power to push it out with her tongue, but it was too large to move and she found herself gagging.

Then, before she scarcely knew what was happening, her assailant had pulled her two arms behind her, squeezing them with brutal force. She felt her wrists being bound, the cord tearing into her skin. Then she was shoved away from her captor, unable to speak, her bound arms preventing her from tearing the gag out of her mouth.

She turned around and stared in shock at her attacker, recognizing him at once. It was the student who had first spoken to her in October, then followed her to Dave's house the evening of Claudette's party, and finally tried to push his way into her own place just two months ago. Not having been bothered by him since, she had though herself safe. But that had been a naive illusion. Once, she had considered him harmless, pathetic even, but the eyes that leered at her now were not the eyes of a sane person.

Janna found herself cowering against the wall as he approached her. She wanted to run, wanted to make some kind of noise that would alert her neighbors, but her body was frozen in fear, her eyes unable to look away from the young man who was coming nearer and nearer.

He began to speak in Arabic, and the thought crossed her mind that she had only heard his broken English before.

"It's my turn now," he said with an eerie calm and matter-of-factness. "I've waited months for this moment. I saw you all last year with Cherqaoui. You must have known that everyone at school was gossiping about how you and he were lovers. I realized then that if you gave yourself to one student, you would give yourself to me too. I don't understand why you've always resisted me. Today I'm going to prove to you that I'm as much a man as Cherqaoui was. And you'll see. He may be gone, but I'm here now, and when I'm through, you'll see. I can do everything Cherqaoui did, and better."

The young man nearly ripped open his pants, and his engorged cock shot out threateningly. Oh God, she thought. This was no dream. She was actually going to be raped! And with this realization, Janna regained her strength at last. The guy might be crazy, but he meant what he said. She had to get away. She had to!

He was blocking her path to the front door, but if she could get to the living room, she might be able to kick against the wall which faced the street or even bang her head against the shutters. Damn, why had she let Halima convince her to keep them closed!

She dashed past her attacker, reaching the living room before he realized what she was planning. He still had to pull his pants back up before he could come after her. Janna had managed to kick the wall twice before he was there, encircling her with his arms, pulling her back, away from the wall, away from her one means of informing the neighbors of her plight.

Now, all at once, the shock and terror she had felt when he had first grabbed her was replaced by a blinding anger. How dare he assume that her relationship with Lahcen meant that she was available to any man? Though he was holding her tight against him, she could perhaps manage to …

With all the force she could muster, Janna raised her right leg, bending it slightly at the knee, and shoved the heel of her shoe back into her assailant's shin.

He groaned in agony, dropping his arms, releasing her from his grip. But only for a moment. If by chance he was not a madman, he certainly had the strength of one, for she had no sooner begun to rush once more towards the outer wall of the room than he was upon her again, spinning her around, thrusting her in the opposite direction.

Oh dear God, she was never going to escape! He was too powerful in his current enraged state for her to fight off. He was coming towards her, his eyes no longer calm but filled with violence and lust. And she was backing away, praying in vain for a miracle.

Reaching out his arm, her attacker grabbed at the blouse she was wearing, tearing it open to reveal her bra. He came closer, and then his hands were on her breasts, attempting to slide their way inside her bra. Janna tried to shove her knee into the young man's groin, but she was off balance, and she hit only his upper thigh. Still, he flinched from the pain, and now there was fury as well as lust and madness in his eyes. He reached out savagely and slapped her across the face.

"Bitch!" he spat out. "I'm gonna fuck your whore cunt if it's the last thing I do!"

Janna kept retreating, recoiling step by step from the maniac, scarcely aware that she was moving towards the door which led to the entry hall where he had first grabbed her, knowing only that she had to postpone the moment of his final victory.

I'm going to have her, thought Larbi Faress, as he advanced towards Janna. She's done her pathetic best to fight back, but there's no way now that she can stop me from getting what I want and what I deserve.

Now she was near the place where he had stood in wait for her, where she had first attempted to struggle against him. She was backing away, but eventually she would reach another wall and be able to retreat no longer. Then he would ...

Suddenly Ms. Gallagher was stumbling against something, and Larbi looked down to see her foot push against the brass candlestick she had dropped earlier. And then she had lost her equilibrium, and she was falling, falling backwards ...

Larbi gasped in horror as she hit the tile floor, her head making a terrible hollow sound as it struck, like a watermelon which someone had dropped.

Oh God, what had happened? He hadn't meant to kill her, but she was lying there motionless, and he could not see her chest moving. She was dead! He had murdered her!

"But it was an accident!" he protested aloud. "It's not my fault that she tripped over something and fell. It was an accident!"

But who would believe him? Who would believe the word of a student? They would find him and put him in jail and he would spend the rest of his life behind bars if they didn't sentence him to death.

He had to get out of here before anyone came in. He had to get away. He ... he ... he would pretend to be someone who had come to ... to repair the hot water heater. That was it! Before the neighbors had a chance to realize that they had not seen him enter, he would be gone.

First, however, he must remove the evidence of what he had tried to do. Barely looking at Ms. Gallagher, afraid to see the results of his actions, he pulled the rolled up sock from her mouth, then turned her over on her side and, shutting his eyes to blot out the sight of her lifeless body, he untied the cord he had wrapped around her wrists. He was about to straighten her blouse when he suddenly thought of what might happen if the maid were to come in on him now. Perhaps she had forgotten something and was heading in this direction at this very moment. He couldn't stay here even another second. He had to get out, and fast!

Larbi moved quickly towards the front door, away from the motionless form of Ms. Gallagher. He stuffed the sock and length of cord into his satchel, which he had left in the entry hall. Then, before opening the door, he took a deep deliberate breath and, gathering up all his strength, called out, "I think you won't have any more trouble with that heater now, *mademoiselle*." As he left the house, he thought to himself with relief that no one would have even the slightest idea that the person he was speaking to was dead.

Leaving with all the calm he could muster, Larbi walked past the neighbors who were sitting outside on various doorsteps, gossiping about God knows what, and away from Ms. Gallagher's house.

It was not until he was several blocks away and safe from immediate danger that Larbi Faress began to tremble uncontrollably at the thought of what he had done.

CHAPTER 30

▼

"Oh shit!" cursed Miranda once again. It wasn't fair that the party which was to have been given in her honor had been canceled because of the deaths of two women whom Dave and Kevin scarcely even knew.

"I'm really sorry, Mandee," replied Dave for the umpteenth time. "I know you were looking forward to meeting people, but you understand. If we had a party now … well it just wouldn't be in good taste."

"You know I don't give a flying fuck about good taste," protested Mandee. "At the moment all I care about is fucking somebody who tastes good."

She reached down to the coffee table where she was sitting with Dave and Kevin after lunch and took a cigarette. Lighting it, she added, "I guess Mandee will just have to find some excitement on her own. If this morning's bore-fest is any example, I'm certainly not going to get any help from either of you."

"You didn't enjoy your visit inside a Moroccan home?" asked Dave.

"I'm sorry, Davey, but sitting around watching middle-aged women knead dough, or listening to a six-year-old recite from the Koran in a language I don't know a word of, or being forced to suffer through music that sounds like a stray mutt howling off-key at the moon … well, I can think of about a million other ways I'd prefer passing my time. And I was hoping to sample at least several of them during and after the party you promised me … before you stabbed me in the back."

"I'd hardly call showing respect for the dead back-stabbing," said Dave. "Would you, Kevin?"

"What?" asked the other American absentmindedly. He had been so busy thinking about this afternoon's lesson plans that he had barely been paying attention to Dave and Mandee's conversation.

"I asked you if you thought that canceling Mandee's party was like stabbing her in the back."

"Why should it be?" replied Kevin distractedly. And why should I care? he added silently, extinguishing the cigarette he had been smoking and lighting yet another. He wondered if his nervous chain-smoking was contributing to the unsettled state he found himself in lately, or if it was merely the result of the strain he was under. Dave never stopped gloating about his and Lateef's upcoming departure for the States, except that is when he was pressing Kevin to make a decision about whether or not to stay in Aïn El Qamar himself next year. Being in the same room with his friend was at times almost too much for Kevin to bear. And as if this weren't enough, he also had the *proviseur* to contend with. Monsieur Rhazwani was doing everything in his power to demean Kevin as a teacher, sending his emissaries to verify Kevin's roll-taking, assigning an unknown student to spy on him, and God only knew what else. Finally, there was Kevin's ever-present fear that his students would betray him once again. All these things had conspired to make Kevin a nervous wreck in recent weeks. No wonder he smoked cigarettes and drank cup after cup of coffee as if his life depended on them. At times he felt on the verge of a nervous breakdown, as if just one more thing would be enough to push him over the edge.

"God damn it, Kevin," Dave was saying angrily. "If I can't count on you to support me, then who the hell can I depend on?" For a moment, Kevin couldn't for the life of him figure out what Dave was ranting about. Then, Lateef walked in with a bright "Hi guys," Dave's eyes shot from Lateef to Mandee, who looked to be nearly drooling at the sight of the tall handsome Moroccan, and Kevin realized the real reason for Dave's irritation.

"I thought I'd stop by on my way to school," Lateef announced casually. "To see if one of you wanted to walk with me." And to get another look at our uninvited guest, thought Kevin, noticing how Lateef couldn't take his eyes off the sultry raven-haired visitor from America.

"Kevin can join you," said Dave. "You know that I only teach from three to four on Monday afternoons."

"It slipped my mind."

Sure it did, thought Kevin, though he refrained from saying it aloud. It seemed incredible to him that Dave still entertained thoughts that Lateef might be in denial about being gay, and just waiting for the opportune occasion to jump into bed with his American best friend. At the moment, Dave was clearly the last thing on Lateef's mind.

The young Moroccan had sat down next to Mandee, who was complimenting him on his English. "Dave says this is only your second year studying the language." She was almost purring in his ear in her husky, breathy voice, leaning close to him to show a good deal more cleavage than was customary in Aïn El Qamar. "I studied French for two years and I can't remember a word. How would you feel about giving me a private refresher course before the end of my visit?"

"Of … of course," stammered an obviously flustered Lateef. Kevin saw Dave's eyes narrow, and to prevent a possible explosion, he stood up and said to the student, "We'd better be getting on to school. I don't want to be late and give Monsieur Rhazwani any ammunition to use against me. Come on, young man." He grabbed Lateef's arm a bit more forcefully than was necessary and jerked him upright and away from Mandee's clutches.

"Lateef," said Dave. "I have a few errands to run after school today, but I should be back here by about four-thirty, I think. Could you stop by a little before five? There are a few things I think we need to discuss."

"All right," replied Lateef, but without much enthusiasm in his voice.

"Hurry up," insisted Kevin. "You'll make us both late." Then, leading Lateef out of the room, he whispered to him, "Dave's not the only one who wants to talk to you." He returned briefly to the living room to grab his materials for his afternoon classes, noticing as he did that Dave had moved over to sit next to Mandee and no doubt tell her once again to keep her hands off Lateef.

Kevin joined the Moroccan at the front door, and they began the walk to school.

"It's getting warm," said Lateef nonchalantly.

"Don't play little mister innocent with me," replied Kevin coldly.

"What are you talking about?" asked Lateef, his voice more defensive than innocent.

Kevin spoke quietly, so as not to be overheard by the students they were passing on the way, but his voice was firm. "Listen, Lateef," he said. "I don't think you understand just how serious Dave is about this Mandee Cox business. You seem to be under the impression that you can do just about anything you want and that Dave will excuse it, but you're wrong. Dave would never forgive you if you tried something with that slut."

"What makes you think I'd even want to?" exclaimed Lateef. "Listen, Kevin. I'm sick and tired of everyone trying to live my life for me. The two of you act as if I owed Dave the world, just because he's going to take me back to the United States with him. But you know perfectly well that he's getting just as much out of that as I am. He'd be miserable if he had to leave me behind, and you know it. So stop trying to make me think that Dave's motives are so pure and unselfish, because that's a bunch of bullshit! And both of you, stop telling me how to live my life because I'm not your fucking slave!"

And with that Lateef called out to a group of friends walking further up the street and Kevin found himself suddenly abandoned, a chill running down his spine. What in God's name was happening to Lateef? Was he merely showing signs of typical youthful rebellion, or was there more to this declaration of independence? Could it be that he had in fact been playing a devious game with Dave from the very beginning, a game which he was only now starting to reveal?

For the first time Kevin found himself questioning Lateef's devotion to Dave, and he wondered if their relationship would survive until the day they were scheduled to leave for the United States together.

CHAPTER 31

▼

Michèle left her classroom, profoundly relieved to have completed her last lesson of the day. It had been torture attempting to teach as if nothing were wrong, all the while knowing that Dominique was dead, the victim of a senseless twist of fate. Whenever Michèle would begin to forget, to let her lesson involve her, she would suddenly see Dominique's face before her as it had been in recent months, her eyes sparkling and her smile radiant, the sour complainer of October and November seemingly vanished, her place taken by a woman gloriously happy and blissfully fulfilled. And the thought of her housemate's life snuffed out in an instant would cast a dark shadow over Michèle's heart and make it nearly unbearable for her to go on with today's class.

Thank God this was almost the last week of teaching. She didn't know how much longer she could go on with today's charade. And thank God for Kacem, who made her life so much richer than it had ever been, and whose comfort and loving concern had made today's tragedy somehow at least bearable.

How she wished he were here at the *lycée* this afternoon, but he had left Aïn El Qamar after lunch for a physics teachers' conference being held in a nearby town and would not be back until early that evening. The memory of their noon-time lovemaking was still fresh in Michèle's mind, and she knew that wherever Kacem might be working next year, she would find a way to be with him as often as she could.

But where, she wondered, would that be? While it was true that friction between Kacem and the *proviseur* had lessened in recent weeks, this might mean simply that Monsieur Rhazwani had already asked for Kacem's transfer to another city, and was only biding his time until the official order came through.

What if Kacem should be posted in Oujda, close to the northern border with Algeria, and a two day's journey from Aïn El Qamar by car, or in Sidi Ifni, an equal distance to the South? Could Michèle bear having Kacem so far away from her that she would only be able to see him during long vacations?

Well, she thought, at least such a move would put more distance between Kacem and Claudette. Incredible as it seemed, Claudette had not yet given up her battle to convert the Moroccan into the latest and greatest of her conquests. Her efforts would be almost comic if they weren't so pathetic, for despite Kacem's unequivocal indifference, she had managed in her desperation to convince herself that he was secretly and hopelessly in love with her.

Though a part of Michèle wished that Kacem would tell Claudette once and for all to simply get the hell out of his life, there was definitely something unstable in the eyes of the statuesque Frenchwoman these days, so perhaps Kacem was behaving prudently by continuing to resist her advances with as much kindness and tact as he could muster.

Still, the situation was becoming harder and harder for them to handle. Their own love affair had been going on for months now, but so discreetly that Michèle was sure that few people guessed that they were anything more than professional colleagues. Lovemaking had become a nearly daily pleasure for them, but it was invariably love in the afternoon, as the two of them had made the deliberate decision not to spend the night together in order to avoid the gossip that would certainly ensue if Kacem's neighbors were to see Michèle leaving his house in the early hours of the morning.

This had been a successful tactic at first, but it left Kacem alone after nine or ten, and recently Claudette had begun dropping by in the late evenings. Though Kacem had no desire to open the door to her, he could scarcely have her standing outside ringing the bell again and again and calling to him for all the neighbors to hear. So he would let her in, and try to remain courteous but distant. Anyone in her right mind would get the message, but not Claudette, who still insisted that Kacem was concealing his true feelings for her. Michèle sometimes wondered if Claudette left Kacem's house convinced that she had actually had sex with him.

Now, as she entered the *salle des profs* and saw Claudette standing there in a demure skirt and high-necked blouse, her hair pulled primly back like a librarian, Michèle knew that nothing was improving in the preposterous triangle. Claudette must really be becoming unhinged to affect such a totally absurd image change, but she had apparently concluded that Kacem found her too blatantly sexual, and it was because of this that he was resisting his "urges," so she had gone to opposite extremes in recent weeks in order to achieve her aims.

Oh God help me, thought Michèle. If all three of us should remain in Aïn El Qamar next year, how will I ever manage to bear the strain?

Michèle looked around the *salle des profs* hoping to see Janna, who had a three o'clock class on Mondays, but her friend was nowhere in sight. Well, perhaps she had been delayed in class. She had told Michèle they'd meet at school this afternoon, hadn't she, and that they'd discuss plans for Michèle to spend the next few nights with her?

Dave was coming into the faculty room now. Maybe he'd seen her.

"Hi," said the tall dark-haired American. "Do you have any idea why Janna didn't make it to school this afternoon?"

"Didn't make it to school?" Michèle asked incredulously. "What are you talking about?"

"I just heard from one of her students that she never showed up for class."

"How can that be?"

"You don't think that …" Dave's voice trailed off.

"Do I think that maybe Janna stayed home to get stoned?"

Dave nodded.

"There's no way, Dave," replied Michèle. "That's why I'm concerned."

"Teachers do lose track of the days and forget they have class … sometimes," said Dave without much conviction.

"It's Monday, Dave. People don't think it's Sunday two days in a row. No, this is just not like Janna. I'm going to run over to her house and see if there's anything wrong."

"I'll go with you," offered Dave. "I'm through for the day, and I'd like to make sure myself that everything's all right."

"There's probably a perfectly logical explanation for this," said Michèle. "But it can't do any harm to check."

"Okay. Let's go," replied Dave, and the two teachers left the *salle des profs* in the direction of the parking lot.

"I'll give you a lift back to your place once we're sure there's nothing wrong," offered Michèle as they got into her car and began the short drive to Janna's neighborhood.

"Everything *looks* normal," commented Dave as Michèle pulled up in front of the American woman's house. They got out of the car and headed for the front door, Michèle ringing the bell as Dave spoke to the neighbor children in Arabic.

"They say they haven't seen Janna since she got home for lunch," translated Dave.

"And there's no answer to my ringing," said Michèle. "I think we'd better use the spare key she gave me earlier in the year."

Dave nodded as Michèle located the key on her key ring and, inserting it into the lock, opened the door. There was no sound coming from inside the house.

And then they saw her, lying on the floor at the other end of the hall.

"*Oh mon Dieu!*" gasped Michèle, and rushed with Dave to Janna's side.

"Is she … is she …?" she stammered as the American placed his fingers on Janna's neck to feel for a pulse.

"She's alive," said Dave, and Michèle cried out "Oh thank God!"

"But her pulse is very very weak," continued Dave. "It scares me to move her, but by the time we locate a telephone to call an ambulance and wait for one to arrive …"

"No, we'd better take our chances and drive her to the Clinique El Qamar ourselves," agreed Michèle. "Oh dear God. Everything was finally starting to work out for her, and now this. What could have happened?"

Dave looked into the living room and said, "There seems to have been same kind of struggle here, and Janna's blouse is torn. It looks like someone attacked her and she fell and hit her head"

"Well let's get her to the Clinique and into a doctor's care," said Michèle urgently.

"Go start your engine and I'll carry her out," said Dave. "I just hope I don't aggravate whatever injuries she's suffered in the fall."

Michèle raced towards her waiting car and turned the key in the ignition. Then she reached back to open the rear door. Dave managed to get in while still holding Janna cradled in his arms. It was a tight fit, but thankfully the Clinique was not far. Michèle lowered her foot to the accelerator, wishing she could slam it down and race there at top speed, but knowing she must make the ride as smooth as possible for Janna.

Oh dear God, she prayed as she moved cautiously towards the Clinique. Please don't take Janna away from me too. I can scarcely believe that Dominique is dead. Don't make me lose my dearest friend as well. Please let her live!

Michèle thought they would never reach the Clinique. She was used to speeding along the streets of Aïn El Qamar, swerving from side to side to avoid children and animals, honking at pedestrians to warn them to clear her path. Now the short distance seemed endless.

Finally, however, they arrived.

Jumping out of her car, Michèle hurried around to the other side to open Dave's door. He squeezed out, holding Janna as steadily as he could, supporting her head in the curve of his bent arm.

Michèle raced to the entrance of the Clinique El Qamar, pushed open the door, and tore past the crowd of Moroccans sitting in the antiseptic, impersonal waiting room.

"*C'est un cas d'urgence*! Emergency!" she cried out to the nurse in attendance. "Call Doctor Marouane, for God's sake!"

"Where can we put her?" asked Dave as he carried Janna's unconscious form into the waiting room.

"I don't know," exclaimed Michèle. "I've just sent the nurse to get the doctor."

"Here he comes now," said Dave, and Michèle rushed up to Doctor Marouane, the clinic director, to explain what had happened. The man called to one of his nurses to prepare the emergency room while an orderly approached wheeling in a gurney. Dave laid Janna down as gently as he could, and watched as she was wheeled away towards a room in the back of the Clinique.

"I'll let you know her condition as soon as I've examined her," said the doctor. "Please sit down and wait."

And then he was gone, following the gurney, the nurse at his side.

Dave took Michèle by the arm and led her towards a pair of empty chairs in one corner of the room. As they sat down, Michèle realized for the first time that they had become the center of attention for the Moroccans sitting in the waiting room.

"Looks like we're the main attraction," she said, and Dave nodded. Michèle glanced down at her watch. It was not even a quarter past four. They had left school hardly fifteen minutes ago, and yet it seemed that an eternity had passed.

"I'm so frightened," Michèle moaned. "I've never seen Janna that pale, and when she was lying there, I thought at first … You don't think there's any chance she won't … she won't …?"

"Janna's not about to give up now," said Dave, "not after what she's been through in the past year, and especially not after the way she's pulled herself together recently. If anyone's got the will to fight back, Janna does. Of course she's going to be all right."

Michèle heard the reassuring words, but she sensed that Dave was saying them as much to convince himself as he was to convince her.

On and on the minutes dragged, and Michèle did not know how many cups of coffee she and Dave had drunk. What was happening in the emergency room?

she asked herself apprehensively. Was Janna still unconscious? Was she finally coming to? Or had they brought her here too late? Was she already …? No! She mustn't let herself think such things. Janna had to pull through this. She had to!

"It looks like …" Dave was saying. "Yes, there's the doctor coming this way."

Michèle and Dave shot up in unison, looking expectantly at the approaching figure. But his face was expressionless, telling them nothing.

"Doctor … Is she …?" stammered Michèle.

"I'm afraid, *mademoiselle*, that it's too soon to say. The young lady appears to have hit her head quite severely and at the moment … well, there's no easy way to say it. She's in a coma."

"*Oh mon Dieu!*" gasped Michèle, suddenly feeling faint, and it was only Dave's strong arms that kept her from falling.

"How long will this last, doctor?" asked the American. "Are we talking days? Months?"

"Possibly. And then again it could be only a matter of hours. In cases like this, there's no way of telling."

"There's nothing you can do, doctor?" cried Michèle.

"Naturally, we're monitoring her vital signs," the doctor explained, "and she's receiving medication intravenously. But other than that, all we can do is wait. And now, *monsieur*," he said, addressing Dave. "Will you come with me? I'd like to get some information about Mademoiselle …"

"Gallagher. *Nous sommes volontaires du Corps de la Paix.*"

"Peace Corps volunteers," repeated Doctor Marouane. "So I surmised. After you've given me information regarding Mademoiselle Gallagher, I'll need to call your health director in Rabat."

"Will you be all right for a few minutes, Michèle?" Dave asked the French-woman.

"I'll try. Just don't be too long," she replied, watching as Dave left with the doctor. She was trembling now, and more frightened than she could ever recall being. Why couldn't the man have been more reassuring? Why couldn't he have told them that of course Janna was going to recover?

Looking towards where Janna had been wheeled out, Michèle suddenly saw the orderly reappear pushing the gurney once again, this time towards a door which opened onto the waiting room. Janna lay there, an IV attached to her arm, her body covered with a blanket, her face still deathly pale.

Jumping to her feet, Michèle dashed over to the orderly as he was opening the door to what appeared to be a private room.

"Please let me stay with her," begged Michèle. "I'm her closest friend … her … her sister. I can't leave her alone."

The orderly answered her in Arabic, his face expressing clearly that he did not understand her. Damn, why hadn't she made more of an effort to learn at least a few basic words of the language!

When Michèle tried to follow the gurney into the room, the orderly pushed her gently but firmly out, saying "*La … la …,*" which Michèle understood. "No … no …," he was telling her.

"Damn you!" cried Michèle, unable to bear the frustration of not being able to communicate with the orderly, of not being allowed to stay with Janna.

"*Qu'est-ce qu'il y a?*" asked a voice in French. "What's all the commotion about?" Michèle turned to find Doctor Marouane standing with Dave.

"Tell that man to let me stay with my friend!" pleaded Michèle. "I can't leave her alone!"

"But I explained to you before that we have no idea how long the wait might be," replied the doctor.

"I don't care," answered Michèle. "You must let me stay with her, at least overnight."

"*D'accord, mademoiselle,*" conceded the doctor, "but I must ask you to maintain both quiet and calm. Speak to her gently if you wish. It will help for her to hear a known voice. But don't get overly emotional. Comatose patients may well be able to sense hysteria and despair. So maintain your composure and be optimistic."

"Yes, doctor," said Michèle gratefully. "Anything you say."

"Very well, then," said Doctor Marouane. "I'll inform my staff that you will be spending the night in Mademoiselle Gallagher's room."

"Both of us will be," said Dave.

"But … there's no need for you to …" protested Michèle, but her words lacked conviction.

"I'm staying too," insisted Dave, and Michèle squeezed his hand appreciatively.

Thanking the doctor for all he had done for Janna, Michèle and Dave entered the room where their friend lay, a tube leading from her arm to a bottle of fluid suspended above her, her face as white as the sheet which covered her.

Oh God, prayed Michèle, as she held Dave's hand tight in her own. Let her pull through this! Don't let Janna die!

CHAPTER 32

▼

Miranda paced back and forth in Dave and Kevin's living room, bored beyond belief and thinking that she had never been so sexually frustrated in all her adult life. These past few days had hardly been what she was expecting when she arrived, and now, with the party canceled, she was sure she would go stark raving mad. So what if she had come to stay with two gay men, who fuckable as they might be—Dave was even more studly now than during his university days, and boyishly cute Kevin was just begging to be seduced—would only be interested in her if she had a sex-change operation? So fucking what? They could still have had some pussy-starved Moroccans anticipating her arrival instead of making her wait for a party that was never to take place.

Dull. Dull. Dull. That's what the past few days had been, and today had turned out to be the most boring of them all. Visiting the little neighbor girl and her family had been as excruciating as watching paint dry and had only added to her anger and frustration.

It wasn't that she hated Morocco. It was a beautiful country, to be sure, mysterious and exotic, but how could she appreciate it fully when she was going out of her mind with horniness.

Mandee lit another cigarette, thinking to herself that it was no wonder so many Moroccans smoked. It was the only way to stop from dying of ennui. Dave had said he'd be back from school around four-thirty. It was still only ten past so it was too soon yet to expect him or his student Lateef.

Now that was some delicious male, thought Miranda. Hair, eyes, smile, skin, body. The whole package was totally desirable; she had thought so from the moment she first saw him. And the fact that he was sexually inexperienced was the greatest turn-on of all. How thrilling it would be to initiate him into the pleasures of sex! Dave had told her that Lateef might be gay, and he had forbidden her to confuse him sexually (those were Dave's words). Bullshit! She wasn't going to traumatize Lateef for the rest of his life!

Now that there was going to be no party, Mandee could see no reason whatsoever why she should not take what was so temptingly within her grasp. If only she could maneuver to get Lateef alone with her, she would not hesitate to make her move. Screw Dave and Kevin and anyone else who thought they could turn her into a fucking nun! She'd had enough of that in Catholic school. She was a normal heterosexual woman with needs and desires to be fulfilled. And if she had her way, Lateef would be the next man in her life to fulfill them.

Just then there was a knock on the door. It can't be Dave, thought Mandee. He'd use his key. The knock came again, and Mandee went to see who was there. It might be …

It might be …

It was!

Just one look at Lateef and Miranda felt her loins begin to tingle and her panties become moist. She glanced at her watch. Twenty minutes ought to be time enough, if she moved quickly. And if they were in the midst of fucking when Dave got home, well it would serve him right! In any case, she'd better get to work fast.

"Come in, come in!" she exclaimed, reaching out to take Lateef by the hand and escort him into the living room.

Lateef sat down on one of the *banquettes* and Mandee took a seat beside him, pressing her body close to his. God, she was surprising even herself at the boldness and rapidity of her seduction.

"When Dave told me he had a favorite student," she whispered in his ear, "I imagined an awkward adolescent. So you can imagine my surprise when I found out how grown up you are. Really, Lateef, how can you let Dave treat you like such a child? How does it make you feel when he bosses you around as if you were his personal property?"

"Lately, he's been acting like he thinks he owns me," agreed Lateef. "I have the same right to be free as he does!"

"You know there is a way you could show him that you belong only to yourself." Mandee's hand was at Lateef's hair, her fingers running through its silky black waves. "A way you could show him how much of a man you are. A way you could show me too."

Mandee's free hand had begun to unbutton her blouse. "Start by showing me here," she whispered. "Show me how grown up you are. Show Dave you aren't his slave."

Mandee reached down to take Lateef's hand in her own. Slowly, she pulled it up to the level of her breasts, guided it into her open blouse, inside her bra, let it caress her smooth white skin, let it feel her hard erect nipple.

"Try pinching it if you want to hear me moan," she suggested and as Lateef was quick to follow her advice, she obliged him with the promised moan.

"I'm yours … if you want me," she told him bluntly.

"Do you really mean that?" asked Lateef incredulously.

"Show me how much you want me," she said, rising to lead Lateef in the direction of Dave's bedroom.

"But … are you sure that …?"

Mandee silenced Lateef's words with her mouth. Ooh, but that felt good she thought. She sucked in his upper lip, then switched to the lower, nibbling on it gently, finally thrusting her tongue into his waiting mouth.

Suddenly, Lateef pulled away. "Maybe … maybe I shouldn't," he said. "Dave made me promise to stay away from you, and he has been good to me, even if he does boss me around at times."

"Dave wants to own you," repeated Mandee. "You're not his slave." Drawing Lateef with her into the bedroom, Mandee continued, "Dave won't let you behave like an adult. Dave won't let you live your own life. Show him how much of a man you are. Show me!"

They were standing by the bed now, and Mandee pulled him down on it beside her. "Take off my blouse," she said. "Look at my skin. Feel my breasts. They're yours if you want them."

Lateef had been fumbling with the buttons, his hands trembling. Mandee, meanwhile, had her own fingers under Lateef's shirt, exploring the hidden delights of his washboard stomach and his rock hard but smooth as silk chest. All the while their mouths were attached, their tongues as deep in each other's throats as was humanly possible.

"Get rid of your shirt while I take off my bra," suggested Mandee.

When they were both naked from the waist up, she whispered, "Now my tits are all yours," and she could see from Lateef's saucer-wide eyes that he was absolutely transfixed by her full rounded bosoms and their hard dark nipples.

Mandee put her hands around Lateef's head and lowered it until his mouth was at her chest, his wet tongue bathing her with his saliva.

Playing with his beautiful dark hair, running her fingers up and down his sleek warm back, kneading and pinching his delicious deltoid muscles, Mandee could not get enough of the young Moroccan she had wanted since the first time she saw him.

And now there was one thing she wanted more than anything, and that was to grasp his rock hard cock in her hand, to fill her hungry mouth with it, to feel it thrust up her pussy, exploding deep inside her with his virile Moroccan cum.

Mandee could bear it no longer. Reaching down to unfasten his pants, she stuck her hungry hand inside to feel Lateef's …

Limp unresponsive cock.

Suddenly, Mandee began to laugh. She laughed and laughed until she was nearly gasping for breath, laughing at her own stupidity, laughing at Lateef's impotence, laughing at the irony of Dave's victory.

The son of a bitch was right. Lateef was clearly as gay as gay could be, and Miranda Cox had had the flaccid proof in her hand.

Lateef meanwhile had flown from the bedroom in shame and confusion, and she now heard the bathroom door slam shut, heard his muffled sobs over the sound of running water.

Wouldn't Dave be delighted by what she had to tell him! Wouldn't he enjoy getting the last laugh!

Unless …

Though she'd done a good job pretending otherwise, Mandee had never forgiven Dave for breaking up with her in college. Idiot coed that she was, she'd gone and fallen in love with a fucking closet case, and the pain and humiliation of his dumping her for a man was, she now realized, a score that had remained unsettled … until today.

She knew exactly what she was going to do.

Rising resolutely from the bed, Mandee put back on her bra and blouse. She could be packed and out of here in ten minutes. She was traveling light.

But first.

Miranda Cox went over to Dave's desk and, taking a piece of paper and pen in hand, began writing the son of a bitch who'd fucked up her life a letter he would never forget.

CHAPTER 33

─────────── ▼ ───────────

There were few teachers in class at this late hour. Those who remained at school were the unlucky ones who had to teach until six o'clock. Kevin had managed to have one of his five o'clock classes changed to eleven in the morning, but he still had to teach until six on Mondays and Thursdays. Mondays especially were difficult as he had two classes in the morning at nine and eleven and four in a row in the afternoon.

Until lately, these long hours had simply meant more time doing what he liked best. He had looked forward to the moments spent with his students as a way of blotting out everything but the present. Only teaching had made it possible for him to cope with Jamey's death. Only teaching had enabled him to get over his shattering misunderstanding with Kacem Hajiri. Only teaching made his life in Aïn El Qamar bearable.

In recent months, however, all that had changed. Each time he arrived at the school, he wondered what new way Monsieur Rhazwani would find of persecuting him. Each time he entered a classroom, he asked himself if today would be the day that his students would once again stage a revolt. Each time he even thought about school, he felt the weight of knowing that he must soon make a decision regarding the coming year, a decision which was becoming day by day more impossible to reach.

Kevin's students were smiling expectantly today as he laid out his materials, eager despite the late hour to begin the lesson. It was ironic, thought Kevin, and a reminder of his shaky mental state, that he could not stop worrying that these young people would betray him once again, when in fact their behavior had been exemplary ever since that dreadful afternoon in March. It seemed that they felt him to be as much an innocent victim of the *proviseur*'s injustice as they had been. The day after Monsieur Rhazwani had chastised Shakiri, Kevin had attempted to apologize to his students for not having defended them against the *proviseur*, but Guirrou, Shakiri's best friend, had led them in a chorus of protests, and Kevin had felt his eyes fill with grateful tears at this unselfish gesture.

Today, it was Shakiri, the very boy whose hands had been so bloodily beaten that awful day, who had the broadest smile as Kevin began his lesson. Would he ever understand these students? the American asked himself. How could they rebel against him one day, and yet be so warm and caring the next?

Well, from their expressions today, they were clearly in a cheerful mood in spite of having been at school since early that morning. Kevin promised himself that today's class would be as lively and fun as he could make it, as well as being instructive. He owed this to his tired but enthusiastic students, who greeted him with such warmth.

He was about ten minutes into his lesson, and pleased with the way it was going, when the door opened suddenly and in marched the *proviseur*, fat and full of self-importance as always.

"Where is Salah Guirrou?" he demanded without preamble.

"Why do you want to know?" asked Kevin suspiciously, wondering what the man could possibly want with Guirrou.

"I have received word that Guirrou was absent from your class twice last week. Since you did not see fit to report this to me yourself so that the boy could be suitably reprimanded, I have come to punish him myself."

Kevin recalled that Guirrou had missed both of last week's five o'clock classes because his mother had been briefly hospitalized and he had asked for permission to leave school early to visit her in the Clinique El Qamar. Kevin had not only consented to let him miss class, provided that he did extra credit work, but had agreed not to report the boy's absences. Guirrou had kept his end of the bargain, turning in two near perfect book reports, and now Kevin felt it was his responsibility to do likewise.

"I excused Guirrou's absences," said the American. "As such, there was no need to report them."

"There are no excused absences in Lycée Mohamed Cinq!" cried the *proviseur*. "In any case, Guirrou is also one of the *externes* who have been boycotting Monsieur Godin's math class, and an example must be made of him!"

Kevin knew of the day-students' recent boycott of their math class, and he supported them wholeheartedly. They were literature majors, and for that reason mathematics was an unimportant and in Kevin's opinion, unnecessary subject.

According to his students, Monsieur Godin was not only a poor teacher but a racist as well. Kevin himself had heard Godin ranting and raving about the "imbecilic Arab sheep-farmers" he was teaching. Even his science-math majors complained of his unfathomable explanations and his bigoted remarks in class. No wonder those among Kevin's literature majors who had the good fortune to live at home and not in the school dormitory had decided to leave campus during their math class and study together in the olive groves.

"You are interrupting my lesson, Monsieur Rhazwani," said Kevin firmly, amazed at his own audacity. "Kindly exit the classroom at once."

"What!" exclaimed the *proviseur*.

"You heard me. Guirrou's absences during my hours were excused, and what he does in another class is no concern of mine. He's studying English now, and that's where he's going to stay."

"Guirrou! Stand up at once!" ordered the *proviseur*.

"Guirrou! Stay seated!" countermanded Kevin.

"Guirrou is leaving!" insisted Monsieur Rhazwani.

"No, *monsieur*. You are!" Kevin heard his students' simultaneous intake of breath, one mass gasp.

"How dare you speak to me with such flagrant disrespect!" cried the *proviseur*, his voice filled with self-righteous anger. "Apologize at once!"

"I will not!" insisted Kevin, and at that moment, the tension and stress which had built up over the previous weeks suddenly exploded inside him like a time bomb finally reaching zero hour. "Not now, not tomorrow, not ever!" he screamed. "And you, you pompous arrogant son of a bitch, you get the fuck out of my classroom! Get out, do you hear me! Get out!"

Possessed by a force almost outside himself, Kevin lunged at the *proviseur*. But he was no match for the man's gorilla-like strength. With both hands, Monsieur Rhazwani picked Kevin up off the ground and, spinning around, hurled him through the open door and to the ground outside.

From the doorway, the *proviseur* screeched, "You are dismissed from all your responsibilities at Lycée Mohamed Cinq! Never set foot in this establishment again!"

Slowly, unsteadily, Kevin pulled himself to his feet, still gasping for breath from the force of impact when he had hit the ground but feeling his anger unabated.

"You vicious power-hungry tyrant!" he spat out. "I hope you rot in hell for all eternity!"

"Get out of my school! Get out of my school!" shrieked the *proviseur*.

"Go fuck yourself, asshole!" replied Kevin, and then, with as much dignity as he could summon, turned to stumble across the courtyard and out of the school. In the distance he could hear a vague rumble growing in intensity. There were voices raised in unison, and little by little the words they were chanting became clearer. "Right on, Mr. Kensington! Right on, Mr. Kensington! Right on, Mr. Kensington!"

Kevin smiled despite himself at their use of the idiom he had taught them. Then his smile faded.

What in God's name had he just done? His impetuous stand against Monsieur Rhazwani, however courageous, however inspired, had backfired against him, had cost him his job. The best he could hope for now was a transfer to another city. The worst was to be thrown out of the Peace Corps in disgrace. And what about his students? This time it was he who had betrayed them. This time it was his own impulsive fault. There was only one thing to do and that was to arrive at Peace Corps headquarters without delay. There was a five-thirty bus to Rabat and Kevin was going to be on it. He looked at his watch. Five-twenty. If he ran, he could be at the bus station before it left. There was no time to pack. He had to reach Rabat before Barry Pennington had gone to bed for the evening. He had to talk to him face to face before a decision was made without Kevin's viewpoint being taken into consideration. Barry was a reasonable man. There was a good chance Kevin could make him see things his way.

But he must leave Aïn El Qamar without delay. Kevin looked back one last time at the gates of Lycée Mohamed Cinq, once the scene of his greatest triumphs, now the scene of his greatest fiasco, and wept.

CHAPTER 34

▼

The minutes passed, but much too slowly, as Dave and Michèle sat waiting in Janna's room at the Clinique El Qamar, their anguished faces revealing the depth of their worry. It was nearly three hours since they had found their friend lying unconscious on the floor of her house, and still she lay in a coma, looking hardly alive at all.

"I know the doctor said she might remain unconscious for … I don't even want to think of how long," whispered Michèle. "But still I couldn't help hoping against hope that she'd have come to long before now."

"I hoped so too," admitted Dave grimly. "But now I'm beginning to wonder if she might be like this for …"

"Don't say it," interrupted Michèle. "Don't even think it. We mustn't even consider the possibility that Janna won't get better. She's got to make it! She can't give up now that she's gotten back to being her old self once again. She's stronger emotionally than she's been in months. She's got to fight now with everything she has inside her in order to pull through!"

Dave nodded, his eyes returning to the bed where Janna lay. Her condition remained unchanged, and Doctor Marouane had been able to offer no new hope on his last visit half an hour ago.

"I've been thinking," said Dave after a long silence, "about what happened in Janna's house today."

"Yes?" asked Michèle.

"At first I thought that someone had tried to rob her, but now I'm not so sure. From the way her blouse had been torn open, well, to put it bluntly, it looks to me now like someone tried to rape her."

"You say 'tried.' Does that mean you think her assailant didn't actually go through with it?"

"I'm almost sure he didn't."

"What makes you so certain?"

"Janna slipped and fell," explained Dave. "She lost consciousness. She was hardly breathing at all when we found her. Would anyone, however crazy, rape a woman who was as good as dead?"

"You have a point," concurred Michèle. "And it's also true that only Janna's blouse had been torn, not her skirt or anything else."

"Thank God," agreed Dave.

"But how much comfort can that be when she's lying unconscious in front of us, when we have no way of knowing if she's even going to … to live." Suddenly it was all too much for the Frenchwoman, and she leaned over sobbing on Dave's shoulder. He stroked her hair gently, saying, "Don't worry, Michèle. Everything will be all right," trying to give her the confidence that he himself lacked.

When finally Michèle had regained her calm once more, Dave noticed her looking at her watch. "He should be home by now," she murmured, half to herself.

"Who?" asked Dave.

"Oh what the hell," said Michèle, and after a brief hesitation, continued, "Kacem and I have been seeing each other for several months now."

"You're kidding," exclaimed Dave, dumbfounded.

"Well, obviously we've been good at keeping it a secret. Really, you didn't guess?"

"I hardly realized that you two even knew each other," admitted Dave.

"We've been together since January," explained Michèle. "Our prudence has been mostly Kacem's idea, though I understand his reasons for not wanting to make our relationship public."

Recalling Kevin's mad infatuation with Kacem, Dave was glad that Michèle and her Moroccan lover had maintained their discretion. Knowing that Kacem had found the woman he was looking for so soon after rejecting Kevin's advances might have been enough to send Dave's best friend off the deep end. On the other hand, how lucky for Michèle to have found someone to love. She was sure as hell more fortunate that he or Kevin or just about anyone else he knew, for that matter.

"I need to let Kacem know where I am," Michèle was saying, "but he doesn't have a phone. I said that I'd drop by his place before going over to Janna's to spend the night, although that's certainly out of the question now."

"There's always a spare *banquette* at Kevin's and my place," offered Dave. "Though at the moment one is occupied by a visitor from the States."

"Thanks so much for the offer, Dave," replied Michèle, "but I've already made up my mind that the only place I want to be tonight is next to Kacem. Screw public opinion, at least this once."

"I understand," said Dave, thinking of Lateef and how much he wished he could throw himself into the young Moroccan's arms for the kind of loving and comfort Michèle would find with Kacem tonight.

"Dave?"

"Yes, Michèle?"

"I hate to ask you to leave Janna's bedside when you're as concerned about her as I am, but I'd really be grateful if you'd take my car and drive over to Kacem's house to let him know where I am, and bring him back with you if possible. I'd go myself, but … I just can't leave Janna's side. I'm so afraid that if I do, she … she …"

It looked for a moment as if Michèle would break down again, but she managed to regain her self-control this time. God, thought Dave, how much more could she take? It was only this morning that Michèle had learned of Dominique's death, and now her best friend lay fighting desperately for her life. If Kacem's presence would help Michèle bear up under the strain, then he could not refuse to go get him for her.

"Give me your keys," said Dave. "I'll get him back here as soon as I can."

Michèle handed him the car keys and kissed him on the cheek.

"You're a true friend," she said. "You find out who your real friends are at a time like this." She gave Dave directions to Kacem's house.

"I won't be long," reassured Dave, and with a last look at Janna's unconscious form, he left the hospital room.

Outside he was surprised to find that it was still light. It had seemed inside Janna's windowless room that it could not still be day. How long had it been since they had found Janna unconscious? Hardly more than three hours? It seemed like thirty.

Despite feeling a slight tinge of guilt at having left Janna's side, Dave was glad to be out in the fresh air, still warm from the afternoon sunshine, and it was good too to be behind the wheel of Michèle's Renault. He only drove these days when he was lent a car, which wasn't often, and now as he got into Michèle's and turned the key in the ignition, he could not help enjoying the feeling of control it gave him. He certainly felt powerless in other respects, unable to do anything to help Janna, or poor Kevin for that matter, and less and less able to influence

Lateef, who seemed determined lately to assert his independence from his American friend.

Oh shit, thought Dave suddenly and nearly stopped the car in the middle of the street as he recalled for the first time that he had told Lateef to meet him at his house this afternoon. If the Moroccan had stopped by as planned, only Mandee would have been there to welcome him. Kevin didn't finish work until six o'clock, and Dave had been with Janna since four. Would Mandee have taken advantage of their absence to …? No, the thought was too horrible even to contemplate. Still, Dave made up his mind that once he had brought Kacem back to the Clinique, he would leave him alone with Michèle—she would appreciate that—and go back home himself just to see that everything was all right. Everything had to be. Lateef would never have … No, the idea was unthinkable.

Pulling up outside Kacem's house, Dave jumped out of Michèle's Renault and ran up to ring the doorbell. Kacem answered shortly after, his face showing surprise at seeing Dave for the first time at his door.

"*Il y a eu un accident*," said Dave to the Moroccan. "Michèle needs you."

Kacem noticed that Dave was driving the Frenchwoman's car. "You're saying that Michèle was in an accident?" he asked worriedly.

"No, it's Janna. Come on. I'll explain to you while we're driving."

"*D'accord*," said Kacem. "Just let me get my wallet and keys."

A few minutes later, they were parked outside the Clinique El Qamar, Dave having told Kacem everything that had happened that afternoon. "*Ah mon Dieu*," the Moroccan had exclaimed when Dave had finished. "As if this morning's car crash weren't enough! Michèle must be going through hell."

Now, as Dave and Kacem got out of the car, the American handed Kacem the keys and said, "I have to run back to my place—just for a few minutes—to … to let Kevin know what's happening."

"You don't want to take Michèle's car?"

"There's no need," said Dave. "We're only a few blocks away, and I think the walk will do me good. I'll be back as soon as possible. Hopefully by then the doctor will have some encouraging news for us …"

"*Insha'allah*," said Kacem, which in Arabic meant "If it is God's will." "And now I'd better get in to Michèle. She's been alone since you left."

Walking away in the direction of his house, Dave noticed how crowded the streets were at this hour. It seemed that everyone was out on an evening promenade through town, smiling, greeting one another, stopping to share gossip. Dave responded mechanically to the friendly hellos he received from those among his students he met on this short walk to his house, but his heart was not in his words and he did not stop to speak to the students as he ordinarily would have. Too much had happened today for him to pretend a cheer he did not feel.

When Dave had reached his front door, he was surprised to see the neighbor girl who had invited Miranda over for tea that morning approaching him, an envelope extended in his direction. Why on earth was she delivering a letter to him?

"Your friend," she said in her slow imperfect English. "The American lady. She gives me this. She say me, 'Give it to Mr. Dave.'"

"Thank you," answered Dave. "Did she go out?"

"She is carrying a suitcase and she told me she left Aïn El Qamar," explained the girl.

"She said she was leaving Aïn El Qamar?" asked, his head swimming. Mandee had been seen leaving his house with her suitcase and saying that she was going away? That didn't make any sense. "Are you sure?" he added.

"Yes. She said me, 'I'm going to my house in American. Give this letter to Mr. Dave.'"

"I see," said Dave. "Thank you." But he didn't see. He didn't see at all. What had been happening here while he was at the Clinique with Michèle? What had made Mandee decide to leave so suddenly?

As the Moroccan girl walked away, Dave unlocked the front door and went in. Then, in the entry hall, his curiosity overcame him. He had to see what Mandee had written before he could take another step. Tearing open the envelope, he read:

"Dave darling,

"I was right and you were wrong. Your darling little Lateef isn't into cock as you were hoping. My pussy was just what he needed, and for a novice, he knew exactly what to do. His tongue went into action like it was on automatic pilot. But that was just a preamble to the main event. That boy had more cum stored up in his nuts than even I could imagine. He shot two full loads in me, hardly even stopping to recharge his batteries.

"You were an angel to let me visit you. Believe me, Dave, it was more wonderful than I could ever have dreamed.

"Now I'm on my way to bigger and better things. Well, maybe bigger than Lateef, but certainly not better.

"Love,

"Mandee

"P.S. We did it in your bed."

The letter fell from Dave's fingers to the floor. Dave stood there frozen, unable to move. It couldn't be true! Lateef couldn't have done this to him! He couldn't have fucked Mandee, not while Dave was sitting at the bedside of a friend who lay somewhere between life and death! Not in Dave's own house! Not in Dave's own bed!

"You son of a bitch!" Dave screamed. "You son of a bitch!"

"Dave?"

The American looked up to see Lateef standing in the living room doorway, his face pale, his eyes red and swollen.

"God damn you!" screamed Dave. "You did it! You fucked her, didn't you! You fucked her under my own roof! You fucked her in my own bed, you God damned son of a bitch!"

"No, Dave, no," whimpered Lateef. "It wasn't like that. I … I'm sorry I hurt you. I love you, Dave."

"Love? You don't even know what the word means. You've destroyed everything there's ever been between us. Some dirty tramp comes into my house and you don't waste a minute sticking your lousy prick up her cunt. The bitch doesn't give a damn about you; she just wants a lay, and you … you bastard … you're only too willing to supply." Dave could hear Lateef protesting, but he was damned if he was going to let him squirm his way out of this. "You sleep with her," he continued in fury, "someone who means nothing to you, when for two years now you've told me you love me and you'd do anything for me and you'll be grateful forever for everything I've done to give you a future. And for two years you still won't let me lay a hand on you. You've seen how much I've loved you and wanted you. And you've made me think at times that you loved me and wanted me too. I know you kissed me back last December. Did it scare you too much? Did it scare you to know that you had feelings for me just like I had for you? Was that why you betrayed me with Mandee, you bastard? God damn you! God damn you to hell! But you're not going to get away with it! Mandee's not going to be the only one to know what it's like to have you. I've waited much too long for this, and I'm not going to wait one second longer!"

Advancing towards Lateef, Dave reached out and grabbed the hair on the back of the Moroccan's head, pulling his face up so that it was at his own level. Savagely, Dave pressed his lips against Lateef's forcing them apart, biting them in his rage. He'd wanted this for so long, to taste Lateef's mouth, to feel the caress of his tongue, to fill him with his passion and need, and if he was doing it now out of hatred and not out of love, well at least, God damn it, he was getting what he wanted at last.

And then, suddenly, amazingly, Dave realized that Lateef had thrown his arms around him, was squeezing him as tight as was humanly possible, and that it was not just Dave who was kissing but Lateef as well, returning Dave's desire with equal fervor, his mouth seemingly insatiable for Dave's lips and tongue.

What was going on here? Was Lateef a raging sex maniac? Mandee had said in her letter to Dave that Lateef had had two orgasms, and that was only a matter of hours ago. Was he some kind of bisexual love machine? No, that made no sense at all. Dave pulled his head away from Lateef's and saw that the young man's eyes were flooded with tears.

"Lateef?" Dave asked, his voice deadly serious. "I have to know the truth. Did you have sex with Mandee?"

At first Lateef did not reply, so Dave insisted, "Did you fuck her, God damn it!"

"No, Dave. No," he sobbed. "I ... tried to. But I couldn't."

"I don't understand."

"I mean ... I ... wanted to," continued the young Moroccan. "I wanted to ... to prove to you that I was my own man. I wanted to prove to you that I *was* a man, because ... because here in Aïn El Qamar, you can't be both gay and a man at the same time! I ... I know now how stupid that that must sound after all the talks we've had. I know now how stupid I've been! You're the strongest, bravest man I know. There's no one I'd rather be like than you. But I didn't want to be ... to be different. I'm sorry, Dave. I've been thinking for the past couple hours ... about how much I love you ... about how important you are to me. If being gay means being like you, how can there be anything wrong with being gay? Anyway, the truth is ... that I guess I've always known I was. I just needed you, and that disgusting tramp Mandee, to help me accept it. Kiss me again, Dave. Kiss me again and let me prove that what I'm saying is true!"

Dave's head was swimming. Part of him couldn't believe what he was hearing. Part of him was thinking that this must be another of those recurring dreams where his fantasies became real, and that he would soon wake up alone and hopeless once again. But the truth in Lateef's eyes and the passion behind his words were too strong to be denied.

There'll be time to talk later, thought Dave as he threw his arms around Lateef, and once again pressed his lips to Lateef's waiting mouth. There'll be more than enough time to talk. Now, there was only this miracle, so long hoped for, so long despaired over, finally coming true. Dave melted into Lateef's embrace, home at last.

CHAPTER 35

▼

Hours had passed since Kacem's arrival at the Clinique El Qamar and still Janna showed no visible signs of improvement. To Michèle, the waiting seemed endless and at times unbearable, and it was only Kacem's presence beside her that gave the Frenchwoman the strength to maintain her vigil. Only Kacem's presence.

How had she ever lived without it? How was it possible that in her years in Southern California and her first months in Aïn El Qamar she had not realized how truly empty her life had been? She had thought that her career and her friends were enough for her, but she could not have been more wrong. Only Kacem truly fulfilled her, completed her.

This was the conclusion she had come to during the last anguished hours of waiting, and if she had previously taken Kacem's presence in her life for granted, it was only the terrible reality of seeing Janna so near death that had made Michèle consciously aware of how profoundly she needed him.

Up to now, though, they had just been playing games with their lives, refusing to make a full commitment to each other, and in so doing they had allowed Claudette to put a wedge between them. But the time had come to make a change. The time had come to …

"Kacem," said Michèle suddenly. "*Nous ne pouvons pas continuer comme ça.*"

"What?" asked the Moroccan.

"I said we can't go on like this."

"What do you mean?"

"The two of us. We've been doing all the wrong things, and thinking they were the right ones. It's time we put an end to it."

"What are you talking about, Michèle? You're not ... you're not suggesting that we stop seeing each other, are you?"

"No, love," replied Michèle, squeezing Kacem's hand reassuringly. "And forgive me for startling you. Actually, it's just the opposite."

"I don't understand," said Kacem.

"It's Janna. It's seeing her lying there, somewhere between life and death, and knowing that ... that it could go either way. It's made me think about us, and about all the time we've spent throwing our lives away."

"What do you mean?"

"You and I, we ... we've been so concerned about our reputations that we haven't thought of the sacrifices we've been making. Hiding a relationship from the world isn't the way to make it grow and stay healthy. In our case, it's just added to our problems with Claudette. She still thinks she can have you, that you're only afraid or shy or God knows what. Kacem, darling, we've got to make some changes in our lives while ..." Michèle glanced over at Janna's motionless form. "While we still have a chance."

"But Michèle, you know as well as I do that if we were to be seen together in public, people would start to think all sorts of terrible things about you. French-women don't date Moroccans in Aïn El Qamar without being called the vilest of names. After that, people begin to think they can do just about anything in the presence of the foreign woman and ..."

"But I can't stand this hiding any longer."

"We don't have any choice, love. It'd be different if we were ..." Kacem suddenly hesitated.

"If we were what?"

"Never mind," said Kacem, and Michèle could feel him retreating from her. Then suddenly it hit her, what he was talking about.

"Are you saying that if we were married, people would accept our being together?" she asked.

The Moroccan said nothing, clearly disconcerted by Michèle's question.

"Kacem," insisted Michèle. "I want you to answer me."

"All right, yes. Things would be different in that case, but ..."

"But you're not ready or willing to make the commitment?"

"I didn't say that, Michèle."

"Then what? Are you afraid that I'd say no?"

Kacem's embarrassed silence spoke volumes. "Are you saying that you'd ask me to marry you, but you think I'd refuse? Kacem! Answer me!"

"Keep your voice down," whispered the Moroccan. "This is a hospital room."

"You're avoiding my question, Kacem. Now, answer me … please."

"I know perfectly well that I can't expect you to accept a proposal of marriage from me," said Kacem. "I've only just started my career, and what with the situation between me and Monsieur Rhazwani, I don't seem to be off to a very good start. Besides, you have your friends and family to consider. I doubt they'd approve of your marrying a man who comes from a different world, a different culture, a different religion."

"That's not true," insisted Michèle. "My family and my real friends would realize that I don't make decisions lightly, and that if I decided to marry someone, that man would be the right one for me, in every way, and they'd respect my decision."

"What exactly are you saying?" asked Kacem.

"I'm saying that seeing Janna here fighting for her life, and knowing that Dominique has … lost hers, has made me think a little bit more about my own. I love you Kacem, more than I ever thought I could love a man, and I need you. So propose to me, will you, and see how long it takes me to accept."

"You'll marry me?" asked Kacem unbelievingly.

"Of course I will, you beautiful man!"

"Michèle. *Ma chérie*! I've wanted you as my wife since the moment I first saw you," exclaimed the Moroccan, and taking her in his arms, he pressed his mouth to hers. Michèle responded to Kacem's kiss with all the love she felt for him, the depth of which even she herself had not been totally aware of until this evening. As she felt the soft caress of his lips, as she felt his love and strength flowing from his soul to hers, she realized suddenly that joy could indeed spring from tragedy.

She was kissing him still when a faint moaning penetrated her consciousness as if from afar. Then, suddenly, she realized that it was coming from only a few feet away, from Janna's bed precisely, and at that instant she pulled herself from Kacem's arms.

"*Qu'est-ce qui se passe?*" he asked in surprise.

"Listen!" whispered Michèle excitedly, looking towards Janna.

"Is that …? Is she …?"

"I dearly hope so," said Michèle, her voice trembling. "God willing our vigil is about to end." She jumped up from where she was sitting and ran to the door, throwing it open and calling out, "*Docteur! Docteur!* Come quickly!"

Seconds later, Doctor Marouane was standing beside Janna, taking her pulse, and smiling at Michèle and Kacem.

"It appears our wait has not been as long as I feared," declared the doctor.

"She's coming around then?" asked Michèle.

"*Oui, mademoiselle.* It certainly looks that way."

Michèle threw her arms around Kacem, kissing him once again, not caring that that doctor was standing there. Soon everyone would know of their wedding plans, and Janna—Janna would be their maid of honor!

Michèle looked at her friend now, watched as Janna's eyelids began to flicker, her lips attempting to move. She hurried to her side, taking her hand and repeating again and again, "We're here, love. Michèle and Kacem. We're here, and everything's going to be all right."

Janna's eyes opened, and she looked up to see Michèle's beaming face.

"Where … where am I?" she asked numbly.

"You're at the Clinique El Qamar. You had a fall, Janna, but everything's going to be all right. Thank God, you're going to be fine!"

"Be fine," repeated Janna faintly, and then closed her eyes once more.

"*Docteur!*" asked Michèle worriedly. "What's wrong?"

"Nothing at all, *mademoiselle*," replied Doctor Marouane. "There's nothing to be upset about. She's sleeping. The crisis has passed."

"But how can she sleep? She's already been unconscious for …" Michèle looked at her watch. It was nearly a quarter past nine. "… for more than seven or eight hours."

"Unconscious, yes, but far from sleeping normally," explained the doctor. "You must understand that Mademoiselle Gallagher's system has suffered an enormous shock today, both physical and emotional. She may very well sleep the rest of the night. That's why I recommend that you and your friend go home and get some rest yourselves. You've been here for hours and it's been exhausting for you too. Come back in the morning. I'm sure you'll find Mademoiselle Gallagher back to being her old self by then. Of course we'll need to perform certain tests and she'll have to remain here in the Clinique for several days—at least until we're sure there are no complications. But—but if I were you, I'd sleep comfortably tonight. The worst is over."

"*Merci, docteur!* Thank you for all you've done," exclaimed Michèle. In France, she would have thrown her arms around him and kissed him, but this was Morocco after all.

Kacem too thanked the doctor, and then, taking Michèle by the hand, led her out of the hospital room.

"Are you still coming home with me?" he asked.

"There's nowhere else I'd rather go," answered Michèle as they stepped out into the night air, finally becoming cooler after the day's warmth which had lasted late into the evening.

"Shall we stop by Dave's and give him the good news about Janna?" suggested Kacem. "He never came back to the Clinique."

"I hadn't even realized," admitted an embarrassed Michèle. "I wonder what came up."

"Let's go find out," replied Kacem. "I'm sure it's nothing to be concerned about, but it won't hurt to check."

"You do the driving, love," asked Michèle. "I'm totally wiped out."

Kacem accepted the keys from her with an understanding smile and opened the passenger side door. Michèle got in, seconds later Kacem taking his seat behind the wheel. Starting the car, he pulled away from the curb and headed in the direction of Dave's house, which was only a few blocks away.

"Everything looks fine," said Kacem as they approached the house. "The lights are on in the living room."

Leaving the car, they walked up to Dave's front door and rang the bell. Soon after, the door was opened by Dave, his face beaming.

"You heard the good news already?" asked an incredulous Michèle.

"Good news?" asked a seemingly uncomprehending Dave. "Oh my God! Janna! How is she?"

"She's fine, but … Dave what's been going on since you left the hospital. You look as if you've won the lottery."

"I have, Michèle! I have!"

Michèle waited for Dave to explain.

"I'll tell you later, okay," said the American. "Really, I'm overjoyed about Janna. It's just that … I'm just plain overjoyed!"

"It's wonderful, isn't it!" exclaimed Michèle.

"Yes," answered Dave, his smile radiant. "I'll see you both at school tomorrow. Have a good night!"

Dave closed the door.

"Now what was that about?" asked a dumbfounded Kacem.

"You've got me," replied Michèle. "But whatever it is, it looks like you and I aren't the only happy people in Aïn El Qamar tonight."

"Speaking of which …" Kacem leaned over to whisper in Michèle's ear. "Why don't the two of us get back to my place? It's been a very long day and … Don't you think it's about time we got down to the pleasure of making love?"

"Anything you say," Michèle smiled up at Kacem, her face aglow. "Anything you say."

CHAPTER 36

▼

Claudette was alone in her living room doing her damnedest to get drunk. There was an open bottle of Johnny Walker on the table in front of the *banquette* where she sat, and she had already emptied about a third of it. The room was lit only by whatever light filtered in from the hallway, and its darkness matched that of her soul.

How much longer could she stand being subjected to the terrible realization that she would never find the happiness she was searching for? Earlier tonight at the dinner table, the nascent bliss of Jean-Richard and Marcie had been almost too much for Claudette to bear.

Not that she begrudged the two of them their happiness. Of course she was glad that Jean-Richard had finally unburdened himself of his nightmarish memories to someone he loved, and if doing so had freed him from the hold his past had exerted over him for so many years, then who was she to deny him that liberating joy?

But why for the love of God was it always others, others and not she herself, whose dreams came true? Why did nothing ever work out for Claudette Verlaine? Why?

First she had wasted months deceiving herself that she was in love with Fareed while all the time she had only been buying his attentions with her gifts. When finally he had tired of her and even those gifts were no longer enough to hold him, revenge had blinded her. She had wanted to prove to both Fareed and herself that she could have any man she wanted, and she had had many, so many in fact that she had lost count of their number. At times, there had even been more than one or two in a single evening.

Now, when at last she had found someone she truly loved, someone whose affection could not be bought but must be earned, her mad behavior after Fareed's rejection was preventing him from realizing what she knew to be a fact—that he and Claudette were destined to be together for the rest of their lives.

Of course that must be the reason Kacem still refused to admit his love for her. Her notorious reputation was causing him to fear becoming just another on her long list of lovers. Not only that, but when she had first become aware that she had fallen in love with him, she had employed the worst possible strategy to win his attentions, foolishly believing that she could do so in the same way she had interested those other men in her, through lavish presents and an obvious display of her physical assets.

Thank God she had eventually come to her senses and seen once and for all that Kacem was neither interested in expensive gifts nor excited by blatant sexuality. If she was to win Kacem's heart, she must first transform herself into a model of dignity and propriety, toning down her wardrobe, restraining herself from public displays of her affection for him, and putting an end to any further attempts to buy his love. Only in this way would she be able to convince Kacem to share his life with her.

But she was beginning to become impatient for results. For some reason, Kacem still seemed resistant to her efforts, despite the modest skirts and blouses she had begun wearing, despite the subtle make-up which looked almost like no make-up at all, despite the demure chignon in which she now wore her hair.

Tonight especially she wondered how much longer she could wait for Kacem to come to his senses. When Jean-Richard had brought Marcie back home with him after their last class this afternoon, Claudette had felt unable to stand her loneliness any longer. How could she bear to watch their contentment, to attempt to partake in it, when she herself was still without the man she loved? Excusing herself briefly, Claudette had hurried out to her car and driven to Kacem's house, intending to invite him to dinner with them. He and Jean-Richard were on good terms. Kacem could hardly refuse her invitation to share in their celebration of the Frenchman's joy. But though she had rung the doorbell repeatedly, there had been no answer, and one of the neighbors had informed her that Kacem was out of town for the day.

Later, just before they were about to sit down for the dinner Marcie had prepared in Jean-Richard and Claudette's kitchen, Claudette had once again slipped away and returned at top speed to Kacem's place. This time, however, the neighbor had told her that Kacem was back in Aïn El Qamar but that a tall dark-haired foreign man had come by in a Renault 4 and the two of them had driven away together.

Reluctantly, Claudette had returned to her own house, forced by her unfortunate bad luck to sit through a dinner of Marcie's bland American food which Jean-Richard could not stop praising to high heaven, forced to pretend to participate in their bliss when all she felt was overwhelmed with anger and frustration.

Now it was several hours later, and Claudette had been abandoned to her solitude. Jean-Richard and Marcie had left, apparently to spend the night together at her place, and the Frenchwoman found herself alone with Johnny Walker her only companion.

Refilling her glass, Claudette watched as the level of the amber liquid dropped lower, and she wondered if by the end of the evening she would reach the bottom of the bottle.

The bottom of the bottle. The expression stuck in Claudette's head. The abyss. Not only of the bottle but of her life. Downward was the direction she was heading, ever deeper into the pits of loneliness and emptiness and despair. That was where she was destined to end. That was where …

No, damn it! She was allowing the day's happenings to cloud her judgment! Before this morning, she had been optimistic about her future, certain that it was just a matter of time until her tactics for winning Kacem's love paid off. How had she let herself begin to think such grim depressing thoughts? How had she allowed herself to make the idiotic decision to drink herself senseless? She should be out realizing her dream instead of abandoning it like a gutless fool!

I will not get drunk tonight! vowed Claudette as she screwed the top back on the bottle of whiskey. It's time for me to start doing something constructive about my future for a change!

Kacem must be home by now. It was nearly eleven, and always before when she had stopped by his place in the late evening she had found him there. Tonight would be no exception. Somehow she would discover a way to convince him once and for all of her love for him, of all she had to offer. Tonight she would break through the barrier Kacem had set up between them. Tonight she would know the same happiness that Jean-Richard and Marcie had found. It would all happen tonight!

Grabbing her car keys from the table, Claudette gulped down the liquor that remained in the glass before her, then rose from the *banquette* and walked purposefully towards the door.

Once in the car, she could hardly control the speed at which she raced towards Kacem's house. Her heart was pounding, her hands clammy on the steering wheel. Tonight, at last, she would win Kacem's heart. Tonight, at last, he would be hers, and the wasted lonely moments would matter no longer.

Slamming on the brakes, Claudette came to a screeching halt before Kacem's door, parking her car behind a Renault 4. Was someone visiting him? she wondered. A neighbor had described a tall foreign man in a Renault 4 who had come by Kacem's house earlier that evening. Were they together now? At the moment, Claudette could not recall which among the French *coöpérants* at school drove *une R-Quatre* but she would find out soon enough and get rid of him without delay.

After checking her hair and make-up in the rear-view mirror, Claudette took a deep breath and got out of the car, then hurried towards Kacem's door. She rang the doorbell twice and waited for an answer. When none came, she rang again, this time more insistently. Again there was no reply.

"Kacem!" she called out. "Kacem, *chéri*! I know you're inside. Please open the door! *C'est moi*, Claudette. I must speak with you! *C'est urgent!*"

Her voice echoed in the stillness of the night and for a moment she wondered if Kacem might indeed be out. But no, there was definitely light coming from within.

"Kacem!" she shouted again. "*C'est* Claudette! *Ouvre-moi la porte!* I'm waiting for you!"

She could hear footsteps approaching now, and then he was there, wearing only his robe, his black hair tousled.

"*Oh, chéri*," said Claudette pouting. "Did I get you out of bed? I had no idea you'd retired so early. The night is still young, *chéri*. Let me in …"

"It … it was a long day, Claudette," said Kacem, holding the door half closed.

"I know," smiled Claudette sympathetically. "I dropped by earlier and was told you'd gone out of town."

"*C'est vrai*," admitted Kacem, running his fingers through his wavy hair to put it in place.

"Don't bother," murmured Claudette, reaching up to take his hand in hers. "You look perfect just the way you are, fresh from slumber."

"Is there … something I can do for you, Claudette?" asked Kacem, removing his hand from hers.

"I told you before, silly boy. Let me in."

"Can't it wait until another time? I … as you said, I was in bed and …"

"*S'il te plaît, chéri*," begged Claudette. "Don't make me stand outside and catch a chill. It's important that we speak. I have things to tell you that simply can't be held back another second."

Kacem opened his mouth to protest again, but Claudette would not let him speak. Gently but firmly, she pushed past him and headed towards the living room, passing his slightly ajar bedroom door through which a crack of light shone. Poor boy, she thought. She really had awakened him from his sleep, but not without reason of course.

"What can I do for you?" asked Kacem when they had reached the living room where, on the coffee table, several candles had burned down almost to their holders.

"I want to ..." Claudette stopped in mid-sentence. There was something wrong here. Kacem had said he'd been in bed, and he was wearing his robe, but then where was the owner of the car she had found parked outside? There were two empty wine glasses on the table? Where was the tall foreign man the neighbor had described, the man with whom Kacem had obviously been drinking?

"Are you alone?" she asked suspiciously.

"*Oui, bien sûr.* I told you I was in bed."

"I know, but ..." She glanced towards the glasses.

"Oh, the wine. We finished drinking quite some time ago, and then my friend went home."

"But his car is still in front of your house," said Claudette.

"Car?"

"Yes, the Renault 4 parked outside your door."

"It must ... it must belong to someone else. The person who dropped by was Dave Casalini, and I don't believe he owns a car."

"Dave?" Suddenly Claudette had the most awful idea. Dave was gay. Kacem was proving immune to Claudette's charms. There were two glasses on the table. The car might not belong to Dave, but could it be that behind Kacem's bedroom door ...?

"You said you had something important to discuss," Kacem was reminding her, but Claudette was paying no attention.

Could it be that Kacem had resisted her advances because he was gay? It hardly seemed possible, but then again who would ever have guessed that Dave, so virile and masculine, would prefer the embrace of another man? The facts were unmistakable. Dave's visit to a colleague he pretended scarcely to know, candles and wine glasses on the table, Kacem wearing only his robe (he had said he'd been in bed, not sleeping, hadn't he?), and the bedroom door behind which a light burned ...

Before Kacem could block her path, Claudette had pushed past him and was heading towards that door.

"Don't go in there!" shouted the Moroccan, but she paid no heed to his cry.

"Please don't!" Kacem shouted again, but to no avail.

Claudette threw open the door and gasped as she saw not Dave but …

Her first reaction was one of relief. So Kacem was straight after all. How absurd it had been for her to think otherwise. Kacem was no more interested in men than she was in women.

But her feeling of relief was short-lived. Almost instantly, fury took its place, rage at the woman who sat now in Kacem's bed, at the lying slut who had been plotting against her all the time she had feigned friendliness.

"You've robbed me of my man!" she screamed at a horrified Michèle, who had crossed her arms to cover her naked breasts. "How dare you steal what's mine! Kacem belongs to me, not you, you scheming conniving bitch! Give me back my man! Give me back my man or I'll kill you!"

Suddenly Claudette's hands were at Michèle's throat, squeezing it tight enough to smother every last breath of life from the woman who had tried to destroy her and turn her dreams into ashes.

"I'll kill you! I'll kill you!" screamed Claudette, her eyes those of a lunatic.

And then she felt Kacem's hands on her wrists, attempting to tear them away from Michèle's neck. She fought hard against him, struggling to keep her fingers around woman's throat, longing to see her face turn blue and her eyes burst from their sockets, but Kacem was too strong for her. Her hands lost their grip and Michèle fell on the bed, gasping for air.

"Get out of my house, Claudette!" shouted Kacem, as he knelt beside Michèle, gently caressing her ravaged face. Then, looking back at Claudette, he screamed out, contempt filling his eyes:

"I've put up with your insanity long enough, Claudette. The only reason I haven't told you how much I love Michèle is because I was afraid you were too unbalanced to handle reality."

"But you're mine!" protested Claudette, refusing to believe the truth that was before her, retreating into the fantasy she had created for herself.

"I belong to no one but Michèle. I'm hers, Claudette, and never have been nor will be nor could be yours. You're a crazy self-deceiving fool, and after what you've just tried to do, I don't give a damn what happens to you! You mean nothing to me! Nothing!"

"Liar!" screeched Claudette. "You're lying to me! You're lying to yourself! You love me! You love only me! She's nothing to you, never can be! I'm the woman you love! You're mine! You're mine! Mine, do you hear me? Mine forever!"

"Get out!" ordered Kacem, rising from Michèle's side to move menacingly towards Claudette. "Get out of my house and out of my life!"

"No!!!" shrieked Claudette. "I belong here! I belong here with you!"

"You belong in the insane asylum!"

Kacem was pushing her from the bedroom towards the front door. She struggled to free herself from his grip, screaming all the time, "I belong here! You belong to me!"

She was still screaming at the top of her lungs when he thrust her out the door. "Do you hear me?" she yelled, her cries piercing the air. "I want everyone to hear me!" She was turning towards the windows of the neighboring houses. "I want everyone to know. Kacem Hajiri is mine! He belongs to me! Kacem is mine! Mine! Mine!"

Suddenly she felt the slap of Kacem's hand burn her face, not once but twice. She looked at him in horror, her face streaked with tears, though she had no idea she'd been crying.

"Don't ever come here again," ordered Kacem, his voice deadly serious. "Don't you ever come here again or go near my fiancée. If you ever try to lay a hand on her, I'll call the police on you so fast you won't know what's happened. Now get the hell off this street and out of our lives!"

Claudette closed her eyes to block her view of the one man she'd ever truly loved, covered her ears with her hands to muffle the sound of his terrible words. But she could still hear the slamming of the door as Kacem went back into his house, never again to be part of her life.

Kacem's hateful words echoed in Claudette's head, signaling the end to everything. Her life was over tonight. There was nothing to live for. Nothing.

And now it all seemed clear. The end had indeed come tonight. The final, bitter conclusion of the most horrible and unbearable year of her life. The end.

Claudette got into her car, turned the key in the ignition, pressed her foot on the accelerator, and headed resolutely in the direction of her house.

There was no other solution. She had reached the end of a one-way street. Though she had survived the loss of Fareed by throwing herself into a series of degrading sexual liaisons, there was no surviving the loss of Kacem. She could never laugh again, never know love again. She was finished, too old to interest the caliber of man she wanted, too tired and bereft of hope to even try.

Claudette wondered as she sped through the deserted streets of Aïn El Qamar why she was not afraid of what she was about to do. Always before the mere thought of suicide had appalled her. But she was not frightened now, only determined not to fail in this as she had so miserably failed in her vain attempts at finding love this past year.

Jean-Richard was away for the evening. She would fill herself with sleeping pills and by morning when he had returned from his night with Marcie, it would be too late to save her. Death would already have brought her the peace she had been unable to find in life.

And now she had arrived home. Pulling to an abrupt stop in front of her house, Claudette ran from her car and up to the front door. She was about to open it when she heard a voice calling her name and saw Miguel Berthaud walking towards her.

"Claudette," called the tall skinny Frenchman, his voice unexpectedly serious. "Claudette, wait!"

"Miguel, *qu'y a-t-il?*" she asked, wondering what he could possibly want at this hour of the night. "I'm … I'm truly quite tired, *chéri*. It's not a good time to talk. Can't it wait?"

"*Je t'en prie*, Claudette. Invite me in for just a while. I need desperately to be with someone, at least for a few minutes."

"Not now, Miguel. I told you, I'm just too tired. I'll … we'll talk another time."

"Claudette, please. I'm only asking for five minutes of your time, and then I'll leave you in peace. Please don't send me away."

Claudette wondered despite herself what was troubling Miguel. Never before had he spoken to her like this, and even knowing that she was about to end her own life, she found herself puzzled and intrigued by this change in her old friend. What would it matter if she spent a few of her remaining minutes on earth with him? After all, nothing he could say or do would prevent her from going through with her plan, once he had left.

"*Très bien*, Miguel. *Entre*," she said, accompanying Miguel into the living room. Then, as they sat down, she asked, "What's put you in such a state?"

At first, Miguel said nothing, and Claudette could tell that he was gathering his strength. When at last he began to speak, his voice was hardly more than a whisper.

"*C'est l'accident* … that terrible accident this morning," he said. "I've been obsessing over it ever since the moment I heard the news, thinking endlessly about Christiane and Dominique, not so much about the way their lives ended as … as what they'd found before the end came. They'd found real happiness with each other, happiness together, a happiness I've never known, never will know, not as long as I live!"

Claudette could scarcely believe what she was hearing. Miguel's feelings so precisely mirrored her own that she might have been speaking them herself. How ironic it was that Aïn El Qamar's funniest and best-loved clown should share her despair. The words that poured from his mouth seemed incongruous with his comic face and its too big eyes and nose.

"And then Jean-Richard came by tonight with Marcie, and for the first time in all the years I've known him I saw love and hope in his eyes and it just made me all the more miserable and depressed. To know that those two have found what … what I'll never find. I thought Dave and Kevin might cheer me up, but when I arrived there was only Dave and that student of his, Lateef I think his name is, and Dave and he seemed hardly aware of my presence, holding hands and exchanging the kind of looks you usually only see in the movies. It was all too much for me, Claudette, you understand? First Jean-Richard and Marcie, and then Dave and Lateef, the kind of one-two punch that you don't get up from. That you never get up from!"

There were tears in Claudette's eyes as she listened to Miguel express the very feelings that had pushed her towards the decision she had come to, and suddenly she knew that she could postpone it no longer. If she had to spend another second listening to Miguel talk—the news of Dave and his new young lover had put the final nail in her coffin—she would lose her mind, she was sure. But she could not take sleeping pills. They would not work fast enough, they would not be sure enough. She had to act at once, and in a way that would end her suffering quickly and permanently.

"*Tu m'excuses*, Miguel," she said. "I … I suddenly don't feel well."

Escaping from the room, Claudette hurried noiselessly up the stairs and entered Jean-Richard's bedroom. It was here, she now decided, that the final climactic chapter of her life would be enacted.

In the drawer of Jean-Richard's bedside table she found the gun that, years before, the Frenchman had bought from a departing *coopérant* who had never fully adjusted to the strangeness of life in Morocco and had felt the need to protect himself. That was when Jean-Richard and Claudette had first lived in Aïn El Qamar, and though in recent years they had often smiled at their early apprehensions, the gun had been kept, just in case. Hidden in the back of the drawer, it had remained ready, waiting, as if for this final, inevitable moment to arrive.

Claudette could not take her eyes off the small but potent weapon which lay cradled in her hand. It could shatter flesh and bone with a single, terrible pull of the trigger, allowing her blood to gush from her body, allowing her useless life to pour from her veins, freeing her from the miseries of another tomorrow.

The gun reflected the light from the street lamp outside Jean-Richard's bedroom window, and in its reflections she could see faces from her past. She could see herself as a school girl, being made fun of because her clothes were not as nice as the other girls', and then as a teenager, discovering that she could use her already alluring body as a way to make friends with the most popular boys, though their "friendship" rarely lasted past the moment when they had satisfied their adolescent lust. Later, she had learned how to make that body her greatest asset, learned how to bring men to the peak of sexual ecstasy where they would offer her anything. Coming to Aïn El Qamar had only increased her feeling of desirability. Here she reigned unchallenged, the epitome of beauty and sensuality, the undisputed center of the town's foreign community. Who in Aïn El Qamar, in most of Morocco, for that matter, had not heard of Miss Claudette Verlaine? Even traveling to Casablanca, Rabat, Marrakesh, her fame preceded her.

The gun reflected many memories of Claudette's distant and recent past, some happy, others sad. The present was simply bleak and absolutely lacking in the promise of better things to come. She had allowed herself to hope this year, but too many disappointments had destroyed her hope, and tonight's was the final blow. The one from which she could never recover. She did not even want to try.

With the slightest pull she would end her impossible search for happiness and fulfillment. With just one pull …

Her hand steady in its determination, Claudette raised the gun to her temple. Now, she told herself. Now.

Claudette heard the empty click, but it was not until seconds later that she realized its significance. It couldn't be, she screamed inwardly. But when she pulled the trigger again, and again, and again, it was the same derisive click that mocked her.

"No!" she cried aloud as she threw the impotent weapon to the floor. It hadn't been loaded! Dear God, it hadn't been loaded!

"No, God damn it, no!" screamed Claudette, and then suddenly, as she stared at the useless firearm lying on the floor, she began to laugh, uncontrollably, at her own ineptitude at doing anything, at living, at loving … God, she was even incapable of killing herself!

Claudette laughed and laughed, her eyes wild with hysteria, tears pouring down her face, the gun still staring at her, taunting her, ridiculing her.

She laughed so hard that her legs buckled and she collapsed to the floor, her hand reaching out to grasp the metal object that was to have been her salvation, her escape, pounding the floor with it, bruising her knuckles.

And then someone's hands were on her shoulders, pulling her to her knees, and she found herself staring through tear-blurred eyes at the confused and distressed face of Miguel Berthaud.

"What in heaven's name is wrong, Claudette?" Miguel was saying. "What are you doing in Jean-Richard's room? What …?" Then, apparently for the first time, Miguel caught sight of the gun which Claudette still held in her hand. "Oh my God! Oh my God, Claudette, no! You can't have been meaning to …"

Miguel ripped the gun from her hand and sent it sliding under the bed beyond her reach.

"And why not?" Claudette shot back at him. "What have I got to live for? Do you know what happened tonight? The man I love more than life itself told me he cares nothing for me! I would have given him anything he'd asked for, anything, but no … I'm not good enough for him, I'm too old and faded and worthless. I can't even find a lousy fucking loaded gun. Why couldn't the gun have been loaded? Why, Miguel? Why?"

"God damn it, Claudette!" said Miguel as he led the Frenchwoman back downstairs with him into the living room. "Have you lost your mind?" He pushed her down on the *banquette* and, dropping to his knees before her, looked accusingly into her swollen eyes.

"Oh Miguel, just leave me alone!" cried Claudette.

"To do what? To try and kill yourself again? I'm not that insane. You made a mistake trying to do that while I was around because as long as I'm here I'm not going to let you do anything to hurt yourself. Anything, do you hear me? If I have to stay with you for the rest of the night and tomorrow and this week and the one after, then I will if that's what it takes to stop you from trying this craziness again."

"It's not craziness," protested Claudette. "I have no other choice."

"*Mais c'est absurde*! Of course you have a choice. You always have a choice. You've just made the wrong ones too often and I for one have been too scared of what you'd say to me to let you know just how stupid your decisions have been. Well, let me tell you now, Claudette. This latest decision of yours is the craziest of them all. You're the most beautiful, vibrant woman I've ever met. Your *joie de vivre* inspires everyone who knows you. This town would be pronounced dead on arrival if it weren't for the life it gets from you. And let me tell you one thing more. If you'd succeeded in doing that horrible thing you were planning, my life … my own life would be meaningless. If you were no longer here, there'd be no reason for me to live either. Do you hear what I'm saying, Claudette? I couldn't live if I knew I'd never see you again or hear your voice. Do you want to be responsible for what I'd do to myself if you … if you left me?"

"I don't understand, Miguel," said Claudette. "I've never seen you like this. You're different somehow. You … frighten me."

"Maybe you're just frightened to find that someone really cares about you. You've been spending so much time with people who've just been using you for their own selfish purposes that you don't know how to deal with someone who loves you more than life itself."

"*Mais tu n'est pas sérieux.*"

"I'm more serious than I've ever been, and if I shock you it's only because I've never been brave enough to tell you how I really feel. Tonight I'm willing to risk your derision. I almost lost you, Claudette, and if I had it would have been too late for words. You can laugh at me all you want tomorrow, but tonight you're going to listen to me and take me seriously for a change."

"*Je t'écoute*, Miguel. I'm listening," said Claudette, her eyes facing a Miguel she did not know, a Miguel she had not given herself time to discover. How had she let herself be misled all these years by his imperfect exterior? How was it possible that she had allowed herself to be blinded to the fact that someone other than Kacem might love her and need her? Hadn't she been selfish in not seeing Miguel as he truly was, a man who cared less about what he could get from others than about what he could give?

"I've dreamed for years of telling you how I feel," Miguel was saying, "and I've fantasized about your reaction. In my dreams you've fallen into my arms and vowed to love me forever. Those were only dreams, I know. They were only my foolish, wishful thinking. Still, regardless of how you react, I must tell you once again, my darling Claudette, that only you give meaning to my life, only you make it worth living. So please, I'm begging you, never … never again try to do what you attempted tonight. I … I couldn't live if you did!"

Claudette heard Miguel's voice nearly choking with emotion. She saw the tears welling in his eyes as he knelt before her. And all at once she was overcome with guilt. How could she have been so self-centered? How could she have let herself ignore the effect that her suicide would have on the friends who cared about her? Miguel was speaking the truth. She did not have the right to inflict that kind of pain and loss on another human being, and especially not upon one who loved her as Miguel did.

"*Pardon*, Miguel. *Pardonne-moi, mon très cher* Miguel," she said, placing her fingers gently on his cheeks. "I … I haven't been seeing things clearly these days. I suppose I've been living in a kind of dream world, believing in things that weren't true, and refusing to believe in those that were. But I … I think perhaps I needed to sink all the way to the bottom, in order to finally realize what's important in my life, or what should be. I'm truly sorry I hurt and frightened you Miguel, so truly sorry. But … oh dear God, how can I be sure that I won't reach this point again? If I could promise you that I'd never again feel so despondent, so desperate, I would … But how can I be sure?"

"Claudette," pleaded Miguel. "If you'll let me, I'll make you sure. I'm prepared to have you laugh at what I'm about to say, but I've gone this far and there's no turning back. Let me love you, Claudette. Let me show you what it's like to have someone love you completely. Let me end your search. The love you've been yearning for, it's right her in front of you, if you'll accept it."

Claudette looked at Miguel, seeing the mixture of hope and stoic resignation in his eyes. He wanted so much to believe that he stood a chance with her, and yet he was prepared to accept her derision.

"I can't laugh at you, Miguel," she said. "I've never found you less laughable than you are now. I see only your sincerity and yes, your love. I … maybe I'll disappoint you. It could be that I won't come up to your expectations. No … don't say anything. Let me finish. It could be that I'll be a letdown to you. You place me on a pedestal, Miguel, but I'm just a woman made of flesh and blood."

"I know that, Claudette. But you're also a woman who needs so desperately to be loved."

"Yes, and I do care for you, Miguel, much more than I ever realized. I'll give you the chance, I'll give us the chance, to make some sense of our lives. I'm willing to try, if you are."

"Oh, Claudette," cried Miguel. "How can you even ask!"

Claudette lowered her face to Miguel's, placed her lips on his, and as he kissed her and she felt the depth of his love from the moment their mouths touched, she knew that making love to him would be unlike any other time in her past. True, he did not possess Fareed's virile physique and his features lacked Kacem's extraordinary beauty, but when his hands would touch her naked body, they would do so in the loving exploration of someone who truly worshiped her and when he whispered words of adoration they would come from his heart, and their sincerity would make up for his physical shortcomings. As Claudette gave Miguel a lover's kiss for the first time, she thanked God she had been given a second chance at life.

CHAPTER 37

▼

The morning light shone through the curtains of Marcie's bedroom window reflecting off Jean-Richard's golden hair as he slept. Marcie lay by his side, having awakened at sunrise, too excited to keep her eyes shut any longer on this, the first of a lifetime of mornings she knew they would welcome together. She had spent the last hour or so staring lovingly at Jean-Richard's face, childlike in sleep, the pain and torment of yesterday's confession erased from it—forever she hoped. Marcie never wanted to wake up in a place other than where she was now, next to the man she loved.

Dave felt Lateef's breath on the nape of his neck as he lay naked cradled in Lateef's arms, his back against Lateef's chest, his buttocks pressed into Lateef's groin, Lateef's legs entwined with his. Dave was the older, the stronger of the two, and yet how secure he felt at this moment, how protected, how adored. The dam which had held back all Lateef's repressed desires over the past months had finally broken, allowing them to surge forth and inundate Dave with the power of the young Moroccan's passionate love.

Although Miguel had dreamed countless times of what had taken place last night, he still could not believe that his fantasies had finally come true. They had been so impossible, so ridiculous. He, the sad and lonely clown, daring to dream of his love being returned by the beautiful and desirable woman of his fantasies. Such things happened only in fairy tales, and he was much too old to believe in children's stories. But come true they had, and now here he was, awake ahead of Claudette, in her kitchen preparing the breakfast which he would serve her in bed, the very bed on which his dreams had become reality.

A new day had dawned in Aïn El Qamar. A morning of miracles.

It was difficult on a morning like this for Marcie not to think about the turns life took. For months on end her relationship with Jean-Richard had been going nowhere, both of them retreating from total commitment until finally yesterday the barriers which had been separating them had been destroyed at last. Yesterday morning she had woken alone and without hope that her life might change. And yet today was unlike any other that had preceded it.

Marcie knew that she would never forget the agony which had filled Jean-Richard's eyes as he had told her of the afternoon when he had discovered his wife in bed with another woman. She had reason to hope now, however, that she would never again have to see that expression. Knowing what had tortured Jean-Richard for so many years was the key which would allow her to keep his love as strong as it was at this moment and to prevent him from ever losing faith in her as he had in Nicole.

It would not be easy. Nicole had played the role of the devoted wife to perfection, so brilliantly in fact that when the truth at last came out, her duplicity had been all the more brutal and shocking. No wonder Jean-Richard had resisted any commitment after such a traumatizing experience.

If he had had any idea of Nicole's true sexual orientation, the shock might have been less wounding, but she must have been a consummate actress, so convincing that when her infidelity was finally discovered, Jean-Richard had been unable to separate fact from fiction. Now it was up to Marcie to prove that her love was true and sincere, to calm his fears, and to demonstrate again and again with her words and her deeds that she would never love anyone but him.

He was waking now, his eyelids flickering. Opening them to catch his first glimpse of Marcie in the morning light, he smiled and whispered, "*Je rêve encore?* I must still be dreaming. You're ... you're too beautiful to be real."

"I'm as real as you are," replied Marcie, leaning down to press her lips against Jean-Richard's. "You're my only reality."

And then his arms were around her, and they were making love once again, and Marcie knew that there was no better way to greet the day than in the arms of the man you loved.

Later, as they lay satiated and content in each other's embrace, Jean-Richard said to her, "We're going to have to make some decisions about the future, you know."

"You mean about the job you've been offered in France?"

Jean-Richard nodded. "When I wrote to René to see if there was a place for me at his school, it was to escape from Aïn El Qamar, to escape from you. I couldn't bear the thought of having to face you every day next year."

"But there's nothing to be afraid of anymore."

"The only thing that scares me now is the possibility of not seeing you every day for the rest of my life."

"A slim possibility," reassured Marcie.

"But you understand my dilemma," continued Jean-Richard. "The job in France is still inviting. I've been in Aïn El Qamar for ten years after all, and another would make eleven. That seems an awfully long time to stay in one place, especially when my reasons for remaining here in the past simply don't exist anymore. Not since yesterday. On the other hand, I know how much you love Aïn El Qamar and that you've been counting on a second year here. Besides, officially I'm still expected to return next year. You can see, there's a great deal to think about, to take into consideration."

"*Écoute-moi*, Jean-Richard," said Marcie, tenderly caressing his cheek with her fingers. "Whatever decision you make will be the right one with me. If we stay in Aïn El Qamar, of course I'll enjoy seeing the things that I've missed this first year, and since I'll be seeing them with you, they'll be all the more special. But if we go to France, things will be just as special for me there, for the same reason. So please, Jean-Richard, take your time before making up your mind and know that no matter what decision you come to, no matter where you choose to go, I'll be glad to be by your side. No. Not glad. Overjoyed."

"There are times," said Jean-Richard, "when I find it hard to believe that I haven't dreamt you."

Marcie heard these words, and knew that behind them was the memory of a woman with whom Jean-Richard's entire relationship had been based on falsehood. And once again she was struck by the enormity of her responsibility towards the man who depended so wholly on her to restore his faith in love and decency.

"Please, Jean-Richard, *mon amour*," she said earnestly. "Don't ever doubt my absolute commitment to you, not for a moment. Remember that whatever you decide, wherever we end up going, not just next year but during all the rest of our years together, I promise you that I'll always be beside you, wanting you, needing you, and giving you all the love that's in my heart."

"Then nothing else matters," said Jean-Richard, and took her into his arms once again.

They had made love most of the night, but, thought Dave now as he lay in Lateef's arms, their bodies pressed together as one, it was the kissing that was the best. It was the kissing that meant the most.

Not that the rest hadn't been extraordinary. For a first-time beginner, Lateef had been a quick and voracious learner. After having spent all but the past several hours of his friendship with Dave in denial about his sexuality, it was if Lateef had now determined to throw shame to the wind. He wanted to try everything, sucking, being sucked, fucking, being fucked, and a few other activities that were new even to Dave. But he did so with such joy and innocent enthusiasm that neither Dave nor he could feel there was anything dirty or indecent about what they were doing.

But it was the kissing that was the best. Dave had had sex before; he was no slut, but neither was he a virgin. Yet with Lateef he realized that not since he came to Morocco had he actually made love. There was a difference, Dave thought to himself now, and even acts that might seem pornographic when described in explicit detail became beautiful when they were shared between two people who truly loved each other. But kissing was the purest expression of the melding of two human beings, and it was with a kiss that he chose to wake Lateef on this, their first morning together as lovers.

Rotating his body so that he was now facing Lateef, Dave touched his lips to Lateef's eyelids, then to his cheeks, and finally to his lips. The Moroccan stirred in his sleep, and his eyes opened to look into Dave's.

"Morning, baby," said Dave lovingly, and their lips met once again. Lateef's breath was sweet even in the morning, thought the American as he savored the magic, the wonder, the splendor of Lateef's kiss.

Later, after breakfasting, they showered together, then got dressed for school.

Now, sitting in the living room waiting for Lateef to finish a history assignment, Dave once again caught sight of the note from Kevin, hastily scribbled at the Aïn El Qamar bus station and given to a former student who happened, fortuitously, to be passing by at that moment. The note read: "Dave. I guess you could say I got fired. I'm on my way to Rabat to talk to Barry. Ask any of the students. They'll tell you what happened. More later. Love, Kevin."

Oh Kev, thought Dave now. You really blew it this time. Several of Kevin's students had stopped by last night—between lovemaking sessions, thank goodness—to fill Dave in on the afternoon's events. They were naturally quite concerned about what had happened to their favorite teacher, but even more than that, they were infuriated at Monsieur Rhazwani's outrageous actions. This was the final straw, they declared. They would "find a way to make the bastard pay."

Dave had managed to reassure them that Kevin would be all right, that this would have little effect on his future career, and they had left, somewhat calmer. But Dave remained anxious about his best friend's well-being. How could he get in touch with Kev? Was he staying in a hotel? He might be crashing with another volunteer, but Peace Corps teachers did not have telephones, even in the big city. Dave would have to wait for a telegram, or a pay phone message left with one of the French teachers in Aïn El Qamar, perhaps with Claudette.

"I'm ready if you are, Mr. Casalini," said Lateef from the living room doorway, and looking up, Dave suddenly recalled an image from last October, Lateef standing where he was now, slender but muscled, dark-haired and heartbreakingly handsome, wiping his hands with a dishtowel, smiling his dazzling smile. Still breathtakingly handsome, still dazzling, but his beauty magnified a hundred-fold, a thousand-fold, a million-fold, in the eyes of the man who was now his lover.

"I adore you, Lateef."

"I adore you, too," was Lateef's reply.

And they were off to school.

Miguel Berthaud checked the milk he was heating for the *café au lait*, but it was only just beginning to get warm. He wanted it piping hot and the coffee too. Everything must be perfect for this first breakfast shared with Claudette.

Miguel shuddered to think what would have happened if he had not visited Claudette last night. If she had gone through with her dreadful suicide plan, his life today would be empty and desolate instead of richer and more joyous than ever before.

Claudette said that she cared deeply for him. This was not the same as love, and Miguel was well aware of the difference, but she was willing to accept his love for her, and if she could not yet give him hers in return, Miguel knew that there was room to hope that she would come to love him eventually. He would certainly do all in his power to earn her love, and for the time being her affection was already more than he had ever hoped for.

Tiny bubbles had now formed around the edge of the sauce pan in which he was heating the milk, and steam was rising from the coffee pot. In a second or two the bread he was toasting would be golden brown, and everything ready for him to surprise Claudette. Miguel put the coffee pot on a large silver tray and poured the hot milk into a pitcher next to it. There were already two coffee cups, a plate, sugar, spoons, knives, butter and jam on the tray. Removing the crisp toast from the oven, he piled the plate high with it and, pleased with his preparations, picked up the tray to carry it into the bedroom which he had shared with Claudette.

As he entered the room, she looked up at him from the bed where she lay, and smiled. Even first thing in the morning without her makeup she was exquisite, thought Miguel, and wondered how she could ever have had doubts about her beauty.

"*Tu t'es réveillée?*" he asked. "I didn't realize that you were awake."

"You didn't really expect me to remain asleep with all that racket you were making in the kitchen, did you?" she asked.

"*Pardon, pardon,* I … I was trying to be quiet," stammered Miguel, ashamed to have disturbed Claudette's sleep.

"Silly man," she said, chuckling softly. "I was only teasing. Show me what you've brought me."

Miguel walked over to the large double bed, sitting down on it next to Claudette and placing the breakfast tray between them.

"*Tu es adorable,*" she exclaimed, and kissed him impulsively. "You did all this for me?"

"Is it such a surprise that I should want to show you how much you mean to me?"

"It's just that … no one's ever made me breakfast in bed before, except for Saadia of course. I'm truly touched."

"I told you last night, Claudette. I'd do anything for you. Making breakfast is nothing, no more than a gesture. Ask me to go with you to … to Siberia and you'll find out how much I love you."

"I'd much rather you accompany me to Tahiti," said Claudette, taking a slice of toast and spreading it with jam. "This is heavenly, Miguel," she exclaimed as she took a bite. "Or to Hollywood," she continued, "or to Rio for *Carnaval* …"

"Would next weekend in Marrakesh do?" asked Miguel.

"*Ce serait splendide!*" declared Claudette, taking a sip of her *café au lait*. Later, when she had finished her coffee and toast, she continued, "Do you know, dearest, this morning I feel as if I'm waking up a new woman, as if the craziness and desperation of the past months had never existed. And I … I'm looking at a Miguel Berthaud I never gave myself a chance to discover. The old Claudette laughed at your jokes and took you for granted. The new me says, 'Thank you Miguel for your love and let me be worthy of it.'"

"No, Claudette, let me be worthy of you," insisted Miguel.

"You'll move in here, won't you? I can't bear the thought of having you even a few doors away."

"Won't Jean-Richard find the arrangement a bit crowded?" asked Miguel, doing his best to hide his joy. It scarcely seemed real that Claudette actually wanted to live with him!

"Jean-Richard, for all I know, may be making plans of his own. I do believe we'll be hearing wedding bells in the near future."

"Jean-Richard? *Marie?*"

"Yes, Miguel. Married. People are going to be quite surprised by the Jean-Richard they'll be seeing in the next few months. Besides, can you see Marcie Nelson settling for an arrangement other than marriage?"

"No, not Marcie," admitted Miguel. "And ... What about you, Claudette?"

"*Moi?* A blushing bride? I don't think so, Miguel. It's just not in my nature."

Miguel turned away, not wanting Claudette to see the disappointment her reply had caused him. Of course marriage had been too much to wish for, but still he had hoped ...

"I've hurt you," said Claudette perceptively. "Please understand, Miguel. It has nothing to do with you. Marriage has simply never been my dream. I've never felt that a march down the aisle dressed in white, ironic as that might be, would bring me happiness, and I don't feel that way even now. Happiness is being with someone who can make me happy, whom I can make happy. And Miguel, that someone is you, because you love me, and because I need so desperately to love and be loved. So live with me, and share my life, *d'accord?*"

Miguel could scarcely choke out a reply. It was so much more than he had ever dared to hope for. "As long as you need me, Claudette," he promised, "I'll be by your side. Just don't let it end too soon."

"It won't, Miguel. I swear to you," vowed Claudette, leaning over to kiss him, her mouth open and passionate.

"We have to get ready for school," protested Miguel, though he did not attempt to pull himself from Claudette's embrace or to stop from returning her kiss.

"To hell with school," replied Claudette, and pulled Miguel down on the bed beside her.

CHAPTER 38

▼

It was the same waiting room they had sat in yesterday, and the faces of those who waited might have been the same anxious ones as had been there before. But it no longer seemed the same depressing, even frightening place. It was morning now, and with the dawn of a new day came hope. Michèle could see that on the face of Doctor Marouane as he strode over to greet her and Kacem. He was smiling broadly as he extended his hand, and Michèle could sense at once that the news was good.

"*Bonjour, docteur.* How's Janna today?"

"*Elle va beaucoup mieux,*" replied the doctor. "Much much better. Sleep is a wonderful healer. You'd hardly recognize your friend this morning as the same young woman you brought in yesterday."

"Then she really is going to be all right?"

"It's as I told you last night," explained Doctor Marouane. "We're still going to keep her here for several more days. I've contacted the Peace Corps health director who's agreed that Mademoiselle Gallagher should spend the next few days in the Clinique, though he wishes to see her in Rabat once she's been released. To answer your question, I truly believe you will find your friend in perfect shape by the end of the week, and that there will be no aftereffects of her fall."

"Thank God," said Michèle gratefully. "Could ... could we see her now?"

"Of course. When I spoke to her earlier, I was able to tell her that it was you, *mademoiselle*, and your American friend who had found her in time and brought her here. She's most anxious to thank you herself."

Michèle and Kacem shook hands with the doctor, then walked towards Janna's room. Michèle knocked, and was surprised to hear the strength in Janna's voice when she answered, "Come in."

The head of the bed had been cranked up to allow Janna to sit comfortably while talking with visitors. Smiling as they entered, she said ironically, "I guess your troubles only start when you think they're over, huh?"

Michèle leaned over and kissed Janna on both cheeks. "Yours really are over now," she said, and Kacem nodded agreement.

"I certainly hope so," said Janna.

"How do you feel?" asked the Frenchwoman.

"Not bad, considering how I bashed my head. But the doctor says the pain will go away soon."

"Do you remember anything of what happened yesterday afternoon?" asked Michèle.

"Unfortunately, I'm not one of those lucky people who contract amnesia from a head injury. I can recall everything much too clearly, up to when I tripped on something and fell. After that, there's nothing. Nothing except the fear that it was then that the really horrible thing happened."

"If you're worried that the person who attacked you finished what he started, then set your mind at rest," said Michèle. "Dave and I are both convinced that whoever did this to you got so frightened when you fell that he decided to high-tail it out of your house as quickly as possible."

"Then I guess it was lucky that I tripped," commented Janna, "though I suppose that in saving my virtue, the fall might have taken my life."

"Don't think about that now," said Michèle. "Just concentrate on getting better. We were all so terribly worried last night. We knew how far you'd progressed from the low you hit a few months ago, and then to see this happen to you …"

"I love you for being so concerned," said Janna. "The doctor tells me that you never left my bedside."

"How could I?" asked Michèle. "Until I knew you were better?"

"You didn't tell the doctor I'd been attacked, did you?" asked Janna worriedly.

"No, we just said you'd fallen," replied Michèle. "I didn't think the doctor needed to know any more details. And as far as the police are concerned, we wanted to wait until we had a chance to talk to you, to find out more about what you remembered, and if you had any idea who did this terrible thing to you."

"I'd rather we keep the police out of this," declared Janna. "In fact, I was only worried about two things when you came in. First, I didn't know if I'd been raped. You've pretty much set my mind to rest about that. Secondly, I was afraid that you might have involved the police in this. Thank God you haven't."

"I don't understand," protested Michèle.

"*Moi non plus*," added Kacem. "*Celui qui a fait ça à Janna doit être attrapé et puni.*"

"Kacem agrees," translated Michèle. "He says the person who did this too you should be apprehended and punished."

"No," repeated Janna. "I don't want the police brought into this. My reputation in Aïn El Qamar has already suffered enough as it is. I refuse to have my last months here ruined by another scandal. You know how all too many people feel about rape. They think the woman wanted it, provoked it. And unfortunately, although it goes against all my most enlightened feminist beliefs, I think that in this case I may have had something to do with what happened, however unintentionally. The person who attacked me was one of Marcie's students, a rather spooky young man who'd convinced himself that if I'd given myself to Lahcen, then I'd do the same for him. That's what put the idea into his head in the first place. I don't feel my actions justified what he tried to do. It's his immature, sick little mind that's guilty. But he might not have gotten his crazy ideas if I hadn't been so public about my involvement with Lahcen. And other people, my neighbors, my students … if they find out that someone tried to rape me, then that'll be the final confirmation that I really am a tramp. No, Michèle, Kacem. I've got to stay in Aïn El Qamar for another couple months, and at the moment the most important thing for me is to be at peace with the world around me."

"Well, if that's the way you want it," said Michèle, "then neither Kacem nor I are going to go running off towards the police station. I can understand that you don't want to be the center of any more trouble. But what about the nutcase who attacked you? We can't just let him get away, can we?"

Janna told Michèle and Kacem about the previous times she had come into contact with the young student. "All we have to do is find out his name from Marcie. Then someone, perhaps Dave, or you Kacem, can have a talk with him. Convince him that it's best he leave Aïn El Qamar. Threaten to go to the police if he doesn't get out of town right away."

"All right," agreed Michèle grudgingly. "It still doesn't sound completely fair to me, to just pretend as if nothing had happened, but I can see your point. I understand how you want your last months in Aïn El Qamar to be happy ones."

"Don't you two have classes this morning?" asked Janna in an attempt to change the subject.

"Not until nine, so we still have a few more minutes," explained Michèle. Then, turning to Kacem, "*Je lui dis notre nouvelle?*" and he nodded, smiling.

"You have news?" asked Janna, who still recalled a bit of her high school French.

"Yes," answered Michèle. "Kacem and I are getting married!"

"Oh how wonderful!" exclaimed Janna, though when she tried to lean over to kiss Michèle, she winced at the pain her movement caused her. "I guess I'd better just lie still for a while longer," she added lamely.

Michèle kissed Janna instead, and explained how she and Kacem had reached their decision, though she deliberately left out mentioning Claudette's later intrusion.

"I'm so happy for you both," said Janna enthusiastically. "I'm sure this will make your whole situation much easier. Have you set a date?"

Michèle nodded. "June 15th. That'll give you enough time to get your strength back. We want you to be our maid of honor."

"I'd be delighted to," said Janna. "Really, I'm thrilled for you both. And then? Have you thought about next year?"

"I think we'll be in Aïn El Qamar for at least one more year," answered Michèle, "though at least now if Monsieur Rhazwani decides to get rid of Kacem by transferring him somewhere else, the transfer will have to be for Michèle Hajiri as well. After next year and maybe the one after that, who knows? Actually, if we can get ourselves posted in Casa or Rabat or one of the other big cities, I don't see any reason not to stay in Morocco indefinitely. We're close enough to France to spend several months a year there during summer vacations. Besides, I'm a bit of an adventurer, you know. I don't really need all the comforts of home."

"*Ce ne sera pas facile,*" said Kacem.

"He says it won't be easy," translated Michèle. "There'll be both French people and Moroccans who'll disapprove of our marriage. But I think we're strong enough to face their opposition. *N'est-ce pas*, love?" She smiled at Kacem.

"*Bien sûr,*" he replied, and then in English, "Of course."

"Of course you'll be strong enough!" agreed Janna. "But shouldn't you be heading for school? It's quarter of nine."

"All right, but we'll be seeing you later today, okay?" replied Michèle, kissing Janna once again.

Kacem extended his hand to Janna, though when the American woman reached out to him, he too kissed her on both cheeks.

And then they were off on their way to school, driving past groups of students walking to class and women heading towards the market. The day promised to be a lovely one, warm and sunny, but not oppressively hot.

"I was just thinking," said Michèle as she drove into the school parking lot, "how lucky we are, and how strange it is that the most tragic and devastating of events can lead to two people finding out that they can't live apart even one second longer. From now on, Kacem, my love, it's straight sailing ahead. I just know it."

"Not quite yet, I'm afraid," answered Kacem grimly. "Look out there, in front of the dormitory."

Michèle peered through the car window towards where Kacem was pointing. Past the spot where the gatekeeper sat, across the courtyard, there was a crowd of several hundred students gathered before the dormitory, standing silent and immobile. Their calm was ominous.

"But they should be in class," protested Michèle. "What's happening?"

"It looks, my love," said Kacem, "as if the twig has finally broken. After spending most of the year buckling under while Monsieur Rhazwani gave his orders, they've finally decided to fight back. The *proviseur*'s got a student strike on his hands."

CHAPTER 39

━━━━━━━━━━━━━━ ▼ ━━━━━━━━━━━━━━

The faculty members who stood in the *salle des profs* numbered perhaps three dozen. They were gathered in a semi-circle around Dave, who spoke to them, quietly and seriously. Ordinarily they would have been casually chatting, smoking, making last minute lesson plans, waiting for the nine o'clock bell to ring. But today they were silent as Dave explained to them what he knew about the strike. Marcie, standing hand in hand with Jean-Richard, had a worried expression on her usually sunny face. Michèle, holding Kacem's hand in public for the first time, also looked concerned. Laurent Koenigsmarck was conspicuous by his absence, but it was said that he was secluding himself until Christiane's memorial service.

"It seems that the strike is due to a combination of factors," Dave explained.

"*Et comment vous le savez?*" asked one of the French teachers who had joined the group late.

"As I said to the others, I was walking to school with one of my students, and as I sometimes do, I was planning to enter through the students' gate, which is closer to my house than the main one is. When we got near school, we could see a crowd standing outside. I wondered what was happening, but since there's no way to see past the metal gate and find out what's going on on the other side of the wall, I asked my student to go up and try to learn what was causing the trouble. I deliberately stayed behind, because if by chance there was some kind of protest going on, I thought they might not take too kindly to finding a teacher in their midst."

"*Oui, d'accord,*" commented the latecomer.

"So, to continue, I waited for a few minutes until my student returned and was able to give me most of the facts. Apparently, a group of boarding students decided to take matters in their own hands after Monsieur Rhazwani literally came to blows with Kevin Kensington yesterday afternoon, and Rhazwani told him in no uncertain terms that he was no longer welcome to teach at Lycée Mohamed Cinq, or even to set foot on campus."

There were several exchanged glances of shock and dismay, and Marcie exclaimed, "But that's absurd! Kevin's a fabulous teacher!"

"I think the whole thing stinks, myself," agreed Dave, "and evidently so did the students, especially the *internes*. Kevin is without a doubt one of the most popular, and most respected teachers on this faculty. A group of *internes* decided to organize a hunger strike in order to protest Monsieur Rhazwani's decision. Not that going without the shit they're served is such a sacrifice."

"*Qu'est-ce que vous voulez dire?*" asked another of the French teachers, and Dave thought to himself how detached his foreign colleagues were from the life their students led.

"Apparently, deals are made with local butchers and vegetable vendors and bakers to provide the school with day-old or two-day-old food, stuff that they wouldn't ordinarily sell. The school pays less than they would for fresh food, the vendors are happy because they're making money they wouldn't normally make, and Monsieur Rhazwani pockets the difference."

"*Sal voleur!*" exclaimed the French teacher.

"Yes, he is a dirty thief," agreed Dave. "In any case, when the *proviseur* heard about the hunger strike, he went over to the cafeteria and told the protesters that if they didn't eat, he'd have them thrown out of the dormitory, not just for the rest of the school year, but permanently. You can imagine the effect that had on the other students, the ones who'd only been watching. They were so incensed that right away they joined their schoolmates in refusing to eat. Then things started getting rough. It wasn't just the food, and Kevin's being dismissed. It was the added height and broken glass put onto the school wall, and restrictions on their weekend passes, and censorship of the Cinéclub films. It was the way Monsieur Rhazwani punishes students by refusing them honors during *conseils de classe*, or by beating their hands with his stick. When you put all of these things together, it's not hard to see why the students reacted the way they did last night."

"You said things got rough," declared Kacem. "How?"

"It seems they started breaking dishes and glasses, throwing food on the floor, even smashing a few windows. Needless to say, Monsieur Rhazwani got out of there fast. Then, later, he sent word via one of the dormitory monitors that all boarding students were to be suspended until they returned to school with a parent. Not only was it unjust to kick them out of the dormitory, but for most of them it's next to financially impossible to bring one of their parents back to Aïn El Qamar. It's not for nothing that they're on full government scholarships. Apparently, when the *proviseur* issued his order, that's when the students decided to organize this morning's strike."

"Then it was just a case of one straw finally breaking the camel's back?" asked Marcie.

"That seems a particularly appropriate way of putting it," said Dave. "Especially in Morocco."

"But what is it they want?" asked Michèle.

"At first it was just to be allowed back into school and also, of course, to have Kevin's dismissal rescinded, but now it seems they're also calling on the head of the school board—the *délégué*—to fire Monsieur Rhazwani. Or at least to reassign him to another city. In other words, they want him out."

"They're not the only ones," said Kacem under his breath.

"Be that as it may," continued Dave, "they've stacked cafeteria tables in front of the gate in order to block it from the inside and keep the day students from coming into school."

"*Mais pourquoi ça?*" asked one of the assembled teachers.

"Because they're afraid that some of the *externes* would want to cross the strike lines and attend class. The kids who live at home have less to complain about, and some of them might not want to support the *internes*. The boarders did send out a couple of envoys before they put up the tables, though, to explain the situation to the ones outside. That's how my student was able to find out this information."

"But what are their plans?" asked Jean-Richard. "Specifically I mean. Up to now they've just been standing quietly outside the dormitory, though I must admit to having heard a few catcalls when some of us entered school."

"From what my student told me, that's all they intend to do. They don't want this strike to get violent, like the ones a few years ago when the whole country was in protest."

"I remember that all too well," commented Jean-Richard. "Those were terrible days."

"These kids were scarcely out of primary school then, but they have long memories. They don't want the police involved. They just want to make it clear to the *délégué* that they're serious about what they're doing. They want him to hear their demands, and they hope that with the weight of the evidence on their side, he'll agree to do as they're asking."

"I hope their tactics work," said Kacem.

Dave was about to answer him when the bell rang, indicating that nine o'clock classes would normally begin in five minutes.

"You don't mean they're ringing the bells as if nothing were happening?" exclaimed the Moroccan disbelievingly.

"*C'est vrai*," said Jean-Richard. "You've just arrived, so you don't know. According to the *proviseur*, we're to go to class as usual, and stay there until the next bell rings."

"But that's preposterous!" exclaimed Michèle. "We can't go and sit in empty classrooms for the rest of the day."

"That's what he expects us to do," said Dave, and many of the other teachers nodded, though it was clear from their faces that they were not pleased with Monsieur Rhazwani's order.

"And did you go to class earlier?" asked Kacem.

"At eight o'clock I did," replied Marcie, "but ..." She looked up at Jean-Richard for his reaction. "Now that I know what's really going on, I'm going to stay right where I am."

"*Moi aussi*," said Jean-Richard, clasping Marcie's hand, confident now that with his job offer in France, he could risk the consequences of Monsieur Rhazwani's wrath.

"I'm with both of you," declared Dave, "and I'm sure Kevin would be too if he were here with us."

Kacem and Michèle had been quietly discussing the matter, and now they announced, "We also will be remaining in the *salle des profs*."

A few other French and Moroccan teachers said that they would follow Dave and the others' lead, but the majority of the faculty members began gathering their things to head towards the empty classrooms.

"Don't you realize that this issue concerns us as well as the students?" exclaimed Dave. "Which one of you hasn't been a victim of Monsieur Rhazwani's harassment?"

"I know I'm being a traitor to those of you who are willing to challenge the *proviseur*," said Paul Durand, one of those teachers who were about to leave the *salle des profs* for their classrooms. "But we who are obeying orders have our jobs and futures at stake. I know I speak for most of my fellow teachers when I say that I hope this strike succeeds, but I don't dare make a public protest in case it fails."

"*Nous aussi*," agreed a number of the other teachers.

Dave nodded that he understood, but Kacem cried out, "You've got no guts, no principles!" Michèle tugged on his arm, but Kacem continued, "If you really wanted to see the last of Monsieur Rhazwani, you'd stay here and fight."

"You're wrong to say that we have no principles," countered Monsieur Durand. "But we also have families to think about. I can't let my wife and my two daughters go hungry."

The second bell rang then, and Paul Durand and most of his French and Moroccan colleagues headed towards their classrooms, leaving only Dave, Michèle and Kacem, Jean-Richard and Marcie, and three or four others in the *salle des profs*.

"Well, now the wait begins," commented Kacem as he and the other teachers took seats, some on the edge of the central table, others on wooden chairs scattered around the room.

"God only knows what the result of all this will be," added Michèle as she gripped her fiancé's hand. "God only knows."

CHAPTER 40

▼

If it was possible, they were even more united in their purpose now than they had been several hours ago when they had first gathered outside the dormitory to begin their strike, long postponed through fear and lack of determination. They were still afraid, but now they were resolved to win. Only one thing was on their minds this morning, and that was for Monsieur Rhazwani's reign of terror to finally come to an end.

For most of these students the past months had been nightmarish. Their freedom had been curtailed and their rights infringed upon. They had been forced to eat stale bread, and meat whose stench occasionally reeked throughout the dining hall. Their soup was often hardly more than lukewarm water with a few hard vegetables tossed in. And for boys coming from families where the woman of the house was invariably an expert at making even the most meager meal delectable, creating tasty spicy dishes from the slightest of ingredients, such garbage being served them was an outrage. Where was the money the government allocated for their nourishment, money which would be ample to feed twice their number were their mothers in charge of spending it? Where else could it have gone but into the pockets of the *proviseur*, who, incidentally, was getting fatter by the month?

It wasn't only their food, though, that had made Monsieur Rhazwani their most loathed enemy. It was their abominable study and living conditions as well. While the *proviseur* claimed that his restrictions on weekend passes were intended to help the students' study habits, there was hardly one of them who didn't feel the severity of these restrictions, and few found it easy to learn their lessons in such an oppressive atmosphere.

Inside the dormitory, things were yet worse, and had been since the very beginning of the year when Monsieur Rhazwani had confiscated their portable radios. Later, he had even threatened to punish those students who attempted to lead group sing-alongs in an effort to brighten the monotony of their evenings and weekends. Occasionally blankets and sheets disappeared, and the *proviseur* refused to replace them, forcing the hapless students to buy new ones or to bring their own from home, or, as was often the case, to go without.

There were other grievances, but the one which had finally provoked this long-delayed protest was the *proviseur*'s firing of Kevin Kensington. Even those students who had not been fortunate enough to study under him and feel his warmth and dedication knew of his outstanding reputation.

No, Monsieur Rhazwani had to be stopped, and striking against him was the only way to make their plight public. The citizens of Aïn El Qamar must be made aware of what the *proviseur* was doing, and the *délégué* must be convinced to send him packing once and for all. There were risks in their protest, and the students were well aware of its potential consequences, but the possible long-desired results outweighed those dangers.

Earlier, a number of students had demanded a more vocal demonstration. Some had suggested that they chant protest slogans or shout obscenities at the administrators or the more unpopular teachers should they catch a glimpse of them. There had even been those who had insisted that they literally go on a rampage, breaking furniture, smashing windows, perhaps taking over the office wing and destroying school documents and records.

Calmer elements had prevailed, though, mainly through the insistence of two students, Mustapha Najeed and Salah Guirrou. Najeed had been one of the first to go against Monsieur Rhazwani. It was he who, back in October, had led a group of students to a meeting with the *délégué* which had resulted in the reinstatement of the student council. It was only later that Monsieur Rhazwani had been able to take his revenge by giving Najeed an *avertissment* at the December *conseil de classe*. Since then, the student had been waiting for the right moment to organize a strike. His co-leader Guirrou was the boy whose best friend had been punished by Monsieur Rhazwani during Mr. Kensington's class last March. He had remained one of Mr. Kensington's greatest champions since then, and it was he who had insisted that the students do something about this popular teacher's dismissal, especially since it had been due to the American's defense of Guirrou's right to stay in his English class despite what the *proviseur* termed his "unexcused" absences.

Together the two had organized yesterday evening's hunger strike, which had led eventually to this morning's protest. And it was Najeed who had spoken to the students several hours ago when a number of those gathered in front of the dormitory had proposed a more radical uprising.

"Listen!" he had shouted above the din. "Listen and remember! Remember what happened only five years ago. We were all too young then to have been part of the strikes that swept across Morocco, but many of us have brothers who were involved in them. Do any of you remember seeing an older brother come home with his head bloody from the club of some police pig? How many of us can forget that group of students who were standing on a third floor landing at this very school when a bunch of police thugs came after them, pushing them to the edge of the landing, beating them with their sticks until three of the students were pushed back so far that they fell over the ledge and to the ground below? Two of them were killed at once and the other died later. That last one to die was my cousin Abderrahim, and I watched him in the hospital as he lay there, death only hours away. Do you want the same thing to happen today?"

During Najeed's impassioned speech, the crowd of students had stood in rapt silence, some of them wiping tears from their faces as they recalled their own memories of those turbulent times. Even the ones who had shouted for a more violent revenge were quiet now, no longer screaming for blood.

"What we want to do today is to show everybody, especially the *délégué*, that we're solidly united in our demand that Monsieur Rhazwani no longer be *proviseur* of this school."

And so they had decided to demonstrate their anger without creating havoc, and as time had passed, they had felt their resolve harden, their unity become tighter. Salah Guirrou had spoken of Mr. Kensington, of his dedication to his job and his love for his students, and Ahmed Shakiri, who had borne the blows of Monsieur Rhazwani's stick, had told of his loathing of the *proviseur*, and of how Mr. Kensington had apologized in tears for not having stood up for Shakiri. Then Guirrou had repeated the story of Mr. Kensington's reaction to the *proviseur*'s surprise interruption of yesterday's class, of the courageousness he had shown in insulting the arrogant self-righteous man to his face. Even Mohamed Hashimi, who had led the students in their refusal to take Mr. Kensington's surprise test last March, was singing the praises of his now favorite teacher, calling for solidarity against Monsieur Rhazwani.

The morning hours had passed, slowly, quietly. The students had seen most of their teachers walk foolishly towards their empty classrooms as the nine o'clock and then the ten o'clock bells had rung, not allowed to return to the *salle des profs* until the ten minute break between classes. Absent from these was a small group who remained in the faculty room, and whom the students could occasionally glimpse through the windows: Mr. Casalini, Mademoiselle Perrault, Monsieur Hajiri, Miss Nelson, Monsieur Moreau, and several others, and most recently Mademoiselle Verlaine and Monsieur Berthaud who had arrived together just before ten o'clock. These dozen or so were among the most admired teachers at Lycée Mohamed Cinq, and the knowledge that they supported the student protest only served to strengthen their resolve to continue their silent struggle to the very end. They must see to it that Monsieur Rhazwani would never again be able to harass and bully them. They must not let him win once again!

CHAPTER 41

—————————▼—————————

As Monsieur Rhazwani sat behind his desk listening to the report being relayed to him by one of his assistants, he began to realize that he had a true battle on his hands, not one of physical force, at least not yet, but one of wills. On one side were the students and a small band of rebel teachers. On the other stood he alone. Not for a minute, though, did he doubt that the final victory would be his. He had not gone from his humble beginnings to becoming *proviseur* of Lycée Mohamed Cinq without learning how to emerge from a struggle triumphant.

"The situation is definitely worsening, *monsieur*," the assistant was saying. "When the last bell rang at three o'clock, there were nearly twenty teachers choosing to remain in the *salle des profs*."

"Twenty traitors, you mean!" exclaimed the *proviseur*. "But how can that be? This morning there were no more than eleven or twelve who dared to side against me."

"That's true," admitted the assistant, a young Moroccan in his mid-twenties who had been doing his best throughout the year to remain in the *proviseur's* good graces, knowing the potential consequences of finding himself in Monsieur Rhazwani's disfavor. "At noon, there weren't more than a dozen in the *salle des profs*, while thirty or more teachers had proceeded to their classrooms as usual."

"As they were required to," said the *proviseur*. "Regardless of whether or not there are students to teach, all faculty members must perform their tasks as is their duty. Did you not announce this earlier?"

"Yes, of course I did, *monsieur*. I was in the *salle des profs* at eight o'clock this morning and again at eleven and I returned later this afternoon when classes resumed at two o'clock."

"You must not have spoken forcefully enough! Go back and tell them again!"

"But *monsieur*," protested the assistant. "I was very forceful. Most of them simply nodded their heads and did as they were ordered."

"As they are obliged to according to their contracts," declared the *proviseur*. "But what about the others, the ones who stayed?"

"They ..." The assistant hesitated, indisposed to repeat the striking teachers' exact words. "They said ... that they preferred to support the students." What the teachers had actually said was, "Monsieur Rhazwani *peut aller se faire foûtre*," meaning, "Monsieur Rhazwani can go fuck himself," but of course there was no way of knowing how the *proviseur* would react to hearing this insult repeated so literally.

"Who is behind this infamy!" asked Monsieur Rhazwani furiously.

"Monsieur Hajiri seemed to be their spokesman, but Monsieur Casalini spoke up too." The administrator felt guilty naming names, but better theirs on the *proviseur*'s black list than his.

"But what about the others? What about those who've started to join this ... this mutiny!"

"I don't think you have to worry about them, sir. I'm sure they're not really against you, just tired of sitting by themselves in empty classrooms."

"But that's their job!" screamed the *proviseur*. Damn them! When was the school faculty finally going to realize who was in charge at Lycée Mohamed Cinq? How long would it take to convince them to bow to his authority? He had been struggling all year to show students and teachers alike that his word and his alone was law. And yet it seemed that some of them remained unconvinced. Well, they would find out when all this was over how much their jobs depended on staying in the *proviseur*'s good graces. Many heads would roll once the present situation had calmed down and everything was back to normal.

"You are to return to the *salle des profs* at four o'clock, and announce that any teacher who refuses to perform his duties will be subject to immediate dismissal, do you hear me!"

"*Oui, monsieur*," said the assistant, though it was obvious from his tone of voice that he had no desire to announce the *proviseur*'s ultimatum.

Monsieur Rhazwani himself, however, had no doubts that the teachers could be cowed into submission. They were rebellious now, but that was only because they were too naive to realize the consequences of their insurrection. They would soon come to their senses and accept the fact that it was on Monsieur Rhazwani's side that their bread was buttered. No, it was not the teachers who were the *proviseur*'s primary concern, but the striking students.

According to reports he had been receiving, their solidarity was gaining in strength, not weakening, and their insistence on non-violence was proving irritating to say the least. How Monsieur Rhazwani itched to get back at them, to punish them for their insubordination as they deserved to be punished. He had ordered the school chef not to serve them lunch, but the students had apparently not even tried to enter the cafeteria at noon, so his first attempt to discipline them had failed miserably.

At two o'clock, the strikers had sent a signed petition to the *proviseur*'s office and another slipped under the gate and delivered to the *délégué*. The petition, which enumerated their grievances, demanded that Mr. Kensington be reinstated to his position and that Monsieur Rhazwani be dismissed from his job, or barring that, transferred elsewhere. When the *proviseur* had received his copy of the petition, he had torn it at once into tiny shreds, then telephoned the *délégué* for his reaction. They had been in contact by phone since early that morning when it had become apparent that a potentially explosive situation was developing. During their most recent conversation, the *délégué* had once again assured the *proviseur* of his support. This had come as no surprise to Monsieur Rhazwani, who was confident that the *délégué* approved of the firm hand with which he had maintained order at Lycée Mohamed Cinq throughout the school year. There had not been a single demonstration or protest rally since the start of classes. Until today, damn it. Until today. The *délégué* cared no more than did Monsieur Rhazwani how well the students ate. Like the *proviseur*, he knew that weekend passes were only an excuse for *internes* to fritter away their time when they ought to be doing their schoolwork. He might make a pretense of being forward-thinking and enlightened, but his primary concern was in outward appearances, and who could argue that Lycée Mohamed Cinq appeared to be running smoothly? Without question, the *délégué* was Monsieur Rhazwani's ally, and a malleable one at that.

On the other hand, the man was an imbecile! How else to categorize someone who insisted that no police be brought in to resolve this intolerable situation? Didn't the *délégué* realize that nothing would get the students back into class faster than the glimpse of a few dozen armed men in uniform, heading in their direction, clubs raised threateningly, guns ready if needed? But no, the man insisted that such an intervention would lead to violence, and the *proviseur* had been unable to convince him that the students, knowing what had happened a few years ago, would be too afraid to fight back. The *délégué* was at best naive, and at worst a fool, and the *proviseur* was incensed at his audacity in trying to tell him how to run his own school.

"Is there anything else, *monsieur*?" asked the assistant, who had remained in the *proviseur*'s office for further instructions.

"No, that will be all for now," replied Monsieur Rhazwani. "Proceed as you have been doing, making note of which teachers are obeying orders and which of them are traitors. Keep me posted on any developments which may occur, and prepare the announcement you are to make at four o'clock."

"Very well, *monsieur*," replied the assistant, nearly bowing as he took his leave from the *proviseur*.

Alone once again in the office he had furnished so plushly at the beginning of the school year, Monsieur Rhazwani felt his resolve toughen. He had not come this far only to relinquish everything for which he had fought and lied and cheated since his childhood, certainly not because a group of rebellious students thought they could impose their will upon him.

He must never capitulate, not to the students, not to the teachers, under no circumstances, not today, not ever. That would only lead to disaster, to his stagnating in small town *lycées* for the rest of his life—if he was lucky. This was what infuriated him so about the *délégué*'s not allowing him to summon the police. This protest would be over in minutes if only Monsieur Rhazwani's wishes were obeyed.

Lighting an imported French cigarette, the *proviseur* leaned back in his thronelike armchair and tried to think of an argument that might persuade the *délégué* to see things more rationally. He was still reflecting on this dilemma when the telephone rang. Picking up the receiver, Monsieur Rhazwani found himself speaking to the very man who had just been occupying his thoughts.

"*Oui, monsieur le délégué*," said Monsieur Rhazwani, giving him a report of the most recent developments as recounted by his assistant. "Yes, I do realize that this is the first student strike at Lycée Mohamed Cinq this year." The fool! Didn't he see that the *proviseur* could in no way he held responsible for today's events, that he had in fact performed miracles in maintaining stability and order throughout the year?

"Have you any new suggestions as to how to end this unfortunate situation?" the *délégué* was asking.

"My proposal remains as originally stated," replied the *proviseur*.

"And I have already given you my answer. If we can find no better solution than to let time take its course, then that is what we shall have to do. You'll hear from me in another hour or so."

Hanging up, Monsieur Rhazwani found himself fuming with rage and frustration. Just because the students were behaving calmly was no reason to believe that they were not determined to carry on with their stated goals until the bitter end, until the *proviseur*'s bitter end. No, the police must be called upon to put a stop to this uprising.

The *délégué* was technically Monsieur Rhazwani's superior, but the man was wrong, dead wrong. Following his orders was the surest way to ruin. If the *proviseur* was going to go down, then let it be on his own terms.

But he would not go down! Once the strike was over, and it *would* be over soon if the *proviseur* had his way, the *délégué* would see how mistaken he had been in indulging the recalcitrant students and their ridiculous demands.

By acting decisively now, the *proviseur* would not only put an end to this mutiny but guarantee his present and future supremacy at Lycée Mohamed Cinq as well.

Picking up the receiver, he spoke resolutely to his secretary. "Get me the chief of police," he ordered. "At once!"

CHAPTER 42

▼

Oh God, thought Larbi. How could he have been so foolish? Only an idiot would have chosen to hide among the *internes* in the school dormitory.

At first it had seemed such a brilliant idea, to be safe and unrecognizable, just one among so many nameless faces. Then had come the students' decision to go on strike, and now Larbi was worried, very worried. It was already nearly four o'clock and the strike showed no sign of coming to an end. He was sitting with a group of *internes* in front of the dormitory. There was little or no movement around him. Students left only when they had to use the lavatories or to get a drink of water. They conversed quietly, the subdued hum of their voices broken only by scattered catcalls and boos directed at those teachers who walked towards their classrooms as if nothing were amiss.

So far there had been no sign of Monsieur Rhazwani, no official response from the school administration, though the sight of the *proviseur*'s messengers occasionally monitoring the crowd indicated that he was well aware of the students' actions. Nor had the *délégué* come to any decision yet. Apparently the student who had delivered their demands to the head of the school board had returned with nothing more than his assurance that he would read their petition carefully. That had been hours ago, and still no answer had arrived.

Larbi sat next to his friend Kébir Azzouzi, who was playing cards with several of the other protesters. Kébir knew nothing about what had happened yesterday, had no idea that his schoolmate was doubtless being hunted for Ms. Gallagher's murder at this very moment. Larbi had told him only that he needed a place to crash until morning without specifying the reason, and Kébir, not a very bright or suspicious sort, had welcomed him unquestioningly.

Larbi had desperately needed last night's sanctuary in order to collect his troubled thoughts, in order to find at least some momentary calm after yesterday's emotional turmoil. Never, though, had he planned to stay this long. But for the strike, he would already be hours away from Aïn El Qamar by now, hiding in Casablanca or Rabat. He would now be one of a million or more faceless strangers, far from the reaches of the Aïn El Qamar police.

But there had been pressure on him to stay among his friends, to join in their demonstration against Monsieur Rhazwani, and Larbi had feared that they would turn against him if he tried to get away. Besides, the gate leading out of school was blocked by the tables piled high against it. He could not even hope to scale the wall, for this had been impossible since the day Monsieur Rhazwani had ordered an additional three feet to be built onto it, and even if he had somehow managed to reach the top, there was barbed wire and broken glass up there. Larbi had no choice but to remain with his friends and fellow students.

All through the morning and the early afternoon, Larbi had watched the main entrance at the other end of the deserted courtyard in the vain hope that he would see Ms. Gallagher walk in, thus proving to him that yesterday had been only a nightmarish figment of his imagination. But there had been no sign of her, as he had known there would not be, and as the hours had dragged by, the reality of what he had done had begun gradually to sink in.

He wanted to cry out to the other students, "I didn't mean for her to die! I only wanted what Cherqaoui had. It wasn't fair that one student should have all the luck and that I should get nothing! I only wanted to fuck her, not kill her! It was an accident!" But of course he could say nothing, not even to his friend Kébir. Who would trust his word against the evidence of Ms. Gallagher's corpse?

So he had sat with the other students in strained silence, willing himself to believe that the strike would end soon, thereby allowing him to steal away from the school grounds and head for the bus station. With luck, he would still have time to escape from Aïn El Qamar before the police uncovered evidence or witnesses to incriminate him. But twelve o'clock noon had passed, and two p.m., and now it was almost four and still there was no indication that the administration would capitulate or that the students' resolve would weaken. And Larbi was beginning to feel real fear. For the first time it occurred to him that this strike might continue on for days, and that certainly by the time it did end, every policeman in Aïn El Qamar would be on the lookout for him. What if someone had seen him entering or leaving Ms. Gallagher's house? What if they had gotten a good enough look at him to give the police a detailed description? What if someone had actually recognized him and had told the police his name? Larbi knew it was madness to remain at school, but there was no exit. He was trapped, powerless to attempt an escape, and fearful of drawing attention to himself by feigning illness or using some other excuse to persuade the strikers to open the gate for him. Oh God, he prayed. What can I do?

"Is something wrong, Larbi?" asked his friend Kébir who had just finished another round of cards with his classmates. "You look upset."

"I … it's nothing," stammered Larbi. "I was just thinking that my aunt and uncle are probably wondering where I am now."

"But I thought that's what you wanted," said Kébir. "You told me you'd had a fight with them and that you needed to get away for a while. I thought you wanted them to worry, so that they'd stop bossing you around you. At least that's what you said."

"Uh … that's right. That's what I said. But I … I guess I've changed my mind since then. They're not such bad people after all. Don't you think I might be able to sneak away from here, just for a few minutes, only to go home and let them know I'm all right?"

"Not on your life," replied Kébir. "And keep your voice down, or the others will hear you. Listen, Larbi, if you tried to leave now, our friends would think you were betraying them. They'd never let you go."

Larbi nodded his head in resignation. It was as he had feared. He was locked up inside the school walls with nowhere to run and nothing to do but wait here until he was found out and arrested.

Kébir turned back to his friends who were starting another hand of rummy, and Larbi lowered his head in despair. He had never felt so terrified or so powerless in his entire life. All year long he had watched Ms. Gallagher behave as if he didn't exist. Even yesterday he had failed in his final vain attempt to have her. And now there was no way for him to flee from school. He wanted to scream out his frustration, but he held back his cries, sitting with his head bowed, hoping against hope for some miracle that would bring the strike to an end.

He didn't know how much time had passed when he became aware of a commotion behind him, and upon raising his head, he saw that Kébir and his friends had stopped their card game, leaving the cards strewn on the ground before them. They were on their feet now, and talking earnestly. As Larbi rose, he noticed that most of the other students were standing as well. Suddenly, he felt the air heavy with danger and a horrible sense of expectancy. What in the name of Allah was happening?

"Police!" cried one of the students, and at that moment Larbi too became aware of the sirens coming closer and closer towards them.

Oh God, he thought in panic, the blood running cold through his veins. Why hadn't he realized that where there were strikers, police would surely follow? The very people from whom he was trying to escape were now heading in this direction, and once they had seen his face ...!

All around him there was commotion and the nervous shouts of his fellow students. They were saying that the hours of calm were over now that the police were on the way to break up the demonstration. There were exclamations of "Let's get the pigs!" and "We'll show them who's in charge!" One student screamed out, "Now's our chance to get back at them for what they did to our older brothers!"

But then the voice of Mustapha Najeed rose among the babel of excited, apprehensive cries.

"No!" he shouted. "We must not provoke them! They'll be armed! We must not make any show of force or they'll be sure to fight back, and rocks and fists are no match for clubs and guns. Everybody, sit down! Sit down and join hands! And let no one make the slightest move to strike back at the police! Our only hope is to remain non-violent. We must show the *délégué* that we mean business and that we will not budge from our position. If we give the police any grounds to hurt or injure us, our numbers will be weakened and we're sure to lose in the end. Our victory can only come from the strength of our numbers and from our courage!"

Najeed was a persuasive orator, and by the end of his speech, the students were once again seated, their hands linked, their cries for blood stilled.

The sirens were nearer now, and there was an expectant hush among the students as the wail grew louder. The police were clearly approaching the main entrance, and as the other students realized this too, they like Larbi were filled with dread.

They're going to trap us! thought Larbi in sudden terror. Piles of cafeteria tables blocked the student gate, and the police would be coming towards them from the only other exit!

"Stay calm!" shouted Mustapha Najeed. "Remember! Our only hope is in non-violent resistance."

But Larbi Faress had already lost hope. He had known from the moment he first heard the sound of the sirens that it was over for him. The police were not only coming to put an end to the strike. They were coming to get him too. No matter how far he ran, no matter how hard he searched for places to hide, they would find him eventually and their punishment would be merciless. Better to end it once and for all than to pursue this pointless attempt at escape. It served no purpose; he was only seeking to postpone the inevitable. The time had come for him to pay for Ms. Gallagher's death. The time had come for justice to be rendered.

Just let it be over quickly, he prayed.

CHAPTER 43

▼

Throughout the long morning and afternoon hours, Marcie had listened as one after another of her colleagues had recounted their clashes with Monsieur Rhazwani during the past school year, and it had slowly dawned on her how fortunate she especially had been. It seemed that she and she alone had somehow avoided the surprise inspections, the bigoted critiques, the unfair judgments. And yet thankful as she was for her luck, not for a moment did she question her decision to stand beside her friends. The stories they had to tell of their countless run-ins with Monsieur Rhazwani had only served to convince her that she was right to support them in their struggle for simple justice. For the strike to succeed, it needed the active involvement of as many teachers as possible and not just those who had been most victimized by the *proviseur*.

And in fact, the twenty-odd faculty members who chose to be in the *salle des profs* now were not only those who had class at this hour. She and Jean-Richard did not teach on Tuesday afternoons, for example, but like several of their co-workers, they had resolved to spend this entire day in the teachers' room, lending their support to the student protesters.

Earlier, Jean-Richard had gone out to buy sandwiches and soft drinks for the striking faculty, returning with a deck of cards as well. Marcie now found herself observing a bridge foursome, Jean-Richard and Dave against Michèle and Kacem. She was doing her darnedest to follow the game, but unfamiliar as she was with the terminology in French, and lacking a sound knowledge of the rules, she was finding this a daunting task.

As she watched the game progress, Marcie thought she caught a faint wailing sound in the distance. Was there a fire somewhere, or had there been an accident near school? Then, as the wailing drew closer, a more awful possibility struck her.

"Jean-Richard!" she exclaimed, interrupting the bridge game. "Listen to the sirens. It sounds as if there are police heading this way."

Jean-Richard put down his cards at once. "*Mais ce n'est pas possible!*" he gasped. "I can't believe it!"

"Rhazwani must be insane!" exclaimed Dave. "Those kids have been sitting there quietly all afternoon. There hasn't been even the slightest threat of violence."

"The man is an animal!" declared Kacem in fury, rising to look through the windows which faced the dormitory where the students were gathered. Earlier in the afternoon, someone had finally pulled the worn and faded curtains across the windows to insure the teachers' privacy, but now Kacem drew them apart in order to see what was happening. The trio of teachers who had been playing cards with him came up from behind so that they too could get a look.

"Those kids know what's about to happen," said Marcie, who could sense the students' fearful anticipation as she watched them. Some had stood up, but one of them was evidently directing his schoolmates to remain seated. She could hear his shouts, but as he was speaking in rapid Arabic, she did not understand his words.

The sirens were nearer than ever now. They must be almost at the gate. "There are two truckloads of them!" shouted Miguel Berthaud from where he stood at the window overlooking the main entrance.

"Oh my God, no!" exclaimed Michèle, who was standing next to Marcie.

"We've got to stay calm," ordered Kacem, his hand gripping Michèle's. "I don't think it's us they're after, but if they should attempt to come in, don't try to resist. They've certainly got clubs and they might even have guns. Stand firm, but don't do anything to arouse their anger."

Marcie was quaking with fear now, not so much for herself, though she realized that she might be in danger, as she was for the students who were, after all, only seeking justice, but would be no match for the police.

And then, suddenly, a swarm of policemen were rushing past the window where she stood, moving not towards the *salle des profs* but straight in the direction of the striking students. The sight of the clubs they carried and of the guns she saw in their holsters filled Marcie with terror, and she could imagine what the students must be feeling now.

Marcie wanted to close her eyes, to block out the image of dozens of uniformed, helmeted policemen advancing menacingly towards the crowd of students who, though outnumbering them, were no match for the armed police. But she could not stop herself from watching the spectacle which was unfolding before her. She felt frozen, paralyzed, unable to turn away.

At first, though, it appeared that nothing was going to happen. The police had stopped perhaps fifty feet from the students, seemingly uncertain of how to react to this mass of peaceful yet determined protesters.

And then she saw him, her student, Larbi Faress, the one who had been pestering Janna that night back in March when Marcie had happened to find herself in front of her friend's house, the same one who had apparently assaulted Janna yesterday. So that was where he had been hiding, among the *internes* in the school dormitory. But if he was hiding, then why was he rising now?

"Oh Lord no!" gasped Marcie as she saw him begin to walk slowly and resolutely towards the police. He was shouting something, but his words were not clear enough for Marcie to make out. What in heaven's name was he saying? What could his intentions possibly be? Was he perhaps making some insane attempt to lead an attack on the police? What was going on in his tormented mind?

It was never revealed who fired the shot, not now, not in the investigation which followed. The information was evidently hushed up in order to protect the policeman who had fired so precipitously. But all who observed the shooting knew that they would never forget the sight of Larbi Faress as his body recoiled from the impact of the bullet, a crimson stain forming at his chest. Marcie would always carry with her the awful memory of his body crumpling to the earth, and of the screams of terror which followed.

Suddenly, everything seemed to be happening at once. The strikers had risen and were pushing towards the solid metal students' gate, attempting to remove the tables which blocked their exit. One of the policemen, apparently the one in command, issued an order to the other men, which Marcie learned later was a plea for no more gunfire. And in fact there was none. But no one tried to stop the police from charging towards the terrified students who were struggling to get the tables out of their way. Wildly, savagely, the police swung their clubs, screams piercing the air. Marcie could see student after student struck brutally, on the shoulder, on the arm, on the head, and bloody faces and bodies were everywhere. Some of the students were attempting to help their wounded friends, but then they too were subject to the swinging clubs of the crazed policemen

Then, at last, the gates were open, finally allowing the students to push their way out of the school, screaming all the time, holding injured arms or shoulders, their clothes drenched with blood, their own and that of their friends.

The police were, however, unwilling to halt their attack. They chased after the students through the open gate, leaving only the seriously wounded, perhaps a dozen of them, lying on the ground before the dormitory. Marcie tried to shut her eyes to the terrible gory scene, but she was powerless to look away. One boy lay with his arm twisted impossibly, and she winced at the thought of the agony he must be enduring. Another was endeavoring to rise, but he did not have the strength and soon fell back to the ground. And there was a third, who Marcie saw in absolute horror had had his skull cracked open, and she wondered in God's name how he would ever survive.

"Someone get in touch with the hospital!" she screamed. "Those poor boys need help!"

"I'm on my way already," exclaimed Kacem, taking Michèle's car keys from her.

Miguel Berthaud had come up behind them and was saying, "Some of us had better go out and see if there's anything we can do to at least let those boys know that help is arriving soon. But don't anyone move them. That will only make their injuries worse."

Jean-Richard joined Miguel and several others who were heading out to reassure the latest and by far the worst victims of Monsieur Rhazwani's reign of terror. Marcie stayed behind with Michèle, gripping her hand, praying that the students' injuries were not as grave as they seemed.

"Marcie," Michèle said suddenly. "I want to tell you something that you might find absurd, but please hear me out."

"What is it?" asked Marcie.

"The student who moved out towards the police right at the beginning, the one who started this whole melee, did you have the feeling that he was … that he was somehow asking to be shot? It may sound crazy, but I can't stop thinking that he actually wanted the police to do what they did."

"I don't know, Michèle," replied Marcie, "but you may be right." The thought had in fact forced itself upon her as well, and though she had tried to push it away, she now had to admit that Michèle's words might very well be the truth. At the moment, however, she was too drained to elaborate on her theory. Later, when she had calmed down, when the students were safe in the hospital, when she had had time to find solace in Jean-Richard's arms, later she would tell Michèle exactly who the student was and why he might have wanted to be …

punished. But for now she could only wait, still trembling, for help to arrive, and for Jean-Richard's return.

Out of the corner of her eye, Marcie thought she caught a brief glimpse of Monsieur Rhazwani peering out through one of the windows in the administrative wing. Before he disappeared, she was almost sure she had discerned a satisfied smirk on his ugly bloated face.

JUNE 1977

CHAPTER 44

▼

Rumors had been circulating for the past month, but when they were finally confirmed, the news spread like wildfire throughout Aïn El Qamar.

Janna was sitting in her living room on this hot June afternoon when she heard the doorbell ring. The maid went to answer it, returning with Michèle.

"I have news," announced Janna's friend as she entered the living room. "News which will turn your world completely upside down and inside out."

"Sit down," exclaimed Janna, turning to ask Halima to make them some iced Lipton tea. The Moroccan woman nodded, though her expression revealed that she still could not fathom why Westerners chose to drink their tea cold. Like most Moroccans, she preferred a glass of piping hot mint tea on even the most sweltering of days. "So tell me, Michèle," continued Janna to her friend, who had seated herself. "What is this earthshaking news? And it had better be good! Or have you forgotten that over the past few months I've been through enough shit to last me the rest of my life?"

"It's precisely because you need some welcome news for a change that I had to come let you know right away."

"Well, what is it?" insisted Janna.

"Monsieur Rhazwani's out, finished, gone from Aïn El Qamar as of this morning!"

"You're kidding," gasped Janna. "I … I'd heard stories, of course, but … I'd never really taken them seriously. How could I? It certainly seemed after the strike that the *proviseur* had come out the winner. You yourself told me that the students were so freaked out by what the police did that the classrooms were full until nearly the end of May."

"They were," agreed Michèle. "But that didn't stop Monsieur Rhazwani from getting what was coming to him."

"But how? When did you find this out? Who told you? I want all the details!"

"Kacem heard about it at school," explained Michèle, "just a while ago when he went in to check on the morning's mail delivery. Of course he had to stay long enough to discuss the news with the other teachers, so I didn't find out until about fifteen minutes ago. Once I knew, though, there was no way you could stop me from coming right over and telling you all about it!"

"Wow, Michèle, this is the first good news, I mean really good news I've heard since … since that pair of wedding invitations I received a few weeks ago."

"It was rather a coincidence, wasn't it," commented Michèle, "both Kacem and I and Marcie and Jean-Richard announcing our wedding plans for the second week in July? But you've got to admit that this news tops everything else!"

"It's … it's terrific news, for teachers and students alike. For all of Aïn El Qamar, in fact. But you still haven't told me what it was that finally made it happen. People have been complaining about the *proviseur* since October. Why now, and not before?"

"Kacem was right all along when he said that Monsieur Rhazwani would eventually end up hanging himself. That, love, is precisely what he's done."

"I don't understand," said Janna.

"Well," continued her friend, "according to Kacem, Monsieur Rhazwani was disobeying the *délégué*'s strictest orders when he called for police intervention in the strike last month."

"Oh Lord no," moaned Janna, thinking of the needless pain and injury and suffering the *proviseur* had so callously brought about. Not only had Larbi Faress, Janna's assailant, been killed; there had also been a second death due to severe head wounds, and nearly a dozen other students had been hospitalized with broken limbs. This did not even begin to count the emotional scars which had been inflicted on all the other students who, if they had escaped serious injury, would nonetheless carry with them the awful memories of their classmates being beaten until bloody, and the sound of the screams which had rent the air.

"Kacem explained it all to me when he got home from school just now," Michèle continued. "And what he said makes sense to me. From the very beginning, all the awful things Monsieur Rhazwani has done have revealed an almost obsessive hunger for power. He would never allow anyone but himself to wield authority at school. When he inspected you and Kacem and Jean-Richard and the others, it was because he wanted the final say in your teaching. When he took it on himself to punish our students, he was usurping our authority as teachers.

When he built on to the wall around school, it was to exert his dominance over the students, to refuse them any control over their own lives. The Cinéclub committee, the *conseils de classe*, the student government, they were all subject to Monsieur Rhazwani's whims."

"I understand all that," said Janna. "But you said it was his decision to call in the police that got him fired …"

"Exactly. Before the strike, the only people he alienated were the students and the teachers and the school staff. I know that sounds like a lot of pissed off individuals, but it wasn't in our power to do anything other than complain, and that was mostly among ourselves. But in going against the *délégué* by calling for the police, he was disobeying the one person in Aïn El Qamar who actually did have the power to get rid of him. Apparently that's just what happened. The *délégué* exploded when he realized that the *proviseur*'s insubordination had caused two unnecessary deaths. He immediately requested from the Ministry of Education Monsieur Rhazwani's immediate demotion, and the official transfer order arrived yesterday. Monsieur Rhazwani, our now ex-*proviseur*, was ordered to pack his bags and report immediately to an insignificant desert village on the other side of the Atlas Mountains! According to Kacem, he's on his way there even as we speak."

"Well," said Janna with a smile, "cliché or not, 'Good riddance to bad rubbish,' and personally, I hope he rots in hell!"

"That's what that little village sounds like," laughed Michèle as Halima returned to the living room carrying two tall glasses of iced tea with lemon. Michèle and Janna thanked her, and the Frenchwoman took a sip of the refreshing brew.

"*Mzian bezaff*," she complimented Halima in Arabic. Then, after the maid's rather lengthy reply, she asked Janna for a translation, promising herself to make a real effort to learn the language next year.

"She told you that she's glad you liked the tea," explained Janna, "but she's sure you'd enjoy a glass of hot mint tea much better."

"I'm not surprised," said Michèle. "Aïsha was always telling Dominique and me the same thing, and these days she's at a complete loss to understand how a Moroccan like Kacem could also prefer his tea iced." Michèle's maid had been working for her and Kacem since they began living together after the events in early May, her disapproval of the couple's premarital cohabitation tempered by her relief that Mademoiselle Michèle finally had someone to take care of her and protect her.

"Halima and Aïsha may prefer mint tea on a day like this," declared Janna. "But I'm much happier having mine iced."

"Iced is better," agreed Michèle. Then her face lit up and she snapped her fingers. "I knew there was something different today! Have you gone and bought yourself a refrigerator?"

"How did you guess?" grinned Janna.

"But that must mean ... Janna, is there something you haven't told me yet?" Michèle asked with an eager smile.

"I made up my mind yesterday morning," Janna announced. "I got out of bed and suddenly I knew that I couldn't leave Aïn El Qamar ... at least not yet. I called Barry Pennington in Rabat and told him this was one post he won't have to fill next year. At first he played devil's advocate and tried to get me to change my mind. But I stuck to my guns, and in the end he agreed to let me stay!"

Michèle put her glass down and leaned over to throw her arms around Janna. "That tops even the news about Monsieur Rhazwani! Janna, I am totally overwhelmed and absolutely delighted!"

"You'll make me spill my tea!" exclaimed Janna.

"Sorry, love," said Michèle, taking her glass once again for another sip. "Anyway, tell me what made you come to this decision."

"It just suddenly hit me that I had made a two-year commitment to the Peace Corps."

"But you've been in Aïn El Qamar for two years," protested Michèle.

"And what have I been up to this past year? I spent Fall trimester whimpering and whining about having lost Lahcen to the United States. Winter trimester I was stoned out of my mind most of the time. And Spring trimester, when I was finally getting back on my feet again, I got attacked, nearly raped, and ended up spending a week in the Clinique and another in Rabat waiting for official authorization of my return to Aïn El Qamar. By the time I was back, there weren't any more students left to teach. Don't you see, Michèle? I've really only had one good year in Aïn El Qamar, and back then I was still such a greenhorn that I hardly knew what I was doing. That's why I've got to stay. There's a year's worth of work remaining for me to do, both as a teacher and as a woman who needs to get back some of her self-respect. I owe it to my students, and to the school, and to Peace Corps, but most of all I owe it to myself."

"But aren't you worried about seeing Lahcen again, when he comes back from his year in the States?"

"I've thought about that, Michèle," said Janna reflectively. "Of course I've thought about that. But I think the only way for me to be sure that I really am over him *is* to see him again, if only for closure."

Michèle nodded.

"But you know what," Janna added with a smile, "I'm pretty sure that once will be enough!"

"Janna, I can't begin to tell you how thrilled I am that you're staying!" exclaimed Michèle, her face radiant. "Now that Monsieur Rhazwani's out, there's no reason for Kacem and me to want or expect a transfer in September. So the three of us will be together for another year! I can't tell you how happy I am. I'd really been dreading your departure."

"Well, you can stop dreading it, love, because I'm not going!"

"Now we really have something to celebrate!" said Michèle excitedly. "And there's even more reason for me to invite you to join Kacem and me this afternoon. We're having a picnic at Lake Bin El Ouidane with Marcie and Jean-Richard. Join us, will you?"

"Oh Michèle," said Janna apologetically. "I wish I could, but I promised Kevin I'd go to a farewell party he's throwing for his students this afternoon."

"So he's really leaving Morocco?" asked Michèle.

Janna nodded. "And he's pretty torn up about it."

"He's going to miss his students."

"That's not all he's going to miss," said Janna.

"What do you mean?"

"Our little Kevin's gone and found himself a boyfriend."

"You're kidding!" exclaimed Michèle. "When did this happen? And who's the lucky man?"

"His name is Jared," explained Janna. "He's an American. He works at the embassy in Rabat. Apparently, it's mutual. Kevin would be in seventh heaven, but he insists that there are just too many unhappy memories in Morocco for him to even consider staying. I've told him he's a fool, but you know Kevin. He's pretty stubborn, and about this he says his mind's made up."

"Since when have you two become so close?" asked Michèle. "I'm a bit surprised he even invited you to his party."

"You mean because of that scene in the *salle des profs* a few months back?"

"It did get rather ugly," commented Michèle.

"When I called him a … well, there's no need to repeat it now, anyway, when I said that, it was the *keef* talking, not me. I've been really unfair to Kevin. Sure, he let himself go overboard in his teaching, but he realizes that now, just as I realize that I let myself go overboard over Lahcen. Kevin's leaving Aïn El Qamar in a couple of weeks, and after the two years we've spent in the same town together, I'd like us to part on good terms. He said his students would be thrilled to have another teacher at the party, especially a woman. So I said sure, why not. That's why, dear friend, I have to turn down your invitation to spend the afternoon with you at the lake. But we'll have lots of other chances to do things together. I'm staying in Aïn El Qamar, remember?"

Michèle smiled. "We've been through some pretty rough times the two of us, love, but I think the road ahead is finally clear."

"Knock on wood," said Janna, tapping on the coffee table, and the two women began to laugh.

CHAPTER 45

▼

This was not the first time he had sat here, but as always Dave found the vista from Marrakesh's rooftop Café de France spectacular. From the table where he and Lateef sat drinking Moroccan almond milk, called *kass d'luzz*, the view they commanded of the Marrakesh *medina* was truly magnificent. From here they could relish the beauty of the thousands of closely packed rose-hued houses which made up the ancient walled city, the color and animation of the Jemaa el Fena square, the excitement of the tourist bazaars, and in the distance the endless palm groves that surrounded the centuries-old Imperial City.

"You were lucky to be assigned to Marrakesh," commented Lateef as he sipped the chilled *kass d'luzz*, his eyes scanning the panorama below them on this warm June day. The heat would have been stifling had there not also been a refreshing breeze in the air.

"*We* were lucky," corrected Dave, thinking that they had indeed been fortunate when he had gotten his assignment to administer the English oral component of the *baccalauréat* exam in Marrakesh rather than in some more remote or less exotic part of Morocco as had Kevin and Marcie. Those two were already back in Aïn El Qamar by now, having finished interviewing students and grading their level of proficiency in spoken English. But Dave, who had completed his last interview earlier this morning, was planning to spend an extra few days in Marrakesh with his new boyfriend before returning to Aïn El Qamar. It might be his last visit to the city, and he did not want it to end.

"I was just thinking," he said to Lateef, "how much I've changed in the past two years, or at least how much my attitude towards this country has changed. In the beginning I don't think I was ever able to forget how alien I felt, or how foreign everything around me seemed. Lately, though, I just feel like a person who happens to live in Morocco. I've stopped paying attention to the looks I get in the streets, and I don't feel so offended when someone tries to hustle me. Now, if I get charged extra for something because I'm an American, I just react like any Moroccan would, bargaining for a better price, and if the merchant won't come down, well fuck him."

"A lot of them probably wish you would," chuckled Lateef, playfully squeezing Dave's crotch under the table. "But you're mine! Especially this part of you."

"Lateef, we're in public," cautioned Dave, but secretly he was delighted in Lateef's quick and easy acceptance of his gayness after so many months, years probably, of denial.

"You were saying ..." Lateef removed his hand from Dave's privates, but kept it on his knee, lovingly.

"I was saying that I've finally adjusted to life in Morocco. Today, when we were walking through the square, did you notice how no one bothered me, even though the tourists were being harassed right and left?"

"Yes," said Lateef, and giggled.

"Oh, cut it out, Lateef," said Dave. "I know what you're thinking."

"What is that?" asked the Moroccan, still laughing.

"You're thinking that it's because you were with me that I got left alone."

"Yes," said Lateef through his laughter. "They figured that I was your guide, and since I'd gotten to you first, they might as well stay away."

"All right," conceded Dave. "That's partly true. But a lot of it does have to do with my own self-assurance. I've been through enough shit this year to know that I won't take any more."

"It hasn't all been bad, has it?" asked Lateef. Dave recalled the hassles he had gone through in obtaining his boyfriend's passport, the numerous trips made to Rabat for his visa and ticket, and finally Mandee's visit and the vicious letter she had written in an attempt to destroy Dave and Lateef's relationship. Her scheme had backfired, though, and in the end the bad times seemed but a brief nightmare. The future looked as bright as the Marrakesh sun which shone down on this glorious June day.

"Today, I only want to think about the good," said Dave, his eyes surveying the many different sights that their rooftop vantage point offered them.

The view was breathtaking indeed, and Dave was glad that he had brought his camera along with him on this trip, for without pictures it would be difficult to describe to his friends, whom he would see in another month, the panorama which presented itself in all directions under today's intensely blue summer sky.

He could already imagine how the pictures would turn out, and what his friends' reaction would be when they saw them. One photo taken by an obliging waiter would show a smiling Dave and Lateef at the cafe table where they sat now, and behind them the countless pink-painted blocks of houses which made up the Marrakesh *medina*, squeezed so tightly together within the walls of the ancient city that occasionally it became actually necessary to walk behind the person you were with, so narrow were the streets and alleys. Jutting up from the hodgepodge of houses were the minarets of mosques, now equipped with powerful loudspeaker systems, so that through the marvels of modern technology the chanting of the muezzin could be carried to all the neighborhood households when the time for prayer had come.

A second snapshot would show Jemaa El Fena square as seen from above, packed as always with locals and tourists alike, Moroccans and foreigners, a carnival-like assembly of snake charmers, fortune tellers, magicians, trained monkeys, and bearded old storytellers spinning enthralling yarns which had been passed down from generation to generation over hundreds of years. Crowds formed constant circles around these performers, and those unwitting tourists who tried to photograph one of the snake charmers or fortune tellers were promptly told that it would cost them twenty *ryals*, about a quarter. If one looked closely at Dave's photograph, one would also notice how many Moroccans in the square were going about their daily business as usual, mindless of the excitement and color of Jemaa El Fena, in many ways unchanged since the Middle Ages. These Marrakeshis had their own lives to live, and so they bicycled on, or trod along beside their donkey-drawn wagons, or headed on foot towards the shops where they worked. Dave's friends, when they saw this picture, would be sure to comment on the multitude of people they saw, for there were people everywhere, and in the distance busses and cars and taxis trying to crowd their way into the square. And finally, shooting up at the horizon, the minaret of the fabled Koutoubia mosque, the tallest building in Marrakesh.

Dave had taken other pictures, of course, one of himself standing in front of a tourist boutique's display of rainbow colored Moroccan shirts, caftans, dresses, *foqias*, and *jellabas*. He was proud of the embroidered shirt he had finally bought after bargaining the price down to nearly half of what the shopkeeper had originally demanded. Another picture would show the modern Hotel Le Marrakesh, where he and Lateef had gone discoing last night. The handsome couple had attracted the admiring and occasionally flirtatious looks of many of the other dancers, both male and female, but their eyes had only been for each other, as later that night alone in their hotel room had been their hands and their mouths and their hearts. Lovemaking with Lateef just got better and better, thought Dave. The Moroccan was gorgeous to start with, but seen through the eyes of love, and with the intimate knowledge of Lateef's most secret places, he was perfection, and Dave could not foresee ever losing interest in him, or desire, or love. This was forever, thought Dave. For always.

"Are you sad to be leaving all this?" asked Lateef suddenly.

Dave thought for a second and then replied, "You know something ... I really am, although at one time I probably would just have thought about how happy I'd be to get back to the States." That had been during the depths of his depression over Lateef's passport, when everything in the country had seemed unjust and putrid and corrupt. "But now I'm really going to miss it."

"I wish I knew how I was going to feel a few weeks from now," said Lateef. "It's hard for me to imagine what my life in the United States will be like. I don't know if I'll feel homesick, or scared, or if I'll be so excited and overwhelmed that I'll completely forget about Aïn El Qamar and everything else."

"I don't think you'll ever forget your roots," said Dave. "But honestly speaking, this isn't the country for either you or me. I want to live my life openly and truthfully. It's only recently that gay people have started being able to come out of the closet, but it's beginning, especially in cities like San Francisco and New York. Chicago will be good for both of us. I just know."

"What are you going to tell your parents about me?" asked Lateef. "I mean, they know you've helped one of your students with his passport and visa and school registration and all that, but ... aren't they going to be suspicious?"

"You make it sound as if we have something to feel guilty about," said Dave. "It's true I didn't come out to my parents before leaving for Morocco, but believe me, it's just about the first thing I'm going to do when I get back."

"Aren't you afraid they'll turn against you?" asked Lateef.

"That's always a possibility," admitted Dave, "but it's a chance I'm willing to take. If they can't love me the way I am, the way I love myself, then that's their problem and not mine."

"Have I told you lately how much I love you?" asked Lateef now, and had they been alone, this moment would certainly have led to a kiss and much much more. As it was, Dave contented himself with a smile and a discrete caress to Lateef's cheek.

"I love you too," said Dave, and then added, "and you know something. I've come to love Morocco as well. For me, Morocco is my school, and my students, and my friends, Kevin, and Janna, and Michèle, and even Marcie."

Lateef giggled. "Even Marcie?"

"Well, you know how all that cheerfulness used to drive me crazy. I didn't think anyone could be that naively optimistic twenty-four seven. But I've come to realize that she's got spunk, guts, inner strength, I don't know quite how to put it, but she's a lot more than I realized. And Morocco too, the way of life here. There's something to be said for the slow easy pace, and the sights and sounds, and the crowds at the *souk*, and of course the people. The past two years have been good ones, all things considered."

"But you'll come back," insisted Lateef. "We both will."

"Someday," agreed Dave. "But for the time being, it just seems to me that one really major chapter of my life is coming to an end, and who actually knows what's coming next?"

"It'll be good, Dave," reassured Lateef. "I just know it will."

"And what makes you so sure?" asked Dave, although he already knew the answer.

"Because we'll be together."

CHAPTER 46

▼

"Alors, le salaud est parti. The bastard finally got what was coming to him," declared a satisfied Claudette from where she sat poolside at the Hotel El Qamar. Miguel was with her, and the two of them had just heard the news of Monsieur Rhazwani's fate from Pierre Arrier who in turn had gotten it from Kacem Hajiri at school earlier that morning.

"Let's not even think about that son of a bitch any more," replied Miguel. "He was nothing but bad news from the first day he arrived at Lycée Mohamed Cinq. The best thing we can do now is just try to pretend he never existed."

Claudette nodded in agreement. "It feels so good to have it all over and behind us," she said lazily as she threw back her head, closing her eyes against the sun's radiance and letting its warmth caress her face.

The effect of the sun's rays was hypnotic, and Claudette found her mind wandering back to the recent past. The phrase "to have it all over and behind us" carried deeper meaning in it than even Miguel knew about, for there were some things she had kept private even from him, not wanting to hurt him, fearing that if he knew all her sins, he would love her less.

But in speaking of having it all over and behind her, she had been referring to a myriad of transgressions, from her liaison with Fareed, whose face, ironically, she could only vaguely remember, to the agony and hatred she had felt the night he had abandoned her, to the legion of young studs she had bedded after Fareed in a vain attempt to reassure herself of her desirability, to the humiliating meetings with the degenerate Monsieur Rhazwani, the thought of which still revolted her, and finally to her lunatic infatuation with Kacem which, she knew now, was mostly due to the fact that he was the one man who had resisted her, and was therefore the one man she must have, even if it meant deceiving herself into thinking that she was in love with him.

She was putting all these things behind her. With Miguel's love and devotion, she was making a new life for herself.

True, there were still moments when she wondered what it would be like if her lover possessed Fareed's hard muscular body or Kacem's exquisite sensitive features. However as their relationship had progressed, she had found her own feelings for Miguel the man, the human being, growing steadily day by day, until the point where now, when they made love, it was the emotionally satisfying experience that she had craved for so long. At one time she might have considered her relationship with Miguel a compromise, a settling for second or even third best, but she now realized that, at least in her own case, destiny had indeed saved the best for last.

"Claudette," Miguel was saying now. "Can you imagine how different Lycée Mohamed Cinq will seem next year without Monsieur Rhazwani? It's going to be like teaching in a brand new school."

"It'll be quite a change," agreed Claudette. But only one of many, she thought. Kacem and Michèle were to be married, which was all for the better. It would help the three of them forget the ridiculous pathetic farce which had been enacted over the final months of the school year. Jean-Richard and Marcie also planned to tie the knot, and in fact the Frenchman had already moved in with his American bride-to-be, astounding his friends with his new-found domesticity. Marcie's decision for them to live together before their summer wedding had come as a surprise to all, but she had declared that with or without a marriage license, she had no intention of spending another night apart from the man she loved. They had scheduled two ceremonies, one in Aïn El Qamar for their friends living in Morocco, to be celebrated the day after Michèle and Kacem's, and a second for Marcie's family in Wisconsin during the summer holidays. Dave and Lateef, the third new couple among Claudette's friends and colleagues, would more than willingly be planning their own wedding as well were it legally possible. Which left only Claudette determined to remain *Miss* Claudette, at least for the time being. Why jinx her happiness with a piece of paper? she thought. The status quo was wonderful and fulfilling enough.

The waiter had arrived now with the lunch Miguel had ordered for them earlier, and Claudette suddenly recalled the day she had heard Christiane Koenigsmarck ranting on about how "lousy" the service was at the hotel. It still seemed scarcely believable that she was dead, though now that Claudette had discovered more happiness with Miguel than she had ever dreamed possible, she found herself more generous in her judgment of Christiane. Laurent had left Aïn El Qamar a few weeks ago, soon after the memorial service attended by the town's entire expatriate community. Claudette had been taken aback, as had everyone else, when he had announced his intention to return to Aïn El Qamar next year. "There's no fucking way I can make this kind of dough in France," the bereaved widower had explained. Claudette didn't know whether to feel contempt for his cynicism or admiration for his courage. Well, he hardly deserved admiration; on the other hand, who was she to feel contemptuous of anyone, not after her own shameful wrongdoings.

"It's going to be a good year for us all, next year," said Miguel, taking a bite of his *croque-monsieur* sandwich. "For you and me, and for our friends, and for everyone at Lycée Mohamed Cinq. So many wonderful things have happened to us in the past weeks. After today's news about Monsieur Rhazwani, I think we have good reason to be optimistic."

"*Oui*, Miguel, *soyons optimistes*," agreed Claudette. "Life is just beginning for us."

The Frenchwoman was about to savor her first forkful of *salade niçoise* when she noticed Annie Forte, who taught geography, heading in their direction, and with her, wearing only tennis shorts, one of the most scrumptious Moroccans Claudette had ever seen. He was tall, handsome and virile, with light brown curly hair, almost as fair as a European, but strong, and with a broad hairy chest glistening with sweat in the summer heat. Just one look at him and she felt herself become moist between the legs, felt that old trembling sensation begin again.

"Claudette, *chérie*," enthused Annie. "*Je te présente* Kader Jebrouni. Kader is our new tennis pro. He's just arrived from Khenifra to work the summer months and perhaps into next year."

Claudette extended her hand, though she knew it would feel cold and clammy. His eyes were deep blue and piercing, his smile luminous and seductive. She was falling again, back into the bottomless pit that had almost claimed her a month ago.

"Kader," continued Annie, "*voici* Claudette Verlaine, our tennis champion. I'm sure she'd be a great match for you—on the tennis courts. And this is her ... friend, Miguel Berthaud."

As Kader Jebrouni shook Miguel's hand, Claudette recognized fear, unmistakable fear, in her lover's eyes. Clearly he had noticed her reaction to the new tennis pro, and was terrified. Suddenly Claudette knew that she must not surrender to her urges, for Miguel's sake and for her own as well. They were still there inside her, and perhaps one day they would become irresistible, but for now, resist them she must. She had come so far with Miguel. She must not go back to where she had been!

"*Je regrette*, Annie," Claudette said coolly. "I'm so sorry, *monsieur*. But you see, I've given up … tennis."

CHAPTER 47

▼

He had lived in Morocco for ten years, but incredibly, this was Jean-Richard's first visit to Lake Bin El Ouidane.

For Wisconsin born and bred Marcie, it was nothing new to spend a summer afternoon swimming and sunning beside a lake, but as there were so few of them in Morocco, today was a special treat.

Kacem still recalled with fondness his many childhood outings here with his family, but those had been years ago, and he had not returned since.

Michèle could not help comparing today's excursion with those she had been on to Lake Arrowhead with her Southern California lover, whose wife naively believed him to be away on business.

Today was, in different ways, a new experience for them all. The weather here in the Atlas Mountains, about an hour from Aïn El Qamar, was perfect, and the "Bin," the largest lake in Morocco, was the ideal place to spend the day, the perfect location for these four to celebrate their newfound happiness.

So this is what it feels like to be happy, thought Jean-Richard now, close to incredulous at the bliss Marcie had brought to his previously meaningless life. The lake beside which he was standing was a deep blue-green, surrounded by rolling hills where there was scarcely a sign of civilization. Occasionally one did catch a distant glimpse of the earthen dwelling of a Berber family, and once a group of young mountain boys had stood looking curiously at the quartet of visitors and listening to them speak their strange incomprehensible tongue. But for the most part the four friends felt peacefully isolated from the outside world, far removed from the pressures of teaching and the noise and bustle of Aïn El Qamar.

There was a Yacht Club down a ways from the small secluded beach where Jean-Richard and the others had chosen to spend the afternoon. Claudette was a member, and she occasionally came here to compete in a regatta. She had offered Jean-Richard the use of her membership card for his party, but Marcie had asked if they might find a more private spot, and the Frenchman, as had become his habit lately, had happily acceded to Marcie's wishes.

Before arriving at the lake, though, they had taken Kacem's suggestion that they visit the spectacular Cascades d'Ouzoud, a set of waterfalls just a half hour further into the mountains, and now, several hours later, Jean-Richard was certain that none of than had regretted the side trip. The falls had been a breathtaking sight he knew he and his friends would not soon forget.

After parking the Frenchman's car in the small lot near the entrance, the four of them had begun the long descent by foot into the gorge where the falls spilled their sparkling foamy water. The day's warmth had vanished as they had walked farther and farther down, along a narrow winding tree and vine surrounded path. Jean-Richard had needed to caution Marcie several times to watch her step, as the way was slippery and the grade steep.

Finally, when they had reached the bottom, they had gotten their first clear view of the falls. From a horseshoe curve in the cliff high above, the water plunged, not in one large cascade, but in perhaps a dozen smaller ones, sending out clouds of mist in all directions, meeting in a large round pool about halfway down, then continuing its rush to the bottom over a second, lower cliff, and finally filling a much larger pool where today there was a group of local children swimming. Beyond that the water continued on as a river which would eventually spill out into the Atlantic Ocean.

The four teachers had found a comfortable spot about halfway between the two pools, overlooking the playful swimmers, and there they had sat for nearly an hour, sharing the picnic lunch they had brought along, and the joy of their isolation from the world outside.

Then, somewhat reluctantly, they had collected their things and climbed back to the parking lot and to the warmth of the afternoon sun. From there they had driven to the lake, and now, another hour or so later, Jean-Richard and Marcie, wearing their swimsuits, stood hand in hand, their feet in the cool refreshing water, the Frenchman thinking how magical this afternoon was proving to be, and how much his life had changed thanks to Marcie.

"You look awfully pensive," Marcie said to him suddenly.

"How much will you give me for my thoughts?" he asked with a smile.

"Would a lifetime of happiness be enough?"

"More than I could wish for."

"So, what are you thinking?" asked Marcie again.

"The usual. That my life didn't end that day back in Paris when I found out the truth about Nicole. That in fact it began the day I met you. I realize now that it was love at first sight, at least for me."

"I feel as if I loved you even before we met," said Marcie, leaning up to kiss his cheek.

"It's taken both of us time enough to find our happiness," said Jean-Richard soberly. "After so long a wait, I think we deserve it."

"It wasn't always easy, *n'est-ce pas?*"

Jean-Richard shook his head, recalling the months he and Marcie had been kept apart by the secrets of his past. But there were no more secrets, and as Jean-Richard stood gazing at the tree-covered mountain peaks around the lake, feeling the breeze play with his hair, he knew that the memory of Nicole had at last ceased to haunt his present, and that he had found a reason to begin his life once again.

"Are you sure, Jean-Richard, really sure that you don't mind staying in Aïn El Qamar another year"

"You know that there's no need even to ask," replied the Frenchman. "Not only do I not mind staying, I *want* to. When I asked René for that job in Lyon, I was still trying to escape ... from my past, from myself I suppose. But all that's changed."

"You won't be bored? After all, it'll be your eleventh year in Morocco."

"*Non, mon amour,*" corrected Jean-Richard. "*Ma première.* My first, because it'll be my first with you. I'll be seeing everything for the first time through your eyes, and doing with you all the things I've never done before. I plan on eating *à la marocaine* at least once a week, and bargaining at the *souk* on market day. I'm going to summon up my courage and ... and learn to ride a camel! Well, at least learn to say something in Arabic other than *La bass* and *B'slama*. I'm ... All right, maybe I'm going overboard, but you know Marcie, even if I'd been in Aïn El Qamar for twenty years, I still would have turned down that job in France."

"Why? It really sounded like a good opportunity for you."

"It was," admitted Jean-Richard. "But René's keeping my résumé in his file, and he sounds pretty optimistic about my chances a year from now. No, Marcie, I would have decided to stay in Morocco in any case because leaving now would have meant depriving you of so much."

"But Jean-Richard, you know that ..."

"Yes, I know that you'd be happy anywhere so long as we're together. I would too. But I wouldn't be happy if I felt that I'd taken you away from a place that fascinates and intrigues you the way this country does. So we stay, and we make next year the best ever. *Et après* …"

"After that," continued Marcie, "we discover France together."

"Yes," agreed Jean-Richard. "And you know, I think I'll be discovering my own country for the first time as well."

"And perhaps someday … *l'Amérique?*"

"*Je ne parle pas anglais*!" protested Jean-Richard.

"I know your English is a lot better than you let on," smiled Marcie. "And it will get even better in time. Everything else has."

"*Comme par example?*"

"Like for example this …" whispered Marcie, and turned to kiss him, tenderly, searchingly.

The two had been wading gradually into the lake as they spoke, and now stood waist deep in the water. Jean-Richard surrendered willingly to Marcie's embrace, his sun-bronzed arms around her, his lips and tongue as eager as hers. It was fortunate that Michèle and Kacem had decided earlier to wander off on their own, thought Jean-Richard now, as he reached into the water to deftly lower the bottom of Marcie's swimsuit and begin a provocative probing between her legs. At one time in her life, Marcie would doubtless have felt compelled to protest, but not today. Today, the two of them were living a sensuous fantasy, Marcie's puritanical upbringing as abandoned as was Jean-Richard's fear of commitment. She was pulling down his own swim trunks now, rubbing against him with her sex, which his fingers had already primed. Jean-Richard could no longer restrain himself; his genitals felt as if they were on fire. Clasping Marcie's buttocks in the palms of his hands, he pulled her close, thrusting himself inside her, shooting his love deep within, filling her body and soul with the very essence of his being. And at that moment he knew, knew with all the sureness of his once wounded heart, that they belonged together, now, in the future, and in whatever lives they might live after this one had ended.

Later, as they stood on the shore drying themselves off, Jean-Richard heard voices approaching, and looked over to see Kacem and Michèle coming toward them. The couple looked absolutely blissful. Which makes four of us, thought the Frenchman, wishing at that moment that everyone on earth could experience what he had found with Marcie.

"I think it's about time we opened that bottle I brought along," he suggested. "Don't you?"

"Michèle and I have been wondering what you're going to treat us with," commented Kacem.

"*Moi aussi*," agreed Marcie. Jean-Richard had not told her what was in the foil-wrapped bottle he had put in the ice chest just before leaving Aïn El Qamar.

Jean-Richard hurried over to where they had left their picnic things on the secluded beach, and returned with the bottle and four wine glasses which he distributed among them.

"Well, open it and show us what you've brought along!" said Marcie excitedly, and then squealed with delight as Jean-Richard pulled off the foil to reveal an icy cold bottle of imported French champagne.

"Is it someone's birthday?" Kacem asked Jean-Richard.

"Does it have to be, for the four of us to celebrate just being together? I think that's reason enough."

"You're right," agreed Michèle. "How many people have the luck to find what we have this year—love, happiness, hope?"

"So open the bottle, will you!" ordered Marcie, and Jean-Richard popped the cork, causing the bubbly liquid to spill over the rim of the bottle.

"Save some for us!" exclaimed Michèle.

"There's still lots left," reassured Jean-Richard as he began filling the four glasses. Then, setting the bottle down on the ground, he raised his glass. "I drink to Marcie, who has proven to me that happiness truly does exist, and to Kacem and Michèle, who have shown us what real friends are. I propose a toast to our future. May every day be as good as today."

The four teachers raised their glasses to their lips, sharing at that moment not only the champagne, but also their closeness, and their friendship, and Jean-Richard's wishes for the future. As the Frenchman drank, feeling the bubbles tickle his nose, he looked at Marcie. Their eyes locked, and at that moment he could read her thoughts.

I don't need miracles, she was surely thinking. I don't need dreams. My miracles have already taken place and my dreams have become reality. I ask only that the future be as good as the present, no more, no less. Please God, don't let that be too much to ask.

And Jean-Richard realized at that moment that Marcie's thoughts were his thoughts as well, and that her wishes were also his own. And the two of them knew, as certainly as they could possibly know anything, that as long as they had each other, sharing their love, sharing their devotion, they need never ask for more. As long as they had each other.

And that would be forever.

CHAPTER 48

▼

His students were having the time of their lives, dancing to the latest music, smoking as many American cigarettes as they wanted, flirting with members of the opposite sex without feeling observed, and filling themselves with potato chips and punch and *café au lait*.

Kevin smiled as he circulated among them, but the sadness in his eyes attested to the pain he felt at seeing them all together for the last time. Kevin was indeed glad to have reunited those of his students who remained in Aïn El Qamar, including even a group of girls who had managed to find a way to come with or without their parents' consent. But at the same time he was filled with an almost physical ache in knowing that within just a few weeks' time, these young people would have become no more than a memory of his two years in Aïn El Qamar.

He was doing his best not to show his mixed emotions, of course, trying instead to be a cheerful host, smiling with pleasure at seeing his students enjoying themselves for a change, away from the hassles and pressures of school.

Kevin's living room was hot and smoke-filled, but no one seemed to be complaining, the students having long become accustomed to the dry heat that lasted throughout the summer months in central Morocco. What was undoubtedly a new experience for them was to be at a party where the music was Motown and Elton John, the punch an exotic American concoction called Kool-Aid (Kevin's parents had recently sent him a "Care Package" in the mail), and the mood free and relaxed. Kevin had attended Moroccan parties where the sexes remained isolated in separate rooms seated on *banquettes* throughout the entire festivities, spending most of the afternoon singing minor-keyed Arabic songs. He had vowed when he decided to throw this party that his own would be different, with movement, and rock music, and plenty of laughter and English conversation. So far everything seemed to be going as he had hoped, even better perhaps. At times he would hear his students speaking together in the language he had taught them, as if trying to make this truly an American party, and at those moments his sense of pride and accomplishment was barely containable.

He had expected a large turnout, but still he had been surprised to find that perhaps as many as fifty of his students had come. Luckily, he had ordered enough snacks from the local *hanoot* to feed them all, filled the small refrigerator with ice and ice water so that the punch would be refreshingly cold, and moved rest of the furniture into the bedrooms. There was plenty of room for the students to dance, and if there weren't enough places for them to sit and relax, so much the better. It just meant that they had to get up and dance again.

Kevin had joined them several times on the floor, and once when he had accepted the shy invitation of a female student to be her partner, he had been surprised and somewhat embarrassed to find the two of them dancing alone, the other students having formed a circle around them, urging them on, delighting in the sight of Mr. Kensington, usually so serious in the classroom, showing that he was as fun-loving as they were.

Most of the time, though, Kevin had been too busy to dance, hurrying in and out of the kitchen to prepare yet another bowl of punch or pot of *café au lait*, filling another serving dish with cookies or crackers or potato chips, and when he was in the living room, choosing another cassette to replace the one which had just ended and exhorting the students to "Get up and boogie!"

Kevin looked at his watch now and saw that it was nearly four o'clock. The kids had been here for almost two hours already, and still there was no sign of Janna. What on earth was keeping her? He'd told her to come a little after two. Why was she so late?

And then, just as he was thinking that she might never come, the doorbell rang, and hearing it over the din of the party festivities, Kevin rushed to see if it was Janna at last.

"I'm sorry!" she exclaimed at once. "I'm really sorry I'm so late, but at first I wasn't sure I ought to come right when you said. You know how Moroccans are about arriving on time. They don't. So I thought I'd be comfortably late, and then just as I was about to leave the house, a group of students stopped by to ask if I knew anything about the results of the *baccalauréat* oral, which I didn't, but I promised to drop by school and inquire for them, which I did just before I got here, but before that the electrician came to repair the bathroom light switch which wasn't working, and I wanted to stay and see exactly how much work he was doing and what kind, so I wouldn't overpay him, and also so that I'd know how to fix it myself if it ever went out again. So that's why I didn't get here on time. Forgive me?"

Kevin was nearly dissolved in tears of laughter.

"What's so funny?" Janna asked.

"You are!" exclaimed Kevin. "Here I was thinking that you'd decided not to come because of … well, because of the problems we had a few months ago, and instead you show up with this long tale of woe which you manage to get out hardly taking a breath between sentences. It's just not what I was expecting."

"Kevin Kensington!" exclaimed Janna. "How dare you assume that I harbor any kind of ill feelings towards you! You know damn well that I didn't mean what I said that day. So just stop jumping to absurd conclusions, and invite me the hell in!"

"Yes, ma'am!" declared Kevin, somewhat taken aback but relieved nonetheless. "By all means, come in!"

He was pleased to see that she'd dressed up for the occasion, wearing a short green summer dress which was elegant and special but not too fine to be appropriate for an afternoon party.

The students certainly appreciated her fresh prettiness as well, for there was a loud and enthusiastic cheer upon her entrance into the living room.

"I feel like a celebrity," commented Janna, as Kevin served her a glass of punch. "Even though I haven't taught most of your students, they all know me, and they seem to like me too. It's a nice feeling."

"I know what you mean," agreed Kevin, a tinge of sadness in his voice. Today would be the last time he saw most of them. "I know what you mean," he repeated.

"Come on, Kevin," admonished Janna. "Today's no day to be maudlin. And if you don't mind, can we sneak over to that corner and see if we can escape the limelight for a while? I think I spot an empty space."

The two Americans walked over to the place Janna had pointed out, and as she had hoped, they were now somewhat less on display.

"This is really good of you, Kevin," said Janna, indicating the partying students. "I've been much too intolerant of your attitude towards teaching. I thought that you were just on some kind of ego trip, but it's obvious how much you care about your students and they about you."

"You're right, Janna," said Kevin. "About both things. Teaching has made me feel special and loved, and so in that way it has been an egotistical thing for me. But that's only part of it. These students gave me back my will to live at a time I felt like I wanted to die. They're one of the reasons it's killing me to know that I'll be leaving Aïn El Qamar in just a few weeks."

"Just one of the reasons?"

"I assume you've heard about Jared," said Kevin, and Janna nodded. "I wasn't looking to meet anyone when I went to Rabat the afternoon before the strike, and I certainly wasn't looking to fall in love, but I did, and he's committed to staying at least one more year in Morocco."

"So change your mind and stay too!" exclaimed Janna. "I told you yesterday about my own decision to up for a third year. Why not do the same? We won't have Monsieur Rhazwani to kick us around any more! Or haven't you heard?"

"Could there be fifty students in my house without my knowing what's going on at school? That was the first thing I was told by the first students who arrived."

"Well, doesn't the news about Monsieur Rhazwani make you want to rethink your decision to leave Morocco? Especially now that you've met Jared?"

"I did push around the idea with Barry Pennington last weekend when I was in Rabat visiting my guy, you know, of maybe transferring to another city, so that Jared and I could be together, but Barry didn't seem too gung ho about it. I think he thinks I'm a bit of a basket case. I did create quite a stink back there, and I suppose in a way I'm to blame for the strike, so …"

"Oh fuck!" Janna blurted out suddenly.

"What is it?" asked Kevin. "Did I say something?"

"No, damn it. I forgot something important." Janna pulled out an envelope from her purse. "This was at school for you when I stopped by earlier. They were going to send over a messenger with it, but I said I'd deliver it personally. Here. Sorry."

It was a telegram from Rabat.

"Well, don't just sit there," Janna exclaimed. "Open it!"

Kevin's heart was pounding and his hands shaking. What if it was bad news? What if something had happened to Jared? Or to his family? What if …?

"What is it, Kevin?"

Tearing open the envelope, Kevin gasped as he read the message.

"What is it, damn it?"

Kevin seemed nearly in shock, so Janna grabbed the telegram from him and read it aloud.

"'Urgent call from Aïn El Qamar *délégué*. *Proviseur* out. *Délégué* insists you stay per student petition. Good PR for Peace Corps. Please reconsider decision to leave. Barry" Looking up, she asked Kevin, "So, what are you going to do about this?"

Tears were streaming down Kevin's cheeks, but his eyes were ablaze with elation and the smile on his face was a foot wide. "It's a miracle!" he shouted. "It's a miracle!"

Suddenly, the only sound in the room was the music of the record playing. The eyes of dozens of students were glued on their teacher. It seemed the appropriate time to make an announcement, impulsive as his decision might be.

"Everybody listen!" he cried, jumping to his feet. "I'm not going back to the United States after all! I'm staying in Aïn El Qamar next year!" And with that a tumultuous cheer went up throughout the room, and he was surrounded by hugs and kisses and pats on the back.

One by one his students came up to him, inquiring about his change of mind, thanking him for his decision. "Later," was his response to their question, but their gratitude he accepted with joy.

"So," said Janna, when things had calmed down a bit and the students had returned to their dancing and socializing. "You've made an impulsive decision? Well so, Kevin Kensington, have I!"

"What do you mean?"

"I've decided to move in with you!" she declared boldly.

"What?" exclaimed Kevin, totally taken aback by her suggestion.

"It makes sense, doesn't it? Dave's leaving. You're staying. His room will be empty. Living alone nearly cost me my life last month. People will gossip, but it can't be any worse than what was said this past year. We can be good for each other, Kevin. We can keep each other level headed. We can give each other support. I think it's just what the doctor ordered."

"You know something, Janna?" said Kevin. "I think you just may be right! Let's be impulsive today. Let's take a chance. Let's do it!"

Janna threw her arms around Kevin. He felt her tears on his neck. He knew that his own were wetting her cheek.

"You feel like dancing?" Kevin whispered in her ear, and then he shouted, "I wanna dance!"

And with that he pulled Janna to her feet. The song on the stereo was "When Will I See You Again?" by the Three Degrees. And Kevin knew the answer!

He would see Janna every morning at breakfast. He would see Jared every weekend, either here or in Rabat. His students he would see again in October. The future was bright, thought Kevin ecstatically. There was more than enough reason to be optimistic. There was more than enough reason to dance!

OCTOBER 1977

EPILOGUE

▼

The pretty redhead seemed to be everywhere in the classroom at once. At one moment she was standing near the blackboard, at the next she was walking between the aisles of desks, the eyes of her thirty-five students following her, their faces bright and smiling, full of eagerness to learn the English language.

Pointing to the cover of the comic book she held, the teacher asked: "Where's the mouse?"

Almost instantaneously she pointed to one of the dozen or so hands she could see raised.

"The mouse is in the cat's mouth."

The classroom was filled with laughter, and the teacher laughed along. She seemed looser, more relaxed than in trimesters past, but she maintained control, not just of her classroom now, but of her life as well, and it was as clear as ever that these students truly loved her.

I'm back! thought Janna. I'm back!

GLOSSARY OF MOROCCAN ARABIC (AND FRENCH) WORDS USED IN *MOROCCAN ROLL*
(French words are italicized)

Aïd Mbrok	Happy Holiday
aïd	holiday
atay b'nanaa	mint tea
atay	tea
avertissment	warning
b'slama	Goodbye
baboosh	Moroccan slippers
bac/	
baccalauréat	examination/certificate indicating successful completion of high school work
banquettes	narrow mattresses on wooden supports
bezaff	a lot, many, much
bsmillah	In the name of God (said just before eating a meal)
butagaz	butane gas, used for home heating
conseil de classe	end of school term teachers' meeting to determine honors
cöopérant	French citizen working abroad for the French government
délégué	school board head
dirham	unit of Moroccan currency
externe	student not living in the school dormitory

floos	money
foqia	sleeveless ankle-length cotton robe worn by Moroccan men during the summer months
haïk	colorful sheet like garment worn over a woman's head and covering her entire body
hanoot	small shop, store
harira	spicy hot Moroccan vegetable and lentil soup
hellouf	pig
hemmam	Moroccan public bath
heshuma	a feeling of shame
Insha'allah	hopefully, if it is God's will
interne	student living in the school dormitory
jellaba	long, long-sleeved flowing hooded woolen robe worn by men and women
jinoon	demon
kass d'luz	almond milk
keef	drug, similar to marijuana or hashish
khobs	Moroccan bread
komira	French style loaf of bread
Kull!	Eat!
La bass	How are you? I'm fine.
Llah	God, Allah
lycée	high school
marabout	shrine
marhababek	welcome (to our house)
medina	ancient walled city
meshoui	a feast of barbecued lamb (the entire carcass)

mijmar	round, smoke-darkened and worn portable barbecue
mirikani/	
mirikania	American (man/woman)
moussem	Moroccan festival
mtihan	test/examination
mushkila	problem
mzian bezaff	very good
mzian	good
nisrani/	
nisrania	Christian (foreign) man/woman
oum	river
pouf	Moroccan hassock
proviseur	school principal
qsar	castle
quartier	neighborhood
ryal	penny
salaud	son of a bitch
salem u alikum	Hello, peace be with you
salle des profs	teachers' room
Salut!	Hi!
Sbah-el-khir	Good morning
serwal	Moroccan trousers
sfinj	Moroccan donuts
shaoush	gatekeeper
Shebaat	I've had enough (food).

souk	weekly outdoor public market
surveillant général	vice principal
tableau d'honneur	honor roll, with honors
tajine	Moroccan stew
tarija	small Moroccan drum
Wakha	okay, all right
Yallaho	Let's go
zamal	man who assumes the passive role in sex with another man
zitoon	olive(s)

978-0-595-45324-5
0-595-45324-4

Printed in the United Kingdom
by Lightning Source UK Ltd.
134375UK00001B/301/A